HOLLYWOOD HEROINE

HOLLYWOOD HEROINE

SARAH KUHN

BOOK FIVE OF HEROINE COMPLEX

DAW BOOKS, INC.
DONALD A. WOLLHEIM, FOUNDER
1745 Broadway, New York, NY 10019
ELIZABETH R. WOLLHEIM
SHEILA E. GILBERT
PUBLISHERS
www.dawbooks.com

First Printing, October 2021
1st Printing

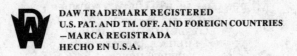

*For Tom Wong, my partner in crime
when it comes to Doing The Most.*

CHAPTER ONE

IT WAS A Saturday like any other when the unthinkable happened—*I slept in.*

Yes, I am aware that sleeping in on the weekend is a highly revered tradition, a simple respite after the long grind of the work week. It's just never been an option for me—after years of strict discipline, my body has trained itself to wake up at six a.m. on the dot. And as a superheroine, I don't *have* a traditional work week. I must be awake, alert, and ready to go whenever duty may call.

In my case, it calls quite a lot.

It had, in fact, been calling so much recently that my body actually moved its wake-up time to *five* a.m. I suppose some might be flummoxed by this, but I welcomed it. It gave me one more precious hour in which to get shit done.

Take the morning when said sleeping in occurred—there was *so much* I could have used that extra hour for. I'd spent the previous night taking down a whole mess of demons who'd disguised themselves as an artisanal meats and cheeses display at a quaint corner butcher shop in the Mission. And I'd had to do it solo, as my best friend and partner in superheroing, Evie Tanaka, wasn't feeling well. Evie was five months pregnant, and while her morning sickness (or, as she liked to call it, "all-the-time sickness") had subsided somewhat, she still had bouts of nausea when confronted with certain foodstuffs. And one of those foodstuffs was cured meat products.

I didn't want to dodge impressive amounts of vomit while

trying to defeat a throng of evil, fanged salamis, so I'd tact-
fully suggested I take this mission on alone. Evie told me to
maybe try calling Shruti, one of our superpowered friends
who helped us out from time to time, but I was extremely
confident in my ability to handle the situation myself. And
I'd been correct.

Even the most evil of salamis cannot help but quake in
their casings when confronted with San Francisco's premier
superheroine—that would be yours truly, Aveda Jupiter (aka
Annie Chang).

After this meaty fracas, I'd returned to Team Tanaka/
Jupiter HQ—a crumbling Victorian in the lower Haight—
and spent the next few hours going through various reports
about suspected supernatural activity in Maui. At some
point, the taxing events of the day caught up with me, and I
fell asleep right there at the kitchen table, my cheek pressed
against the reports, a trail of drool besmirching their fine
data.

I'd briefly stirred awake to my husband Scott gently scoop-
ing me up and carrying me to bed, murmuring in my ear that
whatever I was doing could wait until tomorrow.

Now it was tomorrow. And I was already late.

While my occupation of choice is always demanding, it
had become even more hectic the past few months. This was
thanks to 1) the threat from the demonic dimension known
as the Otherworld taking on some all-new and exciting layers, 2) the hiring of more staff at Team Tanaka/Jupiter, which
I'd taken upon myself to manage, and 3) Evie's pregnancy,
which had thus far been extra nerve-wracking as it was the
first known offspring of a superheroine and a half-demon
(that would be Evie's husband, Nate). Oh, and we'd been
tipped off that some of the most powerful demons in the
Otherworld were after the baby. I'd already been feeling extra protective of Evie, but this kicked me solidly into Mama
Bear territory—another reason I'd suggested I take down
the evil salamis all by my lonesome.

In any case, all of this meant my days were currently

packed to the gills, and sleeping in was not part of my agenda. Hell, "sleeping" was barely part of my agenda, period.

"Annie," Scott mumbled as I popped up in bed and began scrolling through my phone, trying to get a handle on the day. His eyes were still shut tight, his voice thick with sleep as he reached out for me, his hand landing somewhere in the vicinity of my arm. "You should rest more."

"Nonsense." I shook my head even though his eyes were still closed and he couldn't see me. "A good three hours and I'm perfectly rested. I need to finish looking over those reports from Maui, give Nate everything he needs to write up the butcher shop incident, go over the week's tasks with our intrepid Tanaka/Jupiter, Inc. employees, triple check that Evie actually rescheduled her doctor's appointment rather than merely thinking about it and then forgetting entirely—"

"And all of that does not need to be done first thing Saturday morning," Scott countered, his hand finally landing on mine. He tugged gently on my hand, pulling it away from my phone and twining our fingers together. Then he lifted his head, one brilliant blue eye finally popping open. "Put the phone down. And come here."

"But I'm not tired," I insisted—only for a massive, traitorous yawn to interrupt me mid-*tired*.

Scott laughed—a warm, familiar sound that still made my heart flutter after all these years. I'd loved this man since we were both awkward teenagers hopped up on angst and hormones, and time had only made that love more fierce and true than I'd ever imagined. Even now, when my attention was still firmly fixed on my schedule and my to-do list, my gaze couldn't help but linger on him: those sun-kissed muscles rippling over his shoulders, that tousled golden hair. And those blue eyes that looked at me with such pure adoration, making me melt every time.

When he pulled me against him—as he did now, my head fitting perfectly against his shoulder—I always felt like I was coming home.

"Just close your eyes for a minute," he murmured, his

intoxicating summertime scent of ocean and green and sunscreen washing over me. His hand flexed against my back, molding me more firmly against him. "The world's not going to end just because you slept in on one freaking Saturday."

"But what if it does," I sighed as my eyes fluttered closed, visions of fanged salamis and supernatural incident reports and pregnant Evie in peril dancing through my head. "What if it does."

The world did *not* end that day, but I don't like leaving anything to chance. So when I woke for the second time, I immediately ejected myself from the bed. I was unwilling to give Scott an opening to tempt me with further slumber—not when it was already nine a.m. and I had a full day of things to do.

After showering and dressing, I pulled my long black hair into its sleek signature power ponytail and marched down the hall. Tanaka/Jupiter HQ was quiet and eerie, the old floorboards creaking under my feet. Everyone else in the house was still asleep, apparently.

These days, that wasn't many people. At one point, the Victorian had nearly burst with an unruly assortment of residents—always busy, always bustling, always *alive*. But a few months ago, Evie's younger sister (and fellow superheroine) Bea had transplanted herself to Maui to assist with the area's newly formed demon unit. And Lucy Valdez, our trainer/weapons expert/occasional bodyguard, had gotten married and moved in with her wife, Rose. I had campaigned to have the newlyweds relocate to HQ—we had plenty of space, and our sprawling found family of a team had become such a well-oiled unit, it seemed a shame to split us up so . . . definitively. But Lucy had given me a very gentle lecture about boundaries and the healthiness of change, and how this didn't mean she and Rose weren't part of the team anymore, they just wanted some space to exist as themselves. I'd nodded along, but I had to admit—I held out hope that they'd move home eventually.

At least I still had Evie. And as I marched down the hall to the bedroom she shared with her husband, Nate, a spark of pride ignited in my chest. Even though the team we'd built was currently scattered, we were *still* that well-oiled machine. And much of that was thanks to the partnership Evie and I had forged—we'd worked our way through toxic best friend drama and codependence, her tendency to be a doormat and mine to be a steamroller. We'd fought demons of every stripe, saved the city countless times over, and we'd even managed to survive Evie's disastrous grad school reunion several months ago.

That ill-fated reunion was where we'd gotten a troubling clue regarding some of the more recent demonic shenanigans.

It was difficult to imagine a time when there *hadn't* been demonic shenanigans in San Francisco. It all started fourteen years ago, when the very first Otherworld portal opened up in the city. Said portal had actually been opened by aspiring demon queen Shasta—who just so happened to be Nate's mom. Shasta had been attempting some sort of invasion situation, but her portal was so unstable, it snapped shut immediately, killing her raiding party of humanoid demons—and sending their powers directly into the bodies of various San Francisco residents, like mine and Evie's. Evie was gifted with a rather impressive fire power, although at first she found it to be not so much "impressive" as "absolutely terrifying."

I'd received a rather weak bit of telekinesis, which I had initially downplayed as part of my superheroing persona since it simply wasn't that powerful. A supernaturally enhanced earthquake, however, had given many of us power level-ups, and my telekinesis had grown much stronger. And since I am not one to rest on my laurels, I'd also practiced and trained diligently over the years, honing my power into something worthy of the Aveda Jupiter mantle. Now I could lift and move *so many things*, and while I still had to concentrate to maintain a telekinetic hold, it had come to feel like second nature, a simple bit of instinct that switched on whenever I readied for battle.

In any case, it was a good thing some of us had been given powers, because Shasta's original portal led to aftereffects we were still dealing with all these years later. First it had been the aforementioned "puppy demons," who disappeared for a while, but now seemed to be back. More recently, we'd learned that the walls between our world and the Otherworld had rubbed perilously thin in certain spots, giving the demons all-new and exciting ways to cause trouble—and they also seemed to be showing up in new locations, like Maui.

Three months ago, Evie and I had investigated a series of mysterious hauntings and ghostly appearances at Morgan College, Evie's alma mater (well, sort of—technically, she'd dropped out of the graduate program after her burgeoning fire power had burned down the entire library). As it turned out, these "ghosts" were also powered by our not-so-friendly Otherworld demons, and the ultimate culprit was a minion of Shasta. Said minion revealed a larger plan at work: Shasta was most definitely after Evie's baby. We weren't sure what her ultimate scheme was, just that she believed the future Tanaka-Jones offspring would allow her to create a permanent portal between our dimensions.

Thankfully, I was *more* than ready for her—as was that well-oiled machine of a team. Despite this recent ramp-up in danger, I'd never felt more confident.

As I raised my hand to knock on Evie's door, my spark of pride turned into a full-on blaze.

I knocked sharply, and was momentarily distracted by my phone buzzing in my pocket. I fished it out as I listened for the telltale sound of Evie's feet padding to the door. And when I glanced at the screen, the smile that was already spreading across my face got even bigger.

"Whuzzah?" The door creaked open, revealing Evie's bleary-eyed face. Her mass of dark brown curls was matted on one side, and she looked half asleep.

"Wake up!" I exclaimed, clapping my hands together. She winced at the sound. "We have to go brief our adorable employees on the week's tasks."

"And why do we need to do this first thing on a Saturday morning, again?" she protested, running a hand over her face. She shook her head and blinked her cloudy hazel eyes a few times, trying to wake up.

"It's not 'first thing.' It's nine o'clock, practically lunchtime!"

"I . . ." She blew out a long breath and cocked an eyebrow at me. "I am definitely not talking you out of any part of this, right? I should just give up now and get dressed?"

"Only if you want to," I said, putting on my most innocent face and batting my eyelashes at her. "I have become much more skilled in the areas of productive listening and drawing boundaries to prevent a return to the toxicity that once defined so much of our relationship. So if you *really* want to disappoint the bright-eyed college students who look up to us so much—"

"No, no." Evie held up her hands and laughed, finally looking more alert. "I love how I skipped the argument and you're still trying to convince me of something I already agreed to. Just give me a moment to get myself together." She gestured to her unkempt state—faded sweat shorts and a giant old t-shirt of Nate's that draped like a black curtain over her growing baby bump. "Little Galactus Tanaka-Jones has been kicking up a storm, so I might as well get up."

"Please tell me you are *not* going with Bea's baby name," I said, shuddering. "I *still* think—"

"We're not naming the baby Aveda Junior," Evie said, swooping an authoritative finger in my direction. "You need to give up on that dream *now*."

"Spoilsport," I said, sticking my tongue out at her. "But hey, speaking of dreams . . ." I waved my phone around. "My mom actually texted me in a complimentary manner, can you believe that? She saw photos of me kicking that evil salami's ass on 'the social media,' and wanted to tell me that my hair looked very 'neat'—but she's sending me some oranges because citrus has been known to increase shine and body."

"A more Asian Mom compliment I have never heard," Evie said, giving me a little salute. "See you downstairs."

Still grinning to myself, I bounded down to the kitchen. It *was* an Asian Mom compliment—which were usually more like *non*-pliments—but that was progress for me and my mom. We'd always had a very contentious relationship, but we'd managed to reach something of an understanding over the past few years. She tried to show me she was proud of me, and I tried to be gracious about letting her into the superheroing part of my life. And given that oranges were one of the purest demonstrations of Asian Mom love, well . . . I was deeply happy that we'd come this far.

In fact? At the moment, everything was *perfect*. I had the bustling, adventure-packed life I'd always wanted, I was at the top of my superheroing game, my best friend and I had never been closer, and even my mom was giving me compliments.

Honestly, if I kept up my current level of extreme productivity (and worked harder to resist the heady temptation of collapsing against my gorgeous husband and snoring my way through Saturday mornings), what couldn't I accomplish?

I danced into the kitchen, throwing my arms wide in greeting. "Gooooood morning," I sang out. "Are we ready for . . . oh. Where is everyone?" I crinkled my brow at the sole figure stationed at the kitchen table: Pippa Ramos. Who was *not* one of Tanaka/Jupiter, Inc.'s new employees, although she was connected to them.

"Morning, AJ!" Pippa said, beaming and giving me an expansive wave. "Looking fresh and fine as usual."

"Thank you, Pippa," I said. "Not that I'm not happy to see you, but what are you doing here?"

Evie and I had met Pippa during our ghostly investigation of Morgan College. During our stint as undercover TAs, we'd befriended a little gaggle of students: Pippa, her best friend Shelby (who was an actual ghost and involved with the aforementioned hauntings), and their new friends Julie and Tess, who were part of the college's on-campus ghost society. We'd come to think of this foursome as our charges—and taking care of them had helped Evie see that she was cut out for the whole mom thing.

Bea's absence meant we needed extra help around HQ with various administrative tasks, so we'd hired Shelby as our part-time assistant and brought Julie on as our official paranormal consultant. I'd been expecting both of them this morning. I hadn't been expecting Pippa, even though she was very enthusiastic about helping her friends with their new gigs.

Pippa gave me an elaborate shrug and took a long sip from her paper to-go cup of coffee. I noticed she'd set the table, laying out more coffee alongside paper plates piled high with donuts. As part of her assistant duties, Shelby sometimes cooked everyone breakfast—a very balanced, healthy breakfast with lots of protein and greens on the side.

I knew Evie, a junk food connoisseur if there ever was one, would be *much* more in favor of Pippa's version.

"Shel couldn't make it," Pippa said, once she'd downed the rest of her coffee. She set the cup on the table with a vigorous *smack*. "She's, um, well. She's *dating* someone, so she's always, like, occupied at the moment. She said she told you guys she wouldn't be able to come today? And so did Julie—she and Tess are off on some fun weekend getaway."

"Maybe they did tell me," I said, cycling my brain back to the last time I'd talked to Julie and Shelby. What Pippa was saying *did* sound familiar. I just had so much going on, perhaps I'd forgotten. Well, there was a productivity-improving note to give myself: pay better attention when speaking to your charges/mentees/fledgling employees and write *everything* down just in case a small yet crucial bit of information slips from your very full mind. "So you came in their place?"

"Bingo!" Pippa said, shooting me finger guns. "I know I am not technically an employee of Tanaka/Jupiter, Inc., but I'm here so much, I might as well be, huh?"

"I admire your initiative," I said, crossing the room and sitting next to her. I eyed the donut in front of me—a fresh, fluffy maple bar coated in glistening icing. I could not quite stomach injecting such an outrageous level of sugar into my veins first thing in the morning, but I knew Evie would have a different perspective—

"Are those *donuts*?"

Right on cue, Evie shuffled into the kitchen, her eyes widening as they locked on the sweet bounty. She plopped herself next to me, snagged the maple bar, and stuffed half of it into her mouth.

"Oh god," she moaned. "Little Galactus Tanaka-Jones *loves* these. Hi, Pippa!" She grinned at Pippa, her words garbled around her mouthful of donut.

"Hey," Pippa said genially. "I'm filling in as your guys' assistant today. And you have what looks like a very important email at the top of your inbox!" She waved her phone at us, her dark eyes sparkling with excitement. "Can I do a dramatic reading of it? I know that's not what Shelby would do, but I just feel like—"

"Yes, of course," I said, giving her an affectionate smile. Of all the charges we'd gained at Morgan College, Pippa was the most theatrical. Evie had first encountered her when Pippa challenged a particularly terrible college professor—who also happened to be Evie's particularly terrible ex-boyfriend—about his outdated, sexist views on literature. She was never seen without her signature swoopy eyeliner, her platinum hair made her impossible to miss in a crowd, and she always seemed to be having some kind of dating drama. Although at the moment, it appeared she was the only one of her friends *not* dating anyone. Maybe that's why she'd randomly showed up at our kitchen table—she was looking for some not-as-distracted company.

"Ahem!" Pippa declared, sitting up straight in her seat and

brushing her platinum hair out of her eyes. "Dear Ms. Tanaka and Ms. Jupiter, we hope this message finds you well! We are very pleased to inform you that filming has commenced on . . ." Pippa's eyes widened to the size of dinner plates. "The TV show based on your evil-fighting exploits?! Holy cats and dogs and motherfuckin' porcupines . . ." She tossed her phone on the table and threw her arms wide, her incredulous gaze going from me to Evie and back again. "Someone's making a *TV show* about you guys?"

"Oh, right." Evie hoovered the last of her donut and wiped her sticky fingers on a napkin. "We sold those rights a while back, and I honestly never thought anything would come of it—"

"You're saying you don't think we're legitimately fabulous enough for prime time?" I retorted, rolling my eyes at her. "Or, you know, streaming."

"No, I just assumed . . ." She shrugged, her mouth curving into a wry grin. "I mean, aren't *you* surprised they're making a show starring not one, but *two* Asian American superheroines? I thought they'd whitewash one of us—or maybe both."

"Surely our status as Asian American icons is a selling point," I said, waving a hand. "Anyway, Pippa, it's one of those things where we get the occasional update, but between Evie's pregnancy and me trying to put out various superheroing fires—"

"—and taking down the ghosts of Morgan College," Evie interjected, a smile playing across her face.

"Which turned out to be powered by an evil demon and Evie's terrible ex-boyfriend—well, we've been too busy to keep track of it all," I finished. "But I didn't realize they were so close to actually shooting. What else does the message say?"

Pippa picked her phone back up and studied the screen. "They want you to come to Hollywood to observe and consult!" she crowed, her eyes widening again. "I don't know exactly what that means, but it sounds way cool!"

"Mmm, yes. Cool." I absently broke off a piece of jelly donut and popped it in my mouth. Overwhelming sweetness exploded on my tongue and I swallowed quickly, pushing the rest to the side. "But given that we *are* so busy—"

"Are you kidding me?" Evie yelped. She reached over and tugged my sleeve, her eyes sparkling with mischief. "The one and only Aveda Jupiter is willing to miss the chance to see her exploits immortalized on the small screen?"

"The one and only Aveda Jupiter is way less glory-hungry than she used to be," I countered, batting her hand away. "And she's a little hurt you would make such assumptions about her!"

"Y'all talk about yourselves way too much in the third person," Pippa said, eyes still trained on her phone screen. "They're asking if you can come down next week."

"I . . ." I trailed off, hesitating. My fingertips continued to poke at the jelly donut, even though I was finding it less than appetizing.

Evie was right. This kind of fame and glory was something I'd thirsted after for years. And while the current Aveda Jupiter—the one who had learned to share the spotlight and support her friends and did not indulge in the kind of divalicious antics she used to be known for—might not have such things at the absolute forefront of her mind . . . shouldn't she still be a teeny bit excited?

"I guess I'm wondering if it's a good idea for both Evie and me to up and leave the city when we've had an increase in puppy demon activity lately," I said, trying to work out my confusing feelings. "What happens if we're gone and there's an attack?"

"That's why we have reserves now," Evie said, snagging the remnants of my jelly donut. "Shruti's been training more with Lucy, and Shelby's discovering some of the supernatural skills that come with being a ghost girl. I think they can handle things for a few days."

"Mmm," I said, leaning back in my seat. "Then I suppose there's *no* reason not to go, is there?"

"Exactly," Evie said. Her expression had gone from teasing to a tad puzzled as she studied me, trying to figure out the reason for my lack of excitement.

I couldn't help but flash back to her face the last time she'd looked at me so intently—three months ago, when she'd met my eyes during our final battle at Morgan College. She'd been trying to power through, to push aside all her doubts and insecurities, to protect her baby and these new friends we'd made and all the people she loved.

I'd shouted out a desperate pep talk and beamed back that sense of ferocious, unflappable Aveda Jupiter determination— because I knew that if I could only get her to believe in us, we'd make it through no matter what.

And now, she did believe. So much so that she thought we could relax and leave our superheroing duties behind for a few days.

Why wasn't I more excited?

"Annie." Evie brushed her fingertips against my arm, leaving a tiny trail of donut crumbs in their wake. "I know you've been on high—well, *higher*—alert ever since we found out Shasta's after the baby. But we're already taking extra precautions, and we haven't heard a peep about her or her mysterious plan in months. It's entirely possible that we foiled her when we nipped her 'let's haunt Evie until she gives up her firstborn' antics in the bud. And by the way, I *did* remember to reschedule my doctor's appointment. So you don't have to worry about that either."

"That's not . . . I wasn't . . ." I huffed, both irritated and touched that she could read me as well as I could read her.

"We need to live our lives," Evie pressed, brushing away the excess crumbs she'd left on my sleeve. "Being a super-heroine shouldn't mean we're just, like, waiting for bad things to happen. We should celebrate the good things, too. And this is a good thing, right?"

"Right," I agreed, my voice robotic. I was trying to wrap my head around Evie—our resident stick in the mud—advocating for full-on celebration. Was *I* the stick in the mud now?

Maybe observing all of this up close and personal—my superheroic self dramatized for all the world to see—would ignite my excitement.

And as for everything else . . . well, hadn't I just been basking in the glow of my current excellent levels of productivity? Aveda Jupiter may be a burgeoning stick in the mud, but she definitely knows how to get things done. How to get *everything* done. Surely she could witness and celebrate her very own TV show while running an entire superheroing operation, keeping an eye out for increased demonic threats, and protecting her pregnant best friend?

"Okay," I said, smiling back at her. "Let's go."

CHAPTER TWO

AFTER OUR MORNING meeting, I hunkered down at the kitchen table and spent the rest of the day planning for our impending trip and finishing up my review of the latest supernatural incident reports from Maui. As it turned out, they weren't terribly compelling—mostly overexcited tourists claiming that particularly large waves they'd observed were *definitely* demons of some sort.

Still, I read them all several times: poring over each page, dissecting every word for hidden meaning, certain I'd missed something. After all, it was probably within Shasta's power to create particularly large waves. Perhaps she was lulling us into a sense of calm before deploying her evil master plan.

Eventually my eyes started to cross, the words in front of me started to blur, and I very nearly sent Bea my outfit packing list for LA rather than my notes on her reports. It was then that I finally looked up and realized dusk was setting in, casting shadowy whispers of darkness through the window and over my iPad screen. I set the tablet to the side, squeezed my eyes shut, and scrubbed a hand over my face, resisting the urge to bite my nails. It was barely after six, it made no sense that I was suddenly so tired. After all, hadn't I accidentally slept in this morning?

I glanced at my phone, which I hadn't looked at in hours. A cavalcade of texts from my mother popped up onscreen. I squinted at them, trying to make sense of the series of images she'd apparently been sending me all afternoon. They looked to be photos of . . . oranges? Piled high at various corner markets? Yes, she'd mentioned she was going to send me some oranges, but she didn't usually text me preliminary photos for inspection, especially with no accompanying explanation. What on earth was she doing? I scrubbed a hand over my face again, as if that might refresh my brain.

"Annie—sweetheart."

I popped an eye open and peeked through my fingers to see Scott standing in the kitchen doorway, looking as delicious as he had that morning. He was wearing dark jeans and a light blue button-down with a faint pattern of tiny blue and white dots, pressed to perfection and hugging his arms in all the right places.

"Hi," I managed, lowering my hand from my face. "You look so nice. Are you going somewhere?"

He raised an eyebrow, an amused smile pulling at the corners of his mouth.

"I thought I was going somewhere with *you*," he said, crossing the room and settling himself into the chair next to mine.

"I . . ." I frowned into space, my brain doing all kinds of rapid-fire scans and calculations, trying to remember what I was supposed to be doing. What *hadn't* I done today? Were we going to visit Lucy for a special training session? No, that couldn't be right—Scott wasn't part of those, and they usually took place during the day. And as I'd told Lucy many times, the sessions would be way easier to schedule if she'd move back home—

"Annie." Scott jerked my brain out of its cycle, covering my hand with his. "We were supposed to go out tonight—just the two of us."

I shook my head at him, as if that might help call up the memory. "Were we going to do recon on some of the other artisanal meat shops in the area? I thought Nate wanted to analyze last night's incident first."

He squeezed my hand, a shadow of concern disrupting his amused smile. "No. We were supposed to have dinner, see a movie, and maybe take a very cheesy—and probably very

SARAH KUHN 17

cold—walk by the waterfront. Remember? A date night so basic, Bea couldn't stop making fun of us—though there's no one I'd rather be basic with than you."

"Gaaaah." I pulled away from him and leaned back in my chair, my gaze going to the kitchen ceiling. The dingy old tiles glinted in the encroaching moonlight, and I felt like they were scolding me. "I . . . totally forgot. I'm sorry. I have so much to do, and I can't make sense of these reports, and now my mother's texting me mysterious pictures of oranges—"

"Hey." He reached over and took my hand again, giving it a gentle tug. "Come here."

I allowed him to pull me into his lap, his arms going around me as his eyes searched my face. Feeling the warmth of his skin against mine, letting his summer scent wash over me . . . my shoulders instantly relaxed, a long exhale leaving my body. Even though my Hurricane Annie energy had settled a bit over the years, I still had bull-in-a-china-shop tendencies that made me, according to Evie, "a forceful bludgeon for good." Scott, meanwhile, was always so even-keeled, so patient and gentle. His touch was like a balm on my soul, as if he was absorbing all the tension housed in my body into his waiting palms.

"What's going on?" he asked. "You almost never look over these types of reports." He nodded at my iPad screen, and the messy notes I'd scrawled onto various scraps of paper. "That's more of a Nate and Bea thing, no?"

"What's going on is that I'm an asshole who completely forgot our super basic date night," I countered. "And I've been studying *all* reports that come our way recently—I want to be really and truly prepared whenever Shasta deploys her evil plan, and I feel that I can only do that if I have *all* the knowledge. Every bit of information. Because if demons are already getting through in other locations, if the walls between worlds are wearing so thin . . ." I shook my head. "The evil's spreading beyond San Francisco. Who knows how far it could go if we don't figure out how to eradicate it for good? And let's not forget that one of its current primary targets is my best friend and her soon-to-be off-spring. Aveda Jupiter has to be *ready*."

His gaze searched my face again, in that special way where it felt like he could see through my skin. That used to make me feel deeply uncomfortable—I could never take the idea that he knew me well enough to do that, that he might see beyond my confident, assured Aveda Jupiter armor and find the insecure Annie Chang that lurked underneath. That fragile girl who considered every feeling she had to be weakness, who didn't want anyone to know her down to her core.

But now there was a comfort in that. Scott had *always* seen me. And he'd always loved *all* of me, even the tiny broken bits I tried so hard to keep hidden. When he looked at me like that now, I got the same sensation that had bubbled up when he'd lulled me back to sleep earlier that morning: I felt like I was coming home.

If you'd told awkward, uptight fifteen-year-old Annie Chang that gangly, goofy Scott Cameron was totally in love with her and would marry her a decade and a half later, she would have died on the spot.

Because she was, of course, totally in love with him too.

During the course of our childhood-friends-to-enemies-to-lovers romance, our courtship had been rocky and overly dramatic. Scott and I met back when Evie and I folded him into our friendship in sixth grade. He'd been a scrawny little clown with a tendency to get his ass kicked by the bigger kids, but things had changed in high school, when lean muscle rippled over his spindly limbs and admirers of all genders started to take notice.

But I'd *always* noticed him. His kindness, his goodness, his ability to see wonderful things in others. His insistence on sticking up for those who couldn't stick up for themselves—even though he couldn't really stick up for himself, either.

I'd been hurt beyond belief when he'd taken Evie to prom. Even more so when they lost their virginity to each other. And then we'd had a massive fight in our early twenties that had nearly ruined things, but we'd come back together out of mutual concern for Evie when her fire power started manifesting more frequently.

Finally—*finally!*—we'd admitted our feelings to each other during the planning of Evie's wedding. Which, true to form, was *also* extremely dramatic. At that point, I'd been in love with him for so many years, and those first few moments of tender intimacy—the secret smiles he saved just for me, the way his hand would come to rest at the small of my back—were absolutely thrilling. They really did feel like the culmination of a swoony romantic comedy, and sometimes I'd sneak a look at him while he was doing something extra mundane—peeling an orange, watching TV, reading endless dense research tomes for grad school—and feel that surge of blissful happiness. After so many years of pining and misunderstanding and close calls, we finally got to be together. It didn't seem real.

Two years after Evie's wedding, he'd charmed me into taking "just one day off" in honor of my birthday, a holiday I usually loathed celebrating. I know a festive twenty-four hours dedicated entirely to my own fabulousness seems like something I would enjoy above all else, but I've actually never liked my birthday—it's a reminder that I have one less year on this planet, that the time to accomplish all I want and fulfill my mission of stamping out Otherworld-style evil is ever dwindling. Bea had once modified a certain lyric from *Hamilton* just for me: "Instead of 'why do you write like you're running out of time,' it's 'why do you *fight* like you're running out of time,'" she'd teased. "That's the Aveda Jupiter Way."

I could not really disagree with that.

In any case, I never made a fuss about my birthday, and I insisted that those around me simply go about their business as if it was a regular day. No cake, no singing, no excruciating opening of gifts and pretending to be surprised by it all.

But for this birthday, Scott had convinced me to hand the evil-fighting off to Evie and Co. and spend the entire day in bed. With him.

Despite my aversion to birthdays, this was a most appealing prospect.

After we'd spent the morning working up a hearty appetite, he'd presented me with a single slice of delectable cake from one of San Francisco's most twee little bakeries, Cake My Day.

"Mmm—dark chocolate," I'd sighed, pulling the silk sheets around me as I took a bite. I closed my eyes and savored the delicate sweetness, the feeling of silk against my bare skin, and the company of my extremely hot boyfriend. I usually could not stand doing nothing (and given that our current activity was not in any way related to demon-slaying or world-saving, I suppose I would have classified it in the "nothing" area), but the feeling of blissed-out contentment gathering in my chest was a glorious oasis—a pool of calm I wanted to luxuriate in.

"And I swear, Letta's mascarpone whipped cream frosting gets better every year," I continued.

"It does," Scott agreed, piling his own bite of cake onto a fork. "But I still have a particular fondness for the version from two years ago. Right before Evie and Nate's wedding?"

He cocked a knowing eyebrow at me as he slid the fork into his mouth and I flushed. He was referring to A Moment we'd had while planning the wedding, cake tasting at Cake My Day. We'd been sniping at each other—as was our way in those days—and he kept pestering me to try the dark chocolate cake. I'd let him feed me a bite, he'd tried to brush a bit of frosting from my lower lip . . . and I'd sort of, ah, licked it off of his thumb. That single, charged moment ignited sparks between us that had bubbled just below the surface for years.

"Hmm," I said, feigning ignorance—even though my flaming face told a different story. I leaned back against my array of pillows, letting the sheet I'd wrapped around myself slide lower. "I'm not sure I remember. But maybe if you feed me some of that . . ." I nodded at his cake-laden fork. "It'll come back to me."

I cocked my head at him and bit my lip—and was pleased to see his gaze darken as his breathing went rapid and uneven. I *knew* he was a total sucker for that look.

I let the sheet slip just a little bit more.

"Um . . ." He swallowed hard, trying to get his breathing under control. "Let me just . . ."

He fussed with the cake, carefully adding more pillowy crumbs and decadent frosting to his fork. I hid my smile. He was always so mellow and I was so . . . well, the opposite. Hurricane Annie. It was especially gratifying when I managed to fluster him.

He finally got the bite exactly the way he wanted it and held the fork out to me. I leaned in, my gaze never leaving his, prepared to lick the frosting off the fork in the most suggestive way possible—

Until he pulled it just out of reach.

"Hey!" I yelped, falling ungracefully out of the sexy pose I'd been going for. "What was that, are you actually going to make me chase after this bite? On my *birthday* of all days—"

"You hate your birthday," he said, warm amusement lighting his eyes. "Annie. Look at the cake, please. Look really close."

I dropped my gaze to the fork. And there, nestled amidst the swirls of mascarpone, was a flash of garish crimson. Upon closer inspection, I realized it was a plastic ring—the cheap toy Scott and I had won in a gumball machine the summer between sixth and seventh grades. We'd been trying to win a little toy hedgehog for Evie, but kept getting junk like the ring instead. He'd joked all those years ago that he'd use it to propose to me one day.

And now, here we were. And I could barely even see that precious piece of plastic because my eyes were already full of tears.

"Scott," I managed to whisper, my voice shaking. "Is this . . . are you . . ."

His warm smile widened. And since I appeared to be

frozen in place, he gently plucked the ring free from the cake, wiped off the excess frosting with the t-shirt he'd discarded on the floor, and held it out to me.

"Annie," he said—and I realized his voice was shaking, too. The little oasis in my chest radiated outward, happiness overwhelming my entire being. I lunged forward, the sheet finally slipping from my body, and pulled him in for a long, deep kiss.

"Does that mean yes?" he gasped, when we finally broke apart. "I don't think I even fully asked the question."

I held out my hand and waggled my fingers at him. "Of course it's a yes. Ring me."

He slid that hunk of plastic onto my finger, and then he was gathering me against him and pressing his lips to mine. I sank into the kiss, reveling in every sensation—his teeth tugging at the delicate flesh of my lower lip, his hands stroking down my back to bring me closer. I felt consumed by him, insatiable for the feel of his skin against mine and the wet heat of his mouth exploring the most sensitive parts of me.

He eased me back against the pillows, then finally broke our kiss, his eyes searching my face again. Scott's demeanor was so laid back, but whenever we were locked in an especially intimate moment, he tended to get all serious and intense, those blue eyes gazing at me like what was happening between us was the most important thing in the world.

It took my breath away every time.

"I love you," he said, his voice thick with emotion. "I've loved you forever. And I wanted to give you something on your birthday . . ." His voice caught, but he held my gaze. "Something that would maybe make you hate it just a little bit less."

Tears sprang to my eyes again and I reached up to brush his golden hair off his forehead. "I love my birthday right now. In fact, I kind of want to stay in bed with you until my *next* birthday. What do you think of that?"

He answered me with a kiss. And then we didn't talk for a while.

We had to edit our engagement story for my parents, who did *not* need to know that he'd proposed to me with a twenty-five-cent piece of plastic while we were both naked. We'd gotten so caught up in the moment, it wasn't until much later that Scott was able to show me he'd gotten me a real ring to go with the plastic one—a brilliant sapphire surrounded by tiny diamonds, hard edges contrasting with soft lines. It was beautiful and perfect, but I was so deliriously happy, I would've been content wearing a garish piece of plastic around for the rest of my life.

"Annie?" Scott's voice jerked me back to the present moment—the kitchen that was growing darker by the second, the forgotten date night, the pile of reports I still hadn't fully gotten through. I realized I was twisting my sapphire ring (definitely *not* plastic) around my finger, an idle sort of fidget that went hand in hand with all my nail-biting.

"Sorry," I blurted out. "I was, uh . . . thinking about things. I have a lot on my mind."

"And I was saying that maybe you don't have to keep *everything* on your mind," he said, reaching up to brush away a stray lock of hair that had drifted free from my power ponytail. "Let Nate and Bea handle the reports—they love that stuff."

"I know," I said, "but I want to be really caught up on supernatural activity in all locations before Evie and I go to LA, because—"

"LA?"

"Right, right—that just happened this morning," I said, realizing I needed to catch him up. I explained about the TV show and how we were going to witness it all. "I'll only be gone for a few days," I assured him. "And I've already been in contact with Shruti and Lucy about holding down the fort."

He tilted his head, studying me. "Do you want some company? Besides Evie, I mean."

"Oh, that's not necessary." I flashed him a reassuring smile. "I'm sure we can handle all this . . . observing. I'm thinking of it as a short but necessary business trip."

His mouth quirked into a half-smile. "Really? No room for anything more vacation-adjacent?"

"I should think not," I huffed. "I don't even really want to go in the first place, there's so much going on here . . ." I trailed off, all the things I hadn't managed to do today piling up in my brain. I made a mental note to rouse myself at least an hour earlier tomorrow.

"So maybe I could make it a little bit fun for you," he said, his smile widening. "We could steal a few moments, go to the beach—especially if the TV stuff ends up being stressful—"

"It won't be," I said. "I can handle it. And anyway, don't you have a bunch of shifts at the Center next week? Aren't you supposed to present your latest surf clinic plans to management and all that? I thought that was a big deal, you've been working on it for months!"

"Well . . . yeah." He gave me an easy shrug. "But I'm sure I can move stuff around, maybe present some other time. I've always wanted to check out those SoCal beaches, the waves are supposed to be on a completely different level. One of my contacts down at the LA Youth Center says—"

"Oh, wait!" I exclaimed, an idea popping into my brain. "If you want to come with us, maybe you could finally visit the Center down there! Haven't they said they'd love to have you do a mini version of your surf clinic? This might be the perfect opportunity!" I beamed at him, the idea taking more coherent shape as I thought it through.

Like Evie and me, Scott had received a superpower when that first portal opened up—he was able to access and manipulate bits of Otherworld magic with his mind, like some kind of experimental sorcerer. His power, like mine, had been fairly weak initially, but he'd figured out how to do simple spells involving things like glamours and love tokens. When he'd gotten his power level-up, his magic had gotten much stronger, and he'd served as Team Tanaka/Jupiter's resident mage ever since.

Over the past few years, he'd also developed his very own side hustle, and that was where the surf clinic came in. Since earning a Master's in social work, Scott worked part-time at San Francisco's interconnected web of Youth Centers and afterschool programs—and the program he'd developed to teach interested youths how to surf had proved to be a big hit. It was, in fact, such a big hit that a sister Youth Center in downtown Los Angeles kept asking him to do a guest instructor gig.

But he was always getting swept into Team Tanaka/Jupiter's various fights against evil, and there was never any time for him to hustle that side hustle to its fullest potential. I'll admit, I carried some measure of guilt that he hadn't really had the chance to give his all to what could be his dream career.

I *knew* his true passion was working with those kids, sharing his boundless enthusiasm with them and helping them find their places in the world. Scott had grown up the only child of a struggling single mom who worked a variety of crap-paying jobs in order to put herself through law school and keep her sweet, scrawny son clothed and fed. He'd been constantly bullied by the other kids in our grade for his shabby, too-small clothes, his runty physique, and his dreamy goofball demeanor. His mother had given him all the love she had, but Scott's sensitive nature meant he knew that she was exhausted all the time, and he'd dialed up his relentlessly cheerful façade so she'd never know about the boys who beat him up every day at school or screamed insults in his face until he finally broke down and cried. (I'd planted myself between him and those boys during the worst of it, daring them to fight me instead. None of them had wanted to punch a girl, so they'd backed off. For the record, even tiny, non-superpowered Annie Chang would have felled every single one of them.)

I saw the way Scott lit up when his little cluster of surf students gathered around him, yelling questions and demanding pointers on how to make their techniques better. I especially loved watching him whenever he connected with the shyest kid in class, the one too timid to ask for anything at all. He'd approach this kid after the larger group had dispersed or splashed gleefully into the waves, and then he'd gently ask them freewheeling, non-invasive questions about themselves, forging a bond through favorite TV shows or dreaded school subjects. He never made the kid feel like they were weird or wrong for not immediately jumping into the ocean with their more outgoing counterparts, and his mellow demeanor usually got them to slowly open up until they conversed and laughed with him like a lifelong friend.

I knew he saw himself in that kid, and that he wanted to make the world better for them—and my heart swelled watching him make every hard-won connection look so effortless. I adored watching Scott's face whenever that shy kid finally worked up the courage to bound into the waves with all the others. His irresistible lopsided grin would stretch from ear to ear, his eyes sparkling with pride—like he was doing the thing he was meant to do and nothing else mattered in that moment.

I recognized that look because that's how *I* felt whenever I was superheroing. And I wanted him to feel that every day, just as I did.

But over the years, I felt like he'd made his dreams smaller so mine could thrive. His instinct was to put others first, always—faking a happy face for his mom when he was younger, blithely volunteering to rearrange his entire schedule and skip an important presentation simply because he wanted to support me on this LA trip. Hell, every step of his career so far had been driven by his need to help someone else. He'd joined Team Tanaka/Jupiter because he'd been worried for Evie, who was thrust into the limelight when her fire power decided to make a surprise appearance. He'd stayed for me—and because he felt like it was his duty to use his Otherworld-given ability to help protect the city.

I would *not* stand by while this sweet, selfless man pushed his passions aside. He'd told me years ago that he wanted to forge his own path in a way that allowed him to be his whole self, and he deserved for his dreams to come true—he deserved that more than anyone.

"Maybe it wouldn't even have to be a *mini* version of the surf clinic," I continued, warming to the idea. "With a special guest instructor gig, you could probably develop an *expanded* version! Like, different levels? An advanced workshop for the kids who get really into it? Then you could bring that back up here to San Francisco, I'm sure your bosses would love it. Ooh! You could give the kids badges for mastering different skills or something, like in Girl Scouts—"

"Well . . . yeah," he interrupted, giving me an easy grin. "That could be fun."

"It's more than just 'fun,' Scott," I huffed. "This could be *major* for you!"

"I'll call my friend in LA in the morning," he said, his grin turning amused. "But in the meantime . . ." He leaned in, his mouth brushing my ear and making me shiver. "How about that date?"

He cupped my face in his hands, his thumbs stroking down my cheeks as he studied me. Then he pulled me close, our lips meeting, and I sighed against him, letting myself fall into that kiss.

Everything went gloriously hazy, the mundane surroundings of the kitchen falling away, and it was just us, all softness and the beginnings of moonlight through the window . . .

And then the sounds of snores pierced my haze.

"Annie!" Scott pulled away from me, laughing . . . and I realized those snores had been coming from *me*. I'd *fallen asleep* in the middle of our kiss. "Damn, I need to work on my technique," he teased.

"Gah! Sorry!" I blurted, furiously scrubbing at my eyes. "I guess it's been a long day."

"Then maybe we should have a date with our bed," he said, grinning away.

"No." I shook my head vehemently. "I mean. Obviously we'll end up there later. And I will absolutely blow your mind, Cameron." I shot him a suggestive look. "But right now, I'm going to rally. We're going on that date!"

I heaved myself out of his lap, my muscles screaming in protest—probably because I'd been hunched over the kitchen table all day. Perhaps I should book an extra stretching session with Lucy to get all the kinks out.

I marched up the stairs to our bedroom to change, tightening my power ponytail along the way. Yes, I was exhausted after a full day of being Aveda Jupiter. But that didn't mean I was going to ignore my ever-thoughtful husband, who'd barely protested when I'd passed out during what was supposed to be a make-out. I'd thought earlier that everything was perfect, but clearly I was falling down on the job of being a supportive romantic partner.

In order for things to be *truly* perfect, I needed to give every area of my life my full attention, one hundred and ten percent.

Aveda Jupiter could do it all. *That* is the Aveda Jupiter Way.

MAISY KANE PRESENTS: BUZZ BY THE BAY

By Maisy Kane, Half-Demon Princess Editrix

Bonjour, sweet 'Friscans! Now, I know that you're probably about to express concern for your old pal Maisy: is she really updating her li'l ol' blog on a *Saturday*?! Especially after last week's post focusing on the importance of self-care, which just so happened to coincide with a big sale on my new skin care and candle line! (I developed it with us extra sensitive dry-skinned babes in mind, and you can still get twenty percent off with the code ILOVEME, good both online and in store here at Pussy Queen!) While I am still all about seeking rest for those big ol' brains and relentlessly empowered bodies of yours, breaking news waits for no one! And I have the biggest ever scoop to share with y'all!!!

Are you ready? Can you stand the suspense?! Well, your pal Maisy does not believe in burying the lede, so here it is: a mother-freakin' TV show about the lives of our city's dearest superheroines (and my close, personal friends), Aveda Jupiter and Evie Tanaka, is officially in the works!

Could. You. *Die?*

Many details of the series, from casting to storylines, are being kept tightly under wraps—all we know is that it's being produced by Pinnacle Pictures for their new streaming service, it is a fictionalized version of our girls' adventures, and the title has been set. I can exclusively reveal to you that this groundbreaking television show will be called:

Heroine

Simple. Evocative. I am already envisioning the billboard, and cannot wait for the corresponding t-shirts!

Word on the street is that Evie and Aveda are headed down to Tinseltown to watch filming get underway! If any of my LA readers happen to spot them on the street, please snap a pic and give us a scoop on what those two are up to—hijinks seem to follow them wherever they go, and I can't help but feel this SoCal getaway will be no different! Though perhaps they'll be too busy getting mobbed by an adoring public that doesn't get to see EVEDA with the same frequency as we do—we are #blessed here in the Bay! I can only hope they'll be able to enjoy the simple pleasure of a meal out in peace, no fans or paparazzi getting in their way! (At least not until the *Heroine* TV show kicks them into a whole new astronomical level of the fame stratosphere!)

In the meantime, I think I speak for all of San Francisco when I say: please hurry back to us! Evil always seems to be afoot here, and we desperately need our heroines! I've been fielding queries to my podcast about what might happen to this superheroing duo once Evie welcomes the newest little Tanaka to the fold (please subscribe to the Superbaby News tier on my Patreon for the latest on that!). True, we will likely have to lose our favorite firestarter to maternity leave, but as I keep telling everyone: Aveda Jupiter can more than handle it! From the beginning, that girl has built a legendary career in superheroing by doing the most, being the most, and . . . well, pretty much anything that involves "the most," she's there.

Aveda is, in fact, the only person I know of who *never* seems to need self-care! She'd probably scoff at the very thought of it!

But that's why we love her, isn't it? Because she is just that strong, formidable, resilient! Nothing ever gets to her, I have never actually witnessed her sweat, and she just keeps going no matter what! What a (wait for it) *Heroine*!

But let me just say, Aveda—if you ever *do* need some self-care, I would be happy to offer an additional discount on my new skin care and candle line! Kiss-kiss, your pal Maisy's got your back!

CHAPTER THREE

"WHOA! DID YOU see that?! Annie!" Evie jabbed me in the arm, her sharp little index finger piercing through the layers of my silky black bomber jacket.

"Ow!" I protested, batting her hand away. "Why is your pointy finger so *pointy*? And what am I supposed to be looking at?"

I followed her *other* pointy finger, which was gesturing enthusiastically out the window of the sleek Town Car ferrying us from the LA airport to the Pinnacle Pictures studio lot, where our show was being shot. We'd been scooped up by a production assistant named Stacey, who thus far had distinguished herself by being one of the grouchiest individuals I'd ever encountered. She appeared to be somewhere in her twenties, and had a creamy complexion, a mop of red curls, and a consistently sour disposition. She seemed uninterested in speaking to us at length, and sort of grunted in our direction when she had something to say.

Since we didn't have to be on set for a few more hours, Evie had eagerly asked Grouchy Stacey if she could show us LA's coolest sites. Grouchy Stacey seemed very reluctant to show us *any* kind of sites, but had half-heartedly offered to drive up the coastline. The sun-kissed golden sand and brilliant blue waves seemed to stretch on forever, punctuated by the occasional cluster of people frolicking in the water or having a beach picnic.

Or doing the thing Evie wanted me to look at, which appeared to be . . .

"What *is* going on over there?" I said, leaning closer to the window so I could see better. I'd been glued to my phone since we'd landed—checking in on Shruti, Nate, and Lucy back home; texting Bea to see if she had any new insights about the Maui reports; fielding more texts about oranges from my mother.

But now my attention was momentarily captured by the scene on the beach, which appeared to involve a group of very toned humans leading their dogs around on leashes while jumping up and down around a volleyball net.

"It's dog volleyball," Grouchy Stacey called out from the driver's seat. Well, "called" was perhaps an exaggeration since everything she said was delivered in the exact same bored monotone. "It's a thing here."

"Dog *volleyball*?" Evie squeaked, like she couldn't quite wrap her brain around such a concept.

"Just what it sounds like," Stacey said, offering no further elaboration.

"I guess LA *is* different," Evie said, her eyes widening as she watched a particularly rambunctious pug aggressively chase its tail, inadvertently causing it to crash into a pair of Chihuahua opponents. "Oh man, I can't wait to explore more!"

I went back to my phone, a slight smile playing over my lips. I might not be as wowed by the concept of dog volleyball as she was, but I was happy to see her enjoying herself. Evie had been a bundle of excitement from the moment we'd stepped off the plane—eyes darting everywhere, drinking in our new surroundings. Even the wet-blanket disposition of Grouchy Stacey did nothing to dampen her enthusiasm.

She'd even snagged herself a cheesy I HEART LA t-shirt as we were leaving LAX, which she'd promptly pulled on over the rest of her clothes. The HEART rested right above her growing belly, giving her the appearance of a knock-off Care Bear.

I snuck a sidelong look at her. She was craning her neck so hard, her head was practically hanging out the window. I smiled again, a surge of warmth running through me. Evie's pregnancy had been somewhat difficult thus far, and our adventures at Morgan College—where she'd been forced to face both a baby-stealing demon and her complicated past—had put her through the ringer. The final ghost we'd encountered there had been a version of *her*, the personification of all the regrets she still had tied to Morgan. Ultimately, she'd helped her ghost self see that she'd always been strong and worthy of love, and that she needed to forgive herself for imagined past transgressions in order to move forward. This had brought both Current Evie and Ghost Evie some measure of much-needed closure. And now, it was nice to see her *enjoying* something, and in such wonderstruck fashion.

"Look at you, being all excited," I teased, nudging her in the ribs. "Usually you're the worrier."

"Are *you* worried about something?" she said, her brows drawing together.

"Just hoping the Otherworld demons don't decide it's time for another invasion while we're away," I said, going back to my phone. "Especially since Maisy decided to blast out the news of our trip to everyone—just in case there are any demons who want to take this opportunity to fuck up San Francisco."

"You know Maisy, she can't resist a scoop," Evie said.

I grimaced—that was certainly true. The irritating human-demon hybrid gossip blogger loved to stir the pot.

"Shruti and Co. are ready if anything happens," Evie insisted.

"And my mom keeps sending me pictures of oranges," I exclaimed, as another mysterious set of corner-store fruit popped up on my screen in quick succession. I scrutinized the angles, trying to figure out what she was trying to tell me. I'd texted back a few times, asking for clarification. She simply responded with more photos—and she still hadn't sent me any *actual* oranges. Maybe she was scouring every single market in the greater Bay Area, looking for the perfect specimens?

A few more messages popped up, blocking my view of the oranges. "And now Pippa's texting me . . . oh, looks like she just wanted to check in, see if we're on set yet." I frowned at the screen. "She's actually been texting me a lot today, do you think she's feeling neglected by her newly coupled-off friends? Should I speak to Shelby about including her in more things? Or perhaps I could suggest—"

"Annie." Evie laughed and used her pointy finger to jab at the phone clutched in my hands. "You don't need to solve all of Pippa's problems right now. Or decipher your mom's new citrus obsession. Put your phone down—we should enjoy this!" She gestured out the window, toward the ever-extending stretch of beach. "Scott's gonna love those waves, huh? I know we have beaches in the Bay, but none of them are like this."

She beamed out the window, her face lit with unabashed delight.

"Oh, that reminds me, I need to make sure Scott arranged for his own pick-up from the airport . . ." I turned back to my phone. Scott had a shift at the San Francisco Youth Center in the morning, wherein he'd be giving his rescheduled presentation before taking a later flight down to LA. From there, he'd go directly to the LA Youth Center while we were on set. I probably wouldn't see him until the evening.

"Phone. Down!" Evie insisted, batting at my hands. "Scott is a perfectly capable adult person. Now come on, enjoy this with me!" She grinned, her hazel eyes sparkling. "You know what occurred to me this morning? Neither of us has ever taken a *real* vacation."

"I'm sure that's not . . ." I trailed off, frowning. She had to be wrong about that. How was it possible that we'd both reached our thirties without experiencing such a basic rite of passage?

But if I really thought about it, I could not seem to recall a single moment when I'd gone somewhere purely for pleasure. Growing up, neither my nor Evie's family had been able to afford such things. We'd made our own fun every summer, whether that meant scouring Goodwill for weird abandoned treasures or sneaking into R-rated movies at the old Yamato theater in Japantown. We'd gotten our powers at eighteen; she'd gone off to college and I'd become Aveda Jupiter. And as my superheroing star rose, as there were more and more demonic messes for me to deal with . . . I suppose a trip to some glorious tropical paradise with golden sand and endless sea and a beautiful assortment of humans bringing me drinks with little umbrellas hadn't exactly been in the cards.

"You're right," I marveled, my mind stuck on what it might mean to go to a place and not do anything. "Neither of us even went on a honeymoon, really. Duty has always called."

"And our supposed-to-be-relaxing weekend at my Morgan College reunion ended up being an epic stress-fest," she said, making a face. "But remember how it started? You were all gung-ho on the road trip aspect, because you'd never been on one before—you bought all those snacks? And even when we got into the mission, you were excited about being 'carefree college girls.' Where's that spirit *now*?" She gave me a playful nudge.

I returned her smile, even as I flashed back once more to our climactic battle against the forces of demonic evil at Morgan—and Evie's distraught face when she was ready to give up hope. These past few months, I seemed to flash back to that moment constantly. I just couldn't stop seeing her crushed expression . . . how utterly *defeated* she'd looked . . .

It was true, I'd been very into all the fun and hijinks our collegiate adventure might provide. And that had resulted in me letting my guard down. Which had put both Evie and her baby in peril.

I could *not* let that happen again.

I had to remain vigilant, even when there was fun to be had. Aveda Jupiter cannot afford such a mundane luxury as a day off.

"Isn't Nate supposed to take you on a babymoon?" I said, trying to deflect. "You're going to visit Bea in Maui?"

"Yes," she said, grinning and rubbing the little heart above her belly once more. "Hey, maybe I'll get *two* first vacations in the same year!"

"This isn't technically a vacation," I reminded her. "We're still here on business."

She blew out a frustrated breath. "My point is: we should have fun while we're down here. See the sites, do silly tourist things, and goof off as much as possible. Trust the people we've left in charge back home. Trust that Pippa and your mom and Scott don't need you to put out all the fires right at this very moment. And I can't believe that I, the world's biggest stick in the mud, am the one suggesting this to you."

"Mmm." I drummed my fingers on the plush leather of the Town Car seat, a smile tugging at my lips in spite of myself. "Truly, Evelyn, you have come so far—from stick in the mud to hedonistic thrill-seeker, buying cheap, tourist-friendly t-shirts even though you do not yet know if you do, in fact, *heart* LA."

Evie's grin widened and she gestured expansively to her shirt. "It's true, I'm *wild*. But in all seriousness, this whole pregnancy thing has made me really aware of how I never seem to take the time to just slow down and enjoy something." She patted her stomach again, her smile turning dreamy. "Once little Galactus Tanaka-Jones is in the world, I want to be able to enjoy that moment. I know having a kid will make my world bigger—but I also kind of want to make it *smaller*. Move beyond the superheroing of it all."

"Beyond . . . ?" My brows drew together.

"Just, like, we're more than our jobs, you know?" she said, her gaze turning to her baby bump. "We get to have lives. And as our new superheroing reserves get more confident handling things, maybe we'll get that even more. Imagine if your world wasn't saving *all* of San Francisco *all* the freaking time, Annie. What would you do?"

I opened my mouth, closed it. Turned to look out the window so she wouldn't see the expression of total consternation overtaking my face—not that she would have noticed, as she was still cradling her stomach, her face wistful.

"Imagine being able to take, like, a sabbatical," she continued. "Have the whole summer off, and if it's still feeling good, maybe that leads into fall. Maybe Shruti and Co. are so good at that point, we don't need to return at all. Then we'd *really* get to have lives."

I frowned, careful to keep my face turned toward the window. My work as a superheroine *was* my life. And it was more than that—it was my purpose, my driving force, my reason for everything. I'd always felt that way, and the threat to Evie's baby had me feeling *even more* that way.

But for Evie . . . well, perhaps it wasn't the same, especially with her forthcoming life shift to motherhood. She already seemed to be talking about superheroing in the past tense.

I studied her, gnawing at my lower lip and resisting the urge to shove my nails into my mouth. I'd been so caught up in worrying about the impending threat that Shasta might present—and so focused on protecting Evie and her baby from said threat—I hadn't really thought about what would happen after the baby got here. Obviously Evie would want to take some maternity leave, and we'd already discussed that a bit. But what if she was so caught up in her smaller, sweeter world . . . she simply never returned?

It sounded like that might be her ultimate goal—for our reserves to take over, for us to retire into "better" lives full of rest and relaxation and mundane moments to be savored.

"Evie . . ." I began—then trailed off, unsure what exactly I wanted to say. I flashed back to my surge of triumph and pride from just a few days ago, when I'd felt like everything about our superheroing partnership and our friendship was finally absolutely perfect.

Did she really want to change all of that?

Yes, we did have reserves, but . . . I couldn't imagine any of them as my partner. Not the way Evie was. We were so close, we could sometimes communicate through a wordless method she'd dubbed our "BFF telepathy." Looks, shared feelings, a meaningful meeting of gazes: that was all it took.

There was no way I'd have that with anyone else. But how could I say that to her? *Please don't leave me and superheroing behind for the beautiful new life you've worked so hard for and absolutely deserve after all you've been through*, maybe? Somehow that did not sound quite as convincing as I wanted it to.

"You guys want to drive through Topanga Canyon?" Grouchy Stacey's monotone cut into my runaway train of thought.

"What's that?" Evie exclaimed. "Is there more dog volleyball? More places to buy cool t-shirts?"

"It's one of the biggest wilderness-type areas in LA," Grouchy Stacey said, monotone still intact. "And it's only accessible by one road, which runs from the coast up through the hills that surround the canyon. The community up there is like its own little bohemian hideaway. There's tons of art, antique shops, even an outdoor theater. The drive is very scenic, and there are a lot of weird, random art projects by the side of the road."

"That sounds so cool!" Evie shrieked, slapping the leather seat. "Let's go!"

I turned back to my phone as Stacey made a right onto a road that led into a steep uphill drive. I was trying not to fixate on what Evie had said, or to spin some kind of worst-case scenario before we had a chance to talk about it. I didn't think now was the time for that conversation, and I didn't want to distract her from her current state of awestruck glee.

But I could not stop myself from replaying her words—that she wanted to move "beyond the supeheroing of it all," that our sabbaticals would be so blissful we "don't need to return"—as I turned back to my phone.

What did all of that *mean*?

I threw myself into intense study of my mom's orange pictures as Grouchy Stacey maneuvered the Town Car through the hills, the road occasionally narrowing into a ribbon-thin strip of smoky gray asphalt. Evie peppered Stacey with eager questions about every single thing we passed—the gold and green of the rolling hills surrounding us, the whimsical vintage shop storefront festooned with a rainbow of Christmas lights, the array of camper vans selling fresh fruit and homemade trinkets. It did feel a bit like we'd entered another world, as idyllic and fantastical as the beach where dogs played volleyball.

And yet, I couldn't seem to get into the vacation spirit alongside Evie. I just kept studying my mom's orange pictures from different angles. Was she trying to send me a secret message, was it a cry for help? She had mentioned some ongoing irritation with my dad during our last weekly phone call, but I'd assumed it was simply their usual old married people dance. Maybe there was more to it?

"What's going on up there?" Evie queried, straining her neck as she tried to peer out the front window.

I lifted my gaze from my phone screen, and saw that we were stuck behind a long line of stalled cars. The winding one-lane road did not seem to be built for this sort of thing.

"Traffic," Grouchy Stacey said with a noncommittal shrug. "Another thing LA's known for."

Evie and I exchanged a look. We genuinely could not tell if she was joking or not.

We sat there for a moment, the line of cars at a complete standstill. I went back to swiping through my mother's pictures of oranges, my brain working furiously to decode their hidden meaning.

"Do people generally get out of their cars during traffic?" Evie said, breaking the silence. "Is that another thing LA's known for?"

My head snapped up and I saw that a number of our fellow traffic jammers were eagerly ejecting themselves from their stalled vehicles.

"Not really," Stacey said, sounding puzzled. Not puzzled enough to elaborate, of course.

I stuffed my phone in my pocket and leaned forward,

assessing the scene. The people escaping their cars were now rushing ahead, and some of them appeared to be chattering amongst themselves. I narrowed my eyes as a foreboding prickle ran up the back of my neck. This wasn't just a routine traffic jam. Something else was going on.

"Is your Spidey sense tingling?" Evie murmured.

"Aveda Jupiter always knows when the shit's about to go down," I said. "This Mr. Spidey person has nothing to do with it."

"Except what you just described *is*—oh, never mind," Evie said, chuckling. "Shall we go investigate? I'm framing this as a question, even though I know you're going to do it no matter what."

"Thoughtful," I said, cocking an eyebrow. "But you can stay here if you want, Evelyn. I don't know if running through traffic is a recommended activity for pregnant women."

"It shouldn't be a recommended activity for *anyone*," Evie retorted. "Let's go."

We said a brief good-bye to Grouchy Stacey and promised we'd return. She gave us another shrug, as if to convey that it didn't really matter to her either way.

"Wow," Evie exclaimed, as we maneuvered ourselves out of the Town Car. "It is *really* beautiful up here." She smiled at the hills and clusters of trees surrounding us, their branches just starting to flower with the promise of spring. "And the air is so fresh! Everyone always goes on and on about LA smog, but this sky is clear as a freaking bell. I could really see having a perfect little isolated getaway up here. Like, this would be an ideal place for that summer sabbatical—"

"Yes, beautiful," I said, grabbing her hoodie sleeve and tugging her along. All her rhapsodizing about getaways and sabbaticals was getting under my skin and taking me back to her "move beyond the superheroing of it all" statement. I brushed my feelings of foreboding aside and tried to ignore the way the LA sun had begun to break through the morning clouds, my all-black ensemble soaking up the relentless heat—I'd paired my bomber jacket with a simple tank, sleek black jeans, and pointy-toed ankle boots. "But let's do all those relaxing 'vacation' things you're so excited about later. At the moment, we must be in full superheroine mode, ready to save the day as needed."

As I strode forward, winding my way through the line of stopped cars and trying to see what was up ahead, I felt a familiar sense of purpose take root in my chest. While it was true that I'd never really had time for a proper vacation, I also felt that I would not be able to enjoy something so leisurely. I thrived the most when I had things to do, problems to solve, people to rescue. Long expanses of completely unplanned time sent me into a tailspin of restless uncertainty. To be honest, my and Evie's brief forty-five-minute "road trip" over the Bay Bridge had put me at my limit of relaxation. After that, I'd been more than ready to *do* things.

I hadn't anticipated doing any superheroing in LA. But now the possibility loomed large, and I was absolutely giddy at the prospect.

Plus, maybe a little superheroing side-quest would remind Evie that *this* was her calling. Not taking "sabbaticals" in strange corners of LA.

"Annie, slow down!" Evie whined, shaking her sleeve free from my grasp. "We don't need to *run* into traffic in a literal sense."

I forced myself to relax my pace, craning my neck to try to see what was going on up ahead. It looked like we'd almost reached the site of whatever had caused all this commotion. The line of stopped cars led to one spot on the narrow road, and that's where all the vehicles' former occupants appeared to be clustering up. There were about fifty or so of them, buzzing amongst themselves and gazing up at the sky.

Were we about to witness something along the lines of what excited tourists saw in Maui, some gigantic feat of nature? Would the hills around us rise up as the Pacific Ocean waves were doing so often out there? Would something fall out of the sky, a terrifying Otherworld demon that Aveda Jupiter would have to vanquish with her usual panache—

"Is that a *pig*?" Evie squeaked behind me.

I came to a stop right behind the growing cluster of people and followed their collective gaze upward. And that's when I saw it.

It was indeed . . . a pig.

Well, a sculpture of a pig. It was pale pink and very round, topped off by tiny black hooves that were paused in motion, as if the pig was swimming. Or flying through the air. Then I noticed that it did, in fact, have little white wings sprouting from its back.

"Ah, I see," Evie said, as if reading my thoughts. "It's a *flying* pig."

The sculpture was affixed by some sort of wire contraption to a long metal pole, so it looked as if it was dangling over the side of the road. Or, I guess, *flying* over it. This must be one of the weird little art projects Grouchy Stacey had referred to. Perhaps it always attracted this kind of audience?

But . . . no. The buzz running through the crowd was definitely heightened in that particular way I'd become all too accustomed to—something else was going on. Something *dangerous*. Now that we were closer to the small mass of people, I sensed an undeniable strain of tension rippling through the air.

"Watch out!" someone screamed. "She's about to fall!"

I frowned. The pig was about to fall? *That's* what all this fuss was about? But then my eyes wandered to the top of the metal pole and I saw what had provoked the nervous buzz running through the crowd. A very small child—perhaps about four or five years old—was clinging to the pole like a life preserver, her tiny arms clutching the long piece of metal as she stared resolutely at the porcine sculpture. Other than the death grip, she actually didn't appear to be that alarmed.

"Lexie!" Suddenly, a woman wearing a gauzy floral dress and a huge sun hat was running up to join the crowd, her eyes locked on the little girl dangling so precariously above us. "How did you get up there?! I was taking such beautiful pictures of the vista and you just disappeared . . ." She trailed off, panic etched all over her face.

"I wanted to get to the pig, Mama!" the little girl—Lexie—called out. She still didn't seem scared at all, her gaze focused on the whimsical sculpture that was her apparent goal.

"I called 911," someone offered, waving their phone around. "Probably best if she stays in position until they get here, 'cause . . . uh . . ."

We all eyed the drop from pig to ground. It was far enough to damage a body so small.

"They don't have to wait," I murmured to Evie. "Now. We'll have to do this very carefully. I can grab on to her with my telekinesis, but she'll have to let go of the pole in order for me to transport her to the ground. If she resists, my power will respond by putting more physical pressure on her tiny little body, which could end very badly. So you'll need to sweet talk her—"

"Me?" Evie yelped.

"You," I confirmed. "You're a much sweeter talker than I am. So let's stop wasting time and—"

"Hello, glorious Topanga Canyon! Don't you look lovely today!" The voice boomed from the sky, regal and authoritative—like a proclamation from a queen. My head jerked upward, searching for the source. She zoomed into view, a tall, lithe woman with flowing blonde locks wearing a shiny silver spandex bodysuit that covered her from neck to ankles. I squinted up at her as she soared through the air, moving with confidence toward the little girl.

"Is she *flying*?" Evie hissed.

I was having the exact same thought. I wasn't aware of any powered individuals who actually had *that* power. Then again, I hadn't kept up on the power level-ups my superheroic brethren had been granted after that fateful earthquake several years ago. I made a mental note to get caught up immediately.

"Oh, thank goodness!" someone cried out. "Magnificent Mercedes is here! The brightest angel our city has ever seen!"

Evie and I swiveled to look at each other, our jaws dropping in near unison. I turned back to the sky, my brain working overtime as the flying hero gently talked little Lexie into letting go of the pole so she could sweep her to safety. The girl finally acquiesced, wrapping her spindly arms around Mercedes' neck. I watched as she tearily whispered something in Mercedes' ear and Mercedes nodded, then flew her over to the pig sculpture. Lexie's face broke into a gigantic smile as she patted the pig's head, finally accomplishing her goal.

"I wanted to pet the pig!" she squealed, her eyes lighting up with glee.

A delighted "awwww" ran through the crowd, and a zillion phone cameras went off at once.

And my brain went totally blank. Was that really *Mercedes*?

Mercedes McClain had been my one and only rival for superheroine supremacy in San Francisco. Like Evie and me, she'd been gifted with a superpower at eighteen after the failed demonic invasion. The easiest way to describe it was a sort of "human GPS" effect, wherein she had the ability to track vehicles and destinations and to "see" traffic. She'd once told me that the inside of her brain was like a live map, tracking various auto-related incidents everywhere. She had probably sensed the traffic jam happening on Topanga and swooped in to investigate.

Mercedes had been the one to dub herself "Magnificent Mercedes," and in the aftermath of us receiving powers, she'd tried to lock in the position of San Francisco's sole beloved protector. I, however, had known it was my destiny to be a superheroine even *before* I got powers. During one of those hot, hazy, vacation-less summers when Evie and I were kids, we'd watched the Hong Kong classic *The Heroic Trio*, featuring a team of powerful Asian lady superheroines. And I'd felt something like a lightning bolt to the chest—I didn't know *how*, but I knew *that* was what I was meant to do with my life.

I also knew it wouldn't be easy. After a childhood spent defending Evie and myself from sadistic little white girl bullies on every playground we'd dared to set foot on, I was very aware that an Asian American woman was not the first image that popped into many people's minds when you said the word "superhero." But I was determined to change that, and I knew I would have to work my very hardest to do so—I could not afford to show any weakness, to display any flaws, to have a single hair out of place. I knew the ho-hum telekinesis I'd been gifted with was actually one of the least impressive things in my arsenal, so I kept the focus off that and on my sheer amazingness.

I spent hours perfecting my fighting techniques, working until my muscles screamed in agony. I made sure my costumes were fabulous, eye-catching, and beautifully tailored. And I basically *trained* my hair to stay in place.

I also kept tabs on a large cross-section of police scanners, ensuring that I could show up as soon as evil so much as breathed in the city's direction. Mercedes was always hot on my heels, and for a bit, it seemed like she might win the battle and be crowned San Francisco's superheroine supreme.

I still remembered my first triumphant moment as Aveda Jupiter. A bunch of Otherworld puppy demons had leaped through a portal by an old junk shop, imprinted on an ancient tape deck/radio combo, and were terrorizing customers by playing the Kars 4 Kids jingle over and over again. I could still summon the musty smell of the junk shop, particles of dust swirling in the air around me as I took a deep breath and settled myself into the proper fighting stance. I'd spent the last few weeks perfecting a dazzling 360 roundhouse kick, and I was so ready to use it. I managed to draw the radio demons to me by singing the jingle back at them—an extra bit of torture for the cowering customers, as I had an atrocious singing voice, but one cannot be amazing at everything.

The flying radios had circled me like plastic vultures, blaring the song so loud, I was pretty sure it would be embedded in my ears forever. I knew I'd only get one shot at this kick; after that, the demons would likely scatter and start going after innocent bystanders.

I closed my eyes, felt the endless hours of training thrumming through me, sensed in my heart that my power ponytail was as flawless as ever . . .

And then I let loose with the kick, my hip turning with precision, my leg soaring through the air with so much power. I felt each and every one of those radio demons leave a gigantic bruise on my flesh as my leg slammed into them with purpose. But as I returned to my stance, I was too flushed and giddy to care. Especially when I saw the demons lying in sad pieces at my feet.

"Aveda Jupiter!" I whirled around to see Mercedes striding toward me, assured smile in place. We knew each other a little—we'd actually gone to high school together—but I'd never spoken to her at length. Yet here she was, beaming at me as if we were best friends. Both of us had already accomplished minor feats of superheroing—saving cats stuck in trees, nabbing petty thieves—but this was the first time either of us had taken out a whole slew of demons.

And I'd already done that, so why was she here?

"I am just so delighted we were able to save this fine establishment and all these people!" Mercedes continued, her grin widening as she approached me. She slung an arm around my shoulders and beamed at the junk shop's patrons, who were now emerging from their various hiding places. "Lovely teamwork from the superheroines of San Francisco!" she'd added, tossing her shiny blonde locks over her shoulder and flashing a smile worthy of a toothpaste commercial.

I hadn't quite put together what was happening *while* it was happening. It wasn't until later that I realized none of the junk shop customers I'd saved had actually *seen* my incredible kick. They'd all been too busy cowering underneath various shelves. And now Mercedes was coming on the scene *after* the day had been saved to claim partial credit.

I probably should have told her off then and there, but I was still so new to this superheroing game that my interpretation of her actions was quite generous. I reasoned that, like me, she was simply excited to be achieving her dreams. That perhaps she'd taken down some stray radio demons while I was busy with my kick.

Deep down, I also must have known how it would look to the public if the Mean Woman of Color started yelling at the Nice White Lady. So I simply gritted my teeth and made my smile even bigger as a bunch of phone cameras went off at once.

I would learn later, of course, that I should have been much less generous in my assessment of the situation.

"Aveda Jupiter!" Mercedes' voice pierced all that gloriously clear Topanga Canyon air, snapping me back to the present.

I realized that she was striding toward me now, the crowd parting to allow her through. Little Lexie had been reunited with her mother, who was clutching the child and weeping profusely, wailing her thanks to Magnificent Mercedes.

"I knew that was you!" Mercedes crowed, quickening her pace.

My brain was still whirling, unsure of what to make of any of this. I hastily pasted a big smile on my face—and was very aware of all the phone cameras doing their best to capture it.

"Mercedes," I said, pleased that my voice sounded cool and modulated. "That was quite something. Can you, ah . . . *fly* now?"

"Ha!" Mercedes guffawed, drawing me in for a hug. She air-kissed both cheeks, then pulled back and lowered her voice conspiratorially. "It's a modified jet-pack," she whispered. "Strapped underneath my cape. I can only use it for a few hours before it craps out, but the optics are *amazing*."

"I'll bet," muttered Evie. "Well, um. That was . . . cool. What you did up there."

"Thank you so much—Evelyn, right?" Mercedes gave her a queenly nod.

"Evelyn *Tanaka*," I shot back, trying to keep the snark out of my voice. But really, unless she'd been living under a rock, Mercedes should know who Evie was. "We're partners in superheroing now—you might have seen the news about some of our more recent investigations? Like—"

"Oh, I don't read much of the news that comes out of San Francisco," Mercedes said, waving a hand and letting out a tinkling laugh. "LA is a universe unto itself, and I like to focus on the home base, you know? But my parents live up there, and they sometimes fill me in on your exploits, Aveda. It sounds like you are still very much the local darling!"

"I . . ." I forced my shoulders to relax. I didn't need to be snapping at her that Evie and I were definitely known *beyond* San Francisco at this point. True, we were probably still *most* famous there, but our adventures over the years had earned us a very respectable following worldwide, particularly among diehard superhero fans.

"Anyway, my jet-pack is a game-changing enhancement," Mercedes continued. "My human GPS ability has taken me far here in the city of angels. I've been able to assist law enforcement with traffic incidents, high-speed chases, and foiling carjackers, and I've made a lot of progress in clearing up the city's ever-present gridlock problem. But everything is better with a jet-pack, is it not?"

"Sure," Evie said, raising an eyebrow. "But does that mean you haven't gotten any level-ups to your power in the past few years? Because there was at least one supernatural incident in San Francisco that enhanced a lot of the powered folks there—"

"No, no," Mercedes said, waving a hand. "I wasn't anywhere in the vicinity for that incident, you see. I was much too busy protecting my adopted home city. No level-ups for the magnificent!" She flashed us another dazzling grin. "But LA is such a different ballgame, you know? I've been able to build my own brand of heroing down here, and I'm ever so grateful. I mean, Aveda, if you hadn't so immediately captured the devotion of everyone in the Bay, I might never have left San Francisco!"

"Um, right," I muttered.

"Let's get a photo!" Mercedes sang out, whipping back to face the crowd. She slung an arm around my shoulders, and I was hit with the most bizarre sense of déjà vu. It immediately transported me back to her doing the exact same thing after I'd defeated the radio demons all those years ago. "Los Angeles, do you not recognize the most divalicious Bay Area superheroine in your midst? It's my longtime dear friend, Aveda Jupiter!"

A buzz ran through the crowd, fevered murmurings intensifying as people raised their phone cameras yet again. I smiled for the photos, my gaze locking briefly with Evie's as she was shunted to the side. She looked amused, and was obviously trying to stifle a major wave of giggles.

I narrowed my eyes and tried to beam out a message using our BFF telepathy: *If "vacation" means posing for photo ops underneath a flying pig with my one-time rival who seems to be as annoying as ever and now has a freaking* jet-pack . . . *then I want no part of it.*

And if being in LA meant I was going to randomly run into Mercedes at every turn, well, I was so ready to get to the "business" part of the business trip—and then return home as quickly as superhumanly possible.

CHAPTER FOUR

"IS THAT, LIKE . . . the ocean? Or a replica of the ocean?!"

Evie leaned out of the rickety golf cart that was shuttling us around the Pinnacle Pictures lot, her eyes as bright and shiny as they'd been when she'd witnessed dogs playing volleyball next to the actual ocean. This was most definitely not the ocean—it was a gigantic blue backdrop positioned behind a vast concrete basin painted the same blue, with a few little puffs of white to simulate waves.

"It is not the ocean," Grouchy Stacey confirmed from the golf cart driver's seat. "It is part of a standing exterior set. They fill the basin with water to simulate the ocean for filming."

"Whoa," Evie breathed, her gaze still locked on the fake blue expanse.

After Mercedes and I had posed for photos, she'd been swarmed by fans, but had managed to slip me a fancy embossed business card, saying we should definitely "do lunch" while I was in town. It was hard to think of a less appealing prospect. All the more reason for Evie and me to wrap up our business and get out of here.

Normally, I'd probably be annoyed that none of the crowd had swarmed *me*, but I had been very focused on detaching myself from Mercedes and continuing on our way. Grouchy Stacey had seemed completely nonplussed when we'd returned to the car and recounted our adventure with the flying pig sculpture, but at least by then the traffic jam had cleared. She ferried us to the Pinnacle lot, and now she was taking us to set.

I hadn't realized that decrepit golf carts were the main mode of transportation on a fancy Hollywood lot. It seemed very . . . open air? Like there wasn't much protecting our fragile human bodies as Grouchy Stacey careened into a hairpin turn or bounced merrily over a speed bump. I held tightly to one of the metal poles next to our flimsy, exposed seats, the only thing that seemed to be protecting us from going flying out of the doorless side of the vehicle. I also discreetly grabbed on to the bottom of Evie's hoodie, since she did not seem to be operating with the same kind of caution. She was so excited to drink in every sight, every sound, every marvel of constructed reality. We bounced past huge, drafty soundstages housing carefully built fairy wonderlands, dodged actors outfitted in oversized alien costumes, picked up on the scents of bland craft services food being served up for crew lunches.

And her excitement only grew when we finally reached the set—contained in yet another cavernous soundstage—and were ushered inside. Grouchy Stacey disappeared immediately, and Evie and I were given our own director's chairs and seated behind an array of monitors that showed various angles of the scene as it was being shot.

"Can you believe this?" Evie tugged on my sleeve. "Annie. Come on, what did we say about the phone!"

"Hmm?" I looked up from my screen. I was still puzzling over my mother's photos and I'd just sent Shruti a very detailed text about proper procedures to adhere to once a puppy demon attack was vanquished. I'd also received some new texts from Pippa about nothing in particular, just asking for updates on our progress—which I knew meant she was still missing her friends, feeling excluded, looking for things to do. I could relate. Like her, I'd felt left out when my friends were going through life-changing moments that seemed to leave me behind. But I still hadn't figured out how to *help* her, and it was eating at me, a persistent hum in my ear. I knew there had to be some obvious solution that was eluding me, I just had to—

"*Annie.*"

"Hmm?!?" My head snapped up again and I realized I'd unwittingly returned to staring at my screen, trying to puzzle things out.

"I'm going to, like, confiscate your phone," Evie said, rolling her eyes. "You've barely even looked at the set." She gestured to the scene in front of us. "Are you seeing what I'm seeing?! It's like they up and transported Cake My Day to this very soundstage!"

"Yes, yes, most impressive," I murmured, trying to *not* look at my phone, even though that was suddenly the only thing occupying my brain space. I shook my head, trying to clear it, and focused on what Evie was so excited about.

The set itself—which looked like an oversized dollhouse version of real life, constructed within this massive soundstage—was indeed a perfect replica of Cake My Day, the adorable San Francisco bakery where Evie and I had experienced quite a few adventures (and where Scott had obtained the delectable dark chocolate cake he'd proposed to me with). I wondered which of our exploits the show would be dramatizing today.

Many of the elements of the show—from casting to how, exactly, they were choosing to frame our adventures—were top secret. I probably could have asked for more information at some point, but as Evie'd said, we never quite thought it would actually get made.

I had to admit: gazing at that set now was downright weird. Every tiny detail of Cake My Day had been painstakingly recreated, from the sparkly frosting topping the fluffy spread of cupcakes to the somewhat terrifying collection of cutesy porcelain unicorns that served as the bakery's décor.

Staring at such a familiar location . . . housed in a completely *unfamiliar* location . . . well, it was like I was about to watch a bizarro version of my life unspool in front of me.

"What's next, are we going to meet the actresses playing us?" Evie said, poking me in the arm. "Ooh, is that going to be like meeting *ourselves*?"

"Perhaps," I said, my eyes roaming the soundstage. So far, the glamorous Hollywood life seemed to mostly consist of waiting for something to happen. Various crewmembers bustled about, checking equipment and setting up lights. According to the itinerary we'd been given—the one that documented what "consulting" on all this was going to entail—shooting was supposed to start *now*. But the chair positioned in front of us, which was supposed to contain the director, remained empty.

"So what should we do after this?" Evie asked, leaning back in her director's chair and idly rubbing her belly. "I've been making a list of cool stuff I keep hearing about—like the old abandoned zoo in Griffith Park! Or there's this hundred-year-old mochi shop in Little Tokyo. Or! Maybe we can ask some friendly locals for food recommendations? I read about this one Korean taco truck—"

"The one 'local' we sort of know is Mercedes," I said, squashing the impulse to tell her that the only thing I *actually* wanted to do was go home. "And I do not think I'll be calling her to 'do lunch.'"

"Well, yeah," Evie said. "I meant, like, people we're about to meet here on set. Or maybe Stacey will finally warm up to us. I personally don't think we need to see Magnificent Mercedes ever again—the only thing she's actually magnificent at is being a total asshole."

"Ah, I love it when your sweet angel demeanor gets salty," I said, giving her shoulder an affectionate shake.

After my bout of heroing at the junk shop, I'd told myself I'd simply have to try harder to be the absolute best. I tripled my training sessions, added a few more fighting techniques to my arsenal, and made sure a third party was always filming my exploits, so there would be no question as to who had actually saved the day. And I always managed to show up right before Mercedes did, ensuring that the public knew it was Aveda Jupiter who was constantly coming to their rescue.

I wasn't consciously trying to compete with her. I wanted us both to succeed, since double the heroing meant double the protection for San Francisco. I just wanted to be the best at what I do, which had been my basic goal since childhood.

There weren't that many of us who had turned superheroing into an actual vocation—most of the San Franciscans who had inherited their powers from demons used them for much more mundane purposes. And even though I did want to be the favorite of my fair city, I thought that perhaps Mercedes and I could develop some sort of sisters-in-arms-type friendship, sharing wisdom, frustrations, and observations that only a fellow superheroine would understand. My only real friend back then was Evie—I didn't bond with people easily, and at that point, I didn't really see a reason to. But I did wonder if Mercedes and I, having this one extremely specific thing in common, could become friends.

After about the thousandth dreamy headline bearing my name—above a whole battalion of gushing articles that barely mentioned Mercedes at all—she'd finally given up trying to share the spotlight with me. She'd packed her things and moved to LA. Even though there was no supernatural activity to be had down south, her human GPS ability seemed suited to the area. And as I understood it, over the years she'd developed a measure of local fame (one might say she was a "local darling," hmm?) while Evie and I saw our star shine bright enough to merit a whole TV show. But perhaps Mercedes' new jet-pack was helping her star grow as well. It had certainly seemed that way during the flying pig incident.

Evie's saltiness, however, was not inspired by any of this. No, it all had to do with an icy dinner Mercedes and I had partaken of right before Mercedes moved to LA. She'd reached out and asked me if I'd have a meal with her and share my superheroing wisdom before she headed out to brighter pastures.

I'd accepted her invitation eagerly, thinking this was the beginning of our sisters-in-arms friendship—a friendship that would now encompass multiple cities, even.

Unfortunately, Mercedes had other ideas.

As soon as we sat down to our meal of artisanal tapas, she'd started the love-bombing, peppering me with overly effusive comments that felt like grenades.

"You're lucky you're so *beautiful*," she'd said, giving me a brilliant smile with way too many teeth and shaking out her wavy blonde mane. "The way your hair is so shiny, so perfectly straight—it looks great on camera. And you probably don't even have to treat it, right? It just *falls* that way."

"Sort of," I said, my mind flashing to the five kazillion miracle Asian hair serums my mother was always pressing on me.

"So lucky!" Mercedes had cried, slamming a fist on the table. Her bright green eyes were lit with something I couldn't quite put my finger on—something borderline delirious. "And diversity is so *in* right now—that exotic look is actually seen as desirable, you know? Have you thought about trying to do some kind of endorsement with Japantown—to, like, celebrate your heritage? The media would eat that up!"

"I'm Chinese, so no," I'd said, my brain stuck on the word *exotic*.

"No one would know the difference," Mercedes said, waving a hand and giving me what she seemed to think was a "helpful" smile. "Anyway, Aveda, I'm so glad we could do this. I really want to wish you the best. You've achieved *so much*, it's inspiring. And it gives me so much hope for the future."

"How's that?" I murmured, already knowing I wasn't going to like the answer, but desperately needing to see this through to its awful conclusion.

"I mean, I—and probably a lot of other people—assumed that if San Francisco was going to anoint a heroine, it would be someone more *traditional*." She drew the word out, toying with her golden curls. "But the fact that they chose you—it's really progressive, don't you think? Affirmative action at work! I can't be too sad about being rejected for something if it means more Annie Changs get their shot!"

Then she'd smiled at me, patted my hand, and downed three prosciutto-stuffed figs.

This was one of the only times in my life when I'd been rendered speechless.

I guess I'd always thought that in our unofficial competition to win the heart of San Francisco, Mercedes had perhaps recognized that in the end, I'd bested her.

But that hadn't been the case at all. Instead of seeing all my hard work and talent, she viewed me as someone who had only been able to achieve anything because my face was suddenly seen as "desirable." In her eyes, I'd taken what she, as a blonde white woman, was entitled to. And not because I was better than her. Because diversity was "trendy."

While my diva-esque temper has been known to blow at the smallest provocation, I actually didn't lose it on her. I was too shell-shocked by the sheer audacity of the completely wrongheaded conclusion she'd drawn.

I knew I was the better superheroine, no matter what metric we were going by. So I'd simply given her a big, fake smile, cut dinner short, and headed home secure in the knowledge that Mercedes was leaving town anyway, so what did her delusions matter?

I actually hadn't told Evie about this dinner until much later, after she'd joined me in the superhero game. When I'd been injured, she'd suggested we call Mercedes to step in. I'd vehemently refused, and she'd thought it was because I didn't want to share the spotlight. After we'd healed—both my ankle and our friendship—I'd explained the real reason.

She'd been uncharacteristically furious, growling about how Mercedes "knew exactly what she was doing," how she'd been trying to undermine my confidence because I'd gotten something she thought should be hers.

Evie had also demanded to know why I hadn't told her

about that awkward dinner sooner. I suppose I was so used to being marked as a diva that I didn't want to share any anecdotes that might encourage that sort of thinking. Was I simply interpreting Mercedes' comments in a jealous, uncharitable way? Or was she actually trying to sneakily hit me right where she knew it would hurt?

"Her comments were straight-up racist," Evie had scoffed. "And there was nothing sneaky about them."

Even though I wasn't bothered by Mercedes' mediocre whiteness, I still had no desire to see her again.

I really could not wait to leave LA. Maybe I could find a Bay Area–based Korean taco truck to entice Evie with. Maybe I could *invent* one.

"It's *happening*," Evie exclaimed, jolting me out of my thoughts.

At first I thought she meant I'd received some crucial text on my phone—an emergency back home that Shruti and Co. definitely couldn't handle, an SOS from my mother conveying that oranges were the traditional sign for "I've been kidnapped!", a note from Pippa about feeling hopelessly adrift and friendless—but my screen was blank.

I followed her excited gaze and saw what she was so enthused about: two beautiful women with flawless hair and makeup, striding toward us.

One had dark brown curls and freckles, and was clad in a sloppy ensemble of jeans, a hoodie, and battered Chuck Taylors. The other had glittering black eyes and was wearing a sleek black catsuit and a power ponytail.

"Oh my god," I murmured, clasping Evie's hand. "Is that *us*?"

CHAPTER FIVE

AS THE SHINY TV versions of Evie and Aveda moved toward us, I was surprised to feel a tiny spark of excitement ignite in my chest. They looked *so much* like us. This was happening. This was real! Aveda Jupiter's most incredible exploits were about to be immortalized for all the world to see. And just for a moment, sheer giddiness overwhelmed me, washing away my worries about Evie's dream "sabbaticals" and Pippa's friendship problems and my mother's new citrus obsession.

"Well, hello!" TV Evie sang out as the duo reached us, giving an expansive wave. "Wow. It's like looking in a mirror, isn't it?"

"Indeed," TV Aveda said, gifting us with a knowing eyebrow arch—*my* knowing eyebrow arch, I realized! "Hopefully all the studying we've done of y'all is paying off. We've spent oh-so-many hours looking at footage, learning your mannerisms. It's so strange to have you standing in front of us!"

Evie and I slid out of our director's chairs in unison, both captivated by the bizarre mirage we were facing.

"Holy shit!" Evie gasped. "This is both the coolest and the weirdest thing that's ever happened to me."

"I'm Michelle Chong," TV Evie said, a friendly grin crossing her face. "But I go by Miki, not to be confused with the mouse! That's right, my Chinese parents chose a Japanese nickname for my American-slash-French actual name. Diaspora feels, eh? And this is Kat Morikawa."

"Wait a minute," I said, laughing a little. "So TV Evie is

Chinese and TV Me is Japanese? They did an ethnicity switcheroo?"

"Unfortunately, this is the way of things in our industry," Kat said, one corner of her mouth quirking into a weary smile. "They always say they're going to be specific, but in the end, they just see Asian as Asian. In the words of the casting director who did our pilot: 'Close enough.'"

"Ah, excellent, you're *meeting*," a deep voice boomed behind us. Evie and I turned to see a tall, burly white guy with an impressive red beard striding up. "Evies and Avedas all together, just *beautiful*. Love to see it." He stopped in front of us and paused, widening his stance and putting his hands on his hips. Then he flashed us a big smile, as if expecting us to congratulate him on something.

"Um, this is Clint Mayweather, our showrunner," Miki said, once it became clear that Burly Beard wasn't going to offer anything in the way of identifying credentials. Clint shot her an affectionate, condescending look and puffed up in response, even though Miki hadn't said anything particularly complimentary. "He's also directing the pilot—"

"Because I'm a true *auteur*," Clint interrupted, clapping his hands together. "Can't trust anyone else with my vision."

"*Your* vision of *our* lives?" I blurted out. I instantly disliked this man. He was the type of over-assured blowhard I'd been dealing with in various situations for most of my life, so convinced of his own greatness despite absolutely no evidence to back it up. I knew Evie thought I was generally too judgmental, but *come on*.

This was who they'd chosen to shepherd our story to the screen?

"Ha!" Clint gave me finger guns. "I heard you were a pistol, Aveda Jupiter—delighted to see that wasn't an exaggeration! True, this show is based on you. But being an auteur, I had to put my own stamp on it. People expect nothing less from Clint Mayweather!"

I glanced over at Miki and Kat. They weren't saying anything to each other out loud, but the knowing looks they exchanged spoke volumes. Hmm. Perhaps Evie and I could speak to them alone later.

I wanted to kick myself for not following the behind-the-scenes progress of the show more carefully. I'd never expected that of all the people to put in charge, they'd choose a blustery white man who seemed very invested in his "vision." But perhaps I should have seen that coming?

My gaze slid to Evie. Her eyes were locked on Miki and Kat, a mushy sort of expression overtaking her face. She'd barely even registered Clint's overbearing bluster; she was enchanted by these shiny versions of us. And thanks to our best friend telepathy, I could practically hear what she was thinking—about her and me and how far we'd come. About how *unreal* this moment was, mixed-up ethnicities and annoying self-proclaimed auteurs aside.

"Don't you worry that gorgeous head of yours, Aveda Jupiter!" Clint said, clapping a heavy, unwelcome hand on my shoulder and giving me a squeeze that made my skin crawl. I resisted the urge to . . . well, I'd like to say "shake him off," but it was more like "punch him in the face."

Aveda Jupiter is not exactly a master of subtlety. And she does not appreciate when overly confident braggarts invade her personal space.

Evie finally broke free of whatever Hollywood spell she was under and turned away from Miki and Kat, her gaze going straight to Clint's hand on my shoulder. Without hesitating, she grabbed my arm and tugged me to the side, pulling me away from his grasp.

Now she was reading *my* thoughts. And she knew punching was definitely on the table.

"I did take some artistic liberties, but you can rest assured they were *very* artistic," Clint said with a broad wink. "I think you'll find that the *heart* of your story—two strong Asian American women kicking ass and looking absolutely stunning while doing so—is still very much alive!"

I'm not sure why, but that only made me want to punch him *even more*.

"Time to get started," Clint bellowed, clapping his hands together. "Miki, Kat: let's do a run-through, and then we may need to re-light you both. It looks like Nico had a heavy hand with the makeup today."

"I believe these gargantuan false eyelashes were *your* idea," Kat muttered under her breath.

"Places!" Clint yelled, ignoring her. "This is rehearsal, people! But I want those animatronics fully deployed! On a Clint Mayweather production, we go full out *always*!"

He said his name as if declaring himself a brand or a legend. Like I said, I can be judgmental . . . but he was giving me so much to judge him for.

Evie and I sat back down in our director's chairs. And suddenly, the set was *alive*. Bells rang out, people yelled commands at each other, someone clapped one of those clacky slates together . . .

And then Kat and Miki, that bizarro version of me and Evie, stood in the center of the bizarro Cake My Day. Waiting for their cue.

In spite of my simmering annoyance with Clint and his "vision," I felt that spark of excitement ignite in my chest again.

"Look at our girls," Evie whispered. "Look at *us*."

I reached over and squeezed her hand.

"And, action!" Clint yelled.

Miki and Kat sprang to life—Miki crouching behind a counter, Kat throwing her hands up to defend against . . .

"Oh my god," Evie whispered. "They made the *cupcakes*!"

Indeed they had. Tiny fake cupcakes with flashing eyes and snapping fangs burst out of nowhere, raining down on Kat. Those must have been the animatronics Clint was referring to.

And this was the fateful demonic cupcake battle that had taken place right before I'd injured my ankle and Evie had agreed to pose as me until it was healed. *This* was when we'd become true partners in superheroing.

"It's our origin story," I hissed in her ear. She grinned and gave a tiny fist-pump.

"Evie, duck!" Kat called out, her fists flying as she punched cupcakes left and right. I nodded, impressed—her moves were so assured, so powerful. She must have studied the footage of this particular battle extra carefully.

"On your left, Aveda!" Miki cried out, her face crumpling in distress.

Kat whirled around and smacked another cupcake, turning the poor animatronic into a mess of flying smithereens.

"Take that, you befrostinged fiend!" she shrieked.

"Oof," I winced. "That was dreadful. I guess it's part of Clint's *vision*."

"No." Evie met my eyes, lips twitching with amusement. "You actually said that."

"I'm sure I did *not*," I retorted, trying to sound imperious. But my lips were twitching, too. I turned away from Evie before we ruined rehearsal with a mutual giggle fit. And then squeezed her hand again, pride swelling in my chest.

I had to admit—this was cool.

The TV versions of us looked *extra* cool.

And so far, even Clint's depiction of us was cool—and pretty true to life. Though I absolutely did *not* remember coming up with such a corny one-liner.

"That's *it*," Kat cried, her eyes narrowing as another flock of cupcakes swarmed her. "My fists are not enough for these jerks. Time to bring out the big guns!"

"Um, what?" Evie murmured. "Okay, you totally said the 'befrostinged fiends' thing, but you never said *that*."

We both watched in confusion as Kat pulled a massive wooden stake from the waistband of her pants—where it had apparently been tucked the whole time? How had I not noticed?—and went into a spin worthy of classic Lynda Carter Wonder Woman. Her arm flew out and the stake sliced its way through the remaining cupcakes, demolishing them on the spot.

"You know what this means!" Miki cried out, scrambling to her feet.

Kat glowered at the piles of animatronic frosting coating her boots, stake still poised to stab. "Do I ever," she hissed. "These cupcakes aren't just demonic! They're *vampiric*!"

Next to me, Evie let out a little yelp—and I realized I was squeezing her hand so tightly, bones were starting to crunch together.

"Sorry," I muttered, loosening my grip.

Before I could even begin to process everything that had happened in the last five minutes, a poof of smoke exploded in front of Kat and Miki, sending them both into coughing fits.

And then, out of nowhere, there was another figure lurking behind them—swoopy black and red satin cape, flashing red eyes . . . and the barest hint of fangs protruding from his mouth.

"Ahhhh, Aveda Jupiter!" he intoned, eyebrows waggling. I cringed. He sounded like a super exaggerated version of the Count on *Sesame Street*. "At last, we meet. And at last, you are mine!"

And then, without further ado, he grasped Kat by the shoulders and sank his fangs into her neck. She slumped against him, her eyes rolling back into her head.

"Aveda!" Miki screamed, falling to her knees and reaching skyward. *"Nooooooo!"*

I somehow managed not to scream anything. But next to me, I heard Evie yelp again as my hand tightened around hers once more.

Clint's auteur vision had transformed me from Aveda Jupiter, Beloved Badass Superheroine into . . . Aveda Jupiter, Vampire's Shrinking Violet Victim?

What. The. *Fuck*.

CHAPTER SIX

"THIS WILL NOT stand!" I spat out as I stomped down the hall toward our Beverly Hills Hotel suite. Stomping down this particular hall was far from satisfying. The hotel was a century-old landmark done up in whimsical pink and green. The carpet bore a pattern of tranquil green waves, and was plush beneath my heels, muffling the sounds of my decisive footfalls. And the wallpaper surrounding us sported the hotel's signature banana-leaf print, to reinforce the idea that you were entering a tropical oasis with a distinctly LA vibe. If I was feeling more relaxed, I might have been able to imagine a cool breeze ruffling those leaves and sending the scent of wild greenery wafting through the air.

But since I pretty much never feel anything resembling "relaxed," this hypothetical was very unlikely to happen anyway.

"I can't believe it!" I continued, throwing up my hands. "Why did that hack 'auteur' decide our story needed *vampires*? We already have demons! And ghosts, if you really want to get into it. And why did that scene depict Aveda Jupiter being defeated by a vampire? That would *never* happen in real life! Um, if vampires actually existed, I mean."

"We only saw the beginning of the episode, we don't know how it ends!" Evie protested, scrambling to keep up with me.

I took a deep breath and slowed my pace. I didn't need to be making a pregnant lady run a marathon. After we'd witnessed the shooting of that horrifying scene, Grouchy Stacey had appeared by our side like magic and swept us away.

"Clint needs to focus," she'd hissed at us. "So we've been asked to clear the set temporarily. Sorry." I'd never heard someone apologize with less conviction.

I'd wanted to fight her, of course, but Evie had looked woozy and I'd sensed she probably needed a snack and a lie-down. So I'd gone along with it, snagging Evie a granola bar from the craft services table on our way out. (Stacey hadn't noticed my petty theft—I'm guessing I would have been on the receiving end of some serious stink-eye if she had.)

I could battle Clint and his terrible vision *later*. After my pregnant best friend had gotten a nap in.

"Annie?" Evie finally caught up to me and tugged at my sleeve. "Did you hear me? We don't know how the episode ends! Maybe Aveda Jupiter comes back and kicks his ass as, like, Aveda the Vampire Slayer."

"Oh, dear god." I stopped in my tracks, the soothing banana-leaf wallpaper blurring in and out as I parsed her words. "Please, no. The only thing worse than being depicted inaccurately is being depicted as a *copycat heroine*." I narrowed my eyes at the wallpaper. "Aveda Jupiter is *an original*."

"Of course she is," Evie said—and I detected a certain level of soothing tonal nuance enter her voice. It was the same nuance she'd always used when she'd been my assistant, seeing to my every whim. "I'm sure that will come through in the end."

"Ugh." I stared at the banana leaves, forcing them to come back into focus. "I'm sorry, I don't mean to drag out the diva—"

"Just don't make me scrub cupcake frosting off your boots and we're good," Evie said wryly.

"I wish I'd kept better tabs on this whole process," I lamented. "I should have asked them to keep us updated on every move, should have demanded we approve every person on this show. It's odd that we didn't even meet our TV alter egos, didn't even know who they were, until *today*. And Clint—who made *that* choice?"

"You can't—*we* can't—be expected to keep detailed track of every single thing," Evie reasoned. "I'm sure some of the emails that actually *did* update us came in during our break between assistants. You and I aren't great at dealing with all those messages ourselves; there's just no time. Plus, back when the studio first optioned our life rights . . . wasn't that right around when you and Scott got married? So on top of the usual superheroing, you were also busy being in love." She gave me a teasing, hopeful smile.

"No excuses," I said—but I returned her smile as best I could. "Now. Let's find out who we need to speak to in order to fix this train wreck."

As we traversed the remaining green carpet that led to our suite, I actually felt my shoulders relax. Now that my brain had a tangible mission in front of it, something to solve and accomplish, it settled into its groove, assembling ideas for definitive next steps and action items. I could practically feel my power ponytail twitching with excitement.

Maybe this trip wouldn't be so bad after all.

We arrived at our suite and let ourselves inside. Our luggage was already there, neatly stacked in the corner.

Just like the hallway, the main living space was designed to be a calming oasis of pink and green. The centerpiece was a sumptuous curving couch done up in green and white upholstery that mimicked the wallpaper's banana-leaf pattern. Green velvet armchairs flanked the couch on either side, and the glass table perched on the plush carpet sported an overflowing vase of fresh white flowers. An enticing scent of coconut and gardenia floated through the air—I imagined it was piped in from some kind of central system to further enhance the oasis feel.

"Wow," Evie breathed out, her eyes drinking in every detail. "So they may have butchered our life story, but at least the studio saw fit to put us up somewhere *really* fancy."

"A whole suite," I murmured in agreement. "It's supposed to have two full bedrooms—"

"Make that *three*!" a lilting voice called out.

Evie and I both whipped around to see a familiar figure with an eye-catching swoop of platinum blonde hair emerging from the bedroom off to the left.

"Pippa!" I exclaimed as she grinned and toasted us with a mini-sized can of soda. "What are you doing here?"

"And is that from the minibar?" Evie asked, eyeing the tiny soda can trepidatiously. "Because you have to pay for that stuff—"

"Oh, *relax*," Pippa said, waving the soda at her. "You guys are VIP guests, everything's comped! I checked." She took a hefty swig of the soda. "And as for what I'm doing here— well, I was hanging out at HQ because Shelby and Tess and Julie were all busy doing lovey-dovey stuff *yet again*, and Nate was saying how your guys' trip was going to be such a whirlwind, he wondered if you needed, like, a minder. Then Lucy said the studio was supposed to give you someone to handle all that, then Bea said—"

"Bea was there?" Evie interrupted, her brow crinkling in confusion.

"She was on FaceTime," Pippa clarified, taking another swig of soda. "And *she* said that no way would some rando assigned by the studio be able to live up to the great Aveda Jupiter's standards—"

"I'm guessing she said that in a much less complimentary way, but thank you," I interjected. "Did they all send you down to LA as a surprise? I was texting with you earlier and you never let on that you were here!"

"Nope!" Pippa tried to take another drink—only to realize the tiny can was empty. She frowned at it, then set it down on the pristine glass table and marched over to the minibar. "It was all my great idea!" she exclaimed, pulling another tiny soda free. "But I did want to surprise you. I knew that if you guys had any kinds of heads-up, you'd try to talk me out of it. But now I'm here, I'm ready to help, annnnnd . . ." She gestured dramatically with her soda can. "There are *three* bedrooms! So it's perfect!"

"I . . ." Evie opened her mouth, closed it. "Annie, do you . . ."

I stifled a grin. I was always Bad Cop. But in this case . . . well, normally I'd also want to send Pippa home. She wasn't technically employed by us, she had a way of getting into trouble while doing absolutely nothing, and she was already shotgunning her way through the minibar.

But my brain was also slowly coalescing around an idea—and when Aveda Jupiter gets an idea, there's no stopping her.

"Actually," I said slowly, "I think Pippa should stay."

"Oh. Kay?" Evie said, her gaze narrowing suspiciously. She tended to hate it whenever I got what she referred to as my Idea Face.

"She can help us on our latest mission," I said. "You know—the mission to stop this adaptation of our life story from being a total disaster. And say, are we sure there's not some kind of supernatural interference happening? It almost seems like there would have to be for things to be this *level* of disaster. Perhaps we should look into that as well!"

"Ooh!" Pippa said, finishing her second soda. She rummaged around in the minibar for a third. "That sounds right up my alley."

"Hold on," Evie said. "Annie. Why is this suddenly a full-on mission? This trip was supposed to involve *no* missions. You even agreed to do some vacation-adjacent things with me!"

"I don't know that I *agreed*—"

"And there's nothing supernatural happening!" Evie insisted, raising her voice and waving her arms around like she was trying to get my attention in a crowd. "Annie, I know you're still kinda freaking out about Shasta's potential plan—"

"I don't understand why *you're* not more freaked out about it!" I countered. "Since it involves stealing *your* offspring and all!"

"I just don't want to worry about that right now!" she shot back. "Like I said, I want to enjoy our time here, but it feels like you're seeing danger around every corner—"

"Because there usually *is* danger around every corner!" I

retorted. "You've said it yourself—if something seems even a little bit supernatural, it usually is. That's how our lives tend to go, Evelyn."

"But in this case, I really think the only danger is, you know, fictional! Vampires!" She curled her hands like claws and made her front teeth protrude over her lip, to really drive the point home. I stifled a giggle.

"Vampires?!" Pippa shrieked. "There are *vampires* happening and no one told me? AJ, I'm so disappointed in you, you know I am an expert in all things paranormal romance—but especially vampires!"

"*Fictional* vampires!" Evie bellowed.

"That are now part of our life story for some reason," I grumbled.

"Oh, hold up, Shelby's calling me!" Pippa exclaimed, her eyes sparkling as she glanced down at her phone screen. "I gotta take this, I haven't heard from her in *days*."

She scrambled to answer, her overeagerness causing the phone to nearly slip from her grasp.

"Shel!" Pippa screamed, throwing an arm out as she answered the phone. "I have *so much* to tell you! I've been called down to LA on a very special mission with our bosses! And it involves *vampires*! Evie and AJ—say hi!"

She flipped the phone around so we could see Shelby, who was wearing her usual vaguely worried expression.

"Oh, hey," Shelby said, giving us a wave. "That's great, Pips. I was actually calling to see if you could monitor the Tanaka/Jupiter, Inc. inbox for the rest of the day, so I guess it works out perfect, huh?"

"Well . . . yeah," Pippa said, deflating a bit as she swiveled the phone back to face her. "Of course. No problem. But don't you wanna hear about the vampires—"

"Sure, sure—but later," Shelby said, sounding distracted. "I gotta go, me and Kris have reservations at that new hole in the wall just off campus—"

"You're eating at Coy?!" Pippa yelled, her eyes nearly popping out of her head. "The converted gas station that's now a super hot underground and possibly illegal grub spot? I thought they didn't do reservations!"

"Kris got us in," Shelby said. "I don't know how they did it, but that's Kris. They always seem to be surprising me with the wildest things."

"Um, right," Pippa said, deflating further. My heart twisted. Even her platinum hair swoop looked droopy. "It's just. I thought *we* were going to go—"

"We will," Shelby insisted. "Later. And we'll have the best time, because Kris will prep us on exactly what to order. They have an uncanny knack for sussing out menus, knowing what to get. God, they have so many random talents. I still can't believe they wanted to go out with me."

"Yeah, Kris is great," Pippa said, her voice very faint. "All hail Kris."

"I really gotta go, but text me!" Shelby said. "Tell me all about the werewolves."

"It's *vampires*," Pippa said—just as her phone emitted the telltale beep that meant Shelby had hung up. "And you never return my texts these days."

Her hand clutching the phone fell to her side and she gazed out the suite's massive windows, her face going contemplative.

My heart twisted further. I knew what she was feeling. When Evie and I had first partnered up, the public had seemed way more dazzled by her than by old standby Aveda Jupiter. And as her wedding planning progressed and her star shone brighter, I'd felt her slipping away from me. As if I'd been cut out of every photo we'd ever taken together. As if she'd never needed me the way I needed her.

In the end, that hadn't been exactly what was going on, and we'd worked it out. Just as I was sure Pippa and Shelby would. But the slump of Pippa's shoulders and the lost look in her eyes were all too familiar.

Perhaps this was the real reason she'd ended up down here. So I could officially figure out how to help her with this current seismic shift in her friendships.

Which meant I had yet *another* mission. My heart lifted at the thought.

I'd eventually solve her friendship dilemma, but for now, maybe it would help if I kept her busy.

"All right, Pippa," I said, straightening my spine and making my voice as Aveda Jupiter authoritative as possible. "Let's tackle this TV show dilemma. I want to figure out how we ended up with such a disaster in the making. Can you start by going through our assistant email box—gather all the messages from any representative of Pinnacle Pictures and see what they say. I want to know everything we might have accidentally agreed to, everything we might have missed. And more importantly, I want to know who to investigate—and who to yell at."

"You got it, AJ," Pippa said, perking up.

"And why don't you grab another soda," I said impulsively. "You're going to be working so hard, you deserve it!"

She flashed me a peace sign and a big toothy grin as she grabbed another can, bustled into her bedroom, and shut the door.

"Why do I already feel like this is going to end badly?" Evie said, laughing as she collapsed onto the couch. I crossed the room and sat down next to her.

"Let her help us," I said—and now I was trying to make *my* voice soothing. "She's feeling neglected by her friends, left out. Maybe if she has something to occupy her time, she'll feel better."

"Aww, look at you," Evie said, giving me a friendly punch in the arm. "Empathy and insight into the behavior of a fellow human! The old divalicious Aveda Jupiter could never."

"Yes, well." I gave a modest shrug. "Being extra aware of why people do what they do has made me a better superheroine."

"And a better friend," Evie said, an affectionate smile crossing her lips. "Ugh, what time is it? We never got to that Korean taco truck, and I need to eat again. And call Nate."

"I'm impressed he didn't insist on coming with us," I said,

reaching out to toy with the delicate leaves of the flower arrangement on the table. "I know he's been so worried about you and the baby."

"We've been communicating much better," Evie said, her eyes softening into a distinctly mushy expression. "Ever since—"

"Ever since you had dirty desk sex in your old Morgan College TA office, thereby exorcising various personal demons from your past and reaffirming your undying love for each other?" I batted my eyelashes and placed a hand over my heart. "I remember."

"Hey," Evie said, laughing. "Okay, yes, so that was part of it, but the better communication part came about thanks to all the talking we did *before* the sex. I realized I'd been shutting him out and pretending like I had zero concerns about this whole pregnancy business. Meanwhile, he was smothering me and being overprotective. And things have been good ever since. Although . . ." She glanced down at her phone. "I do kind of wish he had come with us."

"You can still have dirty *phone* sex," I countered. "Or Skype sex. I don't know, what do the kids do nowadays? Zoom sex? Is everything on TikTok?"

"Maybe that's something else Pippa can fill us in on," Evie said, grinning at me.

"In any case, I'm glad the two of you are *you* again," I said, giving her a gentle smile. "There's been far too much change at Tanaka/Jupiter HQ recently, and I don't think I could have taken any more of it. We're perfect just the way we are. Although I still think I can get Lucy to move back in—with Rose, of course—if I just—"

"Annie." Evie shook her head at me affectionately. "You have to give that up. Lucy's *not* moving back in."

"It never hurts to try," I said, toying a little more aggressively with the flower arrangement. One of the leaves crumbled in my hand.

I wasn't sure why Lucy moving out and Bea moving away

was still bothering me so much. Perhaps it was because they seemed intent on making all these changes after we'd finally gotten everything so perfect with Team Tanaka/Jupiter. And now Evie wanted to make her life "smaller" . . . and, well, it was hard for me not to feel like all of these shifts in our hard-won infrastructure were the bricks at the base of a massive Jenga pile, and losing just one more would send the whole enterprise into fatal collapse.

My phone buzzed against my hip, jolting me out of my thoughts.

"Ah, it's Scott!" I exclaimed, studying the screen. In all the chaos of the day, I'd forgotten to check in with him. I mentally scolded myself for neglecting yet another part of my life, and vowed to set some kind of reminder for the rest of the week—CHECK IN ON YOUR HUSBAND. "His flight was fine and he's had a busy day at the Youth Center."

"Is he changing young lives already?" Evie asked, peering over my shoulder.

"I believe today was ceremonial. He's getting to meet everyone, filling out boring paperwork. That kind of thing. The actual surf clinic won't begin for another couple days."

"Man." Evie turned to the window that looked out on the city, sunlight cascading through and casting an unearthly glow over the pink and green oasis of our suite. It was late afternoon, right before the sun would begin its lazy descent. "I bet you can surf year round out here—the weather's always gorgeous."

"Pfft, that just means LA has no seasons," I sniffed. "I prefer a bit of a chill myself. Oh, hold on, Scott wants me to call him . . ."

Which you should have done earlier anyway, a little voice nagged at me.

"Annie!" Scott's voice echoed through the line. He sounded excited, almost boyish. I could picture him, all lit up—that passion he displayed whenever he got to do the work he loved was so *present* already. Giddiness surged through me, and I felt my lips curving into a smile. This stint at the LA Youth Center was going to be exactly what he needed.

"Sounds like you're already having a great time," I said.

"Yeah—I hope you are, too?"

"That . . . is a story for another time," I said hastily. "What's up? Do you want to make dinner plans? Oh, Pippa is here as well, I'll explain later—"

"Actually, I wanted to see if you were up for coming down here," he said. "There's a little surprise for you at the Youth Center—an old friend. And she's just dying to see you."

CHAPTER SEVEN

SO YES, IN retrospect, I should have pressed Scott more on this "old friend" business. But my mind was consumed by the utter disaster that was Team Tanaka/Jupiter on TV, as well as the shifting Jenga pieces of Team Tanaka/Jupiter in real life. I also couldn't stop thinking about Pippa's friendship woes. Oh, and the fact that my mother had now gone radio silent. Weirdly, the lack of orange photos was alarming me even more than an excess of them. I would have to call her later.

My brain was spinning so many plates, and Scott had sounded so excited, so *happy*, that I readily agreed to head downtown for whatever "surprise" awaited me.

If I'd had just one less thing on my mind, I'm sure my top-notch Aveda Jupiter investigative skills would have figured it out immediately. Because hadn't Evie and I just encountered the one person we knew in all of LA?

"Annie!" Scott called out as I entered the Youth Center, a worn but sturdy building housed in the metropolitan bustle of downtown LA. "Hey, look who I found!"

"Aveeeeedaaaaa!" For the second time that day, Mercedes McClain made a beeline for me, blonde curls bobbing around her heart-shaped face. And then, before I could do or say anything, she enveloped me in a bone-crushing hug. "We had no time to catch up this morning, hmm? When I saw your handsome husband here, I knew I had to seize the opportunity," she exclaimed, pulling back from our hug and jiggling my arm. "All those paparazzi photos really do not do him justice—luckily I remembered Hottie Scotty from our high school days!"

I cringed at her use of that terrible nickname, something I remembered some of Scott's admirers coming up with after his bemuscled transformation. Also, hadn't Mercedes said earlier that she didn't pay attention to any news items about us? Or did she only notice the ones that featured "Hottie Scotty"?

"I can't believe I haven't seen him since we were all teenagers," Mercedes continued. "I mean, I wasn't invited to the wedding, so . . ."

"It was . . . small," I said, my voice faint.

"And he told me how you two were *estranged* for a while," she said, fluttering her eyelashes and pursing her lips in concern. "Which explains why I never met him when you and I were running around as young superheroines, newly blessed with our powers. But that just makes your love story all the more epic, doesn't it?"

"Yes, epic," I murmured robotically, my voice growing smaller with every syllable.

"He told me *all* about how you came together during Evie's wedding," Mercedes continued, clapping a dramatic hand over her heart. "So romantic!"

I manufactured a smile, even as my brain hooked on to the words that just kept spilling out of her mouth. Had Scott given Mercedes our entire romantic history? The fight we'd had in our twenties, the one that had led to us not speaking for years, was still a painful moment in our past. We'd gotten a little tipsy one night when he was helping me move furniture around in my apartment, and he'd kissed me. I'd been happy for one whole minute . . . and then my annoying brain helpfully reminded me that Scott was probably in love with Evie after their prom dalliance, that I was some kind of second-choice consolation prize because he couldn't have her. That hadn't been true at all, but I'd said things to him I wasn't proud of, things that illustrated just how far I'd fallen into the diva hole.

I'm Aveda Jupiter now, for God's sake, I'd hissed, lashing out in pain. *And Aveda Jupiter can't be seen with some low-rent surfer mage. I have an* image *to consider.*

Thinking back to that fight always poked at the softest parts of my heart—maybe because it was the moment where I really and truly could have lost him forever.

What *else* had he told her?

"Anyway!" Mercedes trilled. "Now that Scott's doing this gig at the Youth Center, he and I can get to know each other! Oh, I just knew seeing you this morning was a sign!"

She linked her arm through mine and guided—well, more like dragged—me across the room and over to Scott, who was grinning at us in the way of men who are completely oblivious to some major shit that's about to go down.

"You work at the Youth Center, Mercedes?" I said, not sure where to start. To be honest, my brain was still stuck on the fact that Mercedes now knew way more about me than I'd ever wanted her to. "I mean, when you're not flying around with your jet-pack."

"Indeed I do!" she preened. "I started two years ago. I had begun to feel empty, always surrounded by the glory of superheroing, you know? My life was so superficial, just endless parties and accolades and admirers. You know how it is—you're Aveda Jupiter!"

"Yes," I muttered. "I definitely know how it is."

"I started asking myself, how can I give back?" Mercedes continued, a thoughtful dent crinkling her smooth forehead. "How can I impart all the wisdom and strength I've gained through the years to today's youth? After all, they're our future!"

"Our future," I mumbled, nodding. I was still so shell-shocked, I could only seem to respond to her by repeating whatever she'd just said.

"So I had my people contact the Youth Center, and they were delighted to have someone of my stature involved!" Mercedes continued. "I've started all kinds of programs here: superheroine arts and crafts for the little ones, self-defense for teens. It's so *rewarding.* But then, I'm sure you do all kinds of charity work up in the Bay Area!"

"Right," I managed, racking my brain for the last time I'd done anything resembling charity work.

"Isn't this great?" Scott exclaimed, his grin widening. "Not only do I get to finally do that LA surf clinic, but it's alongside your old friend Mercedes!"

He threw an arm around my shoulders and pulled me close, his summer scent washing over me. I felt myself soften at his familiar touch and his boundless enthusiasm. Of course Scott had been all talkative and share-y with Mercedes, I reasoned. He was like that with everyone, open and friendly and trying to make a connection. Just like he always managed to do with the shyest kid in his classes. And since Mercedes had characterized our relationship *differently* than I would have, there was no reason for him not to be his usual gregarious self. I tried to smile back at him, but sensed I looked more like an animal baring its teeth.

"Just one day in and he's already showing us all up!" Mercedes said, her tinkling laugh pulling me back to the moment. She reached over and gave Scott a playful swat on the arm. I tried not to fixate on the way her fingers lingered perhaps a moment longer than necessary on his bicep, her expression turning admiring as she felt the muscles rippling underneath the thin cotton of his t-shirt.

While I am quite territorial and protective by nature, I'd spent the last few years trying to stamp out those flares of petty jealousy that always seemed to rise up at the most inopportune moments. I knew in my heart that such things were not worthy of the new, improved, *much* less divalicious Aveda Jupiter.

That said, the new Aveda Jupiter had not exactly planned on watching a former frenemy feel up her husband.

I was jolted out of my trying-not-to-be-petty thoughts by an uproarious laugh from Scott and Mercedes. Her hand, I could not help but notice, was still firmly attached to his bicep.

"That's very flattering," Scott was saying. "But my heart will always belong to San Francisco."

"That is all well and good, but your body could belong elsewhere," Mercedes said, her grin turning teasing. "Just look at me: a born and bred former San Franciscan who's managed to thrive in the city of angels!"

Well, shit. What had I missed *now*?

"We're just kidding around, Annie," Scott said, perhaps picking up on my confused expression. "I've only been here for a few hours, no one's even had time to offer me an actual job!"

"But they will—your talent is undeniable!" Mercedes cooed. "And weren't you saying they only need you part-time up in the Bay? If you moved down here, you could probably be full-time and then some! Really develop your surf clinic, maybe expand it? So many possibilities!"

"We're not moving," I blurted out.

They both looked at me, their expressions turning confused.

"Of course not," Scott said, cocking his head curiously at me. "No one said anything about that."

My face heated and I crossed my arms over my chest. My voice had come out all sharp and defiant and *weird*. Like an exhausted mom telling her kids they couldn't have any candy. And I couldn't think of a thing to say to smooth it over or to even begin to explain why I'd had such a harsh reaction to a conversation I'd barely even heard.

For a moment, we stayed frozen like that, Scott and Mercedes staring at me as I tightened my arms around myself and willed the blush in my cheeks to fade. This of course only made me focus more on their confused faces, and I was struck by how perfect they looked together: blonde, sun-kissed, wholesome. And she was so attentive to him, laser-focused on his every move. She would never fall asleep while he was kissing her—I was sure of it.

Wait, why was I thinking *that*? It was like the vision, this series of beyond-disturbing images, implanted in my brain and refused to leave. I tried to shove them down.

"I don't know," Mercedes finally said, breaking the excruciating silence. Her eyes slid to Scott, her mouth curving into a contemplative smile. "I think a job offer will definitely be coming your way once everyone here absorbs the true scope of your skills, Mr. Cameron." She turned that smile on me, her eyes glittering as she sized me up. "Better watch out, Aveda. LA's got your man's number. And something tells me they'll be calling soon."

I bit my lip as she sauntered off and Scott pulled me closer, murmuring in my ear, asking if something was wrong. I bit so hard that I drew blood—but it was all to keep myself from firing back with a sharp, angry retort.

We'll see about that.

MAGNIFICENT MERCEDES SAVES DAY, PRESERVES PIG

By Sage McDowell
Senior reporter/columnist/editor, *Topanga Times*

Topanga Canyon's renowned flying pig has lived to see another day—and it's all thanks to the greater Los Angeles area's most stalwart guardian.

The famed pig sculpture—which in recent years has been stolen, reconstructed, and enhanced with such thievery-proof elements as a sturdy metal pole—faced further peril today when a young child attempted to (in her words) "pet its cute little pink head." As our Canyon community knows, the flying pig is a symbol of strength and whimsy, guarding us from the occasional dangers of living amidst the untamed beauty of nature (mudslides, coyotes, tourists looking for Coachella-appropriate wardrobes in our many fine boutiques). The thought of it crashing down thanks to juvenile carelessness is way too much for most of us to bear!

Thankfully, the pig was saved by Mercedes McClain—aka Magnificent Mercedes, a true angel in a city full of them. She flew in as gracefully as our pig might, expertly calming the crowd and sweeping the young interloper to safety.

"Trust that I've never seen anything like that," enthused Silver Lake-based social media influencer Bella Dawn, who rushed to the scene as soon as she heard of MM's incredible act of heroism. "This girl taught herself how to fly—how inspiring is that?! I'm actually working with her on an upcoming collab for my channels, and I can't wait to spread the word of Ms. Mercedes out to a bigger audience—she's, like, such an LA icon, but she deserves the world! And I mean that literally!"

Though this old-fashioned reporter likes to stay off the grid (except for the amount of "grid" required to bring you this fine community newsletter), Magnificent Mercedes has come to our attention time and time again, thanks to her generosity of spirit. For over a decade, she has fearlessly shown up whenever Angelenos (or important pig sculptures!) need her help, particularly those who've fallen victim to traffic accidents, road rage, and/or the labyrinthine freeway system so many of us joke about. And she always does it with a smile!

MM also received a surprise visitor in the form of Aveda Jupiter, the famed San Francisco-based superheroine who's in town to witness the filming of a TV show based on her life. The two old friends swapped hugs and snaps as they enthused over Mercedes' incredible act of heroism. Could a potential team-up be in the offing?

"I'd say nah," Bella Dawn commented. "Mercedes is too *real* for glitzy-ass Aveda. Hopefully we'll be getting news about a Mercedes show next—she's the one who really deserves it!"

CHAPTER EIGHT

"I'M SORRY, SHE said what? And *did* what?!" Evie goggled at me from her director's chair perch. It was our second day in LA, and we'd once again been shuttled to set. Apparently our presence had been deemed non-vision-disrupting enough for Clint. I'd also managed to get production to agree to us bringing Pippa (much to the dismay of the ever-grouchy Stacey). She'd been given her own director's chair and was furiously scrolling through her phone and jotting things down in a little notebook emblazoned with glittery vampire fang stickers.

And now we were once again waiting for Clint and other important people to arrive so shooting could actually begin. I'd just briefed Evie on my visit to the Youth Center and my surprise encounter with Mercedes. There hadn't really been a good moment for such conversations the night before. Evie had gone to bed early, citing pregnancy exhaustion, and Pippa had been squirreled away in her room, still digging through our emails. So Scott and I had ordered a quick room-service dinner and gone to bed. I'd studiously avoided mentioning all things Mercedes, and listened to him enthuse about the Youth Center—how engaged the staff was, how they were already so eager for the surf clinic . . .

He was so excited. And he had that same light in his eyes I'd seen before, the one that said *this* was what he was meant to be doing. I couldn't bear to interrupt that with a casual, *Yeah, so actually your new favorite coworker was a raging asshole back in the day! But, um, have fun with that.*

"Annie." Evie tugged at my sleeve. "I'm sorry, but does Scott not know about all the bullshit Mercedes said to you before she moved down here? All the super *racist* bullshit that diminished your very impressive accomplishments?"

"No. He and I weren't really talking when that happened."

And now Mercedes knows why, a little voice helpfully reminded me.

"And since then . . ." I shrugged the little voice off, determined to power forward. "Mercedes has become progressively less relevant to my life. There was no reason to rehash that or bring her up at all. I certainly didn't expect her to show up as a volunteer at the Youth Center. And Scott's having such a good time after just one day there—it feels like maybe he can finally make all his surf clinic dreams a reality, design something to bring back to the Bay with him. I want that for him more than anything, and I don't want to say something that's going to ruin the amazing experience he's having. Since Mercedes works at the Youth Center, she is inevitably going to be part of that experience." I gave Evie a small smile. "I appreciate the outrage on my behalf, though."

She waved a hand. "We-eelllll, maybe these pregnancy hormones are enhancing my rage, or maybe I've just gotten way more comfortable *feeling* rage. But it sure sounds like she was trying to glom on to your sweet but very oblivious husband. You should fill him in on her gross side. Which is kind of all of her sides."

"Oh, I don't know, I probably misinterpreted some of her . . . her . . ." I trailed off, momentarily flashing back to Mercedes' hand lingering on Scott's bicep.

"Sometimes we misinterpret and sometimes people make us *think* we misinterpret," Evie said, narrowing her eyes shrewdly. "So they can better manipulate the situation."

"In any case, it doesn't really matter," I said, trying to make my voice light and breezy. "If all goes well and we complete our various missions here, we'll be back home in a few days and everything can go back to normal."

The thought settled in my chest, as comforting as a warm blanket.

"And in that vein," I continued, "Pippa, have you been able to find anything of note? The sooner we figure out what's going on with the show, the better."

"Everything I've collected so far is totally boring," Pippa said, tapping her pen against her notebook. "Yes, you seem to have received a handful of emails with various updates about the show. There's one telling you about Clint being hired as showrunner, going on and on about his 'auteur vision.'" She made air-quotes with her fingers, her face screwing into a look of distaste. "Another one telling you about the casting of Michelle and Kat, but reminding you of all the NDAs you signed, and how this must be kept under total wraps until the big reveal they're planning at a comic book convention. And a few other bits and bobs, but nothing to indicate supernatural interference. Mostly just seems like the usual Hollywood shenanigans."

"How did we manage to skip over all these emails?" Evie mused. "I know we've been busy, and that period after Bea left was especially chaotic, but it's weird that we missed so much."

"Who are these emails from?" I said. "Grouchy Stacey?"

"They're mostly from the assistant to a Pinnacle Pictures executive with a long, confusing, probably meaningless title," Pippa said, taking her phone out and pulling up an email screen. "The exec's name is Bertram Sturges and his trusty assistant always sounds like he's about to shit himself from excitement, even if the news he's delivering isn't particularly incredible." She tapped on the screen and brought up a message, frowning. "Like here, where he's telling you about Clint's hiring. It starts with, 'Now I know we'd discussed a woman of color showrunner for this, but Clint is just so goddamn fucking good, he transcends all labels. He's going to give the show a voice that's universal.' Or here . . ." She tapped on another message. "This one's about casting: 'Now

I know we'd discussed the importance of these roles being cast ethnically accurate, but these girls are absolutely going to blow you out of the fucking water . . . '"

"I don't remember a Bertram Sturges! Or his assistant!" Evie complained, throwing her hands in the air. "Or any of these discussions, for that matter."

"It sounds like he's the one we should try to talk to, though," I said, my mind trying to grab on to the next logical vine. "How do we do that? Should we respond to one of his assistant's emails?"

"Yeah, done," Pippa said, typing away on the screen. "I'm telling him that *your* assistant is requesting a very important meeting!"

"My gorgeous ladies! Lovely to see you again." We all turned to see Clint swaggering toward us, beard bobbing in a sprightly fashion. He seemed to have no memory of his vision-related meltdown the day before. "And who is this young miss?" he said, his gaze turning to Pippa. I had the immediate urge to throw my body in front of hers.

"This is Pippa, our assistant," I said quickly. "Say, Clint. We haven't seen Mr. Sturges—you know, Bertram—at all. Is he around?"

"Oh no, no," Clint said, throwing his head back as if I'd just asked something completely hilarious. "Bertie almost never comes to set. That's one of the reasons he's considered a prince among executives by all us creative types. He doesn't try to interfere, trusts me completely to knock it out of the park."

"Soooo the vampires weren't his idea?" I said, trying to keep my voice as neutral as possible.

"Nope! That was *all* me!" Clint declared proudly, puffing his chest out. "I looked at your story with a deep, critical eye, and what was missing was a powerful metaphor. I wanted something that would really show the deep beauty of the female experience—how you all see yourselves as vessels, waiting to be fulfilled via men's acceptance—"

"We see ourselves *how*, now?" Evie blurted out, her eyes widening in disbelief.

"—so when that man tries to take from you—to drink of your literal blood—you fight back!" Clint bulldozed on. "It's so feminist, so *empowering*."

"I'd like to empower you to punch yourself in the face," Pippa muttered under her breath.

"And no one had an issue with this?" I said, valiantly trying to keep us on track. "No one thought inserting vampires into a superheroine show already packed with an array of exciting adventures was . . . odd?"

"Bertie loved it!" Clint insisted, his self-satisfied smile growing.

"What about the rest of your writing staff?" I pressed.

"Don't have one!" Clint said cheerfully. "Auteurs are best served by a singular vision. Now. Let's get started!" He pressed a theatrical finger to his lips as if to shush us, even though he was the only one who'd been talking. "Miki, Kat: you ready?"

I shoved down my urge to interrupt, because where would that get us? Clint seemed to have an avoidant non-answer for every question. I suppressed a sigh and turned to the set. We were still in Cake My Day, and it looked like Kat and Miki were getting ready to shoot the scene right after the vampire bit from the day before. They were both clad in the same costumes, but Kat now had bloody crimson bite-marks painted on her neck.

I tried to focus on what was happening in front of me, even though my brain was still replaying every infuriating thing that had come out of Clint's mouth in the last five minutes.

Vessels . . . auteurs . . . metaphors . . .

"And . . . action!" Clint bellowed.

Kat and Miki sprang to life, facing off and regarding each other with concern.

"Are you sure you're all right, Aveda?" Miki said, reaching a tentative hand toward Kat's fake vampire bite. "He bit you *really* hard."

"Vampires are no match for Aveda Jupiter," Kat said, straightening her spine and giving Miki a confident look.

"You should know that by now, Evie. The whole world should know that!"

"Well, the vamp didn't know it," Miki said, giving Kat a sardonic eyebrow raise. "We managed to chase him off, but that doesn't mean—"

"What, he's going to pop back in here like some kind of hokey B-horror movie monster? I think not. Once any man has tasted the wrath of Aveda Jupiter, he will surely have learned his lesson!" Kat declared.

I heard snickering next to me and cast a withering side-long look at Evie.

"Sorry," she whispered. "It's just . . . despite the inaccuracy of so much of this, they *really* captured your essence."

"Hmph," I muttered, sliding down in my director's chair. "I don't believe I've ever used the phrase 'the wrath of Aveda Jupiter' before."

"Maybe you should start," Evie shot back.

"Shhhhh!" hissed Clint.

"Vampires!" shrieked Kat, looking skyward. "If you're lurking out there somewhere, come and face me! I am a strong, powerful woman, and I am not afraid. I! Am! Not! *Afraid!*"

"Aveda!" Miki screamed. "Watch out!"

Suddenly, a hulking blur sped toward Kat, grasping her by the shoulders. I jumped. Where had that come from? But before I could think any further, the blur resolved into a more definitive shape—the cheesy, caped "vampire" from the previous day. And he proceeded to sink his teeth directly into Kat's neck.

"Aveda!" Miki wailed.

"Wow, really?" I hissed.

Kat batted and flailed her arms at the vampire, but it was no use. His grip on her was too strong, his teeth too deeply embedded. She wilted, going limp in his arms.

What the hell?! I straightened in my director's chair, my gaze homing in on Kat—who seemed to have lost the will or the strength to fight back. Was this show really about to kill off *Aveda Jupiter*?

"Aveda . . ." Miki repeated, reaching out for Kat.

The trio appeared frozen in place, Miki extending beseeching arms to "Aveda" and the vampire, Kat limp against her attacker. It looked like someone had pressed pause.

"*Aveda*," Miki said again, but this time she sounded weirdly annoyed? Like she was trying to give the other two actors a cue for something. She stared at them pointedly, but their position didn't change. A thread of panic skittered across her face. "Av—Kat?" she whispered.

"Something's wrong," I murmured, hopping down from my director's chair. I didn't know what, exactly, was happening, but it seemed like things were veering way off script.

"Hey, Director Man, you wanna yell cut?" Pippa said, poking Clint in the arm.

"Never," he said, "I like to let the drama play out organically, when the actors are in the moment—"

"*Kat!*" Miki screamed, charging toward Kat and the vampire—whose fangs were still lodged in Kat's throat. "Get off of her!" She pounced on the vampire and grabbed his arm, pulling hard. "This isn't in the script, you're hurting her!"

The vampire responded by releasing Kat, who collapsed to the ground, her eyes snapping shut. And the blood on her neck now looked horrifyingly real.

The vampire snarled and lunged at Miki, who screamed and dodged to the left, sending a whole pan of prop cupcakes flying.

"Wow," Clint breathed out. "This is so *authentic*. So—"

"Fuck that," I snarled, making a beeline for the stage.

My adrenaline kicked in, singing through my bloodstream and powering me forward, even as Clint yelled for security to restrain me. I dodged the hulking men in uniform easily and bounded onto the stage, planting my body in front of Miki.

"Aveda," she whimpered. "I don't know what happened, but now Kat—"

"It's okay," I said, projecting all the Aveda Jupiter authority I could muster. "I've got you."

"Security!" Clint screamed again, flailing his arms in my direction. "That woman is *destroying* my set!"

"That woman is saving your cast!" Evie countered, positioning herself in front of him. "And if you don't shut up, I'm going to raise a wall of fire around you that will *actually* destroy the set!"

"Hey!" I said loudly, turning back to the vampire. He was hovering over Kat's limp form, as if sussing out the best way to continue his biting spree. "I don't know if you're one of those Method actors or what, but you are *way* too in character right now!"

He turned to me slowly, momentarily distracted from his Kat snack. His face was pale as snow, save for the twin tracks of blood trickling down his face. They looked very much like *real* blood—Kat's blood. His gaze met mine and I felt queasy, like I was about to vomit up my room-service breakfast.

His eyes were red, glowing, and sparked with something undeniably malevolent. Had they actually been *glowing* before? I remembered them being enhanced with colored contacts, but this looked . . . different.

Less Hollywood magic, more *actual* magic.

"Aveda Jupiter," the vampire intoned. His voice was deep, accented. I was hit with the sudden strange feeling that I'd been transported into an old-school horror movie. "At last, my sweet," he purred. "I've been waiting for you."

And then he advanced toward me and I was at last able to fulfill my overwhelming desire to punch someone in the face.

CHAPTER NINE

"WELL, MR. AUTEUR, I am really going to have to insist that you stop giving us non-answers and explain yourself." I glowered at Clint, giving him my best Aveda Jupiter steel. He cowered in front of me, his eyes shifting to the side, and I tried not to revel too much in the satisfaction that gave me.

After I'd clocked the way-too-aggressive actor/vampire, he'd been down for the count. Which just goes to show how *wrong* this TV show's portrayal was: the real Aveda Jupiter was not so easily felled by monsters of any sort.

And then the set was swarmed, a veritable fleet of security people rushing in and sweeping all three actors away. From what Evie and I had been able to ascertain, they'd all been taken to a local hospital. Meanwhile, Stacey the Grouch had tried to herd Evie, Pippa, and me back to our hotel, but I was having *none of that*.

I wanted answers, and once I'd made it clear I was not budging until we got them, we'd been shepherded to a squat bungalow next to the soundstage. I'd insisted that Clint join us, since he seemed to be the only person who might be able to provide an explanation of this very upsetting sequence of events.

"Clint?" I prompted. He was still busy cowering, his beard twitching with distress. I planted my hands on my hips and stared him down.

"I don't know what happened!" he insisted, holding out his hands beseechingly. His demeanor had done a complete one-eighty. Gone was the confident visionary who wanted to lecture us about feminism. Now we had a sniveling coward trying to weasel out of any kind of accountability. "As I said on set, I like to let scenes unfurl *naturally*," he said, a strain of whine creeping into his voice. "So sometimes I allow them to continue past the scripted portion. That's where the real magic tends to happen, because the actors aren't trying to remember their lines or wondering if their makeup's still in place—they *live* in the moment, it becomes real. That's what you want!"

"And all that realness seems to have led to the actor playing your vampire injuring one of your lead actresses and going after another," I said.

"That's Stan, he's just so into his craft," Clint insisted. "It perhaps became *too* real for him, but that's what happens when you are working with a consummate thespian."

"Wait a minute." Pippa raised her hand, like she was in class. She'd been scribbling down notes while we talked. The sparkly fang stickers adorning her notebook glittered in the dim light of the bungalow. "The name of the actor playing your mysterious, scary vampire is *Stan*?"

"Probably not the time, Pippa," Evie murmured.

"He's really the centerpiece of our show," Clint continued, nodding eagerly. "The true beating heart."

"The beating heart of your show about Asian American superheroines is a white man playing a character who doesn't even exist in our actual lives?" I snapped.

"I think he was living as the character," Clint said, clasping his hands as he got really into his theory. "He *was* the vampire, he felt that thirst for blood deep in his bones, and—"

"And so attacking Kat was somehow justified?!" I shook my head. Hollywood was even more savage than superheroing. "If nothing else, doesn't that make him a major liability?"

Clint shrugged. "He's eccentric, yeah. I know he's driven some of his other castmates up the wall, because he insists on staying in character the whole time. You yell 'cut,' whoever he's playing is still there. Stan *disappears*. He's worth it."

I exchanged a look with Evie. Clint's voice had taken on a reverent quality, his eyes glazing over as he waxed rhapsodic about Stan's brilliance. I could not help but wonder if Clint would consider Kat or Miki "worth it" if they decided they *also* needed to stay in character the whole time, to the point of attacking their castmates.

I was pretty sure I already knew the answer.

"So what was actually in the script?" Evie piped up.

We exchanged another look and I shot her a grateful smile. One thing I appreciated about Evie's and my partnership was her ability to steer a conversation back to its original purpose without seeming totally combative. This was not a quality I possessed, so we tended to balance each other well.

"Almost everything you saw up to the point where Miki called Kat by her real name, totally breaking character," Clint huffed.

I clenched my fists at my sides, resisting the urge to strangle him. I'd already punched one person in the face today, I didn't need to make it two. At least not yet.

"The vampire *was* supposed to return and attack Aveda again," Clint continued, steepling his fingers thoughtfully. "She passes out momentarily, and he turns to Evie. But rather than attacking her as well, he uses another one of his vampire powers—compulsion."

"So he tries to, like, mind control her?" Pippa said, her eyes widening.

"Something like that," Clint said, giving her finger guns. "He can plant visions of things that haven't actually occurred to mess with her memories, or get her to do his bidding. Or sometimes they're visions of possible futures, each one designed to lead her down a bad path. Evie has a much more *suggestible* mind—"

I heard the real Evie let out a derisive snort.

"—and so she falls under his spell, and starts to walk toward him. Then Aveda reawakens and manages to sweep her friend away. But the vampire now has control of Cake My Day, which ends up being a problem for our heroines later."

Clint flashed a smarmy grin, reclaiming some of his swaggering bravado. "I'd tell you the rest, but you will simply have to watch the show to find out what happens!"

"If there is a show after this," I muttered. "So it sounds like Stan went, ah, off script when he attacked Kat more aggressively than planned."

"He was *really* in it," Clint said, nodding vigorously. "And when you have such a dedicated thespian, sometimes these accidents happen."

"That was *not* an accident," I growled. "How can you act like this is okay when three of your cast members had to go to the hospital?"

He shrugged. "Art hurts sometimes."

"Oh, for . . ." I bit my lip hard, forcing myself not to fully unleash my temper on this ridiculous man. I got the sense that he'd only withdraw further, get smugger and more self-satisfied. And that wouldn't help us in our quest to figure out what had just happened.

I *knew* I'd seen glowing red eyes on Stan the vampire. And they'd lit up when he was getting really aggressive. Did that mean supernatural interference or really excellent prosthetics? Or was Stan *just so in character* that his eyes had started to magically glow?

I took a deep inhale, trying to rein in my frustration and switch gears to see if we could get anything actually useful out of Clint—

"Ms. Jupiter? Ms. Tanaka?"

Evie and I whirled around to see the most bland, nondescript man I'd ever encountered entering the bungalow. He had a narrow, pinched face, thinning brownish-blond hair hugging his egg-shaped head, and was wearing an aggressively beige suit. And he was looking at Evie and me like we were some sort of minor annoyance, flies to be swatted away.

"Bertie!" Clint exclaimed, jumping to his feet and trotting over to the man as if he were a toddler running to tattle. I thought I saw a quick flash of relief cross his face, but he quickly reset to his usual smug expression.

So this was "Bertie," aka Bertram Sturges, the network executive whose assistant was behind all those emails Evie and I had missed. It was possible we'd met before, when Evie and I had had the initial meetings about selling our life rights. But given that I could barely remember what he looked like two seconds after he'd walked into the room, it was hard to say.

"Heard there was an incident on set, Clint," Bertram said, giving Clint an officious nod. Now that the exec had zeroed in on everyone's favorite auteur, it was as if Evie and I ceased to exist. Perhaps he thought that simply saying our names was enough to swat us away.

This man had no idea what he was dealing with. He'd *clearly* never met Aveda Jupiter.

(Unless he had. I still couldn't remember.)

"Glad to hear no one was seriously injured, and great job following all the proper procedures," Bertram continued. "There will of course be a brief investigation into the incident from Pinnacle's human resources department, but we shouldn't have to pause filming for *too* long."

"Wait a second, what do you mean not 'seriously injured'?!" I interjected, planting my hands on my hips. "Kat was bleeding, and all three of them had to go to the hospital! How is that not serious?"

"Ms. Jupiter." Bertram gave me a thin-lipped smile that didn't touch his eyes. "I appreciate your concern, but rest assured that we're handling this matter thoroughly and professionally. Filming a television show comes with a great many risks, and we have systems in place for this sort of thing."

"And that does not at all address what I'm saying—"

"Ms. Jupiter," Bertram repeated, his lips pressing together even more tightly. "I must respectfully request that you stop addressing me in such an aggressive manner—"

"*Aggressive?!*" I spat out, my spine going ramrod straight. "Oh, I'll *show* you aggressive—"

"Actually, that's what I'm here to speak to you about," Bertram said, totally unflappable.

I heard rustling behind me and glanced back to see Evie and Pippa flanking me on either side. Evie's brows were drawn together and she was studying Bertram intently. She might not be as *aggressive* as I am, but she still didn't like this.

"There were a number of complaints from the crew about how you and Ms. Tanaka responded to the situation," Bertram said. "Perhaps it's because you're unused to being on a professional film set, but the way you charged the actors and tried to insert yourself into a potentially problematic interaction between cast members was completely inappropriate."

"I . . . what?!" Surely I could not be hearing this right. Were we part of some bizarre prank show? Had we been transported to an alternate dimension?

Was *Hollywood* an actual alternate dimension?

The slightest crease appeared on Bertram's forehead. "I'm afraid we will have to restrict your and Ms. Tanaka's set privileges," he said, in the gently regretful way a waitress might tell someone that the diner was out of their breakfast meat of choice. "Clint needs to be able to focus on this project so he can bring his vision to life—"

"His vision of *our* lives," I muttered.

"—and the two of you being difficult, distracting, and confrontational—as you were today—is not conducive to that atmosphere," Bertram continued, unmoved. "The current PA we have assigned to you—"

"Stacey," Clint said, puffing out his chest, as if he should receive a medal for knowing her name.

"Stacey," Bertram said. "She'll continue to serve as your liaison to the production. Whenever it's appropriate, she will bring you to set for short, supervised visits. But you will no longer be permitted to observe filming of any kind, and there are certain areas of set you will be outright banned from."

"Sometimes sacrifices must be made in order for the purest forms of creativity to flourish," Clint said, giving a regretful one-shoulder shrug.

I just kept shaking my head, like a robot whose brain won't stop short-circuiting. My fists were balled at my sides, my shoulders tensed around my ears, and my blood was *on fire*. Were these infuriating men *really* doing this, speaking to me like I was a child who'd misbehaved? And after I'd saved one of their leading ladies?

Maybe I wasn't *that* opposed to punching a second person in the face today. Maybe I'd even make it three.

Words mixed with toxic rage bubbled up in my chest, and I was just about to open my mouth and let both of them have it . . . when I felt Evie's fingers brush my arm. I glanced over at her and she gave me a small, imperceptible headshake. I clenched my teeth together, hearing her BFF telepathy loud and clear.

Not now, that will only make it worse. Let's leave and figure this shit out.

I swallowed my words, returning her nod and forcing my hands to uncurl themselves.

"Of course, Mr. Bertram," I said, making my voice as soft and pliant as possible. I barely recognized it, even though it was coming from my body. "Why don't you call Stacey and we'll get out of your hair."

I started walking toward the exit, Evie and Pippa following me. Then I stopped in the doorway, turning to give Bertram and Clint my sweetest, fakest smile. "And next time? I suppose we'll simply let *murder* happen. Wouldn't want to be *difficult*."

Yes, fine, I couldn't resist giving them a *metaphorical* punch in the face. And even though Evie had claimed to be against such things, I heard her snicker as we finally made our exit.

CHAPTER TEN

"NOW WHAT?" I paced the plush carpet in our hotel suite, annoyed that even my most forceful footfalls refused to produce a sound. I was still *trying* to get my stomp on, though, and winced a bit when the joints in my knee ground together in protest.

Aveda Jupiter was doing all she could to slow the aging process, but her body liked to make it clear that certain things were inevitable.

I really needed to find a good way to work out while we were away from home. We seemed to have found ourselves in a classic, weird, and potentially dangerous Tanaka/Jupiter *Situation*, and I couldn't allow myself to get rusty on the ass-kicking front.

"I'm trying to come up with productive avenues for us to take, but . . ." I stopped in my tracks and gestured around helplessly. "It's like hitting my head against a brick wall. Maybe I should have punched those assholes and been done with it."

"Annie." Evie patted the spot next to her on the soothing banana leaf–print couch. "First, why don't you take a moment to sit down and eat something." She pointed to the massive feast laid out on the glass table, crowding an all-new flower arrangement for space.

After Grouchy Stacey wordlessly deposited us back at our hotel, Pippa had gone on a heroic quest to find us an array of the best foodstuffs LA had to offer. There were spicy tacos with bright, delectable flavors cradled in fresh tortillas.

Chicken katsu sandwiches topped with gooey mac salad. And something called a "potato ball," lightly fried spheres of goodness stuffed with an intriguing meat mixture.

I huffed over to the couch and plopped myself next to Evie with a mighty *whump*. Pippa was perched on one of the chairs flanking the couch, idly popping potato balls into her mouth and scrolling through her phone. I felt a pang of sympathy. I knew that in the midst of all this, she was still waiting and hoping for communication from Shelby. A text, a call . . . just something to reassure her that her friend was still there for her. Now that it looked like we were about to embark on a more action-packed stage of our mission, I'd have to work extra hard to help her find a solution.

Multitasking is, of course, the Aveda Jupiter Way.

"I'm sorry, but what *is* going on here?" I lamented. "Have we encountered a truly evil Hollywood production or are all Hollywood productions evil by nature?"

"Let's do the usual: go over what we know," Evie said soothingly. She waved a potato ball under my nose. "And come on, please eat something. These are *so* good—mmm!" She pulled an over-exaggerated "yummy" face, licking her lips.

"I see you're getting that mom training in," I said, rolling my eyes at her. I opened my mouth and allowed her to feed me the potato ball.

"Hey, at least I didn't do 'here comes the airplane,'" she retorted.

"You should eat some more of this as well," I said, nodding toward the spread. "You haven't had anything since breakfast, and all the vampire drama made us miss at least two of your usual pregnant-lady snack windows."

"Do y'all want to get the rest of the team in on this brainstorm summit type of thing?" Pippa said, snagging the remote control off the coffee table and aiming it at the TV. "I hooked up my iPad to the TV so we can FaceTime them and it will display on here . . ." She gestured to the television screen. "Like we have our own Batcave-esque control center!"

"That's very cool, Pippa," Evie said, giving her a sweet

smile as I chomped my way through the rest of my potato ball. "Why don't we try calling everyone? We can get their input on both our investigation and what other fun things we should check out while we're in LA—since I have a feeling we'll be extending our stay."

Evie winked at me as Pippa pulled up FaceTime on her iPad, her fingertips flying over the shiny surface, her brow furrowing in concentration. She really did look like she was ready for the Batcave—a younger, punkier version of Alfred.

I gave Evie a small smile, trying not to betray how uncertain her breezy demeanor was making me. Was she totally checked out from the superheroing life already? It didn't seem like she was taking the unsettling events of the day very seriously, treating them as if they were a minor annoyance to be dealt with after attending to the more important business of playing tourist.

I filed that thought in my mental Things To Deal With Later folder, and turned to the TV screen as Pippa aimed the remote control and clicked.

A mirror of her laptop screen appeared on the television, and soon Nate and Bea's heads were popping into view, housed in their little FaceTime windows.

Bea was wearing one of her lacy black slip dresses, her mass of blue and purple waves stuffed into a bun so unruly, it looked like it was trying to escape from her head. She was slouched on a battered loveseat in her cluttered Maui bungalow, the expansive picture window behind her framing an influencer-worthy shot of palm trees undulating lazily against the bluest sky I'd ever seen. Nate, meanwhile, was in his dimly lit basement lab—all the surfaces so pristine they practically gleamed with cleanliness. His posture was precise, his piercing dark eyes focused on Evie.

They both looked so much like *themselves*, and my heart warmed at the sight of them, two people I'd come to associate with home. Even though they were both calling in from completely different places.

"Where's Lucy?" I blurted out, my voice strangely plaintive. Evie shot me a curious look and I quickly composed myself, trying to appear unbothered.

"She's helping Rose groom that grouchy old cat Rose has had forever—Calliope?" Pippa said. "Rose will not entrust that fluffy little asshole to any of the professional groomers in the Bay, so Lucy volunteered to help. And it's, like, an eight-hour job."

"True love," Bea exclaimed, clapping a hand over her heart.

"I will fill both Lucy and Rose in later," Nate promised.

"And I tried to get Shelby on here too. I thought maybe she'd have some special ghost girl insights into fake vampires. But I can't get ahold of her," Pippa said, frowning. "It's like she dropped off the face of the earth . . . except her Insta is all full of snaps of her and Kris, like, hiking together, so . . ."

"Let's talk about the real headline," Bea interrupted, leaning forward as her sparkling hazel eyes scanned our surroundings. "That suite is *bananas*. Y'all are total sellouts!"

"Excuse me," Evie said, throwing her an affectionate half-smile, "but we're currently working very hard to *not* sell our souls here, thank you very much."

"Yeah, and if I can scam a few more complimentary beverages out of the The Man, we'll be taking advantage of this fancy hotel thing for as long as possible," Pippa declared, waving around yet another minibar soda with gusto.

"*We'll* be doing that?" I said, arching an eyebrow.

Pippa shrugged and took another swig of her drink.

"Can we discuss the issue at hand," Nate said, his eyes never leaving Evie. "What happened on set?"

I knew that even though Nate had managed to stop smothering Evie and start communicating more effectively, he still worried about her. Maybe he also thought it would be best if their life was smaller. Maybe he also wanted her to take so many extended sabbaticals, she never returned. He'd never have to worry about her getting hurt in the line of duty again, and they could find some peaceful, secluded cabin in the depths of the forest to live out their days as a happy little family.

Considering all they'd been through, I couldn't say that I'd blame him for feeling that way. I just—

"Annie?"

I startled at the sound of Evie's voice, and realized everyone in the room and on the TV screen was staring at me quizzically.

"Sorry," I blurted. "I was just, um, really enjoying the potato balls!" I hastily popped another one in my mouth as if to demonstrate. The infusion of meat and carbs *did* make me feel more energized, so that was something.

"I was saying how we decided to leave the Pinnacle lot, even though we both had a lot more, ah, thoughts to share with Clint and Bertram," Evie said.

I nodded, chewing away. She and Pippa must've finished recapping our experience of the day.

"That's right," I said, swallowing my last bits of potato. "*Many* more thoughts. But before we even go there: Pippa, you said you'd call the hospital. Do we know how Kat, Miki, and Stan the vampire are doing? Are they all okay after today's unfortunate 'incident'?" I couldn't help but mockingly mimic Bertram's disaffected tone.

"Yes!" Pippa brandished her now empty soda can triumphantly in the air. "I called and pretended to be Kat's worried Auntie, and they totally bought it."

"Brilliant," Bea murmured reverently.

"All three are fine, just a bit shaken up," Pippa continued. "Kat has some scratches on her neck, nothing too major. They should all be able to go home soon."

"And then what?" Bea asked. "Will there be some kind of, like, HR investigation? Will that Stan guy be fired for injuring a fellow cast member?"

"Your guess is as good as ours," I snorted, flopping back against the couch. "Apparently the studio has 'procedures' in place for handling this kind of situation. But the very white, very male powers that be seem to think this was simply a little baby accident and that Stan is way too important to lose."

"Sorry, explain to me again how a show about y'all has *vampires*?" Bea said, crinkling her nose. "I mean, I *wish*! Do you even realize how many times I hoped you and Evie might encounter something like Calla, the main character in the *Midnight Dreams* series—"

"Oooh, I just read the fifth book, Bea!" Pippa exclaimed, bouncing in her seat. "Can you even believe they gave her a whole new love interest who is not just a vampire but a weremervampire—"

"A *what*?" I yelped, unable to keep myself from being sucked into wherever this tangent was going.

"Werewolf-mermaid-vampire," Bea said, looking at me with major disdain. The expression was so *teenage*, I flashed back to her actual teenage years, when she'd served both Evie and me that look with impressive frequency. "Totally the best love interest Calla has had thus far."

"Yeah, keep up, AJ," Pippa said, perfectly matching Bea's disdain. "You should probably check out some of the essential literature on vamps if you want to crack this case. I can, of course, put together a recommended reading list of my personal favorites—"

"Ooh, and I can help with that!" Bea enthused. Her messy bun twitched with excitement. "Although weremervamps are pretty advanced, so you should probably start with—"

"Beatrice," Nate interrupted, his gruff rumble of a voice laced with amusement, "this is all very interesting, but may I ask that we address a bigger picture query first: is this something we're classifying as an actual supernatural 'case'? Or simply an unfortunate incident involving a more mundane sort of misbehavior?"

"Let's talk about that," I said, nodding vigorously. "Because the red glow in Stan's eyes looked pretty supernatural to me. I know I'm on high alert since we learned that Shasta has some kind of plan going, but I don't think I imagined that glow."

"You're still seeing Shasta everywhere," Evie said, her voice skeptical. "And those red eyes could have been makeup or prosthetics of some kind."

"I dunno, Clint and that Bertram guy were acting weird too," Pippa chimed in. "No glowing eyes, but it definitely seemed like they were trying to hide something or cover something up or . . . just act like this kind of thing is totally normal?"

"The problem is, we don't know what's normal in this context," I lamented. "This *is* our first experience in Hollywood, and we do know that a certain type of white man tends to be rewarded no matter how bad his behavior. And since everything in this industry is exaggerated, maybe that's just the norm here. Not that that makes it anything resembling okay." My eyes narrowed as I remembered how both men had brushed off Kat's injuries and the danger that had clearly been present on set.

"Forgive my ignorance regarding all things Hollywood," Nate said, his gaze darkening. "But as this show is based on your lives—and as you are perhaps the most prominent superheroine team in the world—can't you simply demand answers?"

"Oooh, you want them to pull a 'do you know who I am?'" Bea crowed, eyes twinkling with mischief. "Damn, Nate, that's such a *diva* solution. I'm kinda proud of you for even thinking of it."

"Aveda Jupiter is no longer a diva," I countered, giving both of them a stern look. "But perhaps more importantly: we seem to have very little say or sway in this fictionalized version of our lives. And no one here seems particularly impressed by our fame."

"Yeah, the locals are way more into Magnificent Mercedes," Pippa mused, toying with a stray platinum lock. "She's built a pretty intense following for herself down here. They view Aveda and Evie as cool-but-distant heroines from a far-off land—and since LA is already full of famous people, Angelenos don't get that excited about a couple more showing up, it's just part of everyday life. And especially since Mercedes *flies* now—"

"Wait, what?!" Bea shrieked.

"It's a jet-pack," Evie said hastily. "She can't actually fly."

"Why don't you have more say in this story about your lives, though?" Nate asked, his brows drawing together.

"An excellent question, and also part of our investigation," I said. "We were in the process of trying to *get* more say when all of this happened."

"That's actually something I wanted to ask you about, Bea," Pippa said, her expression turning earnest. "I've been trying to figure how we ended up here, with all these bizarre things swirling around the production. I've managed to find most of the communication about Evie and Aveda selling their life rights and some of the key steps of the show, but there still seem to be some gaps . . . ?"

"And I sure wasn't the best at handling the inbox," Bea said, her gaze drifting to the palm trees outside her window. "Honestly, all I really remember are those initial meetings about the life rights, selling them and so forth. I think we all assumed an actual show would never happen and therefore paid very little attention to—Scott!"

Her entire face brightened—and then I turned and realized my husband had just walked in the door.

"Hey, Bug," he said, flashing her an easy smile. Scott was the only person in the world who could get away with using Bea's childhood nickname. His gaze went to me, and instantly turned less easy, concern overtaking his expression. "Annie—Pippa alerted me that there was an attack on set, so I left the Center early and rushed back here—"

"Oh, there's really no need for that!" I insisted, as he crossed the room and sat down next to me on the couch. "Evie and I are perfectly fine. We handled it. And now we're trying to figure out how to further handle it." I gestured to Pippa's Batcave-esque setup.

"And I can help with that, as part of Team Tanaka/Jupiter," he said, his easy grin returning as he settled in next to me.

"But . . . you didn't have to leave your actual work early for this!" I protested. "It seems like you're already in such a groove there, getting the clinic going and impressing your colleagues so much!"

Including one particular blonde colleague with a jet-pack who I maybe didn't want him to impress, but I brushed that thought aside.

"I don't want you to feel like you have to get sucked into all the supernatural drama!" I barreled on. "Anyway, we don't know if there's *actual* supernatural drama yet. We're still figuring that out."

"There *better* be weremervampires," Pippa murmured. "That's the one thing I am certain of."

Scott studied me, easy grin still in place. I smiled back, trying to project that trademark Aveda Jupiter confidence. But I could already feel the guilt rising up to claim me. Here we were, less than two days into our big LA adventure, and my life was threatening to overtake his and swallow it up. And he would let it happen—would actively *make* it happen—because he couldn't help but put me first, always.

I had to make sure he stayed on the path that led to his dreams. I wanted him to have that light in his eyes every single day—I wanted that so badly for him, I could practically taste it.

"I guess . . . if you're sure there's nothing I can do to help—" he began.

"There may be, though," Bea piped up, waving her hands around to get our attention. "Aveda, Scott and I have actually been talking a lot about the ways in which his power can access Otherworld magic, and—"

"And that's not important right now since we don't know if this matter is Otherworld related," I said hastily—even though I'd been insisting on the supernatural quality of Stan's red flashing eyes only moments ago. "Until we do, there's certainly no need for him to waste time away from the Center theorizing with us about . . . weremervampires."

"*Never* a waste of time," Pippa said.

"I'll get back to work," Scott said with a chuckle. "We've been making a lot of progress setting up the clinic, and I do want to make sure we have everything in place before it starts. Give those kids the best experience possible." He leaned in to kiss me goodbye, and relief flooded through me as his lips brushed mine.

"Love you!" I called after him as he headed out the door. I grabbed another potato ball and refocused on the team. "So. What's our next step?"

"We could try to get the cast's perspectives on the incident today," Evie said thoughtfully. "Kat, Miki—did they perceive it the same way Clint and Bertram did, just business as usual?"

"And what about Stan?" Bea chimed in. "Y'all should definitely try to speak to him, no? Ooh, I know I've given up my mind-controlly ways, but maybe you could put me on FaceTime and I could—"

"Use your own compulsion-type powers on a vampire?!" Pippa gasped. "Ohmygod, how *cool*."

"Not cool!" Evie insisted, slicing an arm through the air. "We are definitely not doing anything that might tempt Bea to the Dark Side."

Bea's superpower was something we'd taken to calling "emotional projection," and it enabled her to harness and project her own feelings onto others—she could make you feel however she wanted you to feel. In the wrong hands, this was a true supervillain power, and Bea had drifted in that direction during some recent Otherworld-related adventures. But she'd ultimately come back to herself, and had resolved to focus on using her power as responsibly as possible—even when temptation like this dangled in front of her like the most mouthwatering of cakes.

"And anyway, Stan isn't an actual vampire because vampires don't exist!" Evie continued.

"That we know of!" Bea sang out, twirling a purple tendril around her finger.

"The next step is usually observation, information gathering," Nate interjected, trying to get us back on track again.

"Interviewing the parties involved in today's incident is a good start."

"But now that we've been essentially banned from set, I'm not sure how to observe anything," I said, frowning into space.

"I might have an answer for that," Pippa piped up, waving her iPad. She looked up from the screen and gave us a toothy grin. "Because y'all just received a very important email from one Kat Morikawa."

"Oooh!" Onscreen, Bea shot up in her seat. "What does it say?"

"She wanted y'all to know she and Miki are okay and to thank Aveda for stepping in," Pippa said, studying the screen.

"So our efforts weren't seen as difficult and disruptive by *everyone*," I huffed.

"And!" Pippa swooped an index finger through the air. "She and Miki want to make sure you guys know about a 'casual gathering' for cast and crew that's happening tomorrow night. There was apparently talk of canceling it after today's incident, but everyone's decided it would be great to proceed and keep morale up, especially since all of the actors are okay!" A mischievous gleam lit her eyes. "Clearly no one told her you were banned from set."

"I'm presuming this gathering isn't taking place *on* set," I retorted, straightening in my seat. This new information had my brain bashing through its frustrated wall, the possibility of getting closer to the truth sending my synapses firing. "Did she include all the necessary details?"

"Yup!" Pippa said, nodding emphatically. "This li'l shindig is happening at some fancy bar called Edendale. It's on the East Side—oh, and then there are a bunch of directions for different ways of getting to the East Side depending on the time of day . . ."

"Perfect," I said, clapping my hands together. "So we can do our observation thing *and* try to ferret out information from all relevant parties *and* show these egomaniacal men that they can't merely command us to leave and expect us to obey."

"Yes." Pippa pumped her fist and tapped on the screen. "Lemme write back to Kat right now. And for the record, I'd rather watch *this* show—you guys doing vampire-related detective work while eating potato balls—than the one they're actually making."

"Me too, Pippa," I said, grabbing another potato ball and giving the assembled members of Team Tanaka/Jupiter an affectionate grin.

My heart swelled as I chewed my way through a delectable bite of potato and meat, my gaze sweeping over each of the team in turn. Yes, we were missing Lucy, but that satisfying feeling of us being a perfect well-oiled machine was thrumming through my veins now, making me feel confident and sure. My gaze finally landed on Evie, and I tried to catch her eye and make with the BFF telepathy.

But she was back on her phone, and . . .

I peeked over her shoulder and frowned. She appeared to be looking up more LA wonders to visit, colorful photos of quaint little eateries and stunning beach views flying over her screen. As if we hadn't just been talking about potentially dangerous supernatural shenanigans.

I tried to shrug off the prickle of unease running up my spine and refocused on Bea and Pippa, who were back to enthusing about Calla the vampire's many exploits in their favorite books. Once we got the team engaged in our current investigation, I was sure Evie's superheroing instincts would kick in, we would be the incredible partners we always were, and she'd remember how this work filled us with such satisfying purpose.

And in the meantime? I'd worry enough for both of us.

CHAPTER ELEVEN

SHOCKINGLY, THE REST of the day passed without major incident. Pippa went down a research rabbit hole, reading everything she could find on Stan's career up to this point. She came across a lot of glowing profiles with quotes from various directors enthusing about Stan's ability to completely disappear into a character. He'd apparently been making quite a name for himself on the indie film circuit as a celebrated, awards-worthy character actor in very serious films before the vampire gig in *Heroine* came along. I was puzzled as to why a supporting role in a splashy superhero show seemed like a logical step in his career, but then again . . . Clint didn't see Stan as "supporting" anything. In his eyes, this broody indie darling was the clear star.

Meanwhile, Evie enthusiastically made a giant list of all the tourist traps and food emporiums she wanted to visit whenever we had a break from our investigation. Creating said list was so taxing, she'd ended up falling into a late afternoon "nap" that lasted until the next morning. I'd texted Nate that she was dead asleep so he wouldn't think she'd fallen into some kind of treacherous LA pit somewhere, only to never be heard from again.

Then I'd read one of the vampire books Pippa recommended until *I* fell asleep, waking just long enough to receive Scott's peck on the cheek when he returned from work. The book was, I had to say, most fascinating. It was the first in the series Bea and Pippa had been so excited about, chronicling the adventures of Calla, a seven-thousand-year-old vampire who ran a nightclub for supernatural creatures in modern-day LA. As vampires went, she seemed much cooler and sexier than the Count Dracula knock-off Stan was portraying on *Heroine*. Calla reveled in the fact that she'd essentially frozen herself at the perfect moment in time—young, beautiful, never growing old, never changing. She was living exactly the life she wanted, and doing it with style and copious amounts of acrobatic sex. I found myself swept into the story even as I became frustrated at the lack of information it provided about our current dilemma. There was nothing about flashing red eyes being some sort of official vampire tell, for instance. If I was to go by Calla's adventures, the official vampire tell was more along the lines of wearing tightly laced leather corsets and engaging in massive orgies every night.

Then again, why was I looking for "official vampire tells" in the first place? Pippa's books were *fiction*. And what we were dealing with . . . well, possibly it was just as Nate had said. A thoroughly mundane instance of a thoroughly mundane person misbehaving and attacking a coworker.

I just couldn't help but feel that there was way more to it. Because wasn't there always?

Now it was the next day, and I was finally soaking up some of that supposedly pleasant LA weather Evie seemed so enamored with. I found it to be more relentless and unbearably hot than warm and welcoming. In San Francisco, the cloud cover usually kept the sun from shining on us too brightly.

I surveyed my surroundings, trying to pull myself out of my neverending hamster wheel of thoughts so I could better prepare myself for the day ahead. That morning, I'd procured Kat's contact info from Pippa and sent her a text asking if she could help me pick out an outfit for the evening gathering at Edendale. Evie had gotten all excited, thinking I was doing something vacation-adjacent for purely fun purposes. I'd informed her that I was doing nothing of the sort. I thought being able to talk to Kat one-on-one would help us figure out where we needed to focus our investigative energies that evening. I could get her take on the events from set yesterday, learn what it was like working on the show in general, and see if she'd talked to Stan after the whole biting incident.

I also actually did need an outfit. Since our LA journey was only supposed to be a few days, I hadn't packed nearly enough.

And that's how I ended up sitting on a small bench outside a bright pink ice cream shop in a neighborhood known as Highland Park, sunshine beating down on my back as I breathed in the scents of jacaranda, citrus, and spicy street meat being served out of a small cart on the corner.

The main neighborhood drag was a crammed-together cavalcade of cute dessert places, hole-in-the-wall restaurants emitting irresistible smells that made my mouth water, and funky vintage shops I knew Shruti would love—in addition to helping us out with superheroing, Shruti also owned several extremely stylish boutiques and was an expert fashion consultant. I snapped a few photos of the colorful storefronts and sent them to her. There seemed to be a bit of a battle between the old and the new, worn taqueria signs sporting faded promises of tamales mixing with shiny clothing stores featuring bored-looking mannequins in hopelessly hip outfits. But there was also a communal, eclectic neighborhood vibe, people greeting each other by name and petting each other's dogs and stopping to chat at length in front of mom-n-pop boba emporiums.

I glanced at my phone screen, expecting to see Shruti asking me a million questions about the vintage shops. Instead it was my mother, trying to . . . FaceTime me?

I answered immediately, witnessing my brows draw together with worry as my own face appeared in the tiny corner next to Mom's.

"Mom?" I said. "It's not Tuesday, right? Or is it? Did I miss our weekly call—"

"No, Anne," my mother said, tilting her head at me as if this was the strangest observation someone could make. "I just thought I would see how you are doing. On the Face-Time."

I opened my mouth to say something, then pressed my lips back together, studying her expression. What was she up to? My mother *never* called me to "see how I was doing." Our weekly phone call usually took care of that. And we always talked the old-school way. I didn't realize she even knew how to use "the FaceTime."

"So?" my mother prompted. "How are you? Is LA nice?"

"Oh, um. It's fine, Mom. And I'm fine too," I said, deciding to just go with whatever this was for now. "It's very pretty down here. Maybe you and Dad should take a weekend trip sometime."

"Mmm. I do not think so," she said, a nearly imperceptible crinkle appearing on her nose. "Seems very hard to get around with no car, and I do not care for the sun. I prefer a cruise, where the environment is more controlled—"

"Ah, and it's been so long since you and Dad have been on one!" I interrupted. "Maybe that would be fun? For the summer?"

"No time," my mother said, waving a dismissive hand. "And I see your father every day. There is no need for us to see each other in a different place." She frowned at me. "With all that sun, I hope you are wearing the Japanese face sunscreen I sent you—you know the American brands do not calculate SPF correctly—"

"Yes, Mom, I know," I said, trying to keep the Hurricane Annie out of my voice. "I'm all sunscreened up. Not one freckle is getting past this barrier."

"Mmm. How are Evie and Scott?"

"They're good. You know, they're . . . them. Mom, are you okay?" My voice sounded too loud, too *aggressive*. A few people conversing outside the boba shop turned and sent puzzled looks my way. I'd been trying to play it cool, but my mother always brought out the Hurricane Annie. It was that core of intensity that powered me from within, that streak that felt too much and did too much, that instinct I had to hide in casual interactions. Otherwise, I ran the risk of scaring people off.

I *am* just a little too much.

But I couldn't stand not knowing why she was acting so strangely. The sooner I knew what was wrong, the sooner I could help her fix it.

"Of course I am okay," she said, that tiny crinkle appearing again. "Why wouldn't I be?"

"I . . . don't know," I sputtered. "You've been sending me lots of pictures of oranges lately?"

"Yes, the selection at our local markets is quite good this season, I wanted to show you," she said, as if this was a thing all mothers did all the time. "Why is that . . ."

She was interrupted by a faint noise off-screen, and her head turned toward the source.

"What's that . . . ? Oh . . . okay, okay, hold on!" She unleashed a series of words in Mandarin, then switched back to English—for her, this always sounded seamless, a single language that made perfect sense. "I told you not to do that by yourself! Aiyah . . ."

She turned back to me, her expression faintly disgruntled. "I have to go. Your father needs help moving some of his things. I will call you again later. But no more orange pictures, since they are apparently intrusive."

"Wait, *Mom* . . ."

But it was too late. She'd already hung up, her vaguely disapproving face winking out of sight.

Argh. I leaned back against the sun-soaked bench, my gaze still locked on my phone screen. What was going on? Why was she helping my dad move things? My parents never moved anything. I was pretty sure each of their possessions had been in the exact same spot in their modest Pleasanton home for the past thirty years. (Once I'd become a successful superheroine with a regular income of endorsements, I'd offered to buy them a new place. My mother had refused, saying it was a waste of money.)

I gnawed on my lower lip, resisting the urge to bite my

nails. Clearly something was up with my mother. Maybe with both of my parents—why did she seem so irritated with my dad? Yelling at him, moving his things around, not wanting to be "in a different place" with him, even if that place was a luxurious cruise.

I knew she wasn't going to simply tell me what was going on. That was not the Asian way. So I'd have to keep trying to figure it out.

"Aveda?"

My head snapped up to see Kat bustling toward me, a brilliant smile lighting her face. Now that she was out of her Aveda costume, I could see her personal style coming through more clearly. She was clad in a bright pink romper with little cap sleeves and white piping at the cuffs. Sleek white platform sneakers, delicate gold jewelry, and an enormous pair of gold-framed sunglasses completed the look. I was amused to see that her hair was also swept into a power ponytail. Perhaps we had a few things in common out here in the real world.

"Hey, girl," she drawled, plunking herself down next to me. "So happy we can enjoy a little fun time together."

"Hey," I said, my eyes wandering to the one accessory that did *not* match: the small bandage gracing her neck. "How are you feeling today?"

"Not terrible," she said, waving a hand and taking off her sunglasses. "Man, the sun is extra bright today."

"Are those for your celebrity incognito disguise?" I asked, gesturing to her sunglasses. Perhaps we could bond over the necessity of hiding in public when you are of a certain fame level.

"Nah, this is just *style*," she laughed, striking a pose. "I'm not really big enough to get recognized—at least not yet. Also, in LA . . ." She shrugged, giving me a rueful grin. "Celebrities are kinda like wallpaper. Everyone's famous, which means no one truly is. Probably why you don't need incognito-type sunglasses out here, Ms. Superheroic Superstar. But if you do . . ." She waved her gold specs around. "I got you covered."

"Marvelous," I said, returning her smile (and trying not to dwell on the fact that Mercedes, at least, seemed to be *that* level of famous in LA). "And how is your, ah . . ." I gestured to her wound.

"Stan broke the skin, but the bite didn't go too deep." She rubbed the bandage and winced. "Hazard of the job."

"Is that a *regular* hazard of the job?" I countered. "Because I'm familiar with exposing myself to danger at every turn in my line of work, but I didn't realize being an actor involved the same level of risk."

"It happens, especially when you're shooting things like action scenes," Kat said, smiling in a way that didn't quite reach her eyes. "The choreography doesn't account for everything, ya know? And I guess I fainted because it was such an intense moment. Usually I'm tougher than that, but I was really feeling the scene." She was trying to sound breezy, but I could tell there was more going on underneath the surface. And as with my mother's bizarre behavior, I desperately needed to know what was happening.

"I'm so happy you're okay," I said earnestly. "But . . ." I frowned, taking note of the bandage on her neck. "Did Stan explain *why* he actually bit you instead of, like, stage biting you? Was it really just a case of choreography?"

"He's one of those Method actors," Kat said, still trying to sound breezy. "He disappears into the role. And it was probably my fault too, I didn't do my fall in the exact right way, which messed up the angles of our bodies, so—"

"Kat." I shook my head at her, unable to let it go. "I was there. You did nothing wrong, he got *way* too aggressive. And passing out is a perfectly understandable reaction when someone *bites* you. It's not about how 'tough' you are, it's about your coworker straight-up attacking you. That was not okay."

I paused to catch my breath, acutely aware of how loud I was getting, how *intense* I sounded. I was already ruining this. My plan had been to draw her in with the fun and the shopping and my supposed vacation-adjacent casual free spiritedness and then work my questions organically into the conversation. Instead, I was already interrogating her and getting heated. I should have known better; "free spirit" and "casual" were not exactly in my wheelhouse. The Hurricane was always going to come out.

"I'm sorry," I said, forcing myself to lean back and affect a more relaxed pose. "I, um . . . want to go shopping?!" It came out strangled, desperate. Like a last-gasp attempt to salvage this mission.

Kat goggled at me, her ponytail listing to the side. For a moment, I thought she was going to leap off the bench and run away from me as fast as she could. And then perhaps incorporate some all-new and extremely unflattering elements into her performance as Aveda Jupiter.

Instead, she threw her head back and laughed.

I smiled uncertainly, instantly transported back to middle school, when I'd never been sure if the other kids were laughing with me or at me. (It had usually been the second one.)

"Girl," Kat said, giving my shoulder an affectionate shove. "I should have known. We're even more alike than I thought!"

"We are?" I murmured.

"Yes!" she exclaimed, throwing her arms wide. "You have no chill. And neither do I! I was trying to show you my best 'actress' face—you know, the seasoned professional who's so unflappable and resilient, who never lets on that anything bothers her, ever. She's a team player, she rolls with the punches—and if she ever tried to pull any of that Method bullshit like Stan did, she'd be fired in a heartbeat. But Stan's a white guy who does 'important' work, so . . . you know . . ." She shrugged and toyed with her bracelet. "There will be some kind of HR 'procedures' to investigate the incident, but those are set up to protect the studio and the project—not me. I'll smile and nod and agree that it was an unfortunate accident, I have no issue continuing to work with Stan, and I was able to bounce back immediately. Because that's what I have to do."

"Sounds exhausting," I said, flashing back to that moment after my first big battle—Mercedes taking credit, me shutting up and not saying otherwise. Because I knew exactly how it would look if I did anything else.

"I get so fucking sick of being 'professional' sometimes," Kat snarked, rolling her eyes. "Because what that means for me and what that means for Stan are two different things. But I have to keep it in mind always."

"Wow," I said. "Are you sure playing me is worth it?"

"It is indeed, Aveda Jupiter," she said, giving my shoulder another friendly shove. "I've been grinding at this for ten years now. This is the first gig where I'll be able to pay all my bills without driving Uber on the side. That said, there are certainly days where I'm like, damn, this is what I always wanted! I'm living the dream at last! So why am I so fucking tired all the time?" Her smile faded a bit. "But it *is* my dream. So I keep showing up and doing the work. I don't know how to do anything else."

Her expression had now transformed completely, that intensity shining through like a hungry beacon. She *wanted* this. To her, it was more than a career, it was a calling. Even when it didn't feel good.

"I can relate," I said slowly. "I love being a superheroine—it's always felt like what I was supposed to do."

"And you've done it very well," Kat said, smiling slightly at me.

"Thank you," I said. "But I also feel . . . tired sometimes. Like what I'm doing is bigger than me, and that means I *always* have to show up. Demons and the other evils of the world don't take days off—so I don't feel like I can either."

"But you have a team as well, yes?" Kat asked. "Evie and company?"

"And I love them dearly," I said hastily. "But that's another reason I feel like I can't slack off in any way. I can't bear the thought of letting them down."

Like clockwork, I flashed back again to Evie's and my final battle at Morgan College—her looking so lost and scared, me gritting my teeth and trying to show her that I'd *never* give up. I hated seeing that look on her face, that expression that meant she was doubting herself. It made me want to show her that I'd fight doubly hard for both of us.

"I get that," Kat said, nodding vigorously. "I pretty much never complain to my parents about *anything*, because that's how I feel about them. My dad came to this country with nothing, and my mom grew up Japanese American in a teeny tiny town where she couldn't walk down the street without experiencing some kind of racist bullshit. They sacrificed so much so I could have my dreams. And I can't tell them that sometimes those dreams don't feel so good. I just have to push through."

"Seems like that's what you're doing," I said, giving her an encouraging nod. "And if I'd been able to see someone like you in a show like this when I was younger, it would have meant the world."

"Well, hopefully seeing my version of you will mean the world to a whole new generation!" Kat said, a teasing grin spreading over her face. "And you're the only person I've met who I can rant to as freely as I just did, so thank you. That's almost worth more than landing that sweet series lead! *Almost*."

I couldn't help but laugh. I really liked Kat, and it was refreshing to see someone battling with their intensity the way I did. The things I'd said to her were things I usually didn't confide to anyone—but knowing we were the same in this particular way made me feel like I could.

I could actually see myself hanging out with her in a fun-having, vacation-adjacent way . . . but, I sternly reminded myself, I still had a mission. And I needed to remember that.

"So let's actually go shopping," Kat exclaimed, bounding to her feet and extending a hand to me. "You need an outfit for tonight!"

I gazed back at her. Her smile wasn't quite as brilliant as it had been when we'd first met up, but she looked more relaxed, more *real*. Like being able to show me the full force of her intensity had freed her.

I smiled back. "Let's go."

The first place Kat took me to was a candy-colored utopia featuring rows and rows of cute jumpsuits in a rainbow of bright hues. These whimsical displays were accentuated with cheerful, cartoony cut-outs of daisies and suns with smiley faces. The whole place looked good enough to eat.

"I don't think these are quite your style," Kat said, waving a hand at the jumpsuits. "But this place has such brilliant aesthetics, I just had to show you. I got my romper here!"

"Adorable," I said. "And you're right, these aren't necessarily outfits I would wear—I prefer something a bit sleeker to the coveralls cut. But Evie would *love* these. Actually, Bea would too—oh, that's Evie's little sister—"

"I know who Bea is, Aveda Jupiter," Kat said, her dark eyes twinkling with amusement. "Miki and I did *all* the research on you, remember?"

I picked out a kelly green jumpsuit for Evie, a purple one for Bea, and impulsively added a bright yellow edition for Pippa. While it wasn't a solution to her friend problems, maybe it would cheer her up a little. The jumpsuits weren't quite Lucy's style either—she had more of a ruffle-y cottagecore aesthetic. I made a mental note to find things for her and Shruti at one of the vintage places.

I paid for everything, and then Kat ushered me into the shop next door—one of the cool vintage boutiques I'd snapped pictures of earlier.

"This seems more like you," Kat said, gesturing expansively to the racks of sequins, silk, and shimmery cocktail dresses.

"Ooh, yes," I cooed reverently, trying to take it all in. "I can already tell my outfit for tonight's soirée is here. What's the vibe going to be like?"

"It's LA," Kat said, waving a hand. "So there will be people there in full-on formalwear and people wearing sweats and sneakers. Anything goes, no one pays attention to actual dress codes, and sometimes people just don't have time to fight their way through traffic to change outfits at home. It will probably be pretty casual, this is supposed to be a low-key hang. But from all my research, I know that you . . ." She flashed me an amused grin. ". . . like to stand out!"

"I do," I agreed, even though a little voice in the back of my head reminded me that it might be better if I didn't. We were in the middle of an investigation, after all. I kept getting distracted—and didn't want to serve as a distraction myself.

Which reminded me: I really needed to focus.

"So Kat," I said, "did Stan say anything to you after the bite? Did he apologize?"

"He did. He actually got really quiet at the hospital," Kat mused, pawing through a rack of glittery tulle. "And he just kept saying he was sorry. He couldn't seem to explain what had happened from his point of view—which is usually the case with the whole Method thing." She paused, her eyes going to the ceiling as she tried to recall the moment. "It's odd that he apologized at all. That kind of dude, usually he doesn't understand that he needs to. Whatever asshole-ish behavior he's engaging in is part of his process. But Stan actually looked shaken up."

"Did you notice anything unusual about him during the scene?" I pressed.

"Hmm." Kat went back to the dresses, pausing to run her fingertips over the sequins of a particularly vibrant teal number. "Not really. His 'always in character' approach does cause him to go off script sometimes, but it's never ended in injury. I remember that I was extra impressed with the makeup they put on him. It looked really vivid, in a way I hadn't quite seen before. But mostly, it's all a blur." She touched the side of her neck, wincing.

"What do you mean by 'vivid'?" I said, trying not to sound too much like an investigator—then again, Kat seemed to appreciate my intensity. Perhaps an unfiltered approach was acceptable. "How was his makeup different?"

"Ummm . . ." Kat's fingertips lingered on her wound. "Hmm. I'm not sure, exactly. It just seemed so . . . realistic. Like whatever colored contacts they gave him were practically glowing." She laughed a little. "I was just going to say 'he looked like a *real* vampire,' but that's ridiculous."

"Definitely ridiculous," I murmured, imagining how Pippa's eyes would light up at the idea that vampires might exist in our world.

"You know what else is ridiculous: this dress!" Kat sang out, reaching deep into the rack of clothes and pulling out a bright red bandage dress constructed from criss-crossing strips of fabric, all coming together for a body-hugging fit. "I think it's a real Léger!"

"My friend Shruti would flip," I said, reaching out to stroke the rich material. It whispered against my fingertips, as if calling to me. I sighed with something bordering on lust.

"Ha, I know that sigh—this is *your* dress. And I knew you loved clothes as much as me!" Kat exclaimed, shaking the Léger around in triumph. "This is so you, Aveda, you have to try it on!"

And so I did. As I twisted this way and that in the mirror, Kat clapping in delight over the dress, I realized I was doing something actually vacation-adjacent, just like Evie had wanted me to. I tried to recall what other questions I'd wanted to ask Kat, and couldn't think of a single thing.

I was too busy enjoying myself.

"This dress, though," I said, gesturing to the swath of crimson hugging my curves, "maybe it's also too intense? Especially for a casual hang?"

"Yeah, it is," Kat said, beaming at me. "Bitch, that's the point. You *own* that intensity."

I drew myself up tall and lifted my chin, giving the mirror some of that Aveda Jupiter steel.

"I *do* own that intensity," I murmured to my reflection.

And just for a moment, I believed it.

Chapter Twelve

THE NAME EDENDALE conjured visions of a tucked-away magical kingdom—and indeed, the bar seemed intent on projecting that image as hard as it could. Plunked in the middle of a twisty gray LA street, its entrance was a stately iron archway spelling out its name. Once you passed under that archway, the magic started to happen.

The place boasted a charming patio area lit by twinkle lights and shrouded in greenery—that seemed to be where most people were congregating. The inside had a narrow bar area and small dining room, both done up in plush red velvet and wallpaper sporting an intricate pattern of twisting red vines. It had a bit of a Victorian vibe, but it definitely wasn't stuffy—there was an air of laid-back cool wafting over the patio. A fire pit graced the center of the outdoor space, and clusters of airy white umbrellas protected the smattering of tables from all that merciless LA sun (which, thankfully, had finally retreated for the day, giving way to a breezy, balmy night).

This, I sensed, was where the LA hipsterati hung out. It was a far cry from our hole-in-the-wall bar back home, The Gutter, which also had red velvet décor and an impressive roster of regulars, but no other thoughtful touches beyond that. Edendale projected disaffected sophistication; The Gutter wore its shitbag credentials proudly on its sleeve.

Evie and I were somewhat out of our element.

Particularly since I had failed to elicit any further information from Kat during our outing. I'd gotten so caught up in trying on clothes, discussing our shared level of intensity, and then later, lounging on a bench in the shade, eating ice cream and people-watching. It had been lovely, but it meant I was now less prepared than I'd wanted to be for tonight's mission.

I had, however, tried to set things up for us as best I could. I'd asked Kat not to say a word about Evie and me attending. I didn't need Bertram attempting to ban us from additional locations—especially locations where he wasn't even in charge. And perhaps the element of surprise would be useful once we started chatting up the cast and crew. People tend to be more honest when caught off-guard, because they simply don't have time to be anything else.

"Sooooo, it looks like there are a few big parties happening here," Evie said, her brow crinkling in consternation as she scanned the crowd. "They didn't rent out the whole place?"

"Eh, Kat said this was casual," Pippa said. "The *Heroine* crew is just hanging out after work like everyone else. And anyway, as we've discussed, seeing celebrities is just, like, part of daily life round these parts. No one gets excited. No one cares." She pointed to a pod of extremely beautiful people eating bacon-wrapped shrimp and drinking cocktails festooned with tiny flowers. They definitely looked too cool to care.

"What's our strategy, bosses?" Pippa continued, her eyes narrowing. "Divide and conquer? Sock it to 'em? Round robin?"

"I . . . do not know what any of that means," I said.

"Aveda! Evie!" We turned toward the sound of the voice that was ringing out across the patio and saw Kat approaching us, her eyes sparkling. She was wearing the vintage dress she'd purchased during our afternoon jaunt, a silky wrap number with a wild, abstract pattern of blue and purple swirls. With her long black hair swinging around her shoulders and the same delicate gold jewelry she'd been wearing earlier, she looked absolutely perfect.

I tugged self-consciously at the hem of my red bandage dress. My hair was swept into an extra sleek version of its power ponytail, and I'd done a very precise application of a perfect smoky eye. I'd been all about owning my intensity back at the vintage shop, but now that we were actually here, I felt self-conscious. My outfit *was* very attention-attracting, and while that was usually my goal . . . in this case, it might have been better to blend in.

I'd encouraged Evie to go similarly fancy, but she'd just said "Nope—*pregnant*" and that had been that. The Aveda of old surely would have pushed her to don some constricting, flashy garment she hated, but I had learned to recognize her boundaries when she set them—and one of the boundaries we'd agreed on early in her pregnancy was "Nope—*pregnant*" was always a legitimate excuse and the final word on things.

She and Pippa had both been so excited about their new jumpsuits, they'd donned them immediately and refused to take them off. Evie was delighted that the stretchy waistband accommodated her pregnant physique—and that it was an ensemble she could easily accessorize with her favored Chuck Taylors and hoodie. Pippa, meanwhile, had rolled the cuffs and added little ankle boots and dangly feather earrings. I could not fathom how those two elements automatically made the jumpsuit hopelessly hip, but Pippa looked like she'd just stepped out of some kind of influencer photo shoot.

Kat had been right about the crowd. There were people wearing cute cocktail dresses, people wearing sweats and hole-y tees, and everything in between. Everyone somehow fit in perfectly while also not fitting in at all. Maybe that was another LA thing.

I tugged at my dress again, then forced myself to lower my hands to my sides and focused on Kat.

"The dress looks amazing," I enthused, gesturing to her outfit. "It was definitely meant to be yours."

"Yours tooooo," she said. "That was so fun this afternoon, Aveda! Hope we can hang out again."

"Definitely," I said, warmth surging through me. "I would love that."

"Aww, you got Annie to relax and have a good time for a whole afternoon!" Evie crowed. "She's usually completely resistant to anything resembling time off."

"Hey, I get it," Kat laughed. "I'm the same way. I always feel like I'm not doing enough, even when I've been working for twenty-four hours straight." She looked like she wanted to say more on that subject, but a mighty yawn escaped her instead. She clapped a hand over her mouth. "Sorry about that. Guess our shopping marathon wore me out."

"You're also probably still recovering," Evie said, nodding at the small bandage on her neck. "Aveda said the actual cut wasn't too bad, but I'm guessing the whole experience was still very draining."

"Mmm," Kat said, shaking her head like she was trying to rid herself of fatigue. "Why don't we go get some drinks? Or I'll get them while y'all hang out with the gang." She swept an arm toward a cluster of people gathered around a small fire pit. "Miki's over there. I haven't seen Stan—I thought he might come since he was so apologetic and all, but . . ." She let out another monster yawn.

"Has anyone talked to him since you guys left the hospital?" Pippa queried, toying with the cuff of her new jumpsuit. "Did he go home with family? Or does he have a significant other?"

"You know, I have no idea," Kat said with a shrug. "Since he stayed in character the whole time, none of us ever learned much about his life. And I was so caught up in my own situation, I didn't notice if he left the hospital with anyone."

"What about Clint, is he here?" I asked, my eyes scanning the crowd.

"Yeah, I think he's around somewhere," Kat said, waving a hand at the cluster by the fire pit again.

"How do you like working with Clint?" Evie said. "He seems very . . . opinionated."

"Ohhhhh, I need more drinks for that conversation!" Kat exclaimed, giving us a broad wink. "Aveda, why don't you and I make a bar run? Pinnacle set up a tab for us, so it's all on the house. This place has amazing botanical cocktails!"

"Which I sadly cannot partake of," Evie said, patting her pregnant belly. "But I'd love a Coke."

I nodded and raised a questioning eyebrow at Pippa.

"Sparkling water," she said, her gaze following a tray of drinks festooned with beautiful flowers. "With some of those little flowers on top if they'll do that."

"You got it," Kat said, stifling another yawn. "Ugh, I need to wake up. Maybe the botanical cocktails will take care of that."

She looped an arm through mine and guided me over to the bar, where a battalion of servers mixed drinks with vigor.

"You sure you're okay?" I asked her, after she'd put in our order. "You seem really wiped."

"Fine," Kat said, waving a hand and giving me a valiant smile. I noticed she was a bit pale, a hint of dark shadows appearing under her eyes. "I'll rally, it's what I do. More practice for showing HR just how *resilient* I am." She watched the bartenders, transfixed by their quick-moving hands that mixed, shook, stirred, and then topped every drink off with a delicate garnish of those little flowers. "Do you ever get tired of it?" she said abruptly, her eyes still fixed on the aggressive cocktailing happening behind the bar. "I know you said earlier you're a little worn sometimes, but you just get right back to work. I guess I mean 'tired' in a greater sense."

"What kind of greater sense?"

She turned to face me. "Like, the 'getting back to it' part. Do you get tired of being resilient? A strong woman of color? A person who maybe doesn't want to be strong all the time and would probably murder for someone to just, like, bring her a blanket while she watches Netflix for three days straight?"

"I . . . I'm not sure," I said hesitantly. "Even when I'm fatigued, I have a hard time doing *nothing*. I get restless, twitchy. You heard Evie—it's a pretty amazing feat that you got me to do something unrelated to any kind of mission this afternoon."

Even though it was supposed *to be related to the mission*, my guilty conscience reminded me. I brushed the thought away.

"Mmm." Kat smiled at me. "And normally I'm like that too. Or at least I thought I was. But I guess sometimes I wish people would see me as . . . you know, an actual human. Not always strong and fierce and saving the day. Not prized for showing up like a good soldier and doing the work and being oh-so-professional. Everyone always told me I needed a thick skin in order to be in this business. And they were right. But sometimes . . ." She pursed her lips and turned back to the bar. "Sometimes I wish I *didn't* need that."

I didn't know what to say. I always wanted people to see me exactly like that: strong and fierce and saving the day. So tough, nothing bothered me, ever. But her words burrowed under my skin, making me feel itchy. I desperately wanted to help her, and I didn't know how. I shifted uncomfortably as one of the bartenders passed another beautiful creation to a happy customer.

"Kat—" I began.

"No, no." She met my eyes again and gave me a weary smile. "You don't need to try to fix my problem, Aveda Jupiter—and I can see in your eyes that that's all you want to do at the moment. You probably won't be able to rest until you've devised some kind of solution, yes?"

I flushed and shrugged. Perhaps it shouldn't be surprising that Kat, my sister in intensity, had totally figured me out.

"I'm just venting," Kat said, giving my arm a squeeze. "In any case, our drinks are ready, so that should help me feel *much* better."

I grabbed my botanical gin and tonic and Evie's Coke while Kat toted her and Pippa's beverages, and we very carefully made our way over to the fire pit. I didn't see Clint, but Miki was talking animatedly with a tall Black woman wearing a funky tie-dyed jumpsuit. I saw Pippa hanging out next to them, soaking in their every word.

"Aveda!" cried Miki, giving me a big wave and gesturing to the woman in the jumpsuit. "So glad you could make it. Have you met Nico? She's one of the makeup artists on the show!"

"Pleased to meet you," I said, setting both drinks down on a nearby table so I could extend a hand.

"Evie went to the bathroom," Pippa said, jerking a thumb toward the opposite end of the patio. "She said Little Galactus Tanaka-Jones was doing an entire dance routine on her bladder."

"It happens," I said, as Kat passed Pippa her drink. I turned to Miki. "It's nice to see you again. I'm so glad you and Kat are okay after yesterday."

"Ugh." Miki gave a delicate shudder. "What chaos, huh? I was just telling Nico all about it!"

"You know, Kat actually commented on Stan's makeup," I said, recalling our conversation from earlier in the day. Maybe there were some morsels therein that I could follow up on. "How it looked so much more, ah, vivid than usual. Is Stan one of the cast members you work on, Nico? Did you do anything special? It was quite . . . convincing."

"Oh yeah, I usually do him up," Nico said. "The real challenge is the prosthetics—we have to fit him with those teeth and red contacts every day and the contacts irritate his eyes. I've tried using extra drops before and after we put them in, but he still ends up nearly scratching his face off every time— including all the makeup I've spent hours applying."

"What a pain," I said, trying to sound extra sympathetic. "So when you say irritation—do the contacts make his eyes extra red? Almost like they're, I don't know . . . glowing?"

"Not really?" Nico said, her expression turning confused.

"He mostly just looks like a dude with really irritated eyes. Kinda disrupts the magic of television."

"Though come to think of it, his eyes did look super weird during the, um, incident," Miki mused. She stirred her flower-strewn drink, thinking it over. "Kat's right, they were *especially* vivid. I thought I was imagining it because everything was so heightened in the moment, but . . ." She shrugged. "Maybe that's why he lost his mind and charged me and Kat—his itchy eyes were driving him up the wall!"

"You and Kat talked to His Highness Clint about how you were actually scared in that moment, right?" Nico said, arching a perfectly shaped eyebrow. "I know he's always going on and on about how Stan is just so Method, but what he did seems beyond the boundaries of cool."

"Our illustrious showrunner is here somewhere," Miki said, gesturing to the patio. "But Kat and I actually haven't spoken to Clint since we went to the hospital. He didn't even call to check on us. I'm sure he'd just make the same excuses for Stan that he usually does."

"Has Stan done anything like this before?" I said. "Kat was telling me about the whole Method-ness of it all earlier today."

"Not to this extent," Miki said thoughtfully. "But he's your typical 'eccentric' actor who disappears into his characters. As Clint always says, he's 'worth the trouble.'"

"Funny," Nico said, not sounding like she thought it was funny at all. "Because I bet if you or Kat acted like that, the reaction would not be the same. And you two are the stars of the show."

"Not according to Clint," Miki muttered, taking a big swig of her drink.

"Heeeeeeey, are you girls talking about me?!" Clint swayed into view, his face stretched into a somewhat unnatural looking grin. He wobbled on his feet, then swung an arm around Miki's shoulders, as if to keep himself upright. She grimaced and shuffled to the left, extricating herself from his touch.

Good thing, because I do not think I could have kept my punching instincts in check for very long.

"Singing your praises, of course," Miki said, giving him a sweet smile that looked like she was baring her teeth. "Just like always."

"Ahhhhh, you all are too good to me!" he said. He paused, his jovial expression twisting into something more confused. "Do you girls smell something?" He sniffed the air—an oddly animalistic gesture. "Like . . . meat?"

Before any of us could respond, he whipped around and almost crashed into a waiter carrying a precarious platter of food.

"Is that bacon?!" Clint yelped, sniffing more furiously. He reached over and snagged a handful of what looked like bacon-wrapped shrimp from the tray.

"Hey!" the waiter yelled, looking indignant—but also like he wasn't quite sure what to do. "Sir, you can't . . . those aren't . . ."

"I'll pay for them," Clint barked. He stuffed two of the shrimp in his mouth. "Whoa, that's the good stuff. Tastes like it's cured with maple or something?"

"Um, sure," the waiter said, irritation apparent in his every move. "I'll put those on your tab."

"Thanks, brother!" Clint yelled through his mouthful of shrimp as the waiter stalked off.

Time seemed to freeze as Clint continued to chow down on his bacon-wrapped shrimp and the rest of us stared at him in disbelief. What was up with him tonight? Was he wasted? He didn't have a drink in his hand, but that didn't mean he hadn't been partying hard. Apparently drunk Clint was just as annoying as regular Clint—but in a completely different way.

I was almost impressed by this feat.

I glanced across the courtyard, trying to find Evie. She'd been gone for a bit, and even though I knew she could take care of herself, my protective instincts were flaring. I finally found her near what appeared to be the restrooms, chatting with someone I thought I recognized as crew from the show. I caught her eye and gave a subtle head-jerk in Clint's direction. I wanted her take on what was happening with him as well.

"So Clint," I said, turning back to him, "about this whole set ban—"

"Yeah, yeah, sorry about that," Clint said, polishing off another shrimp. He waved a flailing hand in the air. "You know how it is, the suits demanded it! They're very protective of my creativity."

"What's this about a set ban?" Miki interjected. "Aveda saved me and Kat from—"

"From Stan getting a little overenthusiastic with his character—I know," Clint said, frowning as if he was describing a minor nuisance. "But we can't have people attacking cast members—"

"*Stan* attacked cast members!" I blurted out. "Why is *that* okay?"

I felt Pippa's eyes boring into my head. Yes, I was getting all *intense* again, and that was maybe not the best investigative technique. But I couldn't help it. I felt protective of Miki and Kat, and not just because they were portraying Evie and me. Somehow, everything about this show had gone horribly wrong, and Aveda Jupiter would not stand for talented women of color being pushed around, diminished, and dismissed by mediocre men who had done nothing to earn the positions of power they were currently abusing so heinously—

"Annie?"

I was startled out of my reverie by a warm, familiar voice and a gentle hand brushing the small of my back.

"Scott!" I yelped, surprised to see him.

I turned away from the group I'd just been talking to, and took him in. What was he doing here? This night already felt like an out-of-control rollercoaster, and I could barely keep up with all the twists and turns.

He looped an arm around my waist and pulled me close,

murmuring in my ear. "Wow, that dress . . . you look beautiful."

I flushed, momentarily forgetting about Clint, my stewing rage, and my confusion at my husband's sudden presence.

"Aveda!" another familiar voice brayed. And now I saw that Scott had brought someone with him, and goddammit, why did it have to be Mercedes?

The rollercoaster just never ended.

"Hey, lady!" Mercedes beamed at me, curling her golden hair around her index finger. "Damn, look at you—total smoke show!" She glanced around at the crowd, which was currently trending more in the sloppy sweatpants direction. "Did you just come from a super fancy party or something? I'd feel so out of place wearing something like that, but you really pull it off!"

I opened my mouth, closed it. And tried to bite back the several kazillion retorts that were on the tip of my tongue. For one thing, it was nearly impossible to figure out which thing to respond to first.

Embarrassingly, I felt my cheeks heat, and I tugged at the bottom of my dress again. The Clint-related rage that had burned bright just a few minutes ago was back, and I found myself staring at Mercedes as she smiled innocently at me. I swallowed hard, ordering myself to calm down. I didn't need to go full diva right now, not when I was supposed to be ferreting out information like the professional superheroine I am. And anyway, Mercedes hadn't actually done anything wrong. Maybe she didn't realize just how insulting she sounded. Or maybe I was reading way too much into her every word, thanks to our past encounters.

"What are you two doing here?" I asked, trying to keep my voice light. Breezy. Not too *intense*.

"Oh, you knooooow, Scotty said you guys were hanging at a cool bar tonight, and we thought it would be awesome to join you!" Mercedes grinned. "He couldn't remember the name of the place and was going to text you for details. But I told him not to! My human GPS ability allows me to track vehicles, so I searched out your assistant's rental car and pinpointed your location. I thought it would be so fun if we surprised you!"

"Yes . . . fun," I said, my voice taking on a robotic quality.

"Whoa, Magnificent Mercedes!" Clint bellowed, inserting himself into our conversation. He gestured at her so expansively with his drink that liquid sloshed over the rim. "Huge fan, right here. Love everything you do for this city."

"It's an honor," she said, demurely inclining her head.

I tamped down on my annoyance and introduced everyone to each other just as Evie approached our little fire-pit circle.

"Hey, Mercedes!" Evie exclaimed, giving me a sidelong look. "How weird that we keep running into you."

"LA's like a small town when you get down to it. Everyone knows each other, and I'm always running into the same amazing people," Mercedes purred, grinning at Evie. "I've really been enjoying running into this one every day now that we work together!" She leaned toward Scott, brushing her fingers against his bicep and gazing up at him adoringly. "He's so *talented*."

Seriously. What was up with biceps?! Obviously I was a fan too, but . . .

"And I just love hearing what a hopeless romantic Hottie Scotty grew up to be!" Mercedes continued. "Oh, Aveda, the way he proposed to you . . ." She closed her eyes and brought the hand *not* caressing Scott's muscles to her heart. "I can't even imagine anything so beautiful. He told me all about how he came up with it—"

"He *did*?" I squeaked, my mind trying desperately to process everything that was coming out of her mouth. The only person who I'd told the full, true proposal story to was Evie. Even Shruti, Lucy, and Bea had gotten an edited version. It was a moment that felt too intimate, too precious to share. And even sharing it with Evie made me feel extra vulnerable— tears had gathered in my eyes as I'd explained how moved I'd felt when Scott had talked about my birthday, that he knew how much I hated it, that he had fully dedicated himself to making me *not* hate it so much . . .

"The *details*!" Mercedes trilled. "Your much-hated birthday, that plastic ring the two of you got as children . . ." She trailed off, her expression verging on orgasmic.

He'd told her about my beloved plastic ring, too?!

I took a deep breath, and tried to calm the blush that was raging across my cheeks. Scott was grinning at Mercedes, his expression earnest and open. Just being his usual friendly self yet again.

I shook my head, trying to get my petty thoughts under control. Scott was excited about connecting with his new co-workers, which meant he must be feeling really good about his LA surf clinic. Wasn't that what I wanted for him, to pursue his passions with gusto?

I squared my shoulders, sternly reminding myself that in the grand scheme of things, it didn't really matter that Mercedes knew exactly how excited I'd been to receive a cheap plastic ruby. Somehow, I'd completely lost track of what I was supposed to be doing, and I had to get back to the mission. I could not let freaking *Mercedes* of all people distract me from duty.

I turned back to Clint, who now had a pile of sliders he was going to town on. Where had he gotten sliders? Maybe they'd shown up on a special tray for the most overly privileged. The rest of the cast and crew seemed to have broken off into smaller conversation groups. Kat was chatting with Nico, while Pippa appeared to be explaining her latest vampire book obsession to Miki in great detail. Evie was glancing between conversations, assessing which one she should join. As if sensing my discomfort, Kat glanced over at me.

You okay? she mouthed.

I gave her a tight nod and turned back to Clint. "So anyway, Clint. As we were just talking about . . . um . . ." I frowned. What *had* we just been talking about?

"You were about to rip my head off for the way I run my set," Clint said, through a mouthful of burger. He grinned at me, meaty bits lodged between his teeth. Then he turned to Scott. "Your lady's very aggressive," he smarmed. "But I'm sure you know that already. I bet it's even fun when it comes to . . ." He lowered his voice, making it suggestive. ". . . certain things."

"Excuse me?" Scott said. His tone was mostly genial, but I detected a hint of steel underneath. His hand tensed protectively against the small of my back and he pulled me closer.

"Hey, hey, take the compliment," Clint barked, his smile widening. His eyes were glinting with a weird, feverish light, heightened by the flames of the fire pit in front of us.

I wanted to shove Clint *into* the fire pit in response to that disgusting remark, but I was suddenly preoccupied. I turned to Scott as he readjusted the hand on my back, my lips mere centimeters from his ear. The scent of him washed over me, that intoxicating combination of ocean and sunscreen and wild greenery. I found myself breathing deeply, wanting to consume him, *wanting*—

Wait, what the hell was I thinking? Why did I feel so . . . *hungry*. And not for food. Was it because Mercedes still had her fingernails digging into Scott's arm? And was back to prattling on about the plastic ring? Was I really just *jealous*?

Or was it simply due to the fact that Scott looked so fucking hot, his golden hair tousled, his bright blue eyes flashing with consternation, his hand flexing against my back—

"Yeah, so I know we just met," Scott said to Clint, his voice growing cold. "But what you just said was wildly inappropriate."

"Thank youuuuuu!" Clint sang out, toasting Scott with a half-eaten slider.

Scott's frown deepened. "That wasn't—"

"Darling, come with me!" I screeched, grabbing him by the arm that wasn't currently trapped in Mercedes' grip. I tugged insistently, pulling him free from her grasp.

"Watch Clint," I whispered to Evie. "See if you can get him talking more. He's behaving strangely. I'm going to, uh . . ." I nodded in Scott's direction. ". . . see if I can defuse this situation."

"Roger that," Evie said. "But, Annie, are you all right? You look a little . . ." her eyes searched my face, concerned.

"A little what?" I said, my voice twisting up at the end.

"Feverish?" She gnawed on her lower lip, studying me. "Do you feel all right?"

"Of course!" I trilled. Hmm. My voice *did* sound weird. Oh, well, no time to dwell on that now. "Come on, Cameron!" I sang out, dragging Scott away from the group. "I want to show you something."

"Annie," he murmured as I pulled him through the courtyard crowd. "What's going on? And is that asshole really the *showrunner*? The way he was talking to you was . . ." He blew out a long breath. "I was about to punch him in his smug fucking face."

My mouth went dry, my cheeks heating. I could not deny the lightning bolt of lust shooting through me. But *why*? I usually did not respond to the whole "caveman must protect my woman" thing—and sweet Scott was as far from "caveman" as you could get. *I* was the one who was more comfortable punching first and asking questions later. The one who threw myself in front of him when his pack of teenage bullies descended.

But I couldn't ignore the haze descending over me that made my skin feel too hot and too tight all over, the current of electricity that sizzled right where our palms touched.

I spied the bathroom door looming in front of me and pulled him inside. And without thinking much about it, locked it behind us.

"That was very chivalrous of you," I said, turning to face my perplexed husband. "And yes, that man is disgusting in pretty much every way someone can be disgusting, but don't worry—Evie and I have this investigation under control.

Unfortunately, part of the investigation involves *dealing* with that man. But punching him in the face probably isn't going to get anything useful out of him. I mean, probably."

I froze, the extremely satisfying image of me doing just that running through my mind. I brushed the thought away and focused on Scott.

He still looked, well . . . *delicious*. He was wearing a faded light-blue t-shirt that made his eyes more piercing, and I knew without even touching it that it had been rubbed so thin, I'd be able to feel the heat of his skin through the soft cotton. I always loved the way he looked at the end of the day, a little mussed. I reached out and rested my hands on his chest, reveling in that heat I'd been seeking. His irresistible scent was all around me, and I couldn't stop myself from closing those last bits of space between us and pressing my lips to his.

"Annie . . ." he gasped, surprised.

His hands found the small of my back again, drawing me closer to him, our bodies fitting together like they always did. I slid my hands up his chest and over the hard muscles of his shoulders, finally twining my arms around his neck so I could get closer still. Then I nibbled at the corner of his lips, teasing his mouth open and stroking my tongue against his.

He sighed against me, his hands roaming lower, so hot against the silky material of my dress. I slid one of my hands down his chest—lower, lower, lower, until I got to the front of his pants . . .

"Annie!" he gasped again, breaking our kiss.

He met my gaze, his hair even more mussed, his eyes wild. He looked torn between asking me what was going on and allowing my fingers to roam free.

"What . . . is happening?" he finally managed, laughing a little. "If you're done with the party, we can go back to the hotel." He leaned forward, a sly grin tugging at the corners of his mouth. "The suite has a really big bathtub."

"Forget the hotel," I hissed. "I want you *now*."

Then I started kissing him again.

"Fuck," he groaned against my mouth. His hands slid down my waist, fingers digging into my hips. "God, you in this dress . . ."

My fingertips found their way under his shirt, brushing softly against the skin right above the waistband of his jeans. He made a sound in the back of his throat, a guttural growl that sent overwhelming lust racing through me all over again. My fingertips skated lower, my toes curling in anticipation of how hard he was going to be, how he was going to push me up against the sink and take me right there—

"Hey!!!"

Someone banged their fist against the bathroom door.

"Why is this locked?" a voice screeched from the other side. "There are multiple stalls in there and I'm about to piss myself—"

"Hold on!" I yelled back. "We—*I'm* almost done! I need privacy for, um . . ."

I turned back to Scott, our frantic eyes meeting.

"Hurry up!" the voice insisted.

"Y-yes. Of course!" I yelled back.

As Scott met my gaze again, his lips twitched, and I found myself stifling a giggle. What were we doing? I'm adventurous, yes. But sex in a public bathroom was something I'd never attempted before, especially when I was right in the middle of a mission.

"Give us credit—this is a very *not* basic date night," Scott said, cocking a rakish eyebrow at me. "That boring-ass waterfront could never."

I couldn't stop the giggle from escaping me, and I clapped a hand over my mouth, my blush intensifying.

"Hey." Scott pulled me close again, his lips brushing my hair. "While I am certainly *ready* . . ." He pressed more firmly against me to show me just how ready he was, and I let out a little squeak. "I think we can get back to the hotel *really* fucking fast. Mercedes' GPS powers are really something—"

"Oh. Mercedes."

In an instant, all the lust left me. Like air draining from a squashed balloon.

Scott cocked his head at me. "What's wrong?"

"Nothing," I said, completely unconvincingly.

"Annie." He grabbed my hand as I tried to pull away. "What's this about Mercedes? Are you . . ." His eyes widened in disbelief. "Are you *jealous*?"

I huffed out a long exhale, that rage I'd felt when Mercedes manhandled his biceps and yammered on about "Hottie Scotty" rising up again. "I—maybe. Yes. I don't know."

"Sweetheart." His gaze softened and he cupped my face in his hands, his expression terribly tender. "We're working together. That's it. The thing I talk to her the most about— other than the surf clinic—is *you*."

"Yes, you seem to talk about *me* quite a lot," I blurted out before I could stop myself. "And us. Our engagement, our courtship, our . . . everything."

His brow creased. "Is that weird? She's such a big fan of yours—said you two fell out of touch when she moved down here, and she's always regretted that. She loves hearing all these stories about what you've been up to. And since you *are* one of my favorite subjects—"

"Hey!" The banging on the door started up again. "Come on, you gotta open up! There's a line out here."

"Shit." I pulled away from Scott. "Let's talk about this back at the hotel. I can't—"

I was abruptly cut off by an earth-shaking *BOOM* that stopped me in my tracks.

For a moment, I stood motionless, my irrational brain convinced that the person outside—or maybe the whole entire line—had gotten *really* impatient and was slamming their body against the door with incredible force.

Then the screaming started.

My superheroine instincts took over and I darted to the bathroom door, quickly unlocking it and zipping back out to the courtyard.

I'm not sure how long Scott and I were in the bathroom, but somehow all hell had broken loose.

I saw people running for the exits, upended trays of bacon-wrapped shrimp littering the patio. But the mob was having trouble moving fast since there were so many people. I scanned the crowd, trying to find Evie.

The crowd parted a little, and I finally spotted her by the fire pit . . . where the flames were now rising higher and higher, an uncontrolled blaze in the middle of this charming hipster courtyard.

And then, before I could even start to figure out how it had gotten that way, I saw Clint slam a whimsical botanical cocktail into the fire, and the blaze exploded.

CHAPTER THIRTEEN

I DIDN'T THINK. I ran toward the blaze full speed, adrenaline powering me forward.

Nearly everyone else had backed away from the flames and was jostling toward the exits. Evie and Clint were positioned on opposite sides of the pit, facing the fire. She was raising her hands in a placating manner. He still had that feverish look about him, his eyes unfocused and lit with something wild and weird.

"You have to calm down," she was saying, her voice firm. "We're gonna call the fire department, this will all be okay—"

"No, it won't," Clint hissed. He was waving another half-full glass around, his movements jerky. "It will never be okay, not ever again. The suits are probably gonna make me fire Stan, the glue that holds the show together! My vision will be completely destroyed!"

"What happened?" I whispered, sidling up to Evie.

"I don't know," she murmured. "He was already acting weird, and then I think someone asked him something I didn't hear, and . . ." She gestured helplessly at the fire. "He started throwing alcohol into the pit and now . . ." Her features twisted with frustration. "I don't think there's anything I can do since, you know, my fucking fire power will only make this way worse!"

I chanced a look at the blaze. It was climbing higher and higher, orange tendrils licking the velvet night sky. And people were still screaming and trying to push their way to the exit.

"All right," I said, trying to assess the situation as quickly as possible. "Why don't you and Scott . . . oh, where's Scott?" I whipped around and saw him standing on the far right side of the courtyard, trying to herd people toward the exit. "Why don't the two of you get people out of here in an orderly fashion, call the fire department, and I'll take care of this."

"How?" Evie lamented, waving a hand at the flames. "You can't punch a fire!"

"I can try!" I barked, schooling my face into a look of grim determination. "Just trust me. *Go.*"

She looked like she wanted to protest, but took off into the crowd, shouting for them to listen to her.

I faced Clint, who was now staring into his glass like it was some kind of oracle, about to give him all the answers.

"Why . . ." he whispered to the glass. "Why do I work so hard, only to be destroyed like this . . ."

"Hey!" I snapped my fingers at him. "Auteur Man. I know you're in charge on set, but this is not the set, and you need to listen to me. Put your glass down and get out of here."

His head snapped up, his eyes narrowing.

"You don't tell me what to do," he snarled.

And his eyes flashed red. The same red as Stan the vampire's.

I reeled back, shocked. Okay, that *definitely* wasn't Nico's extra vivid makeup at work.

But before I could pursue that line of thinking any further, Stan slammed the remainder of his drink—glass and all—into the fire pit. And the fire roared higher.

I leaped back, scanning the courtyard frantically. My brain was screaming at me to do something, anything, but I couldn't think . . . couldn't *think* . . .

Finally, my searching gaze landed on something that sent the barest wisp of an idea floating through my brain—the breezy patio umbrellas meant to protect from the daytime sun. I took a deep breath and forced myself to concentrate. I had no idea if this was going to work, but I couldn't see any other options.

Everyone else had managed to clear out of the bar, so now it was just me and Clint. He swayed around on the opposite side of the fire pit, occasionally sending me challenging looks. I kept him in my peripheral vision and focused on the umbrellas.

I took one more deep breath, forcing my heart to slow, and reached across the courtyard with my mind, picturing long, invisible feathers unfurling toward the umbrellas—that was how I always visualized my telekinesis in my mind's eye, and I'd worked over the years to refine that technique with as much precision as I could muster. I latched on to the top part of one umbrella, the sturdy white canvas stretched across the pole. Then another . . . and another . . .

Then, slamming all my strength into it, I yanked hard with my mind, using my feathers to pull the huge swaths of canvas free.

Sweat beaded my brow—the bigger the object, the more concentration it took to lift. Also something I'd worked on over the years, and I was pleased that I'd gotten so much stronger. Holding the canvases firm, I swept them across the courtyard, untwisting them so they looked like massive blankets. Carefully—so very *carefully*—I wrapped them around the fire and applied pressure.

In spite of my efforts to keep myself calm and steady, my heart rate ratcheted upward—was this going to work, or was I about to cause an even bigger blaze, thoroughly destroying an entire block of LA?

I must confess that Aveda Jupiter did not pay the strictest attention during the fire safety portion of elementary school gym class. And in adulthood . . . well, fire tended to be Evie's area of expertise.

I could feel the flames fighting me as I wrapped the blaze in the umbrellas, crackling as fire pushed back against my mind. I pressed against the umbrella canvas firmly yet gently—as if I was trying to slowly wring all the water out of a wet rag.

And then . . . the flames vanished. The umbrella tops fell

with an unceremonious *whump* into the empty fire pit. And Edendale was plunged into the dark of night.

I blinked, trying to get my eyes to adjust. After watching the fire cast its ominous orange glow over everything, total blackness was disorienting.

The sound of someone doing a very hearty slow clap pierced the darkness.

"Well done, Aveda Jupiter," Clint intoned, his voice laced with mocking disdain. "We'll definitely have to put a version of that scene in the show, hmm? Even though you tried to ruin my masterwork with all your troublesome meddling. And *aggression*."

"I don't care how much Bertram and his cronies want to kiss your mediocre white man ass," I snarled, frantically trying to catch a glimpse of his shadowy figure in the dark. "After this disaster, you're *done* with that show—"

He laughed—a disconcertingly watery sound, echoing in my ears like he'd managed to multiply and surround me. "Oh, I don't think so. You underestimate how respected and in demand I am in this business—"

"I'm betting there are at least five of those 'auteurs' you keep talking about who can replace you in an instant," I said dryly. I squared my shoulders, trying to reclaim my Aveda Jupiter bravado, even though I had no idea if he could see me or not. "And what you've done here isn't merely 'difficult'—or one of the bullshit terms your executives use to describe actually difficult behavior, like 'eccentric.' You put people's lives in danger—just like you did on set, letting Stan run wild—"

He laughed again, and I resisted the urge to cover my ears. It really did sound like he was all around me.

"I do enjoy your temper, your *passion*," he purred. "We will meet again, Aveda Jupiter—count on it."

"What are you . . . *where* are you . . ."

I saw a flash of glowing red in the dark and heard a loud swooping sound . . . almost like the cheesy vampire Stan had been playing was gathering his voluminous cape around him . . .

And then I heard my name being screamed by a cacophony of voices and blinding light flooded the courtyard. I blinked a few times, trying once again to adjust.

"Annie!"

I still couldn't see anything and was only dimly aware of Scott's voice—ragged, almost teary—and his strong arms sweeping me against the hard wall of his body.

"Sweetheart," he breathed into my hair. "Why did you stay inside? That fire . . . we were all so worried . . ."

"And we couldn't get in!" Evie declared, hugging me from the other side. "Scott and I both tried to get to you, but it was like there was this invisible wall right outside of Edendale, blocking us . . ."

"Where's Clint?" I said abruptly. I pulled away from Scott and Evie, my eyes adjusting to the harsh yellow light. The umbrella tarps were crumpled in the fire pit and singed with soot, a sad pile of wilting fabric. The magic of the place had been totally destroyed.

And I could now see the cluster of people standing in front of me, looking bewildered. Scott, Evie. Pippa. Miki and Kat and Nico.

"He was just . . . there . . ." I said, gesturing to the other side of the fire pit, frustration clawing through my gut. "Did he run outside? Did you guys see him?"

"No," Evie said. "No one came out, we couldn't get in . . ."

"What's that noise?" Miki said, looking around.

I cocked my head, trying to listen—there was a faint smacking . . . no, more like *flapping* . . . sound in the distance. Like a flock of birds beating their wings in formation.

"Y'all," Pippa breathed out. "Look up."

Slowly, we all turned our heads upward.

The night sky was no longer lit by brilliant fire. Now it was ringed by a silent circle of flying bats.

CHAPTER FOURTEEN

"I'M JUST GOING to say what everyone's thinking—
vampires are totally real!" Pippa declared, jabbing an index
finger in the air. "There's a scene in the latest *Midnight
Dreams* book that's *just like* what happened tonight—"

"Is it just like that?" I said. "Because as far as I can tell,
tonight did not end in a massive orgy featuring paranormal
creatures of all types."

"Not *yet*," Pippa shot back, giving me a broad wink. "But
vampires turning into big ol' swarms of bats also happens in
that book." She paused for dramatic effect, her dark eyes
widening. "Clint and Stan are actual vampires, y'all!"

We were back in our suite. We'd searched every corner of
Edendale—and plenty of the corners *near* Edendale—but
Clint was nowhere to be seen. He'd literally vanished into
thin air. And Pippa was convinced he'd turned himself into
the eerie flock of bats circling the sky.

I wasn't sure what to think. Actually, I was starting to
wonder if I'd imagined Clint being there the whole time. Or
at least part of the time. I hadn't actually seen him after the
fire had gone out and plunged us into darkness—just that
creepy flash of red eyes. Had he actually fled much earlier
and my overstimulated brain had hallucinated him talking
to me, laughing at me . . . after all, he'd sounded more car-
toonish than the usual Clint, which was quite a feat.

My runaway train of thought was interrupted by a mighty
yawn—the kind of yawn that feels like it's stretching out your
entire body and rattling your bones.

"Oof." I sagged against Scott. We were curled together on the banana leaf–print couch, him cuddling me close. He had been unwilling to let me out of his sight since we'd left Edendale, and was now idly stroking my hair, as if to reassure himself that I was still there and hadn't been consumed by the blaze. Or magically turned into a flock of bats.

"Annie," he murmured against my hair. "Sweetheart, maybe you should go to bed."

"No, no, I'm not that tired—" Another yawn ripped itself from my jaws, immediately disputing that notion.

I did feel pretty much flattened, like my entire body had been drained of its life force. But that didn't mean I could just go to sleep—we still had work to do.

"So," I said, stifling yet another yawn. "Vampires—"

"Yesssss," Pippa said, slamming her fist against the coffee table. "Clint and Stan are fucking *vampires* trying to take over your show! And when you started to mess with that, Clint tried to take you down for good!"

"That is a lovely theory," Evie said, smiling encouragingly at Pippa from her perch on one of the plush armchairs. "But other than the bats, I don't know that we have much to back it up."

"Pretty sure we can say for sure that whatever's happening *does* seem to have a supernatural element," Scott said.

"Not just a case of mundane misbehavior," I murmured.

I nestled my head against Scott's shoulder and closed my eyes, trying to fit the disparate puzzle pieces together. If vampires *did* exist, wouldn't they have loftier goals than taking over a TV show and turning it into a sexist, racist pile of shit? Were vampires behind all bad TV shows throughout history? That would *really* blow the public's mind . . .

A stray wisp of a thought snaked through my brain, the tiniest bit of an idea I couldn't quite get to cohere.

"What if vampires aren't exactly real," I began slowly, my eyes still closed. "But the Otherworld demons are fucking with us again by using a fictional supernatural creature that humans are known to be afraid of? Just like they did at Morgan College with the ghosts—"

"—and in Hollywood, it's vampires?" Evie said. I could practically hear her skeptical eyebrow raise. "But what are they trying to *do*? Besides make a really bad TV show."

I opened my eyes and sat up straighter, feeling a bit more alert. "What were the ghosts of Morgan trying to do? It was all part of an Otherworld plot to get your baby, Evie. Maybe this is the next step of that. Maybe this was Shasta all along."

"You keep getting stuck on the idea that Shasta is breathing down our necks—well, mostly my neck," Evie said, frowning. "But *you're* the one who's been put in actual danger here in LA. Both times. You almost got attacked by the Stan vampire when you jumped in to protect Miki and Kat, and you were the one facing off against Clint and the fire at Edendale."

"And both of those times I put myself in danger by choice," I pointed out. "I jumped into the fray. But maybe that's part of it—if the demons know anything, they know that that tends to be my instinct. They know I am your greatest protector. And you, of course, are mine," I said, smiling at her as she opened her mouth to protest. "But right now, I have a more heightened interest in protecting *you*, what with the possible baby-snatching plot and all. Maybe her minions are trying to get me out of the way. And they may also know that I've been taking this whole Shasta thing just a bit more seriously than you have," I couldn't help but add.

Evie just rolled her eyes at me.

"Speaking of putting yourself in danger . . ." Scott began.

I twisted in his arms so I could see his face. He was scanning me with grave concern and something else I couldn't quite read.

"Why did you try to handle Clint by yourself?" he asked. "And I'm not saying that because I don't think you *can*, but because you had plenty of superpowered assistance right there—"

"As Evie so astutely pointed out, you can't actually fight fire with fire," I said sardonically. "And anyway, someone with a level head needed to help the mob exit the premises safely."

"I'm not talking about Evie," he said, holding my gaze. "I'm talking about me."

"You?" I murmured, my foggy brain trying to make sense of what he was saying.

"There may have been some spells I could have called up that would've helped," he said. "Remember a few years ago, when you and I were able to combine our powers to better guide one of the puppy demons into a trap? I've been thinking about that a lot lately, especially after everything that happened with you and Evie at Morgan. I'm also concerned about whatever greater plan Shasta has going."

"And to think I used to be the team worrywart," Evie said, idly twisting her curls around her index finger. "How did I switch roles with, well, everyone else?"

"I'm not worried!" Pippa said breezily. "In fact, I'm excited that my paranormal creature expertise is gonna come into super big play here!"

"What do you mean?" I said, still focused on Scott. I remembered the instance he was talking about—I'd still been struggling to use my telekinesis on things I couldn't see, while Scott had been working on a guiding spell that allowed him to isolate supernatural elements in the open air and guide them into our demon traps. But then, one fateful afternoon, I'd managed to get my telekinetic hooks into an invisible puppy demon. It had fought against me, but Scott had used his magic to reinforce my hold and guide the puppy into our trap. "I've worked a lot on my telekinesis. It's so much stronger now!" I continued. "I don't think I need any extra reinforcement."

"That's not the point," he said, his gaze turning exasperated. "Look, Bea and I have actually been talking about this—and no, this isn't a weird secret thing that's going to blow up later and cause all the drama, we've just been experimenting, testing out some theories. Since you and Evie can be a bit . . ."

"Insular?" Evie supplied. "Closed off? Wrapped up in our own two-person drama?"

"Yes. That," Scott said, pointing at her. "Anyway, Bea and I realized that we also kinda combined our powers at one point. Remember, I used that protection spell to encase her when she mentally jumped into the Otherworld—like a supernatural spacesuit. We're devising a spell that could allow for all kinds of power team-ups."

"Okay, slow down—that sounds cool, but we still don't know that whatever's happening with Clint and the show is even connected to Shasta or the Otherworld," Evie said, holding up her hands.

I nodded, even though my mind was already spiraling in another direction. Despite my best efforts, Scott kept getting sucked into *my* issues, *my* problems, *my* drama. Was I not doing a good enough job of encouraging him to pursue his dreams at the Center? Or was Hurricane Annie just way too much of a disruptive, destructive force?

And now he knew I was jealous of Mercedes, which had the potential to disrupt his work even more . . .

"Say we go with the vampires-powered-by-demons theory," Evie continued. She still looked skeptical, but ready to pull on threads, trying to untangle the knotty demon plot. "The Morgan ghosts were powered by demons, yes, but those demons used lingering emotional energy from humans— remember, regrets people had left behind, tied to specific locations. And the ghosts they activated already existed as urban legends of a sort, haunting students for decades. Are we saying Clint and Stan were, what . . ." She shook her head, curls bobbing. "That they were *already* vampires? They just needed to be activated?"

"Maybe they simply possess vampiric *energy*?" I said, trying to rally even as my brain demanded I spiral about how I was clearly ruining Scott's life. "Isn't that a stereotype about Hollywood, that everyone just wants to suck you dry? And those two infuriating men seem pretty in line with the worst stereotypes . . ."

I leaned back against Scott again, another wave of exhaustion overwhelming me. My eyes kept trying to flutter closed of their own accord. I forced them back open.

"How could we begin to investigate that?" Evie said. "And let's step back and look at the bigger picture—because this theory would mean that there is supernatural activity in LA currently, yes? So now we've seen it migrate from San Francisco to the East Bay to Maui to . . . here?" She frowned and curled herself more tightly into the armchair, adjusting to accommodate her pregnant belly.

"Given what we've learned about the walls between our worlds rubbing thin and giving demons various new access points, I don't think that's a bad assumption," I said, my voice grim. I hesitated, another question dancing on the tip of my tongue. I forced myself to ask it, even though I really didn't want to. "Scott, has Mercedes said anything about demon activity down here? Because my impression was that her superheroing has involved more mundane incidents, many of them having to do with LA's legendary gridlock."

"Hmm, no, I don't think she has," Scott said tentatively. I wasn't sure if he sounded hesitant because he was still bothered by me taking Clint on myself or because after our exchange in the Edendale bathroom, he sensed Mercedes was a sensitive subject. "Like I said before, we mostly just talk about work. And you."

"So back to the question of how to investigate," I said, allowing my eyes to close once more. Maybe that would help my brain focus. "Pippa, you started doing some research on Stan—can you do the same for Clint? Find out more about his background, his work history. How he became so in demand in Hollywood."

"And as for Stan, we need to talk to him," Evie said, picking up the thread. "I doubt the powers that be at Pinnacle are going to super helpful with that, so—"

"On it," Pippa said, scribbling in her sticker-emblazoned notebook with relish.

"We could also get Rose and company to make a trip down here, maybe scan the sets?" I said. "If we can get confirmation of supernatural activity, maybe that will be enough to get Bertram and the studio to let us do our jobs. Or—"

I was cut off by a piercing sound, a teeth-rattling jangle that rang out through the air.

"Fuck!" Pippa blurted out, dropping her notebook and clamping her hands over her ears. "What is *that*?!"

"Oh!" Evie exclaimed, getting to her feet and shuffling across the room. "It's the *phone*. Like, the landline."

She gestured to the old-school rotary phone sitting innocuously on a side table, then reached down and lifted the receiver, bringing the jangle to a halt.

"Whoa!" Pippa breathed. I realized that she was young enough to have possibly never encountered a rotary phone before. Or even a phone that simply plugged into the wall.

I suddenly felt a million years old.

"Hello?" Evie said. "Mmm. Yes. This is Evie . . . hold on, please . . ." She covered the mouthpiece with her hand. "It's Bertram!" she hissed at us. "Let me see if this thing has a speaker function . . . since it appears to be a modern replica of an actual rotary phone that's mostly here for the aesthetics . . ."

After some awkward stabbing at buttons, she apparently found the right one and Bertram's unimpressed voice filled the room.

"Mr. Sturges, you're on speaker," Evie said. "Aveda and some of our other colleagues are here."

"Hello to you all," Bertram said, sounding like he was already bored. "I won't waste time with the usual pleasantries—"

"Have a feeling that man's never wasted time on pleasantries in his entire life," I muttered.

"I have been informed of tonight's incident," Bertram

continued. "And I understand that Clint is now missing. We have alerted the authorities, of course, and will make a formal report tomorrow if he is not found."

Evie and I exchanged a glance across the room—how had Bertram heard about any of this? And had the studio managed to do their own search for Clint and come up empty, or was that another lie, a way of protecting the auteur?

"We're going to have to shut down the set for a few days," Bertram continued. "But we are planning on moving ahead once I'm able to install a new showrunner. I've decided it's necessary to think outside the box and find someone who can authentically represent the *experience* of the show. So . . ." He paused dramatically and we all leaned forward in anticipation. "I'll be looking for a *woman*," Bertram said, as if he was making some kind of grand declaration. He paused again—like he was waiting for applause.

"Uh, great?" Evie said, rolling her eyes at me. I smothered a laugh.

"It is great," he said, almost defiantly. "I'm delighted that I had the insight to come up with that. Sometimes you have to step back and look at things in a truly innovative, groundbreaking fashion."

"Mr. Sturges," I said, giving him my best Aveda Jupiter imperiousness. "This is all very interesting, but I must ask: why are you telling us? You banned us from set and do not seem overly concerned with any of our opinions."

"Yeah," Evie said. "And by the way: we're *also* women."

I smothered another laugh. I really did love it when Evie got salty.

There was a long pause on the other line. Bertram cleared his throat.

"Yes. Well," he said hastily. "I'm afraid I must apologize for that. Clearly I did not see the real problem with production, which is Clint's . . . behavior. He's a good guy, has a good heart, but when he drinks, sometimes unfortunate things occur."

Now it was my turn to roll my eyes. Bertram was talking

about Clint like he wasn't at all responsible for these "unfortunate things" occurring, and like none of it really mattered anyway since he was such a "good guy."

"What about Stan?" I pressed. "I know Clint enabled him, but he still attacked Miki and Kat. Surely you can see that that was also . . . unfortunate."

Another pause. More throat-clearing.

"Stan is actually taking a leave from the production," Bertram said. "His representatives communicated to us that he's realized he's gone too deep into his Method, that he needs to take some much-deserved time away for self-reflection. He's on a no-contact retreat out at a facility in Joshua Tree, starting now."

"No contact?" I said, my eyes narrowing. "Because we'd like to speak with him—"

"I'm afraid that's impossible," Bertram said smoothly. "In order to protect his privacy, only his reps know exactly where he is, and they have also been forbidden from contacting him. And as for you ladies, we want to invite you back to set with open arms—with the understanding, of course, that you will not get in the way of the showrunner's work, and will try to rein in those aggressive tendencies. That kind of thing has no place on set."

"Unless you're a lauded male actor, I guess," I muttered.

"Of course," Evie said to Bertram, putting on her placating tone. "We would like to come back, Mr. Sturges. We still want this show to be everything it can be."

Evie and I exchanged a look—best friend telepathy at work again. She was backing down so we could get access, which was the most important thing right now.

"Glad to hear it," Bertram said. "We're all on the same team, after all."

"One more question, Mr. Sturges," I said. "Will Pinnacle be conducting its own search for Clint? Or do you have resources you can use to track him down? His behavior was very troubling, and I'm concerned about his health."

"That is very kind of you," Bertram said. "I will of course

be reaching out to his reps tomorrow morning so we can figure out the terms of his contract termination. All of that needs to be squared away before we proceed with the new showrunner."

"I see," I said, raising an incredulous eyebrow. I supposed I shouldn't be surprised that Bertram's main concern had nothing to do with Clint's health—it was all about absolving himself and his studio of blame. Probably so Clint couldn't pursue legal action—*oh*. That was very likely why we were being invited back as well.

I also noticed that he hadn't actually answered my question.

"Thanks for the call, Mr. Sturges," Evie said. "We appreciate it."

"Of course, ladies!" Bertram said, sounding thoroughly relieved. "I'll be in touch, and whenever we're ready to start shooting again, you can expect Stacey at your hotel. And of course the studio will continue to pay for your stay there."

"Of course," I said. "We'll speak to you soon."

Evie bid Bertram farewell and hung up.

"Wow," she said, crossing the room. She flopped down in the armchair again. "Hollywood really is like another world."

"Truly," I said. "So we won't be getting back on set for a few days, it sounds like. What can we do in the meantime?"

"I'll do more research on Clint and Stan," Pippa said, waving her phone in the air.

"Great idea, Pippa, nice initiative," I said. "And Evie and I . . ." I was interrupted by another jaw-cracking yawn.

Maybe it was because I was so tired, but I really could not think of one useful thing Evie and I could do while we were waiting for Bertram to find a new showrunner. I supposed we could try to track down Stan in Joshua Tree, but it sounded like that was going to be a major undertaking that would lead to a likely dead end.

"You could research vampires!" Pippa said, perking up. "I have loads more books you can read. Maybe that will give you some extra insight. If this is the demons, they're probably going to be inspired by all the classic fictional tropes."

"That's not a bad thought," I mused, lying back against Scott. "I do like to be as prepared as possible for any threat we might face, even if it is the Otherworld demons' *idea* of what that threat looks like." Another thought wormed its way into my brain, a chance to solve a different problem I'd been vexed by. "And say, Pippa, maybe you could have Shelby go with us on this deep dive into vampire fiction. Like a mission-relevant book club."

"Oh . . . that's okay," Pippa said, deflating a bit. "Shel isn't into these books as much as I am. And I'm sure she's too busy anyway." She glanced at her phone screen, as if hoping she might magically discover a new text.

Dammit. In trying to help, I'd only reminded her of her friend drama. I'd have to try harder to find a solution; nothing I'd come up with so far seemed to be working at all.

"That's all right," I said softly, giving her an encouraging smile. "You and I can still be a mission-relevant book club."

"I have another idea," Scott said, stroking my hair. "You could rest."

"Excuse me?" I wiggled away from him, indignant. "Did you really just say that? Don't you know by now that 'rest' is a concept I have little to no familiarity with, and absolutely no desire to change that?"

"I am *very* aware—" he began.

"And anyway," I huffed, "if this is Shasta after Evie's baby again, I cannot afford to let my guard down, even for a second. I will not allow one iota of harm to come to her or little Galactus Tanaka-Jones."

Unlike what almost happened back at Morgan, I thought grimly.

"I agree with Scott," Evie chimed in.

I whipped around to glare at her, my BFF telepathy sending her a clear message: *traitor*.

"Hey, hey." Evie held up her hands. "Don't give me the

Aveda Jupiter Death Glare. Remember how we keep talking about vacation? That's kinda what this was supposed to be."

"And clearly things have changed," I retorted, refusing to give in.

"Maybe they have," Evie said, her eyes wandering to the window. "But that doesn't mean we have to be all work, all the time. We're still in a cool place with lots of cool stuff to see. So let's actually *see* some of it! I've been working on my list of sites and eats . . ." She brightened, pulling her phone out and scrolling through.

"I don't . . ." I trailed off. She had stopped listening to me, and was tapping on her screen with vigor, her eyes lit with excitement.

Once again, I didn't understand her abrupt shift in mood. We'd just been talking about very concerning supernatural happenings, the possibility of Shasta returning, the idea that she might be in danger . . . and now she was back to wanting to blow everything off and play tourist? How did that make sense? And why didn't she seem to get how serious this could be—

"I'm doing the first session of my surf clinic tomorrow— the level for teens," Scott said, interrupting my train of thought. "Why don't you come to the beach with me? It'll still be work, in a way. But we can actually experience a little of that year-round LA sunshine I keep hearing about."

"Yes, excellent," Evie crowed, pointing to Scott. "Go the beach, Annie! That is a vacation-worthy good time."

I studied her beaming face, then turned to look at Scott. He was smiling in that open, earnest way I could never seem to resist. Maybe if I did just *one* vacation-adjacent thing (well, two if you counted my afternoon with Kat), Evie would stop needling me about it and take our investigation as seriously as I was sure she needed to.

"Well . . . all right," I said, my tone trending toward peevish. "I guess I can do that."

"Damn, I've never heard someone so reluctant to go to the beach," Scott said, his voice teasing. "You know I said 'beach,' right? Not, like, 'millipede torture pit' or 'all white guy grad student poetry reading'—"

"Ugh," Evie shuddered.

"Hilarious," I said, giving them both a look. "If there are any millipedes or white men reading poetry at this so-called 'beach,' you will both be in so much trouble."

"Noted," Scott said, chuckling. "Now why don't you finally get that sleep you need."

"Okay, okay," I relented, standing and stretching.

I allowed him to lead me into the bedroom and we settled in for the night.

And then, when he was finally asleep, I snuck back into the living area and read Pippa's vampire books until sunlight winked through the gorgeous hotel windows.

CHAPTER FIFTEEN

I PREPARED AS best I could for my day of relaxation. No, I did not get any sleep, but I slipped out of the hotel in the early hours of the morning to purchase what I presumed was a good beach outfit. I tried texting Kat for her opinion, but she didn't answer—probably still sleeping off the way-too-exciting events of the night before. I also texted my mom to see if I could get some insight into our weird FaceTime conversation. She replied with a photo of my parents' study, which was usually a *Hoarders*-level disaster, but now seemed to be organized in an interlocking series of clear plastic crates.

From the Container Store was her only comment.

So pictures of Container Store merchandise had now replaced giant piles of oranges?

I put that dilemma to the side and assembled my look for the day. By the time Scott woke up, I had already eaten breakfast, showered, and dressed. I was wearing high-waisted navy blue shorts with a nautical flair, a blue-and-white-striped halter top with a sweetheart neckline, and a fetching floppy-brimmed hat to protect myself from sunburns and excess freckling (complemented of course by my mother's revered Japanese sunscreen). Gold sandals and matching gold bangle bracelets completed the ensemble.

Even if I was trepidatious about "relaxing," I could at least appear as if I was ready for such a thing.

Evie, of course, teased me for preparing to relax, insisting that this was somewhat contradictory. I countered that if I *didn't* prepare, it would only add to the tension I was already carrying in my shoulders. At least this way, I could get my overactive brain ready—let it know what to expect.

Or so I thought.

"You're gonna love these kids," Scott enthused as he drove us to the beach, his surfboard rattling around in the trunk of the car he'd rented. Since Scott did not have the benefit of Stacey the Grouch or Pippa carting him all over LA, he'd arranged for his own transportation. "They're so excited about everything. And they still think I'm cool, which I know won't last—I'm enjoying it while I can and hoping Mercedes won't let anything slip about 'Hottie Scotty.' After that . . . forget it, I'm done for. They will *destroy* me."

He grinned, shaking his head ruefully. And despite the unfortunate Mercedes mention, my heart lifted. His voice was full of barely contained excitement—like he relished the idea of his students developing the level of camaraderie they needed in order to tease him.

"Sounds like you're looking forward to getting destroyed," I said lightly.

"It's a living," he laughed. "And no one does complete and total destruction *quite* like disillusioned teenagers. But I'm pretty sure I can buy myself a little extra cool time once I introduce them to you—a few of the kids are big Aveda Jupiter fans."

"That's sweet," I said, flashing a half-smile. "But will that make me distracting? Because I don't want to take away from the very important work you're doing."

I felt a sudden and unexpected spark of hope. Maybe if my presence was *too* distracting, I could get out of this whole "relaxation" thing and wait in the car, burying myself once again in Pippa's vampire books, scanning for anything that might give me a clue about what was happening on *Heroine*. I knew there wasn't much we could do on the ground while production was shut down, but at least I'd *feel* like I was doing something instead of frittering away my time in the blazing sun—

"Of course you won't be distracting—well, maybe to me,

but that's all the time," he said, giving me a rakish wink. "And extending the period of time wherein I am still sort of cool and not that 'how do you do, fellow kids?' meme is vital."

I smiled at him, a flutter racing through my gut. Then I immediately felt guilty. Was I really fantasizing about ditching my sweet husband?

Was I even capable of *not* thinking that way? Or was that just part of being Aveda Jupiter?

I brushed the thought from my mind, smoothing nonexistent wrinkles on my brand-new shorts.

"I'll do my best to ensure you get *all* the cool points," I said, trying to sound breezy.

He smiled, reached over, and twined his fingers through mine, giving my hand a squeeze. I attempted to live in the pleasant sensations bubbling through me: the flutters, the warmth, the fact that this man could still make me feel like a googly-eyed teenager all these years later.

When I thought back to our wedding day a couple years ago, it was never the actual ceremony that stood out to me. Yes, of course it had been grand. We'd rented a glorious estate in Half Moon Bay where we'd been surrounded by lush gardens, stunning vistas, and the sounds of the ocean. I had incorporated various Chinese wedding traditions that were important to me—like the multiple outfit changes. And as the sun set and twilight descended, we'd released a sea of glowing lanterns into the sky.

But the moment I always came back to was actually right *before* the ceremony. I'd been standing in front of the mirror in the estate's sumptuous bridal suite while Evie and Shruti adjusted my veil. I was wearing the first of my dresses: a creamy silk gown with intricate beadwork decorating the back, the neckline, and the delicate cap sleeves. It was a vintage number from the twenties that Shruti had customized to my fabulous specifications. My hair was loose around my shoulders, a shining black curtain that contrasted beautifully with my veil.

"My goodness," Shruti had cooed. "You look like an absolute princess, Aveda Jupiter. No—a *queen*! You would surely give her highness Padmé Amidala a run for her money."

"Oh . . ." Evie swiped a hand over her eyes. "This is no good, I'm already crying." She draped an arm around my shoulders and gave me a teary smile in the mirror. "I'm *so* happy for you. You and Scott . . . it's always been meant to be. And now it *is*."

"It has been for a while now," I reminded her with a laugh. "We're just making it official."

"No 'just' about it!" Evie protested. "This is a huge step for you both! You're embarking on this whole new journey together and I . . ." Her voice caught and she teared up again. "Well, it's gonna be amazing."

"Truly." Shruti nodded decisively. "You have to celebrate every teeny tiny moment of today, Aveda. 'Cause tomorrow, everything will be different. You'll be *married*." She grinned at me and held out a glass of champagne. "Wanna toast?"

"Um . . ." I froze in place, staring at my reflection in the mirror. The color drained from my face, and my mouth flattened into a thin line. And all I felt in my chest was panic, steadily rising and threatening to consume me.

The woman in the mirror looked like a complete stranger.

"Annie?" Evie murmured.

"You don't have to drink the champagne," Shruti said, her bubbly expression turning concerned.

"It . . . it's not that," I managed. My voice sounded tinny and far away, as if I was listening to an old, staticky recording of myself. "I . . . sorry." I shook my head, trying to rid myself of the strangeness that had descended over me. But my face kept getting paler, my mouth flatter. I looked like an extremely displeased ghost. I forced more words out, trying to make my lips curve into something resembling a smile. "I may need a moment to myself. To reflect. Would you mind . . . ?"

"Not at all!" Evie exclaimed. "C'mon, Shruti, let's make sure Bea hasn't eaten all the char siu bao."

"I thought she was testing one—you know, to make sure they taste right," Shruti said.

"Yeah, she's going to 'test' every single one of them if she has her way," Evie snorted. "Let's go."

They bustled out of the room together, chattering all the way.

I took a deep breath and stared at my reflection again, trying to re-orient myself. But the panic only grew, an ugly dark cloud spreading through my chest, down to my fingertips and toes, enveloping my whole body. I shut my eyes tightly, until bright abstract patterns danced in front of my pupils. My blood roared in my ears, and I knew I could not stay here, in this room, facing my ghost-self in the mirror.

I gathered my skirts around me and slipped out the door.

I didn't know where I was going—my legs moved as if guided by some invisible force. I kept putting one foot in front of the other until I was outside, tromping through the garden where the ceremony was to be held. And then I tromped even further, until I found the most gigantic tree I'd ever seen. I scuttled around to the back of the tree and sank to the ground, my breathing coming hard and fast.

A cool breeze ruffled my veil and hair, whispering against my skin. I heard the gentle swishing of the ocean off in the distance. Slowly, my breathing started to return to normal and my chest unclenched. It was then that I realized my face was wet. I raised a hand to my cheek, uncomprehending.

I was crying.

"Annie?"

My head jerked up and I saw Scott. He looked absolutely gorgeous in dress pants and a crisp white shirt. He hadn't added the jacket and tie yet, but seeing him a little mussed, unfinished, shirt tails hanging out . . . it calmed me. My breathing slowed even more.

"What's the matter?" he asked, his brow creasing with concern. He maneuvered himself so he was sitting next to me behind the tree, his perfect pants marred by wrinkles.

"Oh *no*!" I cried, coming back to myself a bit. "Y-you're messing up your nice outfit." I batted ineffectually at his rumpled pants. "And . . . shit, you're not supposed to see me!" My eyes widened in alarm. "It's bad luck!"

"We don't need luck." He tilted his head at me, scanning my face in quizzical fashion. "And I had to find you. Evie and Shruti were freaking out because you disappeared and our guests are going to start arriving soon and . . ." He reached over and took one of my hands in both of his. "Please talk to me."

"I . . ." I looked down at our clasped hands, felt the soothing sensation of his skin against mine. He always brought me back to earth. He could make my out-of-control feelings dissipate with a touch, a look. His natural warmth always made me feel like I could relax into him and let my worries melt away. As someone who was used to carrying herself with tense, ramrod-straight posture and barely knew what the word "relax" meant, this was perhaps the greatest superpower I could imagine.

"Talk to me," he repeated, squeezing my hands.

What had Evie and Shruti been saying, right before I had the sudden burning urge to get out?

You're embarking on this whole new journey together
Tomorrow, everything will be different

I swallowed hard, trying to keep the panic at bay.

"Scott," I said, my voice faint. "Please promise me nothing will change."

I met his gaze, expecting him to stare back at me like I'd lost every single one of my marbles. But he just looked concerned, still.

"What do you mean?" he asked, his voice so tender it made my heart ache.

"I . . ." I pursed my lips, trying to put my thoughts in order. "It took us so long to get here. It took us so long to admit we loved each other. It took *me* so long to let you see all of me—and to trust you with my whole heart. What we have is perfect."

"It is," he said softly.

"And what if this . . ." I gestured broadly to the sweeping vistas in front of us, the beautiful greenery, our ostentatious outfits. "What if it changes everything? What if we wake up tomorrow and everything's *different*?"

"Then it would still be perfect," he said. "Because I'd be with you."

"No." I shook my head vehemently. "That's so . . . god, that's so romantic. But I need to know . . ." I looked at him earnestly, that panic rising in my chest again. "That we'll still be us."

His face softened, his blue eyes brimming with understanding. He reached down and brushed a stray lock of hair off my face, his fingertips skating down my cheek.

"Of course we will be," he said, his voice strong and sure. "Because I know I'll always love you. I couldn't stop if I tried. You're all I've ever wanted, Annie. And sometimes, I can't believe I have you. That we have each other."

Something like relief flooded through me. His words released a pressure valve in my chest, finally making it easier to breathe.

Then he reached into his pants pocket, pulled something free, and held it out to me.

It was the plastic gumball machine ring. The one he'd proposed to me with.

"What if we just say this right here and now," he said. "So whatever happens over *there* . . ." He inclined his head toward the ceremony site. ". . . doesn't matter as much. This part's just you and me, because *that's* what matters."

He brandished the ring, his smile growing wider.

"I love *all* of you, Annie Chang," he said, repeating something we'd told each other near the beginning of our courtship. "And I promise to keep loving all of you. Forever."

"Y-you do?" I squeaked out. My face was wet again.

"I do," he said softly, slipping the plastic ring on my finger.

"And I do too," I whispered back.

He gave me the most gentle smile I'd ever seen, running his thumb down my cheek to swipe away the tears.

"So . . ." My eyes darted to the ceremony site, with its beautiful flowers, its pristine decorations. Then my gaze wandered down to my dress, which was looking about as wrinkled as Scott's pants. I wondered if I had grass stains all over my butt. "Can we just leave?" I blurted out. "If this right here is our real ceremony, is there any need for another one?"

"Unfortunately yes," Scott said, getting to his feet and offering me his hand. "Because if your mother doesn't get to witness her only child getting married, I am fairly certain there will be murder. Hell, even Evie might be pushed to that point."

"True," I groaned, taking his hand and scrambling up off the ground.

"But most importantly . . ." He grinned at me and made a valiant attempt to fix my crumpled veil. "I know you'd have some regrets about that. This is Aveda Jupiter's *moment*, and she will be most displeased if she has to miss it over cold feet."

"Wow, do you know me," I laughed, impulsively pulling him in for a kiss.

"Hey, watch it," he murmured against my mouth. "I just fixed your veil—and if you keep kissing me like that, I am definitely going to mess it up again."

Joy surged through me and I pulled him even closer.

"I don't care," I said.

That same joy welled in my chest now as Scott pulled into the beach parking lot and squeezed my hand, his eyes lighting up at the sight of the ocean.

"Look at that water," he said reverently, gazing out at the sparkling expanse of blue. "This is going to be a perfect day. I'm so happy you came with me! And not just because you're gonna save me from memeification by hopelessly cool teens." He lowered his voice dramatically. "Although that is a fate worse than *death*."

I laughed, shaking my head at him. I had to at least *try* to enjoy myself. For this beautiful man who cared so much about my happiness. Who made me happy every day just by existing.

Scott grabbed his surfboard and other equipment from the back of the car and we were on our way. As we descended on the sand, I quickly realized that my cute gold sandals had perhaps not been the best option. They had a slight heel that sank into the uneven ground with every step, itchy grains sliding easily into the footbed as I walked. I felt like an ungrateful horse stuck in the mud—immobile and sinking deeper as the seconds ticked by.

But Aveda Jupiter was not about to be defeated by something as inconsequential as inappropriate footwear. So I pressed on.

A cluster of teenagers was goofing around closer to the water, and as we approached, Scott gave them a big wave and an eager smile.

I'll confess, my only real up-close-and-personal experience with teenagers had been watching Bea toil through her high school years, and she'd been a tempestuous, moody pain in the ass for pretty much the entire time. (I do not feel bad saying this, as I am fairly certain she would agree with me.)

In any case, my instinct was to expect these teenagers to respond to any display of earnest enthusiasm with extreme surliness, but they all waved back happily—I should have known Scott had already worked his magic, forging true connections with each of them. Despite his claims, he had nothing to worry about on the memeification front.

"Hey, Mr. Cam!" a girl with bright green hair and thick purple eyeliner exclaimed. "Whaddya think? Are the waves choice today or what?"

"We thought they were lookin' a little wimpy, but the wind's definitely picking up!" a boy with a very surfer-esque mane of locks chimed in. "We're ready for you to show us those moves!"

"Thanks, Ezra," Scott said with a chuckle. "We'll definitely get to the moves in just a bit. And Dee, I think the waves look perfect—you probably don't want them to be *too* choppy to start off. The smaller waves will help us ease into things."

As he talked, Scott laid out a couple of big towels for us, carefully arranging his board and the other equipment he'd brought. I stood there awkwardly, trying not to let my heels put me off balance.

"Gang, I want you to meet someone," Scott said, finishing up with the towel and taking my hand. "This is my wife, Annie—you probably know her as Aveda. She's going to hang out with us today."

"Aveda Jupiter," Dee exclaimed, clapping her hands together. "Of course we know who she is! And if we didn't, we would've figured it out. You and Ms. McClain talk about her all the freaking time!"

"Really, Mercedes—er, Ms. McClain talks about me?" I blurted out. I knew Mercedes had talked about me quite a bit with "Hottie Scotty," but I didn't realize this chattiness extended to the students.

"Oh yeah, you're kind of her idol," Ezra said, giving me finger guns. "Is it true you two once took down a rabid gigantic Easter bunny demon with your bare hands?"

"I, er, not exactly," I said, my mind reeling.

Now both Scott and this kid had claimed Mercedes always spoke as if she held me in especially high regard. Yet whenever we were face-to-face . . . she still seemed like the same old Mercedes—passive aggressive and way too interested in giving me neggy backhanded "compliments." And now she had added the great new habit of feeling up my husband.

Or was that just my own petty perception of it? Maybe Mercedes *had* changed. Maybe her inquiries to Scott were just as he characterized them: her wanting to know more about my life after we'd fallen out of touch. Maybe that was her way of trying to make amends for the past.

I tamped down on my frustration and tried to give them my most dazzling Aveda Jupiter smile. "It was actually *seven* Easter bunny demons! A whole swarm!"

"Amaze!" Dee swooned.

"Okay, y'all, let's get ready to hit the water," Scott said, clapping his hands together. "I'm gonna show you guys some basics on the sand—but first, how about a light jog up and down the beach to warm up those muscles? Do whatever movement-type thing you want, at your own pace, to that snack stand . . ." He pointed to a little hut with a cheerful red-and-white-striped awning in the distance. "Then come on back, and we'll get started!"

"Aww, running?!" Dee groaned. "The absolute worst."

"Yes, I am the meanest teacher who ever lived," Scott quipped. "You guys better behave, or I might do something really cruel, like get you all ice cream later."

"Shut up, Dee, Mr. Cam's making sure we don't get any gnarly cramps—let's go!" Ezra exclaimed, throwing Scott a jaunty salute before taking off, leading the cluster of kids away from us.

"Wow, they *love* you," I said, giving Scott a teasing smile. "Why 'Mr. Cam,' though, is 'Cameron' too much of a mouthful?"

"No clue," he said, grinning away. "I can only figure out about seventy-five percent of what they're saying or doing most of the time. The rest is a delightful mystery. You want to sit for a minute while we wait for them to get back?" He gestured to one of the towels he'd spread out on the sand.

"Oh, I . . ." I realized that I'd finally planted my sandal-shod feet in a way that allowed me to remain upright, balanced, and looking as if I was just standing there naturally instead of scrambling to find a comfortable position. If I moved even a millimeter, I was going to topple over—not exactly a good look for being "relaxed."

"Come on," Scott said, his grin widening as he reached out to take my hand. Amusement sparkled in his blue eyes, and he moved closer to me, leaning in to murmur in my ear. "Take the sandals off," he whispered, somehow managing to make that sound both impossibly sweet and impossibly dirty.

I flushed. Of course he'd figured out that my cute-but-impractical-on-the-sand shoes were already making me feel awkward. He was the only one who saw all the uncertainty I'd always tried so hard to keep locked up under the fabulous Aveda Jupiter façade.

I bent down—still awkward, pretzeling my body into a position wherein I could reach the shoes' buckles without flopping my entire body into the sand. I managed to get to the buckles, which were of course extremely tiny and difficult to undo. At least Scott was the only person witnessing this, me bent into a thoroughly unflattering position and rubbing my fingertips raw as I picked furiously at the uncooperative buckles. Otherwise, I could all-too-vividly imagine the headlines that would be produced by uncharitable paparazzi: AVEDA JUPITER BATTLES IMPRACTICAL SANDALS, LOSES IN MOST EMBARRASSING WAY POSSIBLE.

"Almost . . . got . . . it . . ." I muttered, one of the buckles finally coming undone.

"Oh my, what's going on here!" a sugary sweet voice sang out.

Oh god, *why*. Honestly, I would've rather dealt with paparazzi. I raised my head, already knowing what I was going to see—Mercedes McClain, blonde curls bouncing merrily as she approached us.

"Annie's here to watch the surf clinic," Scott said, offering me a hand so I could stand back up. I took it, even though I'd only managed to remove one sandal. Then I faced Mercedes, trying valiantly to plant my feet again.

"Ohhhhh, I'm so glad you're feeling up to it," Mercedes cooed, the slightest of crinkles appearing on her tan brow. "Scotty told me what happened at Edendale after I left last night. He was so worried about you putting yourself in danger like that!"

"I wasn't putting myself in danger, I was doing my job," I said, unable to stamp out the thread of petulance working its way through my voice. *God.* Why did I always have to go from zero to sixty in no time flat? Mercedes was merely expressing concern for my well-being, I reasoned. Just because she'd made it sound like Aveda Jupiter was some kind of helpless shrinking violet recklessly throwing herself into something she knew nothing about . . . just because she'd called my husband by a cutesy, simpering nickname that he did not go by, would never go by, *I* didn't even call him that . . .

Wait a minute. *When* exactly had Mercedes and Scott talked about this? A late-night call, an early morning texting session? I hadn't realized their friendly coworkership had grown into a connection that involved communicating so frequently. Or about things as intimate as his *feelings*.

"Of course," Mercedes said, nodding eagerly. "It was your superheroine duty to step in. I just think it's *so adorable* that he was that worried about you, he honestly could not stop talking about it when I texted to check in last night. The two of you are really keeping the flame alive—from that incredibly sweet birthday proposal to now!" She let out a tinkling laugh that hit my ears like nails on a chalkboard.

"I . . ." I shifted my weight around, trying to remain upright. I was attempting to devise a jovial, tossed-off response, something that would graciously acknowledge her concern and thank her for it.

I could not come up with a single word.

"And that will be extra important when Scotty starts working full time at the Center!" Mercedes gushed. "I know you have your show going, so perhaps you'll be down here as well and the two of you won't have to work too hard at the whole long-distance thing—"

"Long-distance . . . thing?" I squeaked out, my heart dropping into my stomach.

Once again, I could not process any of what she'd said, so I just stood there, mouth agape, staring at her while my one sandaled foot continued sinking into the sand.

"Oh noooo, I guess you guys haven't had a chance to talk about that yet," Mercedes said, her mouth forming a distressed little moue. "Sorry, I'm just excited for our Scotty, he was so absolutely thrilled to get the offer, and I know it gave him so many ideas about making the clinic even more amazing—"

"Thanks, Mercedes," Scott interjected, easy grin in place. "Would you mind checking on the kids? They're taking their sweet time coming back here, and . . ." He nodded in the distance at the snack stand, where the green-haired girl— Dee—was facing off against one of the other girls, hands on her hips. "It looks like they're, ah, dealing with some interpersonal conflicts. That they could use some help with."

I squinted at Dee. She was gesturing wildly now, her index finger jabbing itself toward the other girl in what looked like an aggressive manner.

Were they arguing? What was there to argue about during a surf clinic on this gorgeous, extremely relaxing stretch of beach?!

I swallowed hard, trying like mad to order my face to stop flaming and my sandal to stop sinking into the sand. I was totally failing at this whole "relaxing" thing myself, so I probably shouldn't even attempt to judge a pack of hormonal teenagers.

"Of course," Mercedes said, giving Scott a brisk head bob. "I'll give you two a moment alone!"

"W-what is happening?" I sputtered, as Mercedes jogged off toward the snack stand. "Suddenly we're long distance and you're having late-night texting sessions with Mercedes?! I—"

"Annie." Scott squeezed my hand. His easy grin was still in place, but there was something faint and unsure flickering through his eyes. "I . . . I do actually need to talk to you, but neither of us has really had anything resembling a free moment. Why don't we sit down?"

He lowered himself gracefully onto the towel and tugged me toward him. I managed to maneuver myself down to the towel, pretzeling my body again. When I finally got into a comfortable position, I tangled with my sandal's straps once more and tossed the stubborn shoe to the side.

"So," Scott said, turning to face me and taking both of my hands in his, "the LA Youth Center *did* offer me a full-time gig. They've apparently been thinking about it ever since I first got in touch with them. They're loving my plans for the surf clinic, and they want to give me the resources to expand it into its own thing—a year-round program with different levels. 'Cause, you know, you can actually go to the beach year-round out here." He flashed me a grin. "Remember how you suggested that might be something I could do with this? I never thought it could actually become a reality. I'm still kinda taking it all in."

"And you told them . . . what, exactly?" I said, trying to make sense of yet another huge pile of confusing new information. This relaxing day was really proving to be the exact opposite.

"I told them I had to think about it," he said. "Obviously, we'd have to discuss some things."

I nodded robotically, my mind a whirl. Isn't this what I'd so desperately wanted for him? To finally get to pursue his own thing, outside of Team Tanaka/Jupiter. To be able to explore his passion unabashedly. To light up with that wholesome enthusiasm that told me he was living his dreams.

Well, he was lit up like that now. So why was I freaking out so hard?

I supposed . . . in true Hurricane Annie fashion, I hadn't really thought about what it would mean for him to actually get everything he wanted. I'd pushed him toward this gig at the Center, talked a big game about "expanding" his clinic . . . without fully realizing that all of that might lead to a potentially enticing permanent job offer in LA. Another change in the supposedly perfect infrastructure of Team Tanaka/Jupiter. And, you know, our entire lives together.

"The offer came as a complete surprise to me," Scott continued. "And I know we probably can't come up with a way to make it work. It's not exactly realistic for me or us to consider relocating. Especially with how busy Team Tanaka/Jupiter's been—Evie and Nate are about to have their baby, and we still don't know what Shasta's plan is. But obviously it was really flattering, so I've been fantasizing a little about what it would actually be like to expand the surf clinic, do everything

I want with it—extend my stay so long that I definitely lose any and all cool points with the kids and settle into my destiny as the dorky teacher who insists they learn goofy surfing terms like 'barney' and 'mushburger.'" One corner of his mouth lifted in a half-smile. "Don't worry, I'm not planning on actually pitching long distance to you or anything like that. I was just joking around with Mercedes, and it was so late when she texted, I was probably a little loopy."

Guilt washed over me in rolling waves. Was he making his dreams smaller again so mine could flourish? Allowing himself to be swallowed whole by Team Tanaka/Jupiter when his heart was somewhere else?

And the ugly, petty voice in my brain had to ask: was it true he'd confided all of this to *Mercedes* before he'd even talked to me?

I had a sudden vision of them together, after hours at the Youth Center. Heads bent close as Scott whispered all his hopes and dreams and frustrations to her. Or late-night texting: him lying in bed, looking all sexy with that easy lopsided grin. Finally feeling like he could speak freely to someone who understood and wasn't going to freak out when he brought up the idea of a potential life change. No, Mercedes would only express excitement, she would be *thrilled* about this opportunity for him. That was the kind of reaction he deserved.

He wanted this. I could tell. And I would not be the one to keep it from him.

"Of course you should seriously consider it, this sounds like a dream come true!" I said, pasting a dazzling smile on my face. "And we're mature adults, we can talk long distance. I'm sorry for my initial reaction, I was just . . . surprised."

He stared at me, confusion crinkling his brow. "Really? You'd . . . want that? The other day, when you came to the Center, you said—"

"Why wouldn't I?" I said, trying to match Mercedes' effervescent trill. "I want you to be happy above all else—and as you said, *I* was the one who mentioned expanding the surf clinic in the first place!"

"Well . . . yeah," Scott said, his brow crinkling further. "But—"

"Scotty! Aveda!"

We both turned to see Mercedes approaching, a furious-looking Dee trailing after her. The girl Dee had been facing off against plodded along a few steps behind, throwing poisonous dagger looks Dee's way. And the rest of the kids were following, an unruly line of humanity that seemed to be bickering amongst themselves nonstop.

"I found our charges," Mercedes said, gesturing to the motley crew of teens. "But we seem to have a, um, *situation* . . ."

"This bitch insulted my hair!" Dee wailed, pointing an accusatory finger at the other girl—a petite brunette with adorable masses of freckles.

"You *asked* me what I thought!" Freckles protested. "I gave you an honest fucking assessment, and if you don't like that, maybe you should try making your hair a color that isn't the exact shade of cat vomit!"

"How. Dare. You!" Dee squawked. "You know I *hate* cats—"

"Okay, okay," Scott said, scrambling to his feet, hands held up in a show of peace. "Let's all take a deep breath—"

"*Cats* take deep breaths!" Freckles spat out, eyes sparkling malevolently. She shot Dee an especially evil look. "Maybe that's why Dee is so pissed off, she's realized she's at one with the felines—"

"Fuck offfff!" shrieked Dee, launching herself directly at Freckles.

"Dammit," Scott muttered, stepping forward and kind of dancing around them, like he didn't know exactly what to do.

Luckily, I did. Because while Aveda Jupiter may not know what shoes to wear to the beach or how to graciously respond when the love of her life reveals that he maybe, possibly wants to upend their entire existence together . . . she

does know how to break up a full-on fight between two ci-
vilians who have lost their goddamn minds.

So she jumped into the fray and did exactly that.

Neither Dee nor Freckles—whose real name was Carina—
could explain why they had acted like a couple of hellions
determined to beat the living shit out of each other. Thankfully, I managed to intervene when they were still at the hair-
pulling stage, and no one was hurt.

But when Scott and I tried to talk to them after they'd
been pulled apart and banished to separate beach towels,
they couldn't offer much insight as to what had started the
whole thing.

"I hate cats!" Dee kept wailing. "She *knows* I hate cats!"

"But how did this disagreement *start*?" I said, for what felt
like the trillionth time. I glanced over at Scott, who was trying to talk to Carina. He looked like he was getting about as
far as I was.

"Dee," I continued. "Please. Try to calm down and think
back—it looked like something was going down between you
guys at the snack stand? Was it really just that you asked
Carina what she thought of your hair? Because this argument seems like a lot. For that."

"Mmm, yes," Dee said, her gaze going a little unfocused.
"I . . . hmm." She frowned. "I did ask her what she thought
of my hair. I just dyed it, and it was, like, this multi-step process because I had to bleach it first, I naturally have really
dark hair. Like yours." She nodded at my raven tresses. "It
took a bunch of sessions and a ton of hours before I could
totally achieve my vision. Carina knows how hard I worked
on it!" She glared daggers at the back of Carina's head.
"But . . ." She tilted her head to the side, her gaze going unfocused again. "*I* knew that she'd been very vocally opposed
to me 'ruining' my supposedly perfect virgin hair. So I'm not
sure why I asked that. In the moment, I really, really wanted
to provoke her. I couldn't think of anything else, I just had

to do it. I had, like, a *hunger* for it. That's the only way I can explain what I was feeling. I was also absolutely starving for a deluxe bacon cheeseburger from the snack shack and she kept getting in my way and claiming she was, like, way more starving. So that pissed me off too."

"Do the two of you usually have a contentious relationship?" I said, trying not to let my growing irritation show.

"Sort of?" Dee said with a shrug. "We like to joke around, try to get a rise out of each other. But I don't know why I was suddenly so fixated on that."

I shook my head, not sure where to go from there. I could not fathom what was so appealing about this—defusing fights between hormonal teenagers, then trying to pry any sort of logical reason out of them—that was making Scott consider a move miles and miles from our beloved home.

"Hey, Dee," Scott sauntered up, easy grin in place, obviously trying to make her feel comfortable. "Carina's ready to apologize. And I think maybe you owe her one, too?"

"Yeah, you're right, Mr. Cam," Dee said, getting to her feet. "Sorry 'bout the ruckus."

"Go talk to her," Scott said, jerking his head in Carina's direction. "Then we can get on with the clinic."

"Awww yeah!" Dee hooted, her indignation over the whole hair incident melting away. "Can't wait, those waves are to die for!"

"So what did Carina say?" I asked Scott as Dee trotted off toward Carina. "Because Dee had zero good reasons for why she responded . . . that way. Something to do with deluxe bacon cheeseburgers?"

"I dunno, Carina said Dee knew she wasn't into the green hair," Scott said with an exasperated shrug. "So when she asked for Carina's opinion, all Carina could think of was how to be as insulting as possible. And she was further aggravated because Dee's 'incessant annoying questions' about the hair were keeping her from getting her own bacon cheeseburger. I don't know why those two are obsessing over burgers, they aren't supposed to eat anything right before the clinic—it could upset their stomachs when we get to some of the more demanding exercises. Also, I thought they were both vegan."

"So out-of-control teenagers on the loose, that's what we've come up with?"

"That's the gig." He gave me one of his easy smiles. But there was a glimmer of something uncertain in his eyes I couldn't quite parse.

Before I could respond, Dee and Carina zipped by, arm in arm, chattering at each other.

"Hey, hey," Scott called out, waving at them to get their attention. "Glad to see you two have made up, but where are you going? I'm about to start the clinic—"

"We'll be right back, Mr. Cam!" Dee sang out over her shoulder. "We decided we need to make up with snacks, so we're gonna grab us those deluxe bacon cheeseburgers we were after."

"I can smell that bacon from here!" Carina enthused.

"Okay . . ." Scott studied the newly united duo as they trooped off toward the snack stand, which they'd been about to brawl in front of just moments earlier.

"Maybe they decided not to be vegan today," I said. "Again with the out-of-control teenager thing. At that age, you change your mind about stuff a hundred times an hour."

"You weren't like that," he said, his smile warming. "You always knew exactly what you wanted."

I flushed and smiled back, pleased to feel like some of our usual dynamic was returning.

"No, Ezra, stop that!"

We both turned to see Mercedes waving her arms around at Ezra. He was swaying in the sand, his mane of hair swirling around him, drinking from what looked like some kind of flask.

"Give that to me!" Mercedes demanded. "You're underage, and we're not supposed to have alcohol on the beach, period!"

She was trying to sound commanding, assertive. But her

voice wobbled and she was blinking rapidly, as if trying to stave off tears.

"Oh . . . dear," Scott breathed out, his expression turning concerned. "I better go take care of whatever's happening over there."

I hung back and assessed the scene as he approached Mercedes and Ezra. One of Ezra's friends also had a flask he was trying to guzzle from, both of them dancing unsteadily by the waves.

Scott was so enthusiastic about these kids, so affectionate toward them, and kept talking about how wonderful they were. And yet, one supposed-to-be-relaxing day at the beach and they were all behaving like hellions.

I watched as Scott stepped between Mercedes and Ezra and laid a gentle hand on Ezra's shoulder, murmuring in his ear. Mercedes moved to the side and wiped tears from her eyes, snuffling so loudly I could hear her from several feet away.

I tried to squash the resentment that stabbed through me. Hadn't she been working here longer than he had? Shouldn't she know how to handle this kind of conflict? Or were those big, fat crocodile tears emerging because she wanted Hottie Scotty to swoop in and save her?

Ugh. My judgmental self was coming out full force, and I really needed to get a handle on it. Maybe Mercedes was simply sensitive, like Evie. Evie also tended to cry at the drop of a hat . . . although she was never quite so *theatrical* about it.

It looked like Scott had finally gotten through to Ezra—the boy hung his head as he passed over the flask. A couple minutes later, his friend did the same. No more drunken dance party.

I made a careful approach as Scott consoled the boys, gently patting them on the back. Mercedes was still standing off to the side, snuffling away and dabbing at the corners of her eyes.

"Everything all right?" I said, side-eyeing Ezra and his friend.

"Just fine," Scott said, easy grin back in place. "But since everyone's so, ah, energetic today, we've decided it's best if we head back soon. We'll be cutting the clinic a little short. Instead of the beginners' drills I had planned, Mercedes here is going to do a quick surf demo out in the water, so the kids can see how it's done."

"Mercedes?!" I blurted out before I could stop myself. "But shouldn't the kids watch *you* do the demo? Since you're the expert surfer and this clinic was your idea and all."

"She's right, Scott," Mercedes piped up, delicately dabbing the last of her tears away. "I'm such an amateur compared to you!"

"Not at all," he said. "You're being way too modest. Why don't you suit up, and I'll get the kids all settled on the towels over here."

"Well . . . okay," she said, drawing herself up a little taller and giving him a brave smile. "I guess I can rally—for you."

I squashed the groan that was threatening to escape from me. Staring at them, I was once again struck by how perfect they looked together—blonde, tan, gorgeous. "All-American," as Mercedes would say. If I was a total stranger passing by, I'd assume they were an ideal California couple, out for a beautiful day at the beach.

I managed to rein in my resentment as Scott herded the kids back to the beach towels and settled them in. I sat down on the towel he'd set out for us before, brushing bits of sand from my shorts. My hat had stayed on during the Dee/Carina fracas, and I was grateful for the shade it provided against the sun.

Scott finally got everyone situated and sat down next to me.

"I'm not sure where Dee and Carina got off to," he said, craning his neck to look at the snack stand off in the distance. "I need to track them down before we leave. Turning up with two fewer kids than I started off with will definitely not reflect well on me."

"They're probably just going to town on those bacon cheeseburgers," I said.

"Score another loss for veganism," he chuckled, reaching over to squeeze my hand.

I tried to let the last of my lingering resentment dissipate, to banish the image of the perfect blonde coupledom of Scott and Mercedes from my mind. That was easier said than done, especially since Mercedes chose that moment to waltz back into view wearing a sleek wetsuit and toting a surfboard decorated with soft swirls of blue and green.

There were no tears now. She whipped her golden curls over her shoulder and beamed at us, a perfectly sun-kissed surfer girl silhouetted against the glittering waves. She faced the ocean and walked in until she found a spot she liked, setting the surfboard atop the water and climbing aboard, positioning herself on her stomach.

"Watch carefully, gang—Ms. McClain's technique is excellent!" Scott called out. "We'll be able to actually try some of this next time, assuming y'all can stand to be a little less rowdy."

Some of the kids groaned, sending a good-natured singsongy chorus of "Yes, Mr. Cam" Scott's way. He grinned at them, his shoulders relaxing.

I snuck a sidelong glance at him. He was back to that easy smile, but now it looked more genuine. He was really good at this: making these kids feel like they were well taken care of, but not judged in any way.

"Wow, look at Ms. McClain go!" Ezra whooped.

I turned my attention back to Mercedes and the ocean. She'd paddled pretty far out and was now sitting up on the board, her legs draped over either side. Watching the ocean for that big wave.

"Man, I love this part," Scott murmured, leaning close to me. "The *anticipation*."

I hastily reminded myself that he was most definitely talking about the act of surfing. Not Mercedes, specifically.

She did cut a striking figure, though. She'd paddled so far out that she was the lone speck in her section of ocean, a brave little dot topped by a striking flash of golden hair. She sat up straighter as the perfect wave rolled toward her, a graceful ripple running through the bright blue sea.

Then, at the exact right moment, she stood.

The wave swooped under her, lifting her surfboard to the sky. And she crouched into perfect formation, arms flying out on either side of her to keep her balance.

It looked like absolute magic from afar, her little board skating its way over the sea's brilliant blue expanse, her golden hair flying out behind her.

"Yes!" Scott hollered, clapping his hands together. "Damn, look at her go!"

His charges also responded enthusiastically, leaping to their feet and cheering Mercedes on. I clapped politely and schooled my features into a look of respectful interest. Or at least I hoped it was respectful. Evie had told me that my natural resting expression tended to look rather intense. I supposed Bertram and Co. would have called it *aggressive*.

For one thrilling (well, to everyone else, anyway) moment, Mercedes rode that wave with precision, her board cruising smoothly along the bubbly white foam of the wave.

Then it all came crashing down—literally.

The wave reared up like a giant gaping mouth and overwhelmed her, swallowing her board in its mighty swirl and sending her careening into the water.

"Aw, shit!" Ezra yelled. "Wipeout!"

"It happens," Scott said, laughing a little. "Most surfing triumphs end with you being tossed in the water—just how it goes. Luckily, Mercedes is a pro."

We watched as the wave crested, Mercedes' golden head bobbing in and out of sight.

Then the wave swallowed her entirely.

"It's okay," Scott called out as a concerned murmur rippled through his students. "She'll pop back up. Give her a minute."

Anticipatory silence descended on us as we watched the wave roil with the wind, blue and white crashing together off in the distance. Clouds rolled over the sun, darkening the perfect weather and casting a gloom over the beach. As the seconds ticked by and Mercedes failed to appear, the silence thickened with tension.

"Hmm," Scott murmured, his posture stiffening. "I wonder—"

"*HELP!*"

Mercedes' blonde head popped up in the waves, her arms flailing, scrambling for purchase. Her surfboard was nowhere to be seen, but her screams were loud enough to carry to shore.

"Fuck," Scott exclaimed, scrambling to his feet. "What's she doing? She's usually a strong swimmer . . ." He looked around frantically, but the lifeguard stand closest to us was empty.

"Maybe she's overwhelmed by those giant waves," I said, jumping to my feet as well. My adrenaline spiked, my superheroine instincts kicking in, and I swiftly moved closer to the edge of the water, eyes scanning the sea.

"Mr. Cam," one of the kids piped up, voice wobbly with fear, "is . . . is Ms. McClain gonna be okay?"

"Where's the goddamn lifeguard?" Scott growled through gritted teeth. "I should try to . . ." He eyed the waves, wheels turning.

"No," I said quickly, my heart beating a million miles a minute. "Don't try to swim, it's way too far! I don't know how she even got that far out, but at least she had the board."

"If I paddle out there with my board, it'll take way too long!" Scott lamented, his eyes darting all over the place.

"HELP!!!" Mercedes yelled, thrashing in the water. "Scott, *please!*"

"Let me," I said, stepping forward. "I can do this."

I focused on Mercedes, the tiny dot bobbing in the sea. Just a few years ago, the idea of using my telekinesis in this situation would have seemed impossible to me. She was too far out, she kept coming in and out of view, and I was going to have to maintain a strong hold on her while towing her to shore.

But after spending so much time practicing and honing and refining my unique skill, now I knew I could do this.

I took a deep breath and concentrated, reaching out with my invisible feathers. They stretched across the ocean, brushing against the water. Excitement surged through me, that *knowing* that I was in my element and was about to help someone who couldn't help themselves. Now that I'd finally rid myself of those wretched sandals, my bare feet planted confidently in the sand and my spine straightened with purpose.

Mercedes was becoming less and less visible as she was pulled beneath the current, so I plunged my invisible feathers into the water, searching for a human form. After a moment of sifting through the biting cold of the ocean, I found her.

Her body felt limp as I very carefully wrapped my feathers around her in a telekinetic hold. Then I pulled—I swore I could feel a heartbeat, all that blood beating wildly through her body. Hopefully she was merely unconscious.

I made sure my hold was secure, then channeled all my mental strength into maintaining that grip, lifting Mercedes out of the water.

By now, a small crowd had gathered around us, shouting and pointing as Mercedes floated above the waves. I was vaguely aware of Scott's voice, telling them to stand back, give me room to work . . . and then I heard my name . . .

"Annie," Scott whispered, his tone urgent. "Are you okay? You look like you're struggling . . ."

"Fine," I managed. My voice *did* sound strained. I realized that sweat was pouring down my face, my shoulders were up around my ears, and my hands were shaking. Maintaining this kind of hold was a lot of work, though not so much that it should be affecting me this way . . .

I refocused on Mercedes. The most important thing right now was getting her safely to shore.

I pulled her toward us carefully, keeping her positioned at a decent height, well above the swell of the water. If she hadn't been unconscious before, she definitely was now. Her body was completely still, but I could still feel her heartbeat. I towed her closer and closer . . . one millimeter at a time . . .

That's it . . . that's it . . .

Gradually, the mood of the assembled crowd began to shift. Their concerned murmurs morphed into little cheers and shouts, claps of encouragement. They knew they were watching true superheroing in action, and that made me stand taller—even as my vision blurred and my hands started to shake even more and . . .

A wave of blackness washed over me, obliterating everything else. It was swift and vicious, like someone had just stabbed me in the back.

I gasped and shook my head furiously, trying to get Mercedes back in view, trying to tighten my hold on her, trying to . . . to . . .

Blood roared in my ears and my heartbeat turned labored, my body trying desperately to keep itself upright, my hands shaking so hard I thought they were going to fall off . . .

The harder I tried to regain my vision, the deeper I was pushed into the blackness. I felt my invisible feathers slip away from me, and then there was a scream and a splash and I was falling and falling and falling, my body landing with a bone-shaking *whump* in the sunbaked sand.

CHAPTER SIXTEEN

AND SO, OUR "relaxing" day at the beach ended up being anything but.

After I face-planted in the sand, I was vaguely aware of more screaming and shouting, of my eyes fluttering closed again, of eventually being wrapped in a towel, the familiar feel of Scott's arms around me . . . me trying to say something to him, him frowning in confusion . . . Mercedes saying something . . . wait, was Mercedes okay? How was she all recovered and chatting it up like she hadn't nearly drowned?! Or maybe she *did* drown and I was hallucinating . . .

I drifted in and out, finally falling completely unconscious until much later, when my eyes snapped open and I saw the banana leaf–print wallpaper of the hotel staring back at me. I groaned and rolled over to be greeted by someone shoving a phone in my face.

"Evie!" I shrieked, my gaze going to the wielder of the phone. "What are you doing?!"

"Nate, she's awake! Does she look okay?" Evie bleated.

Slowly, everything came into focus. I was in my bed back at the hotel, and Evie was waving her phone around. Nate was on the screen, his broody expression somewhere between worried and exasperated.

"I told you, I cannot properly examine her over the phone," Nate said, his gruff rumble of a voice endlessly patient. I was guessing this was not the first time Evie had demanded he diagnose my current condition over FaceTime. "But I can come down to Los Angeles—"

"No." I finally found my voice and tried to pull myself up in bed.

Even the smallest movement made me wince—my bones ground against each other, every joint cracking painfully as I tried to arrange myself in a sitting position.

I felt *exhausted*. There were definitely a few more monster yawns in my future. I'd have to try to stifle them so Evie wouldn't worry so much. I was supposed to be watching out for my pregnant bestie, not the other way around.

"I don't think there's anything wrong with me," I insisted, trying to inject my voice with Aveda Jupiter–style imperiousness. "Certainly nothing that Nate has to come all the way down here for. But let's back up, please—what happened? Where's Scott? And Mercedes . . ." I shook my head, trying to make my hazy memories from the beach cohere.

"Annie!" As if on cue, Scott burst into the bedroom. His hair was mussed, his eyes were wild, and his golden skin looked drawn and pale.

Evie turned the phone screen so Nate could see what was going on.

Scott rushed to the bed and gathered me close, his worried eyes scanning my form, as if searching for invisible injuries.

"I shouldn't have left you," he breathed, his voice thick with tension.

"She *told* you to leave," Evie said, rolling her eyes. "And even when half-conscious, Aveda Jupiter can be quite convincing."

"I need you all to back up again," I said, holding up my hands. "I remember being on the beach, using my telekinesis to lift Mercedes out of the ocean and tow her to shore, and then—oh! Mercedes!" My eyes widened with alarm. "Is she okay? What happened to her?"

"You'd brought her close enough that I was able to swim out and bring her the rest of the way in," Scott said, very gently brushing my hair off my face. He was stroking my arm now, his brows still knitted together in concern. "She'd passed out, but I used CPR to revive her. Luckily she didn't hit her head on the board or anything, and she was mostly fine. Just a little shaken up. Everything was chaos, and you were drifting in and out. I wanted to stay with you, but you kept telling me no, I needed to take care of Mercedes and the kids. You got *really* insistent about it. Mercedes suggested we call Evie to come get you so we could take the kids back to the Center and make sure none of them were traumatized. But I . . ." His frown deepened. "I should have stayed with you. I could barely concentrate on anything back at the Center—"

"No," I said firmly. "You did the right thing. The kids should be the top priority. And I don't want you to get fired from your new job before you can even start. I was obviously fine."

"So 'fine' you slept for four hours straight," Evie muttered.

"Four hours?!" I blew out a frustrated breath. "Why did you all let me waste so much *time*?"

"Aveda," Nate piped up from the phone screen. "What do you feel right now? And did anything strange happen right before you passed out? I cannot recall a time in recent years where you've been unable to maintain a telekinetic hold."

"It was very strange," I said, my eyes going to the fancy wallpaper again as I tried to recall the moments leading up to Mercedes plummeting back into the ocean. I'd been feeling so confident, so sure of myself—glad I could make myself useful. But I'd also been struggling, hadn't I? The sweating, the shaking hands, the feeling like I was about to come apart at the seams . . .

"It was harder for me to stay locked on Mercedes," I admitted. "I was definitely exerting way more energy, I could *feel* it. I suppose I haven't had to do anything quite at that level for a while. Maybe my system was simply overwhelmed?"

"And maybe you were still exhausted—remember how drained you were last night?" Scott said, wrapping an arm around my shoulders and pulling me close. "You probably needed more time to recover from the whole Edendale mess."

"Aveda Jupiter can't take time out to recover," I said. "It is true that I didn't get a lot of sleep last night, though. I wanted to study some of those vampire books Pippa provided me with—"

"Annie." Scott shook his head, a thread of irritation creeping into his voice. "You were supposed to rest. The books can wait."

"Not if they contain the key to figuring out what's happening on our show!" I insisted. "Time is always of the essence when innocent people are in danger, Scott, you know that. And anyway, what would have happened if I hadn't been there today? I may not have gotten Mercedes all the way to shore, but I got her far enough that you could then save her."

I bit my lip, forcing the words to stop spilling out of my mouth with such reckless abandon. I sounded defensive, peevish. Qualities I would rather *not* associate with Aveda Jupiter, thank you very much.

I also couldn't stop a certain image from floating through my head. Scott rushing into the surf to save Mercedes, heroically carrying her to safety, giving her mouth to mouth. Her eyelashes fluttering and her lips curving into a grateful smile, tilting her head up so they could engage in *another* kind of mouth to mouth—

Good god. What on earth was my brain doing?! Why was I inventing random scenes of soft-focus romance involving my husband and my sort-of nemesis? Was their overwhelming mutual blondness just too much for me to take?

"Of course I'm glad you were there," Scott said, his lips brushing my hair. "You absolutely saved Mercedes. But I also want to make sure you're taking care of *you*." He gave me a gentle half-smile, but his eyes were still lit with worry. And guilt. He felt *guilty* for not coming back to the hotel with me, even though he'd made the right choice. I threaded my fingers through his and squeezed his hand, trying to reassure him.

"Aveda, if you do not sense anything wrong, then I see no reason for excessive concern or medical intervention," Nate said from the phone screen. "But Scott is correct. If your system was overloaded today, it could be that your body is simply craving rest." A slight smile played around his lips. "Even Aveda Jupiter needs to recharge sometimes."

"Yes, and that's what this beach day was supposed to be," Scott said, squeezing my shoulders again. "But it went all the way wrong, between the kids acting up and Mercedes almost drowning. Apparently I should *not* be the one planning our relaxing outings."

Before he could elaborate on that thought, his phone buzzed in his pocket.

"Oh . . ." Scott disentangled himself from me and fumbled around to pull the phone free, still casting worried looks my way.

"Get it," I encouraged him. "Maybe it's the Center."

"It's not," he said, glancing at the screen. "But I think I need to answer anyway."

He hit the answer button and Bea Tanaka's extremely indignant face filled the screen.

"Scott!" she screeched. "Where's Aveda? Why isn't she answering her phone?"

"Where *is* my phone?" I yelped, looking around frantically. Panic bubbled through my chest—what if I'd missed important calls, texts, alerts? We had *so* much going on right now—

"Relax, it's charging in the main living area of the suite," Evie said, jerking her chin toward the bedroom door. "And obviously there are other ways of reaching you if there's an emergency. Um, is it an emergency, Bea?"

"*Yes,*" she exclaimed, impatiently blowing a lock of purple hair out of her eyes. "It's a code three thousand and two barn burner and I need you to take it extra seriously!"

"What does that mean?" Evie said.

"Beatrice, is this a new system you've invented for classifying emergencies?" Nate asked, looking intrigued.

"Obviously," Bea chirped, shooting him finger guns. "And I'll get into that with you later, big brother, I've already started working on the schematic in my bullet journal. But for now, I need everyone to get out so I can talk to Evie and Aveda."

"But you're on my phone," Scott said, brandishing the gadget for emphasis.

"So give it to Aveda and go," Bea retorted, as if this was the most obvious solution in the world.

"We should all know the drill by now—none of us can argue when faced with the overwhelming correctness of Bea Tanaka logic," Evie said. "Even if the only person said logic is actually comprehensible to is Bea Tanaka."

"Thank you," Bea said, batting her eyelashes demurely. "For exactly half of that statement."

"Sorry, baby, I'm hanging up now," Evie said to Nate. She hit the end call button as he waved good-bye to us, an amused grin overtaking his face.

"I know better than to go all in on a losing battle," Scott said, making his voice light as he passed me the phone. His eyes roamed my face again. "But try not to keep them too long, Bea, Annie really does need rest. Even if she'll never admit it." Those last words seemed like they were trying for teasing, but his voice dipped near the end, turning them low and charged. I manufactured a smile as he left the room and shut the door behind him.

"We need to talk," Bea said, not giving either Evie or me the chance to say anything. "I saw people posting about this whole beach incident on social—"

"What?!" I shrieked. "So me dropping Magnificent Mercedes into the water is plastered all over Twitter?"

"That part, no," Bea said. "The headlines are more along the lines of how 'visiting superheroine' Aveda Jupiter saved the life of local sweetheart Magnificent Mercedes with a timely assist from an 'unidentified wholesome himbo.'" Bea closed her eyes and affected the breathless tones of a star-struck youth. "'Is it just us or does this mouth-to-mouth action look extra hot?! OMG, Romancelandia meet-cute goals! We have no choice but to stan!'"

"They're shipping Mercedes and *Scott*?" Evie's mouth twisted in disbelief. "They don't recognize him as Aveda Jupiter's *husband*?"

"You can't really see his face in most of the pictures people were apparently snapping with their phones," Bea said with a shrug. "And Angelenos may not know who Aveda Jupiter's husband is anyway."

"I suppose that's true," Evie mused. "So why are you calling us, all dramatic-like? What's the emergency?"

"I'm getting to that," Bea shot back. "When I saw this blowing up on social, I tried calling you and Aveda, and nobody answered. So I called Scott. I asked him if there were any oddities with the waves y'all encountered today. I wanted to know if they had any similarities with what we've been dealing with in Maui—especially since we're now thinking supernatural activity has extended to LA as well."

"What'd he say?" I asked faintly. Apparently I wasn't the only one obsessing over how perfect Scott and Mercedes looked together.

"Is *that* the emergency?" Evie interjected. "Did you actually find a connection?"

"Nooooo," Bea said, dragging the word out with force. "If you'll let me finish my story, I'll get to the *actual* emergency." She leveled both of us with a harsh look—the Tanaka Glare, Evie always called it. Something Bea had inherited from their mom. "He said he hadn't really noticed anything unusual, Mercedes just got surprised by an unexpectedly tricky wave. I guess that happens sometimes in surf world. So then Mercedes comes up and starts talking to him and he's like 'I gotta go, Bea,' only he didn't actually hang up. He just thought he did. And I heard *everything*."

"What was Mercedes saying?" I said, even though I wasn't sure I wanted to know the answer.

"Just telling him how sweet he is for being worried about her, how she's totally fine. A lot of the posts on social were urging Magnificent Mercedes to engage in self-care because she's clearly burnt out after being so goddamn magnificent 24-7, and that's the only possible reason the waves almost defeated her," Bea said, voice dripping with disdain. "Then she went on some long, teary tangent about how it's just so *hard* to remember to take care of yourself when you spend all your time taking care of others. But her wellness coach always stresses that she needs to remember that, and so she's going to take a few days off from the Center, and she still feels so guilty for making everyone worry, blah blah, fuckin' blah."

"How is it that white women have managed to turn the term 'self-care' into something I want no part of?" Evie snorted.

"Scott was trying to listen because he's an actual decent person, but he was obviously distracted," Bea continued. "He just wanted to get back to you, Aveda. So *then* Mercedes starts trying to comfort him, telling him he made the right choice to help her bring the kids back, and she knows Aveda will be just fine, because she's so *resilient*. Gets all teary again saying she wishes *she* could be strong all the time like Aveda, but she's much too *sensitive*. And then . . ." Bea leaned in close, her face filling the whole screen. "She put her *hand on his arm* and was, like, stroking!"

"Mercedes seems to . . . really like Scott," I managed. "I don't see an emergency here, Bea."

"It *is* an emergency!" she insisted, her voice twisting up on the last syllable. "Do you not see what she's doing, Aveda? Weaponizing those white woman tears, portraying herself as some kind of sensitive little baby who needs comfort and care while you're the big bad dragon lady, all in the name of *stealing your man*!"

"Scott's not enough of a sucker to fall for that," Evie said. "But Annie, you *really* should tell him about what Mercedes said to you back in the day. I know this stuff can be hard to talk about, and I know you don't want to ruin this supposedly awesome experience he's having, but he needs to know."

"I . . . I think maybe she's changed—"

"No!" Evie growled. "Racists like that don't change, Annie. She's trying to manipulate you again."

"What, 'again'?!" Bea exploded, shaking her head so violently her hair turned into an angry blue and purple storm cloud. "What happened and why have I never heard any of it?"

I sat there numbly as Evie recounted my horrible dinner with Mercedes, too tired to stop her. I stifled another monster yawn and picked at the silky edges of the sumptuous hotel bedspread.

"Excuse! *Me!*" Bea bellowed when Evie was done. "Aveda Jupiter, you are the most bold, badass, flat-out *aggressive*— and I mean that as the compliment it should be—person I know! How have you not brought this to Scott at all? Why are you *shrinking*?!" She shot me a glower, a slightly milder version of the Tanaka Glare.

"I . . ." I yawned again, and tried to get my disparate mess of thoughts together. "I . . . I'm trying not to be *petty*," I finally said. "Diva-like. A self-centered drama queen! Remember when I was trying to plan Evie's wedding and I bulldozed all over what she wanted because I thought *I* knew better? I was trying to be a good friend, but I was a jealous, insecure mess. I . . . I don't want to go to that place again, ever. And anyway, maybe Mercedes *has* changed. She's been perfectly nice to me, she's always complimenting me—"

"No, she hasn't," Evie snapped, crossing her arms over her chest. "Did you not hear everything Bea just said? She's being 'nice' the way that kind of white woman is always 'nice.' With all these little comments that may seem like some warped type of kindness on the surface, but are actually very pointed negs designed to totally undermine your self-confidence. If she *is* being genuinely nice, there's really no need to give her the benefit of the doubt or to forgive all the racist shit she's said and done to you in the past. And even if Scott is not about to let himself be 'stolen,' she's still being completely inappropriate with him."

"Yes," Bea said, stabbing the air with her index finger. "And listen, Aveda, it's true that you've gone full diva in the past. But I'm starting to think that's made you question all of your instincts, or made you feel like voicing any kind of displeasure is wrong." She sent her mouth in a firm line and leveled me with a piercing gaze. "Sometimes what you think of as being 'petty' or 'judgmental' or 'a diva' is actually just you being correct. You have always been a fierce warrior queen and you do *not* need to shy away from that. You're not being 'petty' to Mercedes. *Mercedes fucking sucks.*"

"Let us say I agree with your thesis," I said, still unable to corral my wild storm of conflicting feelings. "What am I supposed to do about it? Tell Scott about some conversation that happened over a decade ago?"

"It's not just the one conversation," Evie insisted. "It's *everything*: The way she tried to take credit for *your* first superheroine triumph. The way she used to undermine you with those totally freaking underhanded compliments about your costume looking 'adorably homemade' or whatever. And were you not listening to *anything* Bea just said?"

"Yeah, and what's with all this reluctance to talk to your husband who adores you above all else?" Bea added. "I know I don't live there anymore, so I'm outta the loop as to whatever weirdo new behaviors all of y'all are engaging in, but it really feels like you've been keeping him at a distance. Like, no interest in our potential power combo spells? 'Cause he and I have been talking about that a ton and we've even done some preliminary experiments, but the other day when he brought it up, you got all weird about him going back to his surf clinic or whatever."

"I don't want him to get consumed by my drama," I said. "That's what always happens—that's why he hasn't been able to pursue all the things *he* wants out of life. Because whatever I'm dealing with as a superheroine and extremely public figure always gets in the way."

"Okay, first of all: we're talking about, like, *the world's* drama," Bea grumbled. "Which I think Scott would agree is pretty important and deserving of his time and energy. He wants to help, Aveda—"

"And that's the problem!" I squeaked. "He *always* wants to help me. He's always going to say yes to whatever I need. But that means his own dreams are getting left behind, and I . . . I just can't bear to see that happen. He's sacrificed so much of his own happiness for other people. I don't want him to do that for me." My voice cracked and I realized that tears had filled my eyes. I hastily scraped them away.

A sad, broken sort of silence descended on us. Like nobody knew quite where to go from there.

"He doesn't see it that way, Annie—I know he doesn't," Evie finally said, her voice very soft. "You have to talk to him. And tell him about Mercedes."

"Too late!" Bea sang out, tapping something on her screen. "I already did."

"What?!?" I exploded, my voice cracking again.

"I sent him a report," Bea said serenely, tucking a stray lock of hair behind her ear. "An official one, like I usually send to Nate and Rose. The title is: Mercedes Totally Fucking Sucks."

"Oh god," I groaned, burying my face in my hands. "Why won't this day just *end*?"

"It probably should," Evie agreed, rubbing her temples. "And Bea, come on, you know better than that—that is a serious boundary violation."

"Like the two of you don't stomp all over each other's boundaries all the frakking time," Bea shot back.

"It's fine, I'll figure out how to take care of it later," I said, slumping back against my pillows. "For now: Evie, can you bring me some of Pippa's vampire books to read while I just lie here like a lump—"

"*No.*" Evie's frown deepened. "You need to *sleep*. Forget Mercedes, you're the one who needs to practice self-care."

"Fiiiiiiiiiiine," I sighed. It came out as the longest of exhales. I was tempted to argue further, but my eyes were already drifting closed. I was so deeply tired, my bones felt like they were about to disintegrate. And I probably should have been even more upset about Bea blowing things up with the Mercedes situation, but I felt too wrung out to care.

My eyes started to flutter closed again.

I was vaguely aware of Evie bidding Bea farewell as I drifted off to sleep. Later, I was also aware of Scott slipping into bed next to me and pulling me close, my face nestling into that perfect spot between his chin and shoulder. That spot where I always fit.

"That's it, sweetheart," he murmured. "Fall asleep on me."

"I love you so much," I said, my voice faint as darkness settled over me like a warm blanket. "You should take that job, you know. Move down here and be all happy and beachy and carefree. And don't pay attention to whatever Bea sent you, it's just her . . . being . . . dramatic . . ."

I don't know how much longer I kept talking, but soon I was snoring away.

I also didn't know if Scott had heard anything I'd said. The only thing I *was* sure of was that he said nothing in return.

DEMON ENCOUNTER REPORT

Submitted to: Scott Cameron (Resident Mage, Tanaka/Jupiter, Inc.; Badass Surf Instructor, Many Generically Named Youth Centers)

Submitted by: Beatrice Constance Tanaka (Senior Researcher and Investigator Type Person, Maui Demon Unit)

Short Summary: Mercedes Totally Fucking Sucks

Long Summary: Please see the attached 27-page spreadsheet detailing Mercedes McClain's (no official affiliation, freelance superheroine for the greater Los Angeles area, pretends she can fly and also be a decent person) gross-ass behavior, particularly toward Aveda Jupiter (lead co-heroine, Tanaka/Jupiter, Inc.). Included are microaggressions, macroaggressions, and just plain old *aggressions*. Report Writer understands that as a white guy, this shit might fly right over your head, so please read extra carefully. Report Writer also preemptively apologizes to Aveda Jupiter for what Report Writer's sister will surely categorize as "a serious boundary violation," but extreme measures had to be taken!

And if Nathaniel Jones (Demonology Expert, Tanaka/Jupiter, Inc.) is reading this—yes, Report Writer is well aware that classifying an encounter with a human (even a superpowered one) as a "Demon Encounter Report" is not usually how we do things around here. Report Writer submits that she is using "demon" colloquially in this case—and if any human deserves the "demon" classification, it's Mercedes.

CHAPTER SEVENTEEN

I SLEPT DEEPLY, my dreams plagued by visions of Scott giving sweet, helpless Mercedes CPR and heroically reviving her from the brink of death. Occasionally I *was* Mercedes in these dream visions, which was extra confusing when the torrid mouth-to-mouth situations inevitably led to something sexier. I'd be all into it, and then I'd remember I was *Mercedes*, kissing my own husband, and I'd remind myself I definitely didn't want that and pull away.

When I rose bright and early the next morning, I was no longer exhausted. I was desperately horny. And Scott had already gone to work, so I couldn't try to fix that (well . . . not with another person, anyway. Unfortunately, when I tried to take care of myself, those pesky visions involving Mercedes just kept intruding, which was a real mood killer).

I also didn't have the chance to talk to him about Bea's ill-advised "report." And he hadn't texted me or anything, so I wasn't sure what he thought of it all.

To my surprise, I also felt something beyond agitated horniness, something more *familiar*: a renewed sense of purpose flowing through my veins, bright as a beacon in the dark. Bea had been right about one thing—I'd been making myself small, second-guessing my every move, and getting tripped up by minor inconveniences like uncomfortable sandals. That was so *not* Aveda Jupiter.

I needed to recapture my mojo. And for that, I needed to return to some of my tried and true tactics of the past, like making my official List of Action Items Needed to Complete a Mission. I used to create this list for every one of my adventures. I'd fallen out of practice in recent years, but what better way to organize all the action items I currently needed to take care of? Then I'd be able to do what I usually do best: *take action.*

So once I'd showered and dressed, pulling my hair into an especially sleek version of my power ponytail, I marched into the suite's living area and settled myself at the dining table.

Solve Pippa's friend dilemma—check!

Figure out what distress my mother's trying to communicate to me via increasingly bizarre photography—check!

Kick all the vampire ass while also saving the show based on your life from being a complete disaster and showing your best friend that superheroing is still the best job ever and she doesn't need a sabbatical and also convincing your husband that he should pursue all of his dreams even if that means he has to move somewhere else and disrupt your perfect life together and—

My train of thought cut off abruptly as I realized I was gasping for air. My vision had narrowed into two tiny white dots, darkness threatening to rise up and surround me. I breathed in deeply, holding myself very still and waiting for it to pass.

When light finally started to filter back in around the corners of my eyes, I looked down at my phone and saw that my mother had sent me a new message. It was another photo; this time, it looked like my parents' kitchen. As with the study, the usually disorganized contents of the room now seemed to be stuffed into a mass of plastic containers.

"What the . . ." I stared harder at the photo, as if that might make it make sense.

All this staring, studying, trying to figure things out was doing me no good. Hadn't I just decided that I needed to reclaim my mojo, to *be* Aveda Jupiter? Time for Aveda Jupiter to turn those action items into true *action!*

I nodded authoritatively, picked up my phone, and Face-Timed my mother.

"Anne?" She looked put out, as if I'd just interrupted her from something important. Like stuffing more things into Container Store receptacles, perhaps. "What's the matter?"

"What's the matter with *you*?" I countered, annoyed at the thread of peevishness weaving its way through my voice. That would simply not do if I wanted to reclaim that mojo. "Why do you keep sending me weird pictures?" I pressed. "And why is part of your house now encased in various plastic bins?"

"Anne, I am simply trying to share with you," my mother said, sounding out each syllable. "Haven't we talked about wanting to do more of that, to connect with each other?"

"Yes," I said, my eyes narrowing in suspicion. "But I'm not sure how much connecting is happening if you won't give me one shred of context."

"Why do you always need so much explanation?" she asked. "Why can't things just *be*?"

"B-because . . ." I sputtered, unsure where to go from there. Any possible words died in my throat, and we found ourselves locked in a staring contest.

"Anne . . ." she finally said, looking exasperated. "I am only trying to make you feel comforted about any changes life may bring. You have always struggled with that. I thought the pictures of oranges would be a comfort, since you are so happy when I send you fruit. And as for the Container Store boxes, I just wanted you to be ready when you see the house next time. It will be, ah . . . different."

"'Different' *how*?" I pressed. "What do you mean? Are you on a Marie Kondo kick? Are things not sparking joy anymore? Or—"

"Anne," my mother said again—then cut herself off abruptly, head cocking to the side. "Oh. Your father needs me. He can't tell which boxes are his." She turned to yell at someone offscreen. "No! Don't touch those, I *told* you, we cannot keep our things together. Must be separate! No, *not* like that . . ." She blew out a breath and turned back to me. "I have to go. I will stop sending the pictures if they bother you."

She hung up before I could respond, just as she had the other day.

"Mom!" I howled at the phone in frustration.

What on earth was happening with her—and with my dad? Why were they putting all their things in boxes? *Separate* boxes. And why was my mother yelling at him so much . . .

Oh . . . *oh*. The answer dawned on me so swiftly, I nearly got whiplash.

My parents were having *marriage problems*. Maybe they were even separating? That would explain all the boxes.

It sort of made sense. They'd always seemed more content than happy, two people who got along well enough to get married, have a child, and live out their golden years in not-totally-unpleasant silence together. Perhaps my mother was trying to reach out to me about their issues, but didn't know exactly what to say.

She needed my help.

The revelation that my parents were maybe, possibly on the verge of splitting up should have upset me. Instead it galvanized me, that *purpose* thrumming through me more strongly than ever. I found myself sitting up straighter, reorganizing my list of tasks with vigor. Now that I had identified the problem, I could actually solve it. I had a target, a goal. A *mission*.

I grabbed hold of my phone, eagerly scrolling through various travel websites. Perhaps my parents just needed something to reignite—or ignite, period—their romantic spark. My mother had mentioned cruises . . . and even though she'd claimed she didn't want to go on one with my father, maybe that would be just the thing. I could send them on a beautiful, luxurious cruise packed to the brim with spa treatments for my mother, golf in gorgeous locales for my father, and plenty of romance for both. Once they were away from their plastic container–stuffed home, they'd be able to see each other in a more swoony context. The champagne would flow, the moonlit deck walks would lead to dancing . . . okay, maybe not dancing. My mother had only agreed to dance at my wedding because she adored Scott so much, and he'd made a big show of asking her for the first dance.

But still. *Romance.*

I nodded to myself, pleased, and started bookmarking things to pull together later. I'd give them the perfect vacation. And when they returned to their weirdly organized home, they'd be like newlyweds.

And then, because my mother was so fond of playing this downright bizarre pic-sending game with me, I sent her a splashy photo of a cruise ship sailing through waters of perfect sapphire blue. No caption, no context.

Satisfied, I was preparing to move on to my next action item when Pippa crashed into the living area, her eyes lit with glee. And possibly sleep deprivation.

"There you are, AJ, so happy you're refreshed," she crowed, plopping herself dramatically into the seat next to me. "I would've checked on you last night, but I got way too into my research!" She waved around the iPad she was toting, her grin stretching from ear to ear. "I read all about your thrilling escapades on the socials, though. That was so badass the way you saved whatshername, Magnificent Mercedes."

"What did your research turn up?" I said, skating around the topic of Mercedes.

"Clint's reps finally got back to me," she said, scanning the iPad screen. "I guess he's now *also* at that super fancy celebrity 'retreat' in Joshua Tree—the place where Stan is supposedly reflecting on all his life choices. But it's *so* fancy, it basically doesn't exist for normies like you and me—or I guess just 'me' since you're also a celebrity! But I've been doing more research on his career as well as Stan's, and it's super interesting. There's this whole interview I found with Clint that was part of a series—*Masters on Masterworks*? And he actually talked about developing *Heroine*."

"Oh, really?" I muttered.

"Yeah," she said, setting the iPad on the table and leaning back in her chair. "It's a lot of the same stuff he's already said to your face, about his auteur vision and all that garbage. But he also dropped something that I think could lead us to . . ." She paused, lowering her voice for maximum drama. ". . . a *clue*."

"And what's that?" I said, trying not to let my impatience show. I didn't want to destroy her youthful zest for life. After all, Aveda Jupiter was also young once.

"He claims he drew much of his inspiration from a particular 'classic of vampire literature,'" Pippa said, reading off the iPad screen. "It's this book I've heard tell of for *years* in the paranormal romance community. It's called *Zacasta's Revenge*, and it's all about this woman who becomes obsessed with being the only vampire in the whole entire world!"

"And you've never read it?" I asked, surprised. "I thought you'd read every vampire book in existence."

"It's super rare," Pippa intoned, her eyes drifting closed in reverent fashion. "Out of print for decades, unavailable in digital. It's like this holy grail that no one's ever been able to locate an actual copy of. The text seems to have disappeared into the ether."

"Then how did Clint get ahold of it?" I queried, resisting the urge to gnaw on my nails.

"An excellent question," Pippa exclaimed, swooping a finger through the air. "I've been all over the paranormal fan chat circuits and online forums, trying to figure out how to track down a copy. We might not be able to find Clint, but if we can find this book . . . well, maybe it will give us some clues. Unless that's not an, um, effective line of investigation?" She shot me an anxious look.

"I think that's a great idea," I said, giving her an encouraging smile. "And this is all wonderful work, Pippa—you're a natural at this supernatural investigating business!"

She beamed at me. "Awesome. 'Cause I also got a good tip on where we can go look for the book . . ." She tapped on the iPad screen, then turned it to face me. The screen showed a photo of a corner storefront with a bright pink awning and a window displaying what looked like an actual fainting couch. "This is an all-romance bookstore on the west side of LA—it's called The Ripped Bodice, and it will take us about thirty minutes to get there, depending on traffic. They have the most well-stocked used and rare romance book room known to man, and so many people have reported finding totally unexpected treasures there." She hugged the iPad to her chest, her expression turning dreamy. "It's basically my personal heaven on earth. And some of my fellow fans in the paranormal romance community have reported spotting *Zacasta's Revenge* amongst the stacks—but whenever they go back to purchase it, it's mysteriously disappeared. I thought we could go paw through their collection, see if we can find it. Or I can do that myself if you and Evie are too busy with more important stuff . . . ?"

"Not at all," I said, smiling at her again. "We have no updates on what's happening with the show, correct? No new showrunner or communication from Bertram or Grouchy Stacey?"

"Correct," Pippa chirped.

"Then this sounds like a great next step in our investigation. I'm all for it, and I'm sure Evie will be too."

As I spoke, a plan was slowly but surely coalescing in my head. This was how I was going to solve *two* problems that had been vexing me. Possibly three.

Going on this expedition to the bookstore would give me some bonding time with Pippa. If her current best friend didn't have time for her at the moment, then *I* could be her best friend. At least until Shelby emerged from her blissful cloud of new love. And if Evie came along too, so much the better—we could make a girls' day of it, and I'd be able to show my BFF and irreplaceable partner that superheroic investigation and fun went hand in hand. Definitely not something she'd ever want to leave behind.

And if we made headway on our whole vampire mess? Even better. Three birds with one stone!

"I should ask Kat to come with us too," I said, impulsively grabbing my phone. Because why not make it a full girls' day? Perhaps Pippa would have so many best friends at the end of this thing, the (hopefully temporary) loss of Shelby would sting less.

I swiped over to my texts, noting that my mother had simply "liked" my cruise ship photo. *Argh.* I'd been trying to shake her up a bit, but her response only confused me more. Never try to go toe to toe with a master of manipulation—aka an Asian mom.

"What are you guys yelling about?" Evie mumbled, shuffling out of her bedroom. "Did I hear something about Kat?"

"I'm inviting her to join us on the latest step of our vampire investigation," I said, tapping away on my phone. "Pippa here had the most amazing notion, so we're headed to a bookstore to dig through stacks and stacks of romance novels!"

"Oh, um. That sounds . . . great," Evie said, settling herself into the third seat at the table. "But given that we haven't heard anything new from Bertram and no one seems to be in immediate danger, I thought maybe we could spend today doing something fun. Like, tourist fun. Not supernatural investigation fun."

"So you admit supernatural investigating is fun!" I crowed, sending my text to Kat. I'd meant for that to sound light, teasing. Instead it sounded like I was yelling some version of *"in your face!"*, all gloaty and shit.

"Sure," Evie said, looking weary. "But aren't you still recovering from yesterday, Annie? I was thinking of something more mellow."

"This can be mellow," I insisted, my voice sounding

strained even as I tried to make it breezier. "We're just going to a bookstore, after all!"

"Yeah!" Pippa said, pumping a fist. "And there's this really awesome Chinese restaurant across the street that makes something called *cheeseburger potstickers*! We gotta try that, right?"

I gave Evie a look, trying to invoke our BFF telepathy. She had to see that this was for our young charge, who was going through a hard time. Her butter-soft heart wouldn't be able to resist that. And I had a feeling she also wouldn't be able to resist the idea of cheeseburger potstickers.

She met my gaze, something unreadable passing through her eyes. For a long moment, she was silent, looking at me in a way that made me think she was trying to come up with some elaborate reason for doing anything except what I'd just suggested.

Then, thankfully, her face softened and she gave me a quick nod.

"Say no more," Evie said, smiling genially at Pippa. "You've convinced me."

As soon as we set foot inside the plush pink wonderland of The Ripped Bodice, Pippa's eyes widened with delight and she made a beeline to the opposite end of the store, where the checkout counter was located.

"Look how happy she is," Evie marveled, as Pippa launched into an animated conversation with the smiling woman behind the pink marble slab that served as the checkout area. "This is better than Christmas. Or multiple trips to Disneyland."

"I'm so glad to see it," I said, as Pippa began gesticulating wildly—she appeared to be reenacting a scene from one of her vampire books. The woman behind the counter was nodding furiously in recognition. "She's been so down about this Shelby thing. And we appear to have finally discovered something that will cheer her up."

"Aw, and look at *you*," Evie said, nudging me in the ribs. "Thinking so intensely about the well-being of our charges. And maybe slipping an actually fun activity into our investigation."

"You know Aveda Jupiter loves to multitask," I said, flashing her a breezy grin as I took in our surroundings. Soft white walls emblazoned with patterns of dreamy pink roses. Freestanding shelves crammed with books and surrounded by little tables of candles and trinkets. And in the middle of everything, a velvet pink couch that was just begging to be lounged on. "That looks exactly like the couch at It's Lit," I said, naming the Bay Area bookstore where Bea used to work. "Actually, the whole place has a very similar vibe."

"Yeah, I was texting with Bea on the way over here and she said they're kind of like sister stores. Alike in spirit, and dedicated to promoting all kinds of happily ever afters," Evie said, glancing at her phone. "She also wanted to know if Scott's said anything about her 'report' on Mercedes."

"He hasn't," I said, trying to keep my tone light. "I fell asleep so hard last night, and then he left early . . ." I manufactured a smile. "I'm sure we'll talk tonight."

Evie studied me for a moment longer than necessary, the silence between us punctuated only by a shriek of uproarious laughter—Pippa was still having the time of her life. Out of the corner of my eye, I saw that she'd already stacked a teetering pile of books on the countertop.

"Remember back at Morgan?" Evie said, her eyes narrowing. "When I kept saying I was totally fine and you knew I totally wasn't? Because I think the same thing is happening here—in reverse."

"It's not so much 'I'm fine' as 'I can handle it,'" I said, rolling my eyes at her. "You were avoiding your problems with all your might. Whereas I'm running headfirst toward them, ready to tackle them to the dirt. That is the Aveda Jupiter Way, after all."

"Is it, now?" Evie said, the corners of her mouth twitching with amusement. "All I'm saying—"

"Oh hey, girls. This place is cool, huh?"

We both turned to see Kat striding toward us, giant sunglasses affixed firmly to her face. She was wearing another jumpsuit—this one full-length and jet-black with bright lime green piping. Her hair was pulled into an artfully sloppy topknot and red plastic earrings shaped like bunches of cherries dangled from her ears. She'd topped off the outfit with gleaming silver sneakers featuring zippers in place of laces.

She looked as stylish as she had the other day, but I noticed her energy seemed diminished. Her gait was a little less peppy, her shoulders slumping. When she took off her sunglasses to greet us, I suppressed a gasp. Dark circles had taken up permanent residence under her eyes, contrasting with the general pallor of her face. I recalled that she'd seemed a bit worn back at Edendale, but now she looked like she hadn't slept in forever.

"Hey, Kat," I said, taking a tentative step toward her. "Are you okay? You look, ah . . ."

"Freakin' exhausted? Probably because I am," she said, blowing out a long breath. "I've barely been able to sleep the past couple days, I'm so stressed about this whole showrunner situation."

"But isn't Clint being fired—well, MIA, but *also* fired—a good thing?" Evie asked.

"Not necessarily," Kat said, frowning into space. "Because whoever they bring on next could be way worse. They could try to re-cast me or Miki. They could make the writing even more atrocious than it already is . . ." She cut herself off. "Sorry. Don't mean to doom spiral."

"You can show the full breadth of your intensity around me, remember?" I said, giving her shoulder a light squeeze. "I honor your intensity. I relate to and make space for it."

"And hey, what you're describing does really suck," Evie added. "Here's hoping they go in the other direction and bring in someone way better than Clint."

"What a dream," Kat said, her eyes getting a far-off look.

At first I thought that far-off look was a result of her getting lost in a new doom spiral—but then she sniffed the air and turned abruptly to face the exit, her forehead crinkling.

"Does anybody else smell the most absolutely luscious cheeseburger?" she asked. "Only . . ." She sniffed the air again. "Like, crossed with something? This sounds wild, but I'm picking up the scent of . . . a cheeseburger stuffed inside a dumpling? Is that a thing?"

"Ooh, you must be sensing the presence of Ms Chi Cafe's cheeseburger potstickers!" Pippa enthused, marching back over to us. "We're totally getting that after we're done here. You must have a very sensitive sniffer."

"I'm picking up faint meaty undertones as well," I said, giving the air a slight sniff. "The power of these potstickers must really be something."

"I hope so, because I am *starving*!" Kat said, her gaze drifting back to the exit.

"Hopefully this mission will be a breeze," I said. "And then we can go get all up close and personal with some fine local cuisine."

"Looks like this is your favorite thing about LA so far," Evie teased Pippa, nodding at the growing pile of books she'd stacked on top of the counter. She seemed to have added a few more since I'd last looked.

"I told you, it's my heaven," Pippa exclaimed, swooning. "And gotta say, it's even more heavenly than I could have imagined. The rare book room is up those stairs near the back—it's supposed to be like a giant attic stuffed to the brim with old romance novels." Her eyes fluttered closed and I reached out to grab her arm, worried she might actually faint.

"And we're looking for what, a particular book?" Kat asked. I'd explained the basics of our investigation to her without getting into the gory details. I'd told her how we suspected something odd was happening related to Clint and

Stan's recent behavior, and how it was our duty as superheroines to investigate whenever we sensed anything amiss. I hadn't told her that Pippa was convinced they'd turned into actual vampires, just that we needed to find this one book to get some insight into Clint's terrible brain and how he'd developed *Heroine*. She'd agreed to be discreet about what we were up to and promised not to breathe a word about our investigation to anyone except Miki.

"That's right—we're looking for a very special tome," Pippa breathed. Her whole body was buzzing with anticipation. It was so nice to see her excited without reservation, her current sadness over Shelby momentarily forgotten. And my plan was actually *working*—soon I'd be able to cross all kinds of tasks off my list. *Check, check, check!*

Pippa led us to the back of the store and up a narrow, creaky staircase. This should have perhaps caused me to recall Evie's and my time at Morgan, when every structure we entered seemed to resemble a haunted house—creepy, creaky, and cobwebby. But this particular staircase had an undeniably cozy feel. The walls were lined with torn-out pages of books, painstakingly decoupaged so they resembled wallpaper. A tiny light at the top of the stairs cast a gentle glow over us, guiding our journey.

We reached the top and entered a door set off to the left, which took us into this quaint attic of a used and rare book room. Shelves lined every wall from top to bottom, each of them absolutely bursting with well-loved paperbacks. Still more books were stacked haphazardly around the room—crowding the floor, piling onto an old-fashioned metal library cart, nestling in a comfy-looking armchair crammed into the back corner.

I cast a sidelong glance at Pippa. She was practically vibrating with excitement. I thought she might ascend to another plane of blissful existence right then and there.

"Are these books, um, organized in any way?" Evie said, faint alarm crossing her face as she scanned the piles and piles of paperbacks overwhelming the space.

"They are not," Pippa said, swooping an index finger through the air. "That's part of the charm. You hunt, you discover—and hey, maybe you accidentally find your true book love in the most unexpected of places!"

"Oh," Evie said, unable to conceal the dismay that was dawning in her eyes.

I could practically read her thoughts: she'd likely been hoping this would be a *quick* task so we could enjoy whatever touristy delights The Ripped Bodice had to offer, then move on to eating delicious dumplings and exploring other fun LA sites.

"There are four of us," I said quickly. "We'll simply split up the room and go through every volume. And we can, you know, talk while we're doing that. Have fun girl bonding time!"

"Ew," Kat snorted. "Why do you suddenly sound like a wine mom t-shirt from the more depraved sections of the Target sale aisle?"

"Sorry, I may be feeling a bit 'rosé all day,'" I said with a laugh. "All I really meant to say is that even the most tedious tasks of the superheroing life have the potential to be fun. First of all, you're superheroing. Second, when you have a team, you're always guaranteed fabulous company!" I flashed them a winning smile, lingering particularly long on Evie. She finally broke into a resigned sort of laugh.

"You're right," she said. "I'm sure this will be big fun. Why don't we get started? Only a room full of thousands of books stands in the way of our cheeseburger potstickers!"

And so we got to work, pawing meticulously through shelf upon shelf of dusty paperbacks. And it did start out fun, Pippa enthusiastically describing the plots of various classic romances in great detail whenever she came across them. As someone who was about to have a baby, Evie was fascinated by the whole secret baby trope, as well as how various fictional paranormal creatures handled their unusual pregnancies. Kat, meanwhile, found quite a few especially dramatic passages she wanted to use as future audition monologues. I was happy to see some of her exhaustion fading as she paged through different novels, a delighted smile stretching across her face as she took in every word.

For a while, the energy in the room *was* nothing but fun— light and bubbly, everybody throwing themselves into the galvanizing mission of a shared task. But as the hours stretched on, as we found absolutely nothing resembling *Zacasta's Revenge*, the tedium of said task took over. We fell into dreary silence, shuffling from one shelf to another. My eyes started to cross as I stared at the umpteen-millionth book spine, then methodically moved on to the next. And the dark circles under Kat's eyes returned—she looked like she was on the verge of falling asleep.

"Ugh, this was obviously a terrible idea," Pippa moaned, shoving aside a pile of books that was littering the middle of the floor. "Forget 'needle in a haystack,' this is more like 'needle in a haystack that is *also made of needles*.'"

"Very evocative, Pippa," I said, trying to sound encouraging. But my words came out dull and flat, like I was trying to convince myself of something.

"I'm sorry," Pippa blurted out, flopping back on the floor. Her limbs sprawled outward, nearly toppling several piles of books. She looked like she was trying to make a very irritated snow angel. "I thought I was being all cool, making this suggestion. I thought it would actually help our mission, give us some insight into what happened with Clint the other night. But all I've done is waste everyone's afternoon on what was clearly a wild goose chase." Her entire body deflated, and now she was just lying on the floor, looking like she never wanted to move again.

I studied her, idly rubbing my thumb against the book I was holding, smearing dust around. Maybe we should give up for the day. Pack it in, have some cheeseburger potstickers, and shuttle Evie back to the hotel for a much-needed afternoon nap.

"Not every mission we embark on is successful," I began

tentatively. "That's part of being a superheroine—or an assistant to a superheroine. You have to follow all relevant leads, because you never know which ones are going to end up providing you with useful information. That doesn't mean it's a waste of time, but . . ."

I stopped talking, still studying Pippa's motionless form. She seemed determined to remain flopped on the floor for as long as humanly possible.

I did not think my fumbling speech was giving her the encouragement or inspiration she needed. Perhaps I'd better quit while I was ahead and proceed with the whole giving-up thing. I'd peel Pippa off the floor myself if I had to, and she could indulge in all the minibar sodas she wanted back at the hotel.

I forced myself to stop fiddling with the book in my hand and slid it back onto the shelf. Kat sidled up to me, her eyes also on Pippa's deflated body.

"Girl, you gotta pep talk her," Kat whispered to me. "She looks up to you. *Admires* you. But she can't rally if her hero is *also* defeated. Bring on the intensity, Aveda Jupiter. She needs it."

I stared at the book I'd just put back on the shelf. The problem was, I *did* feel defeated. After my big morning plan to run headfirst toward all my problems and conquer them handily, I was batting a big fat zero.

I focused on the book's spine, as if that might give me some sort of clue. It was a paranormal romance that looked right up Pippa's alley—*The Weretiger Queen*. I pulled it off the shelf again and studied the cover, which featured a fierce-looking woman who was in the midst of transforming into an actual tiger, her flowy white dress disintegrating off her body as her hands turned into claws. Her mouth was open in a silent scream, fangs stabbing through her gums. I started to put it back on the shelf, frantically searching my brain for words that were more pep talk–adjacent . . . when the book right next to *The Weretiger Queen* caught my eye. This one was called *My Duke the Lion*, and looked like a historical romance with a hint of the supernatural. Intrigued, I plucked it from the shelf and examined the back copy. The story followed a young woman in Regency-era London who discovers that her paramour transforms into a lion when night falls. (So the title was apparently quite straightforward in its description.) The book had been published several decades before *The Weretiger Queen*, and the author, publisher, and cover style were completely different. But thematically, they certainly had a lot in common.

"Pippa," I said slowly. "Are you sure there's no organizational system at work here?" I scanned the rest of the shelf and saw that it was mostly stocked with books based around characters who transform into different animals.

"There's not," Pippa said glumly. "I asked several times at the front. And okay, then I got caught up in fangirling over Nalini Singh with the nice lady behind the counter, but . . . no. It's all random." She let out the mightiest sigh I'd ever heard. Not even the sullen teen version of Bea would have been able to match it.

"Then maybe we should cut our losses," Evie said, her eyes scanning the endless piles of books we hadn't even gotten to yet. She'd settled herself in the attic's cozy armchair, and she was looking worn and bored. It would definitely be time for a pregnancy-induced nap soon.

But not yet.

"No," I said, making my voice as determined as I could. "Because I think there's a *secret* shelving system at work here! Perhaps that's something the store's proprietors wish for you to discover on your own."

"What do you mean?" Pippa asked, turning her head so she could meet my eyes. It was the most movement I'd seen out of her in the past five minutes, so I decided to run with it.

"This shelf," I said, gesturing to the books I'd just been perusing. "It's not arranged by author or title or color or series or anything that would make sense, really. It's organized by *theme*. All of these books are about shapeshifting human-animal hybrid people. Other than that, they have absolutely nothing in common. Maybe every shelf and/or stack is like that?"

Very slowly, Pippa lifted her head off the floor. "You think?" She still sounded defeated, but there was an intrigued spark flitting through her eyes.

"I can't say for certain, but if anyone can figure it out, it's you, Pippa," I declared, pinning her with my best Aveda Jupiter Stare. "You know everything about these books—the genres and subgenres, the nuances, the history, all of that! What theme do you think our dear *Zacasta's Revenge* would be part of?"

"Well," Pippa said, resting her head back on the floor so she could gaze up at the ceiling, "of course we could go with the idea of *revenge*. There are a lot of great books, both classic and new, that would certainly fit the mold. But I feel like that might be too obvious."

"More obvious than something called *My Duke the Lion*?" Kat murmured, glancing at the shelf.

"It's such a rare book," Pippa continued, her eyes going a bit unfocused. "Whoever shelved it wouldn't want to make it obvious. Discovering it would be like such a holy grail to so many people . . ." She seemed to be talking mostly to herself now, working it out. She sat up, still looking deep in thought. "What else could be a theme for that book? Zacasta is the most powerful vampire in the world, but then this other lady she *hates* gets turned into a vampire too and starts to slowly steal Zacasta's chosen one shrine. Our girl Zacasta has to step it up and go fang to fang with this bitch, or risk losing her entire vampire empire!"

"So . . . what, rivals?" Evie said, fidgeting around in the armchair. "Or is there, like, a *Single White Female* theme we can run with?"

"What's that?" Pippa asked.

"Aw, you're so young," Kat cooed. "It's an old-ass movie about a white woman trying to take over another white woman's life."

"Oh, sorta like that, then!" Pippa said, nodding.

"Are there other books with that theme?" I prompted. "Uh, life stealing?"

"Hmm." Pippa scrambled to her feet and bustled over to one of the shelves in the dustiest corner of the attic. "Let's see . . ." she muttered, running her fingertips along the procession of spines.

"I feel like I'm watching a master code breaker at work," Kat whispered. "Or a great detective. Or, like, an expert bomb defuser!"

"All of those things," I agreed.

"The theme we're looking for isn't revenge," Pippa said, her voice becoming more confident as she scanned the titles on the very bottom shelf. "And it's not 'life stealing' or whatever that old movie is about. It's about the idea of sharing power." She nodded to herself and began pulling books from the shelf. "This one's about sisters, both destined to be queen, but they don't want to share the throne. And this one's a contemporary enemies-to-lovers story about two people fighting for the same promotion—and then getting together in the end."

"Who actually gets the promotion?" I couldn't resist asking.

"Neither of them. They decide to leave and start their own company." Pippa set the books to the side, then started rifling through the rest of the shelf. "Hmm . . . no, no . . . no . . ." She shook her head in frustration, her rifling growing more intense.

We all just watched her—the master code breaker at work. I realized at some point I was holding my breath. It seemed like she was on the verge of a major discovery, but she was also getting perilously close to the end of the shelf . . .

"Nooooo," Pippa breathed out, reaching the last book. "Maybe I was wrong about . . ." She trailed off as she spotted something stuck behind the rest of the books. She dug around on the shelf, rearranging books so she could see better . . . then, very slowly, she pulled something free.

It was another tome, crammed so far back in the shelf it wouldn't be visible unless you looked extra closely.

"I can't believe it," she whispered. She raised her head and met my gaze, her eyes sparkling. "AJ. Look! It's *Zacasta's Revenge!*" She jumped to her feet and waved the book in triumph, doing a little dance around all the romance novels littering the floor. "We found it!" she shrieked.

"*You* found it," I corrected, giving her a warm smile. "Incredible investigating, Pippa! And only you could have put all those pieces together. We would have been completely clueless without you."

"Thanks, AJ," Pippa said, her expression turning shy. "Shall we go get cheeseburger potstickers?"

"Yes, please," Evie said, rising from her seat. "Oof." Her knees wobbled and she grabbed the armchair for support.

"I think it's naptime," I said, rushing to her side to help her stand.

"No," she insisted, shaking her head vehemently. "I've been looking forward to these potstickers—and doing something *not* work-related—all freaking day!"

"Mmm," I said, my brain already working out how I was going to convince her to take the nap she clearly needed. "Let's purchase this tome for whatever exorbitant amount it may cost, and then we'll head across the street for lunch."

As we filed out of the cozy attic, Kat grabbed my arm. "That was so cool," she said, smiling at me.

"It was," I agreed. "Pippa's knowledge of this genre and her deductive reasoning skills saved the day."

"I meant *you*, bitch," Kat said, laughing. "She couldn't have gotten there without your encouragement. She was ready to give up, and you knew just what to say to bring her back."

"Oh." I shrugged, unsure how to respond. "Well. She would've gotten there herself eventually."

"I don't know, I think she'd still be lying on the floor," Kat said, her grin widening. "That was absolutely superheroic mentoring, Aveda Jupiter."

I smiled back, my spine straightening as purpose flowed through my veins once more. I'd succeeded in getting Pippa's mind off Shelby for a bit, just as I'd hoped. And perhaps I'd shown her that I could be her BFF as well.

No, I couldn't completely check "help Pippa with her friend dilemma" off my list just yet. But at least it was a start.

CHAPTER EIGHTEEN

THE CHEESEBURGER POTSTICKERS were to die for.

As she flipped through her new copy of *Zacasta's Revenge*, Pippa explained to me that they were the creation of Chef Shirley Chung, the owner of Ms Chi Cafe, and that she'd even won some sort of reality TV challenge with the recipe. One juicy, delectable bite confirmed that she'd certainly deserved to.

The restaurant was bright and airy, big windows inviting the light in to illuminate the cheery red-and-white-striped front counter, the long wooden tables accented by vibrant turquoise chairs, and the whimsical wall art—close-up photos of cherry blossoms overlaid with light-up neon sculptures twisted into the shape of fluffy clouds. It was cool and offbeat, the breezy energy so very LA.

Evie had been falling asleep on her feet, and even though she'd protested mightily, I'd managed to convince her that she really did need that nap. So we'd ordered her a veritable truckload of potstickers and Pippa had called an Uber to take her back to the hotel. Kat had also started feeling poorly, her insomnia catching up to her, so she'd grabbed her food to go as well. The dark circles seemed to reappear under her eyes in an instant as she gathered her takeout bag and waved us a weary goodbye. I made a mental note to check in on her later.

"Spotting any clues yet?" I said to Pippa around my mouthful of cheeseburger potsticker. "Also, how are you already halfway through the book?"

"I'm a speed-reader," Pippa responded, her eyes never leaving the page. "That's how I'm able to consume double-digit romance novels every week on top of all the crap I have to read for school."

"Impressive," I said, cocking an eyebrow at her. "I guess Shelby isn't the only Morgan College student with super-powers."

Her expression faltered and I immediately knew that I'd said the wrong thing. I shouldn't have mentioned Shelby at all. *Dammit.* I couldn't let her lose the high of her triumph—she'd barely gotten to bask in it.

"So how is the book?" I said, attempting to redirect her thoughts. "Has Zacasta gotten her revenge yet?"

"Not gonna lie—it's absolutely dreadful." Pippa winced and set the book down. "Zacasta is a simpering ingénue of a white lady who is also somehow the most powerful vampire in the world, ruling her empire of dutiful vamps. Every single person in the book wants to sleep with her, even though she's about as exciting as dry toast with mayo spread on top."

"Doesn't the mayo make it . . . not dry?"

"Yeah, true, I fucked up that metaphor," Pippa said with a laugh. She toyed with the remnants of one of her cheese-burger potstickers. "Anyway, Miss Mayo loves being a vam-pire because she'll stay youthful and fabulous forever, and nothing about her amazing, romance-filled life will ever change."

"To be fair, her life does sound kind of awesome," I said.

"I guess. So she hears tell of some other lady vamp who's started building her own empire on the other side of the world. She sets out to 'make friends' with this lady vamp. Other Lady Vamp, by the way, is also white and living in some generic 'Asian' country that is actually the grossest mashup of, well . . . multiple Asian countries? Everyone wears kimonos and, like, kabuki-style makeup while also bloviating about 'zen' and using their magic chopsticks—"

"Magic *chopsticks*?!" I spat out.

"Yup." Pippa nodded vigorously, warming to the topic. "Tons of nebulous 'mysticism' at work, too."

"So was Clint's inspiration the massively offensive Orientalist tropes at play in this book?" I groaned. "Because I can see that."

"Yeah, kinda surprised he didn't have Evie and Aveda using magic chopsticks from the jump," Pippa said. "Anyway, this other lady actually loves Zacasta's ass, looks up to her, thinks she's the coolest thing ever. But Zacasta can't stand that there's another lady vamp who might be as special and powerful and ever youthful as she is. Plus, other lady vamp has all this Asian set dressing, which makes her like a thousand times 'cooler.' So at first, Zacasta develops this plan to use magic to literally pull this lady's vampire powers out of her."

"Is that a thing you can do?" I asked. "Is that, like, a regular part of the vampire mythos?"

"Sometimes?" Pippa said, shrugging. "I think the author of this book just kinda made shit up as she went along, to be honest."

"Does Zacasta succeed?"

"Yes and no." Pippa leaned forward, her eyes widening. "She ends up being driven so mad with power that she decides she's not just going to pull the vampy powers out of this one lady. She's going to pull them out of literally every vampire in existence! Then she will *truly* be the only one."

"But aren't the other vampires her minions?" I exclaimed. "Doesn't she need them to assure her of her own fabulousness?"

"She's so delusional, she thinks they'll keep being her minions anyway," Pippa said, rolling her eyes. "And she does succeed in pulling the powers out of all of them—but they revert to their human forms, so some of them just drop dead on the spot from old age. Whoever's left is so broken, so betrayed . . ." Pippa shook her head solemnly. "That's it for poor Zacasta. Yeah, she gets to stay hot and live forever, but she's totally alone and miserable. Not really how one generally wants to spend eternity."

"Huh." I took the book from her and flipped through the pages. "I realize not all vampire books are romance books, but isn't this one billed as such? I thought books of this sort always had a happy ending."

"They *do*," Pippa declared, slamming her palm against the table. "The ending is a total betrayal of the genre! Although given that Zacasta sucks so hard, I guess it's kind of a happy ending for the reader. Who is me." She grinned and popped her last potsticker in her mouth. I was happy to see her spark filtering back in, my Shelby comment forgotten.

"Hmm." I leaned back in my seat, my gaze running over the pink and white petals of the cherry-blossom art. "Maybe *that* was Clint's inspiration—the idea of upending an entire genre with your 'auteur' vision simply because you think certain kinds of stories and characters are beneath you."

"This book does scream 'I'm trying to do serious art, but am actually quite bad at it and do not understand my audience at all,'" Pippa said, her mouth full of potsticker.

I ran my fingertips over the cover. There were no actual vampires depicted on it; it simply announced the book's title in sweeping, lurid cursive rendered in metallic gold. While the book sounded godawful—and like something that definitely would have inspired Clint in all the wrong ways—Pippa's description of the plot had also sparked a memory that was now winding its way through my brain.

It was the moment right before Evie's wedding, when she was possessed by a demon, trying to destroy both her own nuptials and all of San Francisco. I'd been desperate, overwhelmed, and out of options—and in a wild flash of inspiration, I'd tried something I'd never done before.

I'd used my telekinesis to reach inside her body and *pull* the demon out.

I'd never been able to replicate that feat—in part because there was no way to safely test it. But I'd always wondered, when push came to shove, if it was something I'd be able to do again.

Was there a way to "pull" vampirism out of people?

If we were dealing with vampires, that is. If we figured out how the vampirism was working. If this was Otherworld magic all over again. If, if, if.

I always hated "if."

"Oh . . ."

My head snapped up and I saw Pippa gazing at her phone, her platinum hair swoop drooping a bit.

"What is it?" I asked, my brain immediately going to Evie, all alone back at the hotel. My shoulders tensed, preparing for emergency.

"Nothing," she mumbled, slumping back in her seat. "I, um. I thought Shelby was finally texting me back, but she just, like, butt-texted me. It's literally a string of random letters, and then . . ." She held up the phone so I could see the screen. Shelby had a sent a hasty follow-up text that simply read: *Oops!! Sorry!*

And that was it.

"The first time I hear from her in days . . ." Pippa sighed and set the phone down, her mouth twisting into a mopey frown.

My heart clenched—her disappointment was so palpable I could practically feel it myself. Perhaps I'd been foolish to think that I could distract her from the Shelby of it all. I couldn't replace her best friend any more than Pippa could replace Evie if our positions had been reversed.

"Hey, Pippa," I said softly. "You want dessert? Evie was excited about the mochi donuts . . ." I frantically waved the waitress over, racking my brain for ways to make Pippa feel better.

"Sure, AJ, that sounds great," Pippa said, idly tracing the wood grain of the tabletop with her fingertip.

She kept circling the same bit of wood grain as I ordered one of each kind of mochi donut—black sesame, matcha, and strawberry.

We sat in silence as the waitress returned with our treats, Pippa staring resolutely at the table. She seemed to have lost interest entirely in Zacasta and her various offensive adventures.

I cast a sidelong look her way as I bit into the black sesame donut. It was delicious, light and chewy with rich sesame flavor in every bite and a gentle sweetness that complemented rather than overwhelmed.

How could I help Pippa? I kept coming back to that question, but everything I tried seemed to be a total bust.

"AJ?" Pippa's quavery voice snapped me out of my intense spiral of thoughts. "Have you ever had . . . I mean, has a friend ever, like, dumped you? Or were you ever worried they were going to? Nah, what am I saying—you and Evie are ride or die. Silly question." She gave me a shaky smile.

"Ha!" I exclaimed. "Funny you should say that, Pippa. Because there was a period of time where I was absolutely convinced Evie was going to dump me. Our relationship had developed into something unhealthy and toxic. She was always avoiding conflict, I was always willfully creating it. She was a doormat, I was a bulldozer. And right before she got married . . ." I took another bite of my donut, calling up the memories. "I was jealous of her because she'd been revealed as this new, shiny superheroine and I felt like yesterday's news. But there was more to it than that." I cocked my head to the side and regarded Pippa thoughtfully. "We had neglected our friendship. We let it coast along, we allowed ourselves to sink into these set roles, and it eventually became very unhealthy."

"How did you come back from that?" Pippa asked, toying with her matcha donut.

"I think there was a point where we both had to make a choice—work on this, or leave the other person behind forever. The second one was never an option. We love each other too much—and we *are* ride or die." I smiled at her. "I think you and Shelby are, too—Evie and I could see that the minute we met the pair of you. And I don't think whatever's going on here . . ." I nodded at her phone. ". . . is actually as serious as what transpired with Evie and me. Shelby is experiencing a lot of new things as a ghost girl made real, and one of those things is falling in love for the first time. It might be hard, but you two will work it out. Of that, I am very sure."

Pippa's smile widened the tiniest bit, and she swiped a tear from her eye. "Wow, I . . . thanks, AJ. That's something I needed to hear." Her gaze skittered to the last bit of black sesame donut on my plate. "Are you gonna eat that?"

"Have at it," I said, pushing the plate over to her.

"All this change has really freaked me out," Pippa said slowly. "I know I'm the one in our friend group who's, like, the life of the party. Like, the fun one, the adventurous one, the one who's up for literally anything. But I actually like stability. I need some of that in my life." She gave me a small smile.

"I very much get that," I said, recognition pinging through me.

"I like this supernatural investigating stuff," Pippa said, tapping the cover of *Zacasta's Revenge*. "It's so cool when your brain just, like, assembles a bunch of disparate shit in an instant and the picture becomes clear."

"You're a natural." I gave her an encouraging smile. "What you did back there was incredible. If you'd like to make your position more permanent when we return to the Bay, I'm sure we can make that happen. Shelby has been assisting us in many of our administrative duties, but perhaps you could help out on the investigatory side?"

"I'd looooove that," she shrieked, her eyes widening. "Oh my god, AJ, I will do you so proud!"

"I know you will, Pippa," I said, grinning at her as she crammed the rest of the donut into her mouth. "I know you will."

CHAPTER NINETEEN

EVIE WAS STILL napping when we returned to the hotel suite, and I could tell Pippa was itching to get into the massive stack of books she'd purchased from The Ripped Bodice, so I decided to retire to my own room for further research. Since Pippa had managed to finish *Zacasta's Revenge* at lunch, she passed it on to me. I dove in immediately, eager to scour its pages for further clues.

Twenty pages in, I was ready to throw the book across the room.

It was as atrocious as Pippa had stated, faux empowerment wrapped up in an insufferable lead whose central trait seemed to be delusions of grandeur. Frustrated, I skipped to the end, and to the scene wherein Zacasta finally figures out how to take everyone else's vampire powers away. Even though this sequence was written in such a way that we're supposed to sympathize with Zacasta, her odd self-centeredness made it extremely difficult. It mostly played out as if she simply couldn't stand for anyone else to be happy or powerful. She had to be the only one, the chosen one, the prettiest princess at the ball. And she didn't care who she had to hurt to get there.

I set the book to the side. I wondered if anything else from this literary abomination had been part of Clint's vision.

I leaned back against my pillows and closed my eyes, trying to think. What could I take from this that was actually useful? I just kept staring at the words on the page until my eyes crossed and the letters swam together.

I also kept coming back to that climactic part where Zacasta used her power to literally pull vampirism out of her minions. Even though it was horribly written, I couldn't seem to stop reading that particular scene over . . . and over . . . and over . . .

The next thing I knew, my eyes were fluttering open to a darkened room, and a shadowy figure was rustling around near the window.

"Who's there!" I growled, shooting straight up in bed. "Don't even *think* about trying to steal anything or launching an attack, Aveda Jupiter may have been sleeping just now, but she—"

"It's me, Annie."

I blinked a few times, my eyes adjusting to the shadows. I'd managed to unwittingly fall asleep again right in the middle of the day. I really had to stop doing that.

The figure finally came into focus, limbs and features resolving into a familiar shape. It was Scott, and all the rustling around was due to him shoving clothes into a suitcase splayed out by the window. Dusk was falling outside, casting shadows over the walls.

"What are you doing?" I croaked, scraping a hand over my bleary eyes. "And what time is it? God, have I really wasted *hours* again—"

"I'm going home," he said, cutting me off.

I studied his back as he stuffed more clothes into the suitcase. His posture was rigid, his shoulders stiff—in direct contrast to his usual easygoing stance.

"Why?" I asked. "Did something go wrong with the clinic—"

"Fuck the clinic."

He whirled around to face me—and even in the shadowy dark, I could see the tension around his eyes, the tight set of his mouth. His voice was low and cold and his expression was absolutely furious.

"I got Bea's report," he said.

"Oh . . . no." I slumped back against my pillow, and tried to shove down the panic rising in my chest. In all the commotion of the day, I'd completely forgotten about Bea's Mercedes Totally Fucking Sucks screed. In addition to falling dead asleep at the most inconvenient of moments, I also couldn't seem to stop *forgetting* things. Despite my best efforts, my checklist mojo had definitely *not* returned. Quite the opposite.

"I'm sorry," I said, scrubbing a hand over my face. "You know how Bea is—our little chaos monster. She meant well, but as usual, she acted rashly and . . . well, please don't let that throw you off the amazing thing you have going at the Center—"

"Is it true?"

I cocked my head at him, confused. "What?"

He crossed the room and sat down on the bed, his shoulders slumping even more. It appeared as if all the fight was slowly leaching out of him, like air sadly leaking from a balloon.

"Is it true?" he repeated, his voice barely a whisper. "That Mercedes said all those fucking terrible things to you? That she was never your friend, that she . . ." He trailed off, and shifted to face me. The tension had left his expression, but something much worse had taken its place. Now he looked *hurt*.

"It was a long time ago—" I began.

"I don't *care*!" He shook his head vehemently, anger filtering back into his eyes. "Why didn't you tell me?"

I tugged at the pillow-squished end of my power ponytail, desperately trying to put my thoughts in order.

"This is such an incredible opportunity for you, and you were having such a good time, and I . . . I just didn't want to disrupt that or get in the way or . . . or . . ."

"Annie." He raked a hand through his already mussed hair, mussing it even further. Frustration radiated from his every pore. "Do you really think so little of me? That my first thought would be about you *disrupting* something? That I'd be upset at *you* for sharing that someone else disrespected you like that and acted like a complete piece of shit?!"

"N-no," I said hastily. "Of course not, I just . . . Scott, I want you to have all your dreams. You deserve to have the absolute best life in the world, you're just the most . . . the most *good* person I've ever known. You never put yourself first, ever—and that's so wonderful, so fucking kind, but I don't want you to miss out on your dreams because you keep putting them to the side—"

"I'm not a *child*, Annie," he snapped. "I can figure out my own dreams."

"But you'll never actually prioritize them!" I exploded. "You'll always let yourself get sucked into Team Tanaka/ Jupiter's drama, and you'll always shove whatever *you* want to the side because you want to help *me*." I leaned forward, trying to meet his gaze, trying to get him to see how important this was. "The way you talk about this job, this possibility of expanding your teaching—I can tell you really want it. And I don't want to be the thing getting in your way."

"Getting in my . . ." He shook his head again and jumped to his feet. Then he started pacing the room, staring hard at the floor. I idly wondered if he also noted how the sheer plushness of the carpet made stomping such a difficult endeavor. Maybe he didn't even notice since he wasn't usually the hardcore stomper that I was.

I just let him stomp because I could not think of a single thing to say.

After a few moments of unbridled stomping, he stopped abruptly in his tracks and turned to face me again.

"Am I not enough for you?" he said.

"Wh-what . . . ?"

"Is that why you keep pushing me to take this LA gig? Before we've even had a chance to talk about how it would work?" He blew out a long breath, his eyes going to the ceiling.

"Scott." I leaned forward and held out a hand, trying to get him to come back to me. "What are you talking about?"

"Every time I bring it up, you just say I should take it," he said, ignoring my hand. "That I should take something that would definitely upend our lives, and that . . . would apparently be completely okay with you?" He took a few steps toward me, and now I could see his face more clearly. His eyes were full of confusion and anguish and hurt, and my heart felt like it was crumpling in on itself. "You're still not over Bea moving out. You still talk about Lucy moving back home, even though that's never happening. And I can tell you're freaking out about Evie's maternity leave and whatever's going to happen after that. I *know* you," he said, as I opened my mouth to protest. "I can tell that's bothering you, Annie. But a potentially huge life change that would take me hundreds of miles away from you . . . that's just fine? You don't care?"

"Of course I care!" I insisted. How had he gotten this so wrong? And what could I possibly say to make it right? "I love you more than anything—"

"Then why do you keep trying to push me away?" His voice cracked, and he resumed his pacing. "You won't let me help with anything related to Team Tanaka/Jupiter, you came up with this whole LA Center idea when all I wanted to do was spend time with you, and you're straight up not talking to me about things I know are important to you—"

"That's not true!" I protested—but my voice sounded thin and wavery, even to me.

He came to a stop in front of the window and leaned against the frame, his figure silhouetted against the glittering maze of taillights LA transformed into during rush hour. His broad shoulders drooped again as he crossed his arms over his chest, keeping his back to me. Even though we were in the same room, only a few feet apart, I had never felt farther away from him.

"I keep thinking about what you said to me during the fight we had all those years ago," he murmured, his voice so low I had to strain to hear it. "Right after I kissed you for the very first time."

"Oh no," I murmured. "Please don't—"

"You said," he continued firmly, "that Aveda Jupiter couldn't be seen with some low-rent surfer mage."

He whirled to face me and I swallowed hard, tears pricking the corners of my eyes.

"Do you still feel that way?" he demanded.

"I *never* felt that way!" I insisted, pushing myself out of bed and to my feet. "I lashed out because I was terrified of how much I felt for you. And I was even more terrified that you only kissed me because you couldn't have Evie. You know that. I *told* you that—"

"And yet, I can't help but think there was some sliver of truth in there," he said, his mouth pressed into a thin line. "Because you seem to want me to achieve some weird, invisible marker that will prove that I want things the same way you do. If you think I'm not claiming my dreams right now, well . . . I don't think you understand what my dreams actually are. I don't think you understand dreams that aren't exactly like yours."

"So tell me!" I spat out, my voice twisting into a desperate yelp. My heart felt like it was cracking wide open, radiating every bit of hurt I'd felt when Mercedes smugly informed me of all the precious, intimate things he'd shared with her. "*Please.* Because lately it seems like you're going out of your way to confide in everyone *but* me. You talk about me pushing *you* away, but you haven't told me any of this. And yet, you're always talking to Mercedes—"

"And how stupid do you think I feel about that now?" he shot back, taking a step toward me. "I thought, being your old friend, maybe she could help me understand the things you've been going through—"

"I'm not going through anything!" I exploded, throwing my hands up in frustration. "I'm just . . . *busy* . . ."

"You're running yourself into the ground," he said flatly. "You're trying to do *everything*, you're clearly exhausted, and you brush off anyone who suggests you might need rest or help." He frowned, his frustration morphing into concern. In a way, that was even worse—now he was scrutinizing me with that worry I could never bear, that worry that told me his life was being consumed by mine.

He took a few more steps toward me, closing the distance between us. Those brilliant blue eyes met mine—he was looking at me in that way that made me feel like he could see through my skin. But this time, it wasn't comforting. This time, I didn't want him to see me or *know* me as well as he did. The very thought made tears spring to my eyes.

"You go so hard, always," he said, his voice softening. "And I love that about you. You've achieved so many of your dreams already. But what you can't see right now is that your own dreams are killing you."

"Scott," I whispered, the tears in my eyes finally spilling over. "I . . . "

"You didn't trust me enough to tell me about Mercedes," he continued, his voice still heartbreakingly soft. "I don't know if it's because you think I'm so weak-willed that I wouldn't be able to handle it, or so unambitious that I'd quit the Center on the spot . . . or if I'm just so unimportant in your life, you didn't think it was necessary. Like I said, maybe I'll never be enough for you. And I don't know how to forgive myself for getting close to someone who was so hateful to the person I love the most."

I bit back a sob, tears flowing freely down my cheeks.

"I'm going home tomorrow," he said. "I don't want to continue at the Center. And I think . . . I need some space."

With that, he turned and started walking toward the door.

"Wait . . . Scott . . ." I managed. His name came out as a sob. "Don't throw this amazing opportunity away because of me. Please—"

"It's not because of you," he barked. He stopped at the door, his hand resting on the knob. But he wouldn't turn and look at me. "This is *my* choice, Annie. Please respect it."

And with that, he was gone.

I collapsed on the bed, at last allowing my sobs to escape into the empty air. I cried until my pillow was soaked and the maze of taillights gave way to late-night darkness. And when I didn't have any tears left, I finally fell asleep.

Chapter Twenty

I SLEPT FITFULLY, plagued by vivid dreams where I was chasing entire mobs of faceless vampires—only for them to turn into hazy flocks of bats as soon as I caught up to them. Occasionally, this was punctuated by interludes similar to my dreams from the night before: sexy mouth-to-mouth sessions on the beach that morphed into Scott and Mercedes making out on the beach . . .

When I finally started awake, I was drenched in sweat and clutching a pillow to my chest like a life preserver. My eyes felt puffy and dried-out from crying, and I was fairly certain I was severely dehydrated after releasing so much moisture via my tear ducts. I groaned and rolled over in bed, smashing the pillow over my head to block out the light streaming in from the window.

How had I managed to so thoroughly fuck everything up when I'd been trying to do the exact opposite?

I couldn't get Scott's hurt face out of my head. He'd looked so *defeated*.

And I couldn't help but remember the only other time I'd seen him look that way.

It was on our wedding day, after we'd recovered from my runaway bride fiasco. The beautiful ceremony had proceeded without drama, the sun cascading down on us as the waves in the distance created a gentle soundtrack. When we'd said our vows, Scott had given me the sweetest secret smile and thrown in a little wink, reminding me of the more intimate vows we'd said only moments before.

Afterwards we'd posed for pictures and then I'd headed back to the bridal suite with Evie and Shruti to don my first reception gown—a silky red qipao embroidered with an intricate blaze of gold patterns. Evie and Shruti had begged me to tell them what Scott had said to get me to return to the wedding instead of hightailing it outta there, but I kept deflecting. That moment felt so private, more intimate than the first time we'd kissed, the first time we'd seen each other naked. It was a moment just for us—I instinctively knew that, and I wanted to keep it secreted away in the most hidden part of my heart.

So they'd settled for teasing me, and we'd laughed and had more champagne as they helped me change and get my hair in order. I felt giddy, carefree, drunk on more than just mere alcohol. I couldn't believe I'd married the love of my life, and that I'd fallen even more in love with him over the past few hours.

It was yet another thing too magical to actually feel real.

I was so wrapped up in my giddy, giggly bubble with two of my best friends, I barely registered the door to the bridal suite creaking open.

"Aveda . . ."

All three of us turned to see Nate poking his head in, his dark eyes lit with concern.

"She's almost ready, baby," Evie said, fussing with an ornate gold hair ornament she was trying to pin in my hair. "You can tell Scott we'll be out in—"

"There's a problem," Nate said abruptly.

"What is it?" I said, my superheroine instincts kicking into gear. "Because if demons are trying to disrupt my wedding day, I have some very strong feelings I am more than happy to share with them, and those feelings will probably take the form of my *fists*—"

"Not demons," Nate said hastily. "Sorry, I probably should have said that up front. No, it's, ah . . . Scott's father? He showed up and tried to force his way into the reception."

"Excuse me, *what*?!" I batted Evie's hands away and

adjusted the hair ornament myself as I took a step toward Nate. "That man hasn't seen or spoken to his son since Scott was a child. He skipped out on Scott's mother, on child support, on fucking *everything*. How did he even know we were getting married? How did he . . ."

I shook my head, all-consuming rage descending like a haze over my vision.

"Maisy and a lot of the other local outlets have written and posted about your engagement and all the wedding planning," Shruti said, her usual exuberant expression twisting into a frown. "Maybe Scott's dad saw the photos of you two looking all happy together?"

"What does he want?" I asked Nate. "And has Scott seen him yet? Maybe I can get him out of here before—"

"Too late," Nate said, his expression turning stormy. "Unfortunately, Charlie—that's Scott's father—did not exactly make himself inconspicuous. He barged in, headed straight for the bar, and declared that he was ready to, ah, party. That he couldn't believe his only son was getting married to a big, famous superheroine, and he couldn't wait to meet her."

"Oh, he'll be meeting her," I snarled, gathering my skirt around me. That rage pulsed through me now, red-hot in its fury. Hurricane Annie was about to come out full force, and I would do nothing to stop her. "Where is he now? And where's Scott?"

"Scott's first concern was getting his mother away from Charlie immediately," Nate said. "I don't think she even realizes her ex-husband is present, despite the scene he was making. Charlie tried to approach to her, but Scott blocked him at every turn and managed to redirect his mother to the greater kitchen area, where *your* mother—"

"Is trying to tell the chefs how they're doing everything wrong?" I let out a deep sigh. "That's actually good—my mom and Scott's mom get along. And my mother is probably being extra enough to distract Lynne from the Charlie-ness of it all."

"I attempted to escort Charlie from the premises myself,"

Nate said, his stormy expression morphing into a full-on glower. "But Scott returned and intervened, and now they're . . . talking . . ."

"I'll handle this," I growled, starting for the door.

"Oh wait, Annie—your hair thingy!" Evie cried, reaching for me.

The gold ornament was trying to slide its way free from my locks yet again. I yanked it out of my hair and set it to the side.

Nate turned and wordlessly led me, Evie, and Shruti out to the reception area—a beautiful, flower-laden courtyard right next to the ceremony site. People were milling around, sipping drinks and chatting. I didn't see Scott's mother—or mine—but I finally spotted Scott at the very edge of the courtyard, facing off against a tall man in a rumpled gray suit.

I was struck by how much he looked like an older carbon copy of Scott. He had the same lean muscle, the same broad shoulders, the same tousled golden hair—though his was going gray at the temples, and crinkly lines surrounded his bright blue eyes. I'd never even seen a picture of Charlie; Scott preferred to treat him as if he simply didn't exist.

I marched over to them, vaguely aware that Nate, Evie, and Shruti were right behind me—a much less festive version of the bridal procession. A few guests spotted me and called out hellos and congratulations, but I was too focused on my target to respond.

"Please just go," I heard Scott saying to his father as we approached. His shoulders were tense, his fists balled at his sides. And he was trying to keep his voice low, so as not to cause a big scene. "I'll talk to you later if that's what you really want, but—"

"Awwww, come on, son!" Charlie brayed, his speech slurred. I noticed he was swaying on his feet, and that those blue eyes were cloudy and unfocused. I wondered how he'd been able to get wasted so fast. "Lemme meet the beautiful bride, it's the least you can do after spiriting your mother away from me so fast—"

"You don't need to talk to either of them," Scott hissed. "Do you even know how many nights Mom spent crying over you, how she'd apologize to me for you not being around and refusing to send any money? Like it was her fault—"

"Maybe it was," Charlie shot back. Something broke through his cloudy vision, something hard and mean. "She drove me away, insisting on having you in the first place. I knew she was gonna raise you into some kind of crybaby mama's boy—and I was right." His mouth twisted into a cruel sneer. "Just look at you. Soft. Sensitive. *Worthless.* I was always hoping my genes would assert themselves, make you into a real man—"

"*Leave.*"

The word tore itself from my throat, a full-blown roar that caused the festive cacophony around us to cease. I felt several hundred sets of eyes on me, silence descending across the beautiful courtyard as everyone turned to watch the scene that had ended up being unavoidable.

Scott and Charlie both swiveled to look at me. My new husband's face was pale and pinched, and the eyes that had gazed at me so adoringly only moments earlier now looked haunted. In contrast, a big, shit-eating grin stretched across his father's face.

"Ah, this must be the little missus!" Charlie bellowed, clapping Scott much harder than necessary on the back. "Well, son . . ." He looked me up and down, a leer crossing his face. "Looks like you did *something* right."

"Don't talk to her," Scott growled, shaking his dad's hand off. "I told you to leave."

"Actually, *she* told me," Charlie said, his shit-eating grin getting even wider. "You just let your wife call the shots like that?" He took another step toward me. "Where's your purse, little miss? I assume you need something to hold my son's balls."

"We both told you to leave," I said, refusing to let him rattle me, even as my rage thrummed against my breastbone, bright and sure. "And given that this event is pretty focused on the two of us, I think you should listen."

"All right, all right, I can tell when I'm not wanted," Charlie said, holding up his hands in a placating manner. His grin morphed into a full-on smirk. "But maybe you could give me a little incentive." He leaned in close, as if he and I were about to share a particularly juicy secret. "You're a big, famous superhero, huh? I've read all about you. And I'm thinking you might wanna share some of the wealth with your new father-in-law. Especially if you'd like to never see him again."

"Oh, I definitely never want to see you again," I shot back, my voice cold as ice. "But I'm certainly not paying for that privilege."

I took two more steps toward him, closing the distance between us. Then I planted my hands on my hips and looked him dead in the eye. That rage was pulsing through me at a more controlled speed now, powering me forward.

"If you've read about me, then you also know about my telekinesis. And if you don't leave now, I will use said telekinesis to transport you somewhere much less pleasant. Like the ocean over there." I jerked my chin toward the glorious view of the water. "And if that doesn't work . . ." I allowed my lips to curve into a chilly smile, then gestured toward Evie. "That one can light you on fire." I pointed at Shruti. "That one can entrap you in her freaking *hair*." I turned to Nate. "And that one . . . is, uh, really smart." I heard Nate cough in an attempt to hide a snicker. "And if none of that works, well! We have at least one other member of the family who can basically mind control you and make you feel however she wants you to feel."

I crossed my arms over my chest and leveled him with my best Aveda Jupiter Stare. "You're lucky *I* don't have that power. Because if I did, I'd make you feel how you actually should feel—like a worthless excuse for a human being." I took another step, completely invading Charlie's personal space, and felt a sharp stab of satisfaction when he stumbled backward. He was trying to maintain his smirk, but his expression faltered into uncertainty. "You abandoned the most incredible man I know—he's stronger than you'll ever be. And his *balls* are just fine." I looked down my nose at Charlie—quite a feat, since he was taller than me. I stared at him like he was the most inconsequential bug I'd ever seen and was pleased to see him shrink before me, practically cowering. "You are going to leave now," I commanded. "And if I ever hear so much as a whisper of you trying to worm your way back into Scott or his mother's life . . ." I narrowed my eyes and made my voice *roar* again. "I'll use my power to send you to the depths of the fucking earth. So don't. Test. *Me*."

Charlie stared at me as if hypnotized. Then he stumbled backward and spun on his heel, muttering to himself as he made a hasty exit. I couldn't hear everything he was saying, but I was pretty sure *psycho bitch* was peppered liberally throughout.

Hurricane Annie strikes again.

But this time? She was pretty proud of all that fucking destruction.

I took a deep breath and turned around . . . to find our entire wedding staring at me. But I only cared about one person. I finally spotted Scott standing off to the side, next to Evie. He seemed to have retreated while I was laying into his father. His expression was dazed, shell-shocked. Almost like he didn't know where he was.

I shifted my gaze to Evie, trying to send her a message through our BFF telepathy.

Luckily, she picked up on it immediately.

"Um . . ." Evie turned to face the gawking guests and raised her voice. "Sorry about that, y'all! You know we can't have any kind of Tanaka/Jupiter event without there being some kind of drama! But at least no one's possessed this time—wait." She whipped back around and raised an eyebrow at me. "No one's possessed, right?"

"No," I confirmed, giving her a slight smile.

"Awesome!" She shot me a thumbs-up and turned back to the crowd. "Everyone grab a festive beverage, dinner will start soon!"

As our guests went back to chattering amongst themselves, Evie looped an arm through Nate's and nodded at Shruti. "Let's also go get a festive drink," she said. "And give our newlyweds a moment alone."

I smiled gratefully at her as she led them away, then went to Scott and slipped my hand into his.

"Come on, Cameron," I murmured, guiding him to a spot hidden by a pair of tall flower arrangements. Once we were reasonably hidden from view, I faced him, my eyes anxiously searching his. "Are you all right?"

He stared back at me blankly—like he was still confused about how he'd gotten here. Like he barely knew who I was.

"Scott?" I reached up and brushed his hair off his forehead, worry blossoming in my chest. "Please talk to me. Tell me what you're feeling. Tell me how I can help—"

He cut me off by gathering me against him, holding me so tightly I forgot to breathe for a moment. "I . . . I'm scared," he managed, his voice hoarse and broken against my hair.

"Of what?" I whispered.

He released me and studied my face, his eyes brimming with terror. "I'm scared that someday I'll turn into . . . that." He gestured toward the empty space his father had occupied only moments ago.

"I . . . what?" I shook my head. "No. No way. You aren't like him at all—"

"I could be," he insisted. "Th-that's my father—"

"Your sperm donor," I insisted. "You are *all* your mother—"

"—and I know I could become like that," he pressed on, not hearing me. "I know because . . ." His voice cracked and he stepped back from me, covering his face with one hand.

I held myself very still, my heart aching for him. I didn't know how to help. I didn't know what to *do*.

He finally removed his hand from his face and met my eyes again. "I know because when he showed up, when he started making a scene, making everything awful . . ." His jaw clenched and he blinked back tears. "The first thing I thought was: I should leave. I should go now, before I turn into *this* and ruin your life, Annie. I should spare you all of that. I love you too much not to." He turned away from me. "I can't believe I thought that. That I thought about leaving you on our fucking *wedding day—*"

"But you didn't," I growled.

I closed the distance between us, took his hand and tugged, forcing him to turn and look at me.

"You're different from your father because you *didn't*," I insisted, reaching up to cup his face in my hands. I gazed at every single one of his features I loved so much, ending on those eyes that always saw me better than anyone. "And you wouldn't. I am very certain of that, Scott. The only reason it even entered your mind is because you were trying to put me first again. And because seeing that man for the first time in . . . well, ever . . ." I leaned in closer, trying to get him to see how sure I was of him. Of *us*. "That's going to fuck with your mind no matter what. He looks like you, he may have certain mannerisms that are yours—but that's where any similarity ends." We were pressed so close together now, I could feel his racing heartbeat through his shirt and suit jacket. And I wasn't going to let go of him until he heard me. "Evie and Bea have a shitty dad. Lucy has a shitty dad. And Nate . . . holy fuck, he has the worst mom in the entire universe. And yet, they're all wonderful."

"They are," he murmured.

"And so are you."

I pulled him into a deep kiss, the kind of kiss where I needed to *show* him how I felt—words just weren't enough. He stiffened, surprised . . . but then he softened against me, his hands going to my back to draw me even closer.

When we finally broke apart, breathless, color had come

back to his face and he was looking at me in that awed, adoring way that always made my heart melt.

"God, I love you," he said fervently, touching his forehead against mine. "Thank you for standing up for me like that."

"By threatening to throw your dad into the ocean, right after Evie possibly sets him on fire?"

He laughed a little and pulled back, his eyes dancing.

"I can't believe my dad made me miss you in this dress—I feel cheated out of a first reaction," he said, gazing at the red silk of my qipao. "You look . . ." He trailed off, his eyes misting over as he took me in.

I smiled at him, my heart lifting as I saw the Scott I loved so fiercely come back to me. "Well," I said, sliding my fingertips up his chest, "You could *show* me your reaction. We already messed up one wedding dress. Why not make it two?"

He laughed, a bit of huskiness creeping into his voice. "I love the way you think, Mrs. Cameron."

And then he did show me how he felt—so much so that we were late to our own reception.

I lay in my big hotel bed for a few moments more, curling myself around the pillow I couldn't seem to stop clutching. Somewhere in the midst of my stroll down memory lane, I'd started crying, tears streaming silently down my face.

Scott's wretched deadbeat dad had caused all that horrible hurt to etch itself across his son's face. And now, I'd done the same.

I was the cause of Scott's hurt. And I didn't know how to fix it.

My wallowing was interrupted by a sharp knock on the door. Before I could say anything, Evie was barging in, waving her phone around.

"Annie!" she sang out. "Man, I can't believe I slept all the way through afternoon *and* night *and* part of the morning again! But I thought today we could finally go see some cool sites, and . . ."

She trailed off, a crinkle appearing between her brows as she took in my teary, unkempt state. "Hey, what's wrong?"

I pulled the pillow tightly to my chest. "I . . . I had a fight with Scott . . . He read Bea's Mercedes report and . . ." I couldn't get any more words out. I burst into tears.

"Oh . . . Annie . . ."

I buried my face in my security blanket pillow and sobbed as Evie carefully maneuvered herself onto the bed next to me and pulled me close.

"It's okay," she murmured, rubbing my back. "All couples fight. And knowing Scott, he's probably mostly mad at himself for getting all buddy-buddy with Mercedes. Tell me what happened?"

I haltingly recounted the fight for her, my voice muffled by the pillow and punctuated by the occasional hiccup.

"Oh, Annie . . ." she repeated when I was done.

She pulled back, her hands on my shoulders, studying my face.

"Look, you should have told him about Mercedes—you should have trusted him with that," Evie said. "And yeah, you guys really need to talk about what this whole job offer thing means for both of you. But . . ." She regarded me thoughtfully. "You weren't totally wrong."

"Excuse me?!" I spat out, my voice twisting into a hysterical shriek. "I cannot fathom any scenario in which I was *right*. About anything."

"You were right about Scott," Evie pressed. "He does put everyone else first, and he does have a tendency to shove his own wants to the side. And if you'd tried to talk to him about it in a direct, honest sort of way, he probably would have nodded along and then just kept doing the same thing." She settled back against the headboard of the hotel bed, a smile playing across her lips. "We're talking about the guy who took me to prom because he felt so bad when that loser

I was crushing on asked someone else. He wanted *you* the whole time, Annie, but he gave that up to make me feel better."

"That's the way he is," I murmured.

"Or . . . remember his fourteenth birthday? His mom saved up some money so he could have a party. Only she didn't quite realize that fourteen is a little old for the kind of themed birthday party you might have when you're a kid. And then, when she asked him what theme he wanted—"

"Oh," I muttered. "I remember this. He said *The Heroic Trio*."

"That's! Right!" Evie exclaimed, pointing at me triumphantly. "*Our* favorite movie. He let his mom throw him a cheesy kiddie birthday because he didn't want to hurt her feelings. And he chose a theme that we would like so it would be fun for us."

"That *Heroic Trio* birthday cake was really something, though," I mused. "I still don't know how they rendered Michelle Yeoh so convincingly in icing."

"It was a thing of beauty," Evie agreed, closing her eyes as she brought her hand to her heart. "My point is: Scott is so used to being selfless, I don't know that he understands how to even recognize his own needs and wants sometimes. You were trying to get him to go after those dreams, Annie. You were ferociously trying to get him to make space for himself, and you want him to feel like he's living his best life. He'll see that once he's cooled down."

"I don't know," I said, picking at a loose thread on my pillow. "He left, Evie. He said he needed space—but, like, space away from me—"

"He slept on the couch," Evie said, rolling her eyes. "I saw him snoozin' away when I went in search of croissants this morning. And then he was gone when I got back. I assumed he had to get up really early for work and didn't want to bother you."

"It appears that his suitcase is still here as well," I said, spotting the half-packed luggage splayed out on the floor. A tiny bit of hope sparked in my chest. Maybe things *would* be okay once we'd both had a little time.

"Mmm-hmm, you guys are so having make-up sex later," Evie said, pretending to swoon. "Now. I have the perfect thing to take your mind off all this." She waved her phone in my face. "I found this online guide for doing a Little Tokyo walking and eating tour. It takes about four hours, and there are so many delicious-looking spots packed in—including that hundred-year-old mochi shop I've been dying to visit! And this will make up for yesterday, wherein I basically passed out before getting to even sample a cheeseburger pot-sticker!"

"Oh . . ." My gaze went to our precious copy of *Zacasta's Revenge*, plopped facedown near the headboard. "I was actually going to try to do some more vampire research today. I know I'm missing something in that terrible book, but if I am able to read it super closely with no interruptions—"

"Annie." Evie shook her head at me, her wild curls whipping around her face. "Okay, so the other thing Scott was right about is this: you *are* running yourself into the ground. And you *are* trying to do everything!"

"I'm trying to do *my job*!" I argued. "Which is to get to the bottom of this vampire nonsense before someone gets seriously hurt!"

"Fixating on some moldering old vampire book isn't going to do that!" she shot back. "And it's not just the vampire stuff. You're running yourself ragged trying to solve literally everything. Your mom's orange obsession, Pippa's friendship issues—hell, you're still trying to come up with a scheme that will get Lucy to move home!"

"I'm multitasking!" I insisted. "That's the Aveda Jupiter Way. And what am I supposed to do, Evie, when you're . . ." I bit my lip, cutting myself off before I could complete that thought.

When you're doing everything you can to avoid superhero-ing and investigating this latest supernatural fracas—which is supposed to be our job. That we do together.

"When I'm what?" she demanded, crossing her arms over her chest.

I swallowed my words down, determined to keep them inside. I couldn't say that to her—not after everything she'd been through, not when she'd been so close to losing all faith in herself back at Morgan. Not when she was just trying to envision a peaceful life for herself and the sweet little family she was in the process of creating.

A vision took shape in my head: Evie and Nate, ensconced in some remote cabin in the wilderness. Finally leaving all the demons and the fighting and the death-defying battles behind. Evie looking ever so angelic, cradling her baby while her husband looked at both of them with pure love. No one to bother them, nothing to penetrate their perfect bubble of happiness.

This gave way to another vision—a vision of what *I* would be doing while all this blissful love bubbling was happening. And all I could see was me sitting by myself in one of the big, drafty rooms at HQ—alone.

No Bea and Lucy, because they'd left long ago. Evie and Nate off in their own little world with their new family. And Scott down in LA, where he'd be so much happier . . .

I realized I was gasping for air, just as I had the previous morning. My vision narrowed again, those twin pinpoints of light floating in front of my eyeballs—

"Annie!"

I breathed deeply, blinked a couple times . . . and realized Evie had grabbed my hand and was squeezing tightly. I breathed again, trying to bring myself back to the present moment.

"Mmm," I said. "Sorry, I started feeling weird. Perhaps I *am* a bit stressed."

"You were having a panic attack," Evie said, unwilling to release my hand from her iron grip. "I used to get them all the time, mostly related to the fire power. Sometimes I still do." She looked at me intently, worry written all over her face. "Have you been having those a lot lately?"

"Just once—yesterday morning," I said, trying to make my voice calm and neutral. "I breathed through it and everything was fine."

"Everything is *not* fine," Evie insisted, squeezing my hand. "This is what I mean—"

"Hey, boss ladies!"

We both whirled around to see Pippa framed in the bedroom door. She was striking a triumphant pose, her iPad held above her head like a trophy.

"Oops," she said, taking in our tense expressions. "Looks like I barged in on y'all doing a drama, but this can't wait. Bertram Sturges called." She leaned in and lowered her voice dramatically. "You have been summoned back to set."

CHAPTER TWENTY-ONE

AS PIPPA BREATHLESSLY explained to us, Bertram's summons did not contain much in the way of context or accompanying information. He'd simply said we needed to be on set by a certain time and that Grouchy Stacey would be arriving shortly to pick us up. I supposed he was accustomed to his orders simply being obeyed—and normally Aveda Jupiter would have challenged that and demanded an explanation for this mysterious summons. But as returning to set also meant we could return more fully to our investigation, I simply pulled myself together as quickly as possible, and hustled Evie through her getting-ready routine. She complained the whole time about how Bertram's summons meant we'd have to skip our Little Tokyo plans, and how she'd already been deprived of an actual vacation moment since we'd spent all of the previous day on work.

I made sympathetic noises as I hurried her along, shoving clothes into her hands and making sure her purse was stuffed with extra snacks. At least all her bellyaching meant she wasn't pressing me on the whole panic attack thing, and our interactions seemed to reset themselves to mostly normal.

Grouchy Stacey picked us up, swept us onto the golf cart, and drove us to set. For a moment, it seemed like an exact repeat of our very first day on the lot. But as soon as we entered the stage, things took a different turn. The set was now completely new—gone was the cheery, pastry-laden façade of Cake My Day. In its place was a different set that looked like an enchanted castle crossed with a Goth bordello. Blood-red damask covered the stately walls, and elaborately carved dark wood furniture was upholstered in black velvet. Fake cathedral-style windows punctuated the sea of red, and an excess of decorative flourishes—ostentatious clocks, curlicued candelabras—were done up in bright gold. Someone had even tossed a bunch of fake cobwebs in there, just in case the atmosphere of Halloween-adjacent cheese wasn't coming through strongly enough.

"Damn," Pippa breathed. "This looks like some real vampire shit." She whipped out her phone and started snapping pictures.

"Wow," Evie murmured. "What part of our life is *this* from?"

"Much like the vampires, I'm guessing some part that's totally made up," I said dryly. I craned my neck to see if there was anyone lurking in the shadowy corners of the set. "But more importantly: where is everyone?"

That was the other, more jarring element that was different today. In direct contrast to the bustling chaos that had been a hallmark of our previous set visits, today the place was completely empty. There were no director's chairs, and no people to go *in* the director's chairs. No crew lighting the place and hauling around sound equipment. No auteurs smarming about. No Miki or Kat or . . . anyone.

Naturally, Grouchy Stacey hadn't prepped us for this at all. The silence was positively eerie, punctuated only by the *clicks* emanating from Pippa's phone as she snapped picture after picture.

"I don't know," Evie said. "But maybe that means this is just more bullshit from Bertram and we can leave?" She took her phone out and began eagerly scrolling through. "We can still do most of the stops on the Little Tokyo walking tour. That mochi shop is open *super* late."

"Or we could try calling Bertram," I countered. "I'd really like to know—"

As if on cue, the side door to the soundstage creaked

open, its rusty joints sending a very unpleasant *screeeech* echoing through the vast space.

"*There* you are, ladies." Bertram's bland voice boomed through the stage. Interesting how he made it sound as though we'd been purposefully hiding from him. He strode across the stage, flanked by two people I hadn't seen before. One was a tall, broad-shouldered man with mussed blond hair and perfectly straight white teeth. The other was a striking woman with golden brown skin and long black hair twisted into a complicated formation atop her head.

I studied this unlikely trio, trying to figure them out. Was one of these people the new showrunner?

"Evie, Aveda." Bertram gave us a businesslike nod. "And, ah . . ."

"Pippa!" Pippa said, waving enthusiastically. "I was here the other day when you, uh . . ."

"Banned us from set," I said cheerfully. I knew we were trying to not totally antagonize Bertram, but I simply could not help myself.

"Yes. Well." Bertram cleared his throat and adjusted his tie. "That was an unfortunate miscommunication."

I squinted at him. Was that really how he was going to characterize it? When he'd been the only one "communicating" and he'd been crystal clear that we were no longer welcome on the set of our own show?

"But now we're ready to move forward," Bertram continued. "We have a new showrunner—a woman." He smiled slightly and once again did that weird pausing thing, as if holding for applause. "She's currently ensconced in one of our bungalows, rebreaking the whole season."

"Oh, so . . ." I tilted my head, confused. "We don't get to meet her?"

"You will," Bertram said. "But the beginning of her process requires total isolation, and we want to respect that. In the meantime, I thought I could introduce you to some cast members you haven't had the pleasure of meeting yet."

He stepped to the side and gestured to the duo he'd brought with him.

Ah. Now *this* made more sense. These were two of the most beautiful people I'd ever seen—of course they were Hollywood actors.

"This is James Hill," Bertram said, sweeping a hand toward the blond man. "He's our Scott—Aveda Jupiter's husband."

I winced, remembering the fight I'd had with the real Scott the night before. I still hadn't heard from him at all today, and I couldn't quite bring myself to text him. I didn't know what to say.

"And this is Naira Mishra," Bertram continued. "She's playing Shruti."

"Nice to meet both of you," I said, nodding politely. "Are you involved in whatever scene is going on here?" I waved a hand at the Goth bordello set. "Because we are very curious about that."

I turned to Evie, expecting her to pick up the thread. But she was still looking at her phone. Probably trying to figure out how fast we could get out of here and get to the ever-important mochi.

"James and Naira *are* part of the next scene we want to shoot on this set," Bertram said. "In fact, that's why I brought them here. We can't actually shoot anything until our new showrunner emerges from her creative retreat—she's still workshopping this scene. But I thought they could soak up the atmosphere in the meantime. And since Aveda is also in this scene, they wanted to ask you some questions about your experience."

"Yes," Naira said, nodding eagerly. She had an earnest, enthusiastic spark in her eyes that reminded me very much of the real Shruti. "This scene has been really tough for me and James to get a handle on—"

"Especially with all the, ah, turmoil going on with the show," James said.

"So we jumped at the chance to meet with the real Aveda Jupiter." Naira beamed at me. "You can tell us how it *really* happened, and that will help us truly ground ourselves when it comes time to shoot this very important moment!"

"I see. Well . . . lovely," I said, returning her smile. "I'm happy to help. Evie can stick around, too, maybe she'll have some extra insights—"

Evie's head jerked up from her phone and she grimaced at me, as if this was the last thing in the world she wanted to do.

"Oh." Naira blushed and looked at her feet. "We were actually hoping we could explore this scene *privately*. Since it's a bit on the intimate side!"

"I . . ." My mind was racing. What scene was this? When had I been in a Goth bordello with Scott and Shruti, and what had we been doing that was so "intimate"?

I was guessing that this, like Clint's fever dream of a vampire attack, was going to be a scene where some extreme creative license was being taken with my life. But still, it could be a perfect opportunity to get more insight into the bizarre happenings on the show and the possible vampires we'd encountered, and to question two cast members I'd never met before.

I needed Bertram gone, though. His presence was not going to be conducive to an Aveda Jupiter–style interrogation.

I glanced over at Evie, trying to convey all of this through our BFF telepathy.

But she was back to her phone.

"Um, maybe Mr. Bertram here could show us around the lot!" Pippa piped up, giving me a little nod. "I've heard the Pinnacle commissary is *to die for*. Is it true that they set aside special artisanal pastries for VIP execs? Because I was under the impression that execs don't go to the commissary themselves, they send their assistants—"

"Well, uh . . ." Bertram sputtered, looking thrown off kilter. "I was actually planning on observing Aveda's take on this scene. I like to be very involved with every element of the show—"

"Aw, but that means Evie and I will be dumped out onto the lot all by our lonesome," Pippa said, throwing him a faux pout. "We'll be totally left to our own devices, just wandering into all sorts of places we're probably not allowed to be."

"On second thought," Bertram said hastily, "why don't I give you that tour. We'll return in about an hour . . . ?" He gave Naira and James a questioning look, and they both nodded.

"Okay, then," I said, turning to the actor duo as Pippa practically dragged Bertram off the soundstage. Evie trailed behind them, still wrapped up in whatever was on her phone screen.

I tried to catch her eye, but she didn't look up.

I turned to James and Naira and gave them my best can-do smile. "Tell me about this scene, and what insights I can provide."

"We'll be here, on the couch," Naira said, leading me and James over to one of the most ostentatious pieces of furniture. We all settled into the black velvet depths, Naira and James pulling out scripts. "Now," she continued, looking at the pages in front of her, "this is one of the big, climactic moments in the pilot—or at least, we think it is. Like Bertram said, the new showrunner's been workshopping it."

"There's been so much chaos with this production," I said, schooling my features into a sympathetic formation. "I imagine that's been hard on both of you?"

"It has been wild," James said, shuffling through his script pages. "This is the first pilot for both Naira and me as series regulars. So we've kinda bonded over that."

"It's nice to have someone who feels like an ally," Naira said with an exuberant head bob.

"Yeah, and neither of us wants to rock the boat or anything. We know we're not exactly the most important people on the call sheet," James said. "You'd think that would be Miki and Kat, but . . ."

"But it's Stan, right? Or it was, until he decided to take his 'leave,'" I said. "From what I understand, Clint saw him as the true star."

"Right," Naira said, pointing an index finger at me. "It was weird how that happened, too. Because initially . . ." She rolled her eyes to the ceiling, as if trying to recall the specific memory. "It wasn't that way. He kept gassing on and on about the importance of female empowerment—and Evie and Aveda were definitely the center of things. As they should be on a show that's about, you know, their *lives*."

I smiled. I liked her already.

"Yeah, you remember that moment?" James said to Naira, a sardonic grin tugging at the corners of his mouth. "We were doing our first big table read, the whole cast together. Clint wasn't there at the start, and that seemed super weird— he was the showrunner and all—but everything was going really well. Miki and Kat had amazing chemistry right off the bat, the jokes were really working, all the touching moments were hitting just right . . ." He frowned into space. "And then all of a sudden, Clint barges in during this really heavy scene between Evie and Aveda, and out of nowhere he screams . . ."

James and Naira reenacted this moment in perfect unison, throwing their arms wide and doing a spot-on imitation of Clint's self-important tone.

"I'VE GOT IT! I'VE BROKEN THE SHOW WIDE OPEN!"

They both dissolved into laughter, exchanging an affectionate grin. I watched them, wondering if their bond went beyond friendship. They were both adorable; I could certainly see it. (I tried to not dwell too hard on the fact that I seemed to keep picturing my husband with other perfect partners. Even the fake version of my husband.)

"He made us stop the table read," Naira recalled. "And he basically ordered us to hand over every copy of the original script so he could destroy all of them—because they were no longer his vision."

"Sounds extreme," I said. "But also very much like the Clint I met."

"It's weird because he didn't go all in with the 'vision' talk until that day," James said. "Actually, Naira and I both kinda noticed a change in him after that. Before, he'd been sorta collaborative, wanted to hear our ideas."

"Yes," Naira said, nodding. "And as blustery and annoying as he could be, he really seemed to care about the final product. And the female empowerment business." She cocked a bemused eyebrow. "But after that table read, he never wanted to talk to any of us, for any reason. New script pages would magically appear every day, and we'd have no idea what they might hold."

"And then suddenly there were vampires," James said, chuckling in disbelief. "Which seemed completely out of left field, to be honest."

"We tried to ask about that once," Naira said, looking puzzled as she turned back to her script. "And he swore up and down that it all had some basis in truth—the real truth, the one the 'corporate superhero machine' didn't want the general public to know about."

"That's another thing we wanted to ask you about," James said, turning to me hopefully. "Is there a superhero conspiracy to cover up the existence of vampires?"

"We won't reveal anything you tell us to the general public," Naira said, leaning forward, her eyes eager and inquisitive. "We just want to know what your experience is, so we can play this scene as truthfully as possible."

"Uh, what *is* this scene?" I asked hesitantly. The situation was getting more and more bizarre with every word they uttered, and my mind was already a whirl.

"It's a big one," Naira said, straightening in her seat and turning back to the first page of her script. "And if it did actually happen this way, well . . ." She tapped a spot on the page, her lips curving into a knowing smile. "I'm *sure* you'll remember."

"That's right," James said, nodding emphatically. "It's the scene where Aveda Jupiter finally takes the throne as Queen of the Vampires!"

"Excuse me, *what*?!" I looked at Naira, then James, trying to figure out if they were joking.

They just stared back at me, script pages clutched eagerly in hand.

"Clint said this was a very important moment in your life, for you as a superhero *and* a person!" Naira enthused. "It certainly reads very dramatically on the page."

"I . . ." I rested against the ornate couch, the velvet rubbing against my back. This was all so weird. I'd thought Clint's vision of the show—complete with Aveda the Vampire Slayer—had been a product of his fevered auteurish imagination and his unbridled desire to make the show all about his pet Method actor. It was strange to hear that he'd actually been writing a more straightforward—and truthful—account of my and Evie's lives. And then started acting strangely . . .

I drew in a long breath and studied Naira and James once more. They were still leaning forward, gazing at me expectantly. Waiting for me to relate the truth of Aveda Jupiter, Queen of the Vampires.

I had to play this cool—traditionally, something I am not very skilled at.

I wished Evie had found a way to stay for this. Between the two of us, we would've been able to figure out the best possible way to interact with James and Naira and approach this piece of the mission.

"Why don't you tell me about the scene?" I began, feeling it out. "I, ah, don't remember all the details, but once you get into it, I'm sure it will come rushing back."

"So you're saying it *is* true! There are vampires and this *did* happen!" Naira exclaimed, her eyes lit with glee.

"Not confirming anything just yet," I said, giving her a broad wink. "So . . . the scene?"

"Right, right," James jumped in. "Hey, why don't we read

it for you? That'll probably be way more evocative than trying to describe it."

"And actors are so self-centered, we'd mostly just focus on our bits," Naira said, letting out a tinkling laugh. "Oh, but we don't have Kat here. Aveda . . . ohmygod, I can't believe I'm even saying this, but would you read *you*?"

"Holy shit," James said, nodding in agreement. "That would be an honor. Here, sit between us and read off our scripts."

"Of course," I said, trying not to let myself get wrapped up in the sheer bizarreness of what was happening. I was about to read a scene from the TV show based on my life—a scene I was pretty sure was entirely fictional. I definitely did *not* remember ever frequenting a velvet-draped Goth bordello.

"And that's where we are when this starts," Naira was saying.

I shook my head, snapping myself out of my rambling train of thought. Oh, shit. I'd apparently just missed the part where she'd provided important context for what we were about to read.

"Sorry, can you say that again?" I said. "I was lost in thought—er, trying to get into character."

"Getting in character to play yourself, I love it!" Naira said, throwing me a wink. "Are you sure you're not an actor, Aveda Jupiter? Maybe that's something you should consider if you get tired of the whole superheroing thing."

"I bet you're a natural," James agreed. "We've watched so many videos of your personal appearances, and that charisma is something that can't be taught. So many of us thespians-for-hire would kill for an X factor like that!"

"This scene comes near the end of the pilot and sets up the series," Naira said. "After Aveda is bitten by the vampire—the one Stan's playing—she starts having strange visions. Visions of an elaborate, velvet-covered lair." She gestured to the set. "She's sensitive to sunlight, and she finds that she can't enter certain places unless she's specifically invited. And there's this *hunger* consuming her. She's insatiable and she longs for blood all the time!"

"Yeah," James said, nodding. "And then she realizes that her true love Scott and her good friend Shruti have gone missing. She has a vision of them *in* the lair, and so she sets off to save them—"

"And she doesn't wait for Evie because time is of the essence and she thinks she can handle it herself," Naira chimed in. "But as soon as she enters the lair, she senses something's wrong. And that's where our scene starts!"

She grinned at me as she and James shifted around on the couch, cueing their scripts up to the right spot and scooting closer to me so I could see. We were all jammed close together now, and I picked up on something light and floral—probably Naira's perfume—as well as a beachy, summery sort of scent wafting off James.

Weird. He even smelled like my husband. These two had *really* done their research.

"Ready?" James said, giving me an inquiring look.

I nodded briskly and once again tried not to spiral about how strange all of this was. An anticipatory flutter thrummed through my gut, my shoulders tightening up, my breath becoming shallower. I felt like I was about to jump out of a plane, not knowing if my parachute was going to activate.

"Aveda!" James exclaimed, reading the first line off the page. "You came."

I bit my tongue, resisting the urge to correct him. Scott never called me Aveda—it was always Annie. So maybe they hadn't done *that* much research.

"We knew you would," Naira cooed, capturing Shruti's bubbly demeanor perfectly. "We were told that if we sent out the call . . ."

She trailed off and there was an awkward pause.

"Aveda," she finally hissed after a beat or two. "That's you! You have the next line!"

"Oh, right!" I squeaked, my eyes scanning the page. "Sorry, I guess I'm already caught up in the moment. Let me see . . ." I found the line I was supposed to say and sat up straighter in my seat, trying to project my best Aveda Jupiter bravado. "Er . . ." I cleared my throat. Ridiculously, I wanted to do a good job, even though no one was filming us. "Scott! Shruti! You aren't in trouble? I came here to save you!"

"It's not us that needs saving," James said, meeting my gaze. "It's you."

His eyes held mine, smoldering with intensity. There was something very *probing* about the way he was looking at me—I could practically feel his gaze stroking against my skin. Then his eyes wandered to my neck . . . and his tongue darted between his lips. Like I was a delicious pastry and he was ready to devour me.

"Um . . ." My voice came out as a tiny squeak, my face flushing. I sternly ordered my racing heart to get itself under control.

Was I really getting *turned on* playing this bizarre fantasy version of myself, opposite a bizarre fantasy version of my husband?

"It's true, Aveda," Naira purred.

I turned to look at her, feeling like I was in slow motion, my heart still hammering in my chest.

"You're here because you're about to fulfill your destiny," Naira continued, leaning forward and brushing her fingertips against my arm. Her hand was cool, but that small patch of my skin was now burning up, yearning for more of her touch. I breathed in sharply, little shivers racing up my spine. I tried to let out a long exhale, but my throat turned thick and heat flashed through my belly. The light floral scent of her perfume washed over me, and I couldn't look away from the warm, liquid brown of her eyes—

I shook my head again, trying to dispel the cloud of lust that seemed to have descended over me in the last few seconds. I was acutely aware of the heat of both of their bodies pressing in on me, my nipples tightening against the cool silk of my sleeveless black shirt, my mouth going dry . . .

"You are meant for so much more," James intoned, his

voice rough and husky. Very gently, he slipped a finger under my chin and turned my head to face him again. "I always knew you were a queen—and now you'll be *our* queen."

"Y-you're both vampires?" I managed to gasp out. I wasn't even looking at the script anymore, I was literally responding as if all this was happening in real life.

"We have become *better*," James said. "We'll never grow old, never die, never *change*—"

"And we need you here with us," Naira said.

"We need you to *lead* us," James agreed. "It's your destiny, my love."

He was staring at my neck again, as if he'd never seen anything more enticing. And somehow I just knew Naira was looking at me the same way.

I tried to take in a long breath again, to get my swirling hormones under control, but my brain was spinning all sorts of scenarios now, tantalizing images flashing through my mind. They descended over me like a hypnotizing fog, and suddenly I could think of nothing else.

I pictured James swooping in at last, his lips finally pressing against that smooth column of neck he was so obsessed with. I knew his mouth would be as hot as a brand, that his kiss would make me feel like I was burning up from the inside. Then Naira would brush my hair out of the way, her soft lips finding the other side of my neck, her fingertips caressing my arm in that way that made every nerve ending in my body come to life. I'd close my eyes, letting them cradle me between them, gasping as Naira slid the silk of my shirt aside to drag her tongue over my aching nipple . . .

Their mouths would explore my bare skin, their intoxicating scents comingling—ocean, flowers, just a hint of citrus . . .

And when James . . . or was it Scott . . . pulled back from sinking his teeth into the most delicate part of my neck, his eyes would flash bright red . . .

"Annie?"

My eyes fluttered open and Scott's face swam into view. The *real* Scott.

I blinked once, twice. Where was I? What had just been happening . . . why was pure lust raging through me like wildfire . . .

I looked around, but my vision was hazy and my head felt like it was wrapped in cotton balls. I was still on the soundstage, lying on the velvet couch. Scott was leaning over me, his hands on my shoulders, his face creased with concern. And we were alone.

I blinked again. That couldn't be right. Hadn't I just been here with someone . . . *someones* . . . else? Where had they gone? Where was Evie? And why was Scott here . . .

"Annie," Scott said again, bringing his face closer to mine. "Please talk to me."

His brilliant blues eyes scanned me. He was leaning in close enough for me to pick up on his summertime scent, sea and sun and citrus swirling around me and making my head spin. His hands were warm against my skin, his golden hair was deliciously mussed, he just looked . . . *so* . . .

My skin felt tight and tingly all over and I could only think of one thing . . . so I moved closer and pressed my lips to his. He made a surprised sound deep in the back of his throat, a guttural groan that only inflamed my lust even more.

I wound my arms around his neck, deepening our kiss. My tongue stroked his with wild abandon and he groaned again, his hands sliding to my back so he could pull me firmly to him. I pressed eagerly against the hard wall of his chest, my nipples tightening again, the sensation so overwhelming it was almost painful.

I wanted to feel his mouth on my neck, for him to ignite the most sensitive parts of my skin. I wanted him to feel the hot blood rushing through me, that irresistible life force, that—

"Ow!"

He pulled away abruptly—his hair even more mussed, his eyes clouded with lust. We were both breathing hard, the combined sound of our fevered exhales echoing off the high ceiling of the cavernous soundstage. He brought his fingertips to his lips—and I saw now that I'd gotten a little too enthusiastic with our kiss . . . and drawn blood.

I heard something in the distance, like a fluttering up by the rafters. My head jerked up and I swore I saw . . . what was that? Indistinct shapes flying near the rafters. Birds? No. More like . . . bats . . .

And before I could get my mind around what was happening, I heard the door to the soundstage open and an enraged Bertram was striding toward us, his face a storm cloud of fury.

"Ms. Jupiter," he said, his voice like ice. "I had a sneaking suspicion I was right to ban you from set the first time. And it looks like I will have to do it again."

CHAPTER TWENTY-TWO

IN SHORT ORDER, Evie and I were banned from set once more. And from all of the Pinnacle lot, period.

Grouchy Stacey shuttled all of us—me, Evie, Pippa, Scott—back to the hotel. We were silent on the ride, and I was pretty sure all of us were bursting with a million questions. But none of us wanted to speak *too* candidly in front of Grouchy Stacey.

I tried to get my thoughts in order on the ride back, but I could not get them to cohere into a clear picture. Perhaps I was still experiencing a massive hallucination wherein I was about to engage in a vampire threesome.

"Okay," I said, as we all piled back into the hotel suite. "I am very confused about the sequence of events that just occurred, and instead of us all talking at once . . . why don't we try to break it down chronologically?"

"Right," Evie said, flopping down on the couch. She gnawed on her lower lip, her eyes rolling skyward. "So our favorite person of all time, Bertram, summoned us to set, totally ruining our Little Tokyo walking tour plans. Grouchy Stacey dropped us off at the set, which was now done up as some kind of . . . I don't even know what to call it . . ."

"Goth bordello?" I offered helpfully.

"Yes," Evie said, laughing a little as she pointed at me. "Then Bertram showed up with those two actors and they wanted to talk to you. So he took me and Pippa on a tour of the lot—"

"Hold up," Pippa said, switching on the TV and fussing

with her iPad. "Let's get Bea in on this. She'll be super mad if we talk Goth bordellos without her."

"What's this about Goth bordellos?!" Bea shrieked, her face popping up onscreen.

We filled her in, and then I asked Evie and Pippa to tell us what had happened on their lot tour.

"It was extremely booooring," Pippa said, rolling her eyes as she drew the word out. "And Bertram was definitely *not* into it. I asked all kinds of questions, trying to get a feel for just how sus this guy is—"

"Pippa was fantastic," Evie chimed in. "A real pro."

"Thank you," Pippa said, beaming at her. "All of his answers were totally bland and not at all informative. I thought as this big-time executive, he'd know all kinds of history and lore about the lot. I mean, the Pinnacle lot is one of the oldest studio lots in Hollywood that's still functional. So many classic movies have been filmed there and you know there have *got* to be stories!"

"Or at the very least, you'd think he'd know his way around," Evie said. "He kept going the wrong way and leading us into these weird dead-ends. He almost walked right into a film shoot!"

"Yeah, and he didn't know anything about the bomb-ass commissary," Pippa said. "After he was done with his little non-tour, he dropped us off at the car with Grouchy Stacey— but I managed to sneak off and find the commissary myself. I scored some of those sweet artisanal cupcakes!"

"And she didn't save even one for the pregnant lady," Evie said, cocking a teasing eyebrow. "Doubly egregious since I also never got that mochi."

"Crammed 'em all in my mouth in one go," Pippa said, not looking guilty in the slightest. "They were just too scrumptious."

"Pippa, I think you have the best supernatural investigative technique I've encountered so far," Bea enthused. "Very impressive."

"So what ended up happening with you, Annie?" Evie

said. "And Scott, where did you come from? How did you end up on the lot?"

"You called me," he said, giving Evie a confused look. "You said Annie was in danger and I needed to come right away and to go to this one specific soundstage. When I got there, my name was on whatever list I needed to be on for security clearance and they sent me over to the stage."

"I definitely did *not* call you," Evie insisted.

"What did you see when you entered the stage?" I asked, turning to Scott. "Was I, ah, alone?"

"You were," he said, looking even more confused. "You looked like you were sleeping on that weird velvet couch thing. It was so eerie—like I had stumbled into a scene from an actual movie. You woke up when I touched you, and then, um . . ."

He trailed off, his gaze drifting to the side, and my face flushed. Oh, right—he'd touched me and then I'd pounced on him and we'd made out in the Goth bordello.

"So someone pretending to be me called you and told you to rescue Annie," Evie said slowly. "But from what? She wasn't in any danger—wait, were you in danger?" She cocked her head at me, her face scrunching up in confusion.

"No," I said. "Well . . . I don't think so." I forced myself to think back to the beginning, to what had happened right before Evie and Pippa left for their tour with Bertram.

"James and Naira—those are the actors playing Scott and Shruti—were very, um, enthusiastic," I said, my cheeks heating. "They were most inquisitive about my experience, and how realistically it was being portrayed in the script."

I recounted the rest of our conversation for them—the actors' description of Clint's bizarre change in attitude, the way he'd had the sudden stroke of genius to add vampires to the show, his insistence that the creatures were real and being suppressed by some kind of great superhero conspiracy.

"James and Naira actually wondered if there was any truth to that," I explained. "It was all very strange."

"So then, what, did they ask you more questions?" Bea asked, leaning forward.

"No, they wanted me to read the scene with them. I played myself, obviously. Apparently in Clint's version of my life, I eventually become a Vampire Queen."

"Holy shit!" Pippa exclaimed. "*Are* you a Vampire Queen? Because that would make you even more goals than you already are!"

"Pretty sure I'm just me," I said dryly. "So we read the scene and, um . . ." I stopped abruptly, heat racing through my body as the memories came flooding back. How did I explain the next part? I'd basically fantasized an orgy with fake vampiric versions of my husband and one of my best friends and all of it had ended with Fake Husband sinking his teeth into my neck. Which I had enjoyed very much.

"I started having these weird visions," I said slowly. "Like, um . . . sexy visions. I think it was supposed to be a sexy scene between these three characters—"

"Between Aveda, Scott, and Shruti?" Bea squeaked, her voice somewhere between disbelief and awe.

"Yes," I said, my blush intensifying. "So—"

"Holy frakballs!" Bea interrupted. "Aveda, your imagination is getting down and dirty—this is just like in the third book of *Midnight Dreams*, wherein Calla invites some of her closest vampire friends over and—"

"*Anyway,*" I said, trying to keep us on track. I couldn't even look at Scott; I wondered what he thought of my brain's vivid fantasizing. He had, I noticed, positioned himself as far away from me as possible, settling into one of the plush armchairs as I paced the opposite side of the room. "I felt like I'd fallen into this weird dream state, where I wasn't sure what was real and what wasn't. I envisioned them, um, biting me. Presumably to turn me into that Vampire Queen. And then, the next thing I knew, Scott was there and James and Naira were gone and . . ." I trailed off, trying to remember more. There was something else, something dancing around the most shadowy corners of my mind . . .

"Bats!" I exclaimed, jabbing an index finger in the air. "Again, I'm not sure which parts I imagined or if everything was a dream *or what*, but I swear I saw bats flying around, up by the rafters of the soundstage. Just like at Edendale."

"This is some *real* vampire shit!" Pippa exclaimed, slamming her hand down on the glass table. "See, I told y'all Clint turned himself into that flock of bats. And now . . ." Her eyes widened as she worked it out. "James and Naira are probably also real vampires! Trying to ensnare Aveda in their web of seduction, until Scott turned up. Then they transformed into bats!"

My hand went instinctively to my neck, remembering how part of my vision . . . hallucination . . . web of seduction?!? Whatever we were calling it, it had ended with James/Scott drawing blood from my neck. But my skin felt smooth, unblemished. So that had definitely been part of some weird vision/fantasy.

"So now we know of four people connected to this show that have displayed some kind of vampiric quality," Bea said. "Stan, Clint, James, and Naira. And are we still theorizing this is possible Otherworld interference, a la what happened at Morgan?"

"It has to be," I said. "And I still think this has something to do with trying to get Evie's baby."

"By, what, trying to distract you with horny vampire visions?" Evie said.

"I mean, do these demon plans ever make sense?" Pippa countered.

"Good point," Bea said, letting out an explosive giggle.

"Whatever the goal—the Otherworld is definitely part of it," Scott said.

I stopped my pacing, and we all turned to look at him. He'd fallen silent for most of our discussion about bats and horny fantasies. Now he met my eyes across the room, and I forced myself not to look away. His expression was sedate, guarded. I had no idea what he was thinking.

"Why do you say that?" Bea piped up.

"Because . . ." He hesitated, his eyes going to the ceiling. "I think I've described before how I'm able to access those bits of Otherworld magic to power my spells and stuff like that. Sometimes I have to reach out with my mind and find that magic. And sometimes . . . it finds me." He met my gaze again. "When I was on that set, I felt Otherworld magic brushing against my mind. It was faint, very gentle. But definitely present."

"So we can confirm one part of our hypothesis," Pippa said, gnawing on her bottom lip. "It's those fuckin' demons again."

"And this could be like the ghosts of Morgan, as we said before," I said, trying to work it out. "Demons taking the form of another supposedly fictitious supernatural creature."

"But again, the demons at Morgan were animating bits of emotional energy to bring ghosts people already believed in to life," Evie pointed out. "These humans presumably existed before, in one hundred percent mundane human form—right? Or, like we discussed, was there something vampiric within them that just needed to be activated?"

"I put together all my research on Clint and Stan if you want to hear it—everything I've compiled the last few days," Pippa said, raising her hand. "Um, sorry, I would have presented it earlier, but I wanted to make sure I had a really full picture—"

"That's all right, Pippa," I said, giving her an encouraging smile. "Tell us what you've learned. Perhaps we'll be able to glean some clues from that."

"So these guys both have pretty straightforward mediocre white man careers," Pippa said, twisting a lock of platinum hair around her finger as she studied her screen. "That is to say, they seem to have been lauded as important for doing the bare minimum. Clint started his career with a low-budget indie film funded mostly by his wealthy parents. It got into Sundance, was picked up for distribution, and even though all it really proved was that he could shoot two actors in a single location having the same boring conversation for two hours straight, it opened up a lot of doors for him. He made a couple more films, then landed an overall deal with Pinnacle. The only real blip was that the first show that was supposed to be made under that overall tanked hard before it even got out of the gate. Execs hated the script he was trying to write, and eventually scrapped the whole project. The *Heroine* series was . . ." She made a face at her screen. "Okay, this is a direct quote from some snarky underground gossip site, just so we're clear. These are *not* my words—"

"Yes, yes, we got it, get on with it," I said, impatience threading its way into my voice.

"It was seen as 'a consolation prize,'" Pippa said. "A way of honoring his deal without celebrating his vision."

"How lovely," I muttered. "Maybe that's why he kept trying to smear said 'vision' all over the thing. Although . . . James and Naira seem to think he was originally trying to be a bit more faithful." I turned this information over in my mind. "What about Stan? You mentioned before that he'd been making a name for himself as a celebrated character actor type, but was there anything more?"

"Indeed," Pippa said, deepening her voice and throwing some dramatic heft behind it. "So Stan's the kind of guy who's always up for best supporting actor awards, is constantly lauded by his peers, and has had *at least* a few reaction shot memes created in his honor. A lot of people know his face—like, hey, it's that guy!" Her brow furrowed as she studied the screen more intently. "He's had a few rough years with not a lot of work. And unfortunately, he was passed over for the villain role in an upcoming summer action movie—potentially a big blockbuster—and that apparently sent him into a bit of a depression. This *Heroine* gig was supposed to be something of a comeback role."

"So both of these white men were coming off of failures right before they landed on our show?" I said, trying to draw a connection. "Or at least what counts as 'failure' to this type of white man."

"I guess, yeah," Pippa said, her gaze turning thoughtful.

"So . . ." I squeezed my eyes shut and pinched the bridge of my nose, trying to think. My brain still felt muzzy from the events of the day, like it was trying to grasp on to every relevant fact and put them all in some kind of order. But so many little bits of information just kept slipping away, and I could not seem to hold them all in my mind at the same time. "Let's continue with the theory that this is like the Morgan ghosts. If both of these men were dealing with recent failures, maybe they were feeling sad, alone, hopeless. Maybe the Otherworld demons figured out how to access *that* emotional energy and . . . turn them into supernatural creatures?"

"That is such an *interesting* way of doing the vampire turn!" Pippa cried.

"Would the humans be aware that that's what was happening?" Evie mused. "Like, are they actively in cahoots with the Otherworld forces, like Richard was at Morgan?"

"Oh man, I would be *so* aware if I was a vampire!" Pippa enthused. "I would *die*. Well, I guess that's part of the process anyway. But, like, I would die both physically and metaphorically."

"Pippa, can you also do some research on James and Naira?" I said. "I'd love to know if they also experienced anything like this—a failure, a loss, something that would make them feel hopeless—before being cast on the show."

"On it," Pippa said, tapping away on her iPad with relish.

"And . . ." I frowned, a wisp of a thought swirling through my brain. I couldn't quite grab on to it, though, so I resumed my pacing. "I read parts of *Zacasta's Revenge* yesterday—"

"My condolences," muttered Pippa.

"I can't believe y'all actually found a copy," Bea said reverently.

"And there was one part that really struck me," I continued. "It's that thing at the end, where Zacasta uses her power to pull vampirism out of all her minions."

I stopped pacing and stood by the massive hotel window, gazing out into the blazing sun of afternoon LA.

"It reminded me of using my telekinesis to pull that

demon possession out of Evie right before her wedding. Despite my hours of practice, honing my power, I've never been able to replicate that feat."

"Well, also because we've never been able to figure out how to replicate it safely," Evie murmured.

"But maybe that's something I could try on these supposed vampires," I continued. "If it's Otherworld magic activating some kind of emotional energy inside of them—"

"Then maybe you could pull that magic out?" Bea said.

"Yes." I nodded at the sparkling cityscape outside the window, turning the idea over in my mind, trying to look at it from all angles. "Shasta's potential connection to our world was severed when Evie figured out how to give the last ghost closure, the ghost that was essentially Evie herself. The lingering emotional energy evaporated, and that was that."

"So why do you have to telekinetically *pull* the Otherworld bits out of the vampires?" Scott said. "Why is something supernatural the answer, when before it was simply about talking to someone?"

"Aw, Scott," Bea said. "Are you saying you want to give the vampires therapy so they can resolve their issues as well? That's so wholesome!"

"I don't think that will work this time," I said. "I actually tried to reason with both Clint and Stan, remember? They straight up did not listen. And James and Naira . . ." I flushed again as the memories surfaced. "They possibly hypnotized me with some kind of sexy vampire vision powers, so I doubt I could maintain the concentration I would need to talk to them in a meaningful way."

"But you can maintain the concentration you need for telekinesis?" Scott asked, his voice tipping into skepticism.

I whirled away from the window. "What are you saying? You don't think I'm strong enough?"

"No, I . . ." Scott blew out a long breath and got to his feet, crossing the room to stand in front of me. "The other day at the beach—you were focusing so hard on maintaining the hold, and you passed out and it scared the living shit out of me. And now you want to do that again, only with a certain technique that you've only successfully deployed *once*? And during a time when you've been so *drained*—"

"So you *don't* think I'm strong enough," I snapped. "I've trained all my life for this sort of thing, Cameron. I'll make sure I'm at one hundred percent, that I'm fully prepared and ready and have practiced as much as I possibly can—"

"Evie just said there's no way to actually practice this!" he cut in, shaking his head in exasperation. "So why do you think—"

"Why do *you* think I can't do this?" I demanded, crossing my arms over my chest.

"I do," he growled. "But . . ." A shadow passed over his face, and his shoulders slumped. When he met my eyes again, his expression was haunted, ghosts of that hurt I'd seen the night before flitting across his face. "I don't know if you'll still be here after."

Silence descended over us, thick as San Francisco's morning fog. His eyes roamed my face like he was trying to memorize it. I just stood there, frozen, at a loss for words.

"Um . . ." Bea's voice cut through the quiet, and she made a few fussy coughing sounds in the back of her throat. "What about a different plan? You know, Scott and I have been talking more about the whole power combo thing—"

"No," Scott said, his voice low and defeated. "Annie will never go for that. Because she thinks she has to save the entire world all by herself."

He turned away from me, running a hand through his already tousled hair.

"I have to go," he said—and he sounded so sad, so utterly *exhausted*, my heart clenched.

"Go where—home?" I managed, my voice a tiny squeak.

"Back to the Center," he said, still not looking at me. "I got called in this morning because two of the students didn't show up and nobody's been able to reach them. I'm going back to find out where the situation stands and see how I can help—unfortunately, none of my locator spells turned anything up."

"Can I . . . can *we* do anything?" I murmured. Of course he hadn't quit the Center, as he'd said he was going to. Because now they needed him for something, and as usual, he was all too ready to put his own feelings to the side.

He turned and gazed at me for a long moment, his blue eyes unbearably sad.

"I'd rather you didn't," he finally said.

Silence enveloped us yet again as he shuffled to the door, the seconds stretching out in such excruciating fashion, I wondered if the Otherworld demons had figured out how to set humans up with slow-motion powers.

"Well," Bea finally said once the door had clicked behind Scott, "nice to see that y'all are as dramatic as ever."

I swallowed hard, ignoring the tears that were pricking my eyes. Aveda Jupiter had a job to do, a *mission*. Everything with Scott would have to wait until later.

"Evie," I said, keeping my tone brisk and businesslike, "are you hungry? Right about now is usually one of your pregnant-lady snackie times."

"Yes," she said, her voice hesitant. "But, uh . . ."

"But nothing!" I barreled on. "Pippa, can you order us something? Then perhaps we can discuss *Zacasta* in more detail, figure out how my plan might work."

"Um, sure," Pippa said, her eyes going from me to Evie and back again.

I settled myself on the couch and took my phone out, trying to think of what else I could do right this second. My phone, as if reading my mind, let out a loud buzz, indicating that I had a new text.

"Oh, Kat messaged me . . ." I said, tapping on the screen.

But before it could open and reveal its contents, my phone buzzed again—this time with a call.

"Kat?" I answered.

"Aveda," she breathed out. Her voice sounded thick and watery.

"What's going on? Have you been crying?"

"Y-yes," she sniffled. "God fucking dammit, I've worked so hard, and now it's just . . . *nothing* . . ."

"Slow down," I said, trying to sound soothing. "Tell me what's happened."

"It's the show," she managed, a sob rising in her voice. "I was just fired."

CHAPTER TWENTY-THREE

KAT WAS CRYING so hard, I spent an hour on the phone, just trying to calm her down. She couldn't manage much in the way of a coherent explanation, so we finally agreed to meet up and talk, and Kat suggested a ramen shop in the heart of Little Tokyo.

Evie, of course, had perked up at the thought of being able to go on some version of the walking tour she'd been yearning for. But as it was now late afternoon, it was officially her naptime, and she passed out before the words ". . . and we'll finally get to see the mochi shop!" left her lips.

So Pippa and I hopped into the rental car and hightailed it down to the outer edge of downtown LA and the famed historic neighborhood known as Little Tokyo. Pippa spent most of the ride telling me all about it: how it had once contained the largest Japanese American population in the United States, and remained an important cultural hub for LA Asians.

"And there are like *a thousand* good restaurants—ramen, musubi, curry, okonomiyaki, you name it!" Pippa crowed. "There's a mochi emporium. A taiyaki place. Ooooh! A spot where you can get ice cream served *in* taiyaki—"

"This all sounds amazing, but where are we meeting Kat again?" I said, giving her an amused look.

"One of the ramen places," Pippa said, her face lighting up. "It's teeny-tiny, never takes reservations, and apparently has a wait of, like, *hours*. But I called ahead and told them Aveda Jupiter, a true A-List Asian American celebrity, wanted to dine there and they said they'll have a table waiting!"

"Excellent assistanting," I said, giving her an approving look. "And we'll have to bring some food back for Evie. Hopefully that will soften the blow of her missing this little adventure."

Pippa parked in a garage near the ramen spot—which, true to her word, had a massive, hungry crowd assembled outside even though it was well past lunchtime.

We threaded our way through the crowd and managed to get inside, where a stern-looking elderly Auntie of a waitress ushered us to a minuscule booth in the very back. I took a moment to study our surroundings. As Pippa had promised, it was "teeny-tiny," a cramped corridor of a restaurant lined with several of these equally cramped booths. The warm brown wood of the walls and tables was chipped and weathered, and the basic vinyl covering the booth seats looked about a million years old. The only wall décor was a smattering of hanging scrolls with faded kanji.

"Oh, there's Kat!" Pippa exclaimed, giving an expansive wave toward the entrance.

I craned my neck and saw Kat hustling inside, her black hair swept into a messy topknot. Some of her cute personal style seemed to have fallen by the wayside today—she was clad in ratty leggings and an oversized sweatshirt that said ASIAN AMERICAN GIRL CLUB, and most of her face was covered by her usual enormous sunglasses.

"Hey, girls," she said, slipping into the booth. She looked around furtively, as if expecting the paparazzi to pop up behind her.

"Hey, Kat," I said tentatively. Her shoulders were hunched up around her ears—a state of being I was all too familiar with. Even though the sunglasses were obscuring her eyes, she looked like she hadn't slept in days. What I could see of her face was pale and drawn, her mouth set in a tight little line.

"So bright outside," she muttered, looking down at the menu. "That LA sun is doing the freaking most today."

"Why don't we order some of this delicious-looking ramen?" I suggested, waving the Auntie waitress over. If nothing else, I was hoping food would cheer Kat up a bit.

"I already did a deep dive on the menu," Pippa said. "Any food allergies, dietary restrictions?"

Kat shook her head no, and Pippa grinned at the waitress. "Then if everyone's cool with it, I suggest we get three of the most gargantuan bowls of chashu ramen you can manage— with *extra* chashu! And a side of gyoza for us to share, please."

The waitress gave her a terse nod, then marched off without writing anything down.

"So," I said, turning to Kat and trying to sound soothing again. "Do you want to talk about what happened?"

She snuffled and finally took her giant sunglasses off. Her eyes were red-rimmed and puffy, and my heart twisted for her—what terrible things had the unending horror show that was this television program subjected her to? How had it drained all of her vivacious spirit? She looked a bit like a faded old photo, all her color and vibrancy dimmed to nothing.

"They fired me," Kat said, her voice flat. Her gaze went to the table and she fiddled with the chopsticks in front of her. "Just like that. And *over the phone*. Bertram called my reps, made them conference me in. Then he told me that while he appreciated my 'hard work,' they'd decided to go in a different direction."

"Who is 'they'?" I asked, resting my elbows on the table and leaning forward. "Like, is it just Bertram making this decision? Was the new showrunner involved—have you spoken to her at all? Do you know her name, even, because—"

Pippa cleared her throat loudly, cutting me off. I shot her an accusing look, but she leveled me with one of her own, as if to say—*chill out.*

But Kat had appreciated my intensity, and I was surprised to find that I felt I *could* actually be that intense with her. Because she'd do the same, neither of us hiding our truest selves.

"I haven't met the new showrunner either," Kat said,

blowing her nose on a napkin. "Miki and I were actually just talking about this: the way that ultimately went down was so weird. We were both worried, but got kinda tentatively excited when Bertram said he wanted to hire a woman. Although I wish he also thought it was important to hire a woman of color."

She paused again to blow her nose, the loud *honk* cutting through the bustle of the restaurant. A few of the other diners turned and looked at us. I gave them my best imperious stare, as if to say, *Yes, my friend is having a total fucking meltdown in the middle of a cozy ramen joint. But you know what? It's necessary.*

The surly Auntie waitress chose that moment to slam a piping hot plate of gyoza down in front of us. Kat seemed to perk up as the delectable smell of sizzling pork wafted from the dish.

"Ahhh, thank god, I am *starving*," she exclaimed, using her chopsticks to spear a crispy-bottomed dumpling. She bit into it and let out a small moan, pork juice and fat oozing onto her chopsticks. "Well, that's one advantage of being fired," she said, a sardonic smile crossing her lips. "No more leading lady diet."

I smiled back, happy to see her reclaiming some of her snarky bravado.

"Anyway," she said, popping the rest of the dumpling in her mouth, "we thought it was going to take some time to find this person. But then Bertram announces he's found someone and we'll be restarting production right away. Miki and I were stoked. Until five minutes later, when Bertram called to fire me."

"What does 'a different direction' mean?" Pippa asked. "'Cause it seemed to me that you were the perfect Aveda Jupiter."

"Thanks, lady," Kat said, snagging another dumpling. "Bertram also said they wanted someone with a 'more universal' look. Someone 'less niche.' Someone All-American—"

"Oh dear," I said, flashing back to Mercedes' words to me

all those years ago—and then realizing, with slowly dawning horror, exactly what that meant. "I think I know how to decode this. He wants to replace you with someone white."

"Ding ding, girl!" Kat exclaimed, pointing her chopsticks at me. "That's right." She plucked another dumpling from the plate and crammed the whole thing into her mouth in one go. "They're whitewashing Aveda Fucking Jupiter!"

I sat back in the booth, my brain trying to parse what she'd just told me. I should be more upset. I should be *enraged*. But I was surprised to find that I mostly just felt a queasy sense of inevitability. Maybe it was because this show had already turned into an utter raging (and possibly vampire-infested) disaster. Or maybe it was because deep down, I hadn't necessarily seen this turning out any other way. No matter how much I accomplished, how much I succeeded . . . a white woman would still always be seen as all of those code words Kat had just spit out.

More universal. Less niche. All-American.

Perhaps I should've just let Mercedes have San Francisco and been done with it.

"Did they fire Miki too?" Pippa asked.

Kat frowned, her mouth still full of dumpling. I glanced down at the plate and realized she'd wolfed down *all* the dumplings. I imagined she was extremely freaking happy to be free of the leading lady diet, if nothing else.

"I don't know," she finally managed. "It's possible they'll want to keep Evie as a handy woman of color sidekick so they can say they're totally committed to diversity."

"Evie is not my *sidekick*!" I bristled.

Kat shrugged. "Welcome to Hollywood. They'll make what you think of as 'your' story whatever they want it to be."

The Auntie waitress returned to plunk three steaming bowls of ramen in front of us. The chashu did look particularly delicious, its crisped fatty edges floating in a sea of heavenly broth. I would definitely have to take some back for Evie. Maybe I could find that mochi shop she was interested in as well.

"And no info on the new showrunner?" I said, trying to circle back to my initial questions. "Not even a name?"

"Nothing," Kat said with her mouth full of chashu. "I suppose I'm no longer on a need-to-know basis regarding anything about the show."

"Do you have any idea who they're replacing you with?" I said. "Or is that also need-to-know information?"

"Dunno," Kat said. "All I was told was that they had an 'exciting newcomer' in mind."

She threw her napkin down on the table and glared at her bowl. I noticed she'd wolfed down all the chashu, but nothing else—the broth, noodles, and vegetables were all still intact.

"*I* was supposed to be the 'exciting newcomer,'" she growled. "Ten years of grinding, auditioning, pursuing this stupid dream of mine. Constantly getting sent the most racist two-line roles possible—and still going in for them, because hey, what else am I supposed to do? I finally get my break, I'm so ready for it, I get fucking attacked on set but return like the trouper that I am . . . and it all ends like this."

"I'm so sorry, Kat—you deserve so much better," I said, racking my brain for something more comforting. "Um. Do you want my chashu?"

"Yes, please," she said, perking up. I slid the bowl over to her. Then tried to think of what I could possibly say—what I could *do*—that would fix this for her.

"Maybe I don't know any better and all Hollywood productions are like this, but it seems like *Heroine* has been very dramatic," Pippa said.

"It has," Kat said. "Aveda, you mentioned you were looking into Clint and Stan's weird behavior—are you thinking it's all connected? That something more is amiss than just regular-type drama?"

"Perhaps," I said. "I must say, it's been a bit hard to tell since this world is so alien to Evie and me."

"Yeah, and normally I *love* drama, but . . ." Pippa frowned at Kat. "You and Miki getting attacked? The showrunner acting like a complete loon and nearly burning down an entire bar? Firings, recastings, assorted other disasters . . . oh, and we haven't even gotten to the part where Aveda almost had a sexy vampire threesome on set—"

"Hey!" I yelped, pointing my chopsticks at her. "That is *not* what happened! I was helping them with a scene, and then I just, uh . . . anyway, I had the chance to talk to some of your castmates, and they mentioned that when Clint started working on the show, he actually seemed to be doing an okay job of it?"

"Yeah," Kat said, poking at the limp vegetables that were still floating in her ramen bowl. "After that first table read, I guess that's when Miki and I started feeling kinda pushed to the side. I assumed he'd just started feeling more comfortable, realizing what kind of 'auteur vision' he could push on the studio. Testing the boundaries, the way a toddler does." She turned to my ramen bowl, picking out the chashu. "Maybe I didn't think it was weird because it was what I'd been expecting all along. It felt . . . inevitable."

My heart twisted. Hadn't I just been thinking along similar lines? I felt her pain so deeply, and I hated that this was the way her dream seemed to be dying.

I opened my mouth to say something hopefully comforting, but was cut off by an ear-piercing scream from the front of the restaurant. My head whipped around just in time to see our Auntie waitress leaping out of the way of something near the ground, something I couldn't quite see . . .

The scream rippled through the restaurant as others started jumping out of the way of whatever it was. I looked around frantically, then trained my gaze on the floor, trying to make it out.

Then a tiny, fuzzy gray blur skittered over my foot. I recoiled, yanking my foot under the table.

"Mouse!" Pippa shrieked helpfully.

"What mouse?!" Kat exclaimed, her eyes going to the floor.

"Everybody calm down!" Auntie waitress barked. "We do *not* have a rodent problem! That one was just, uh, passing through! Already out the back door."

But the damage was done. Now people were frantically talking amongst themselves, rushing for the exit. No one wanted to eat in a possibly infested restaurant. Or even one that had a single tiny mouse who might possibly skitter over your foot.

"Hey, at least now the wait will be shorter," Pippa muttered.

I couldn't help but laugh. I glanced over at Kat, expecting her to be laughing too. But she wasn't. Instead she was still staring at the floor, as if hypnotized. Her eyes had the strangest gleam, like she'd transported herself somewhere else entirely.

"Mouse . . ." she whispered, her voice high and breathy.

It happened in a flash. Suddenly, she was leaping out of the booth and bolting for the back door, still whispering to herself in that strange voice. She moved so fast, she turned into a Kat-shaped blur, her gigantic sunglasses bouncing wildly on top of her head.

"Kat!" Pippa squealed, clambering over me and zipping after her. "What are you doing?!"

"All right, so I guess takeout for Evie is out of the question," I groaned, getting to my feet and preparing to go after them.

I was instantly blocked by Auntie waitress, who planted herself in front of me, hands on hips, judgmental glower firmly in place.

"You haven't paid," she spat out, her eyes flashing. "No dine and dash here, not even for fancy celebrities." Her eyes narrowed. "Although *I've* never heard of you. Is this some kind of con? You pretend you're famous, try to scam a free meal? That doesn't work here. You eat, you pay. Simple as that."

"This is a lot of attitude, considering that you just had a *mouse* in here and many people left without paying," I retorted, gesturing to the door. "Anyway, I will pay, I just need . . ." I frowned, patting my hips. Oh, right. I'd given Pippa my wallet to hold since my sleek black jeans didn't have any pockets. "I need to go get my wallet. My friend has it, I just have to . . ." I pointed toward the exit, hoping she'd cut me some slack.

I should have known better. "Slack" is never on the menu when it comes to Asian Aunties.

"You eat, you pay," she repeated, crossing her arms over her chest and giving me the most stubborn look I'd ever seen on anyone.

"I fully intend on paying," I said through gritted teeth. "If you will let me by—"

"No!" she said, slicing an arm through the air. "Now!"

"*Listen* to me, I—"

I was cut off by a scream from somewhere outside, near the back door. And the voice was unmistakable—it was *Pippa's* scream.

I looked around frantically, as if my wallet might magically appear. I really didn't want to have to get into a physical altercation with an elder just to get outside. But I sensed there was no way I was going to convince her of anything, including the fact that I actually *was* a celebrity.

I stared at her as the seconds ticked by—and then realized there was something else I could do. I took a deep breath, homed in on her, reached out with my invisible feathers . . . and then, very gently, used my telekinesis to move her to the side.

"*Hey!*" she screamed. "What are you doing?! What . . ."

I released her from my hold and bolted for the back door.

I heard her yelling after me, all kinds of colorful insults, but adrenaline was powering me forward now, screaming through my bloodstream and overwhelming everything else. I zeroed in on the door, on my goal, my *mission*, and blocked out whatever salty insults she was hurling my way.

I pushed open the door and landed outside in a small, fairly nondescript parking lot. I blinked rapidly, trying to get my eyes to adjust to the too-bright midday sun.

Finally, I saw Pippa. She was facing off against Kat, both of them glaring at each other and breathing heavily.

And then I saw that Pippa was bleeding.

It looked like a deep cut on her forearm, which she was clutching to her chest like a wounded animal.

"Aveda! She bit me!" Pippa jerked her head at Kat.

"Kat . . . ?" I approached both of them carefully, arms outstretched as if to say I meant no harm. "What's going on?"

"I'm just . . . so . . . *hungry*!" Kat growled, her gaze still laser-focused on Pippa. "No matter how much I eat, I just want *more*. The mouse got away—"

"You were going to eat *the mouse*?" I asked. "Um. I really don't think that's necessary. I can simply order you more chashu—let's go back instead, hmm? If I'm not banned from this restaurant now, that is . . ."

"No!" Kat roared. "I . . . I don't want that. I need life! I need *blood*!"

And with that, she lunged for Pippa again.

Pippa stumbled backward, screaming, and I closed the last bit of distance between me and them, throwing myself in front of Kat.

"Kat." I clamped my hands on her shoulders and tried to meet her eyes. "Come on, what are you doing? You don't want to, um . . . eat Pippa!"

"Get out of my way!" she snarled, struggling in my grip.

Her eyes finally met mine and they looked positively feral. Like she didn't even know where she was, she only thirsted for blood . . .

Oh. *Shit*.

And just as I was finally putting those pieces together, her eyes flashed red.

I released her shoulders and scrambled backward, keeping my body between her and Pippa.

"I think all of the weird stuff happening on the show has finally gotten to you," I said, holding my hands out, trying to soothe her. "But this is happening to other people, too— you're not alone, Kat. We can help you. I need you to calm down and . . . and . . ." I shook my head, frustration raging through me.

And *what*? I knew how to deal with demons. Vampires

were a whole other fucking story. Should I offer to find her another mouse?

Kat looked like she was about to lunge for us again, but then she froze in place, her wild eyes scanning me up and down. She kept that stance for a moment more, as if suspended mid-air. Then she threw her head back and screamed—right before her body exploded into a flock of bats that took off into the sky.

My jaw dropped, my gaze glued to the ominous circle of bats that was now winging its way around the incongruously bright LA sun.

"I . . ." I turned to face Pippa, tearing my eyes away from the Kat bats. "I actually have no idea what to say or think right now, but . . ."

Pippa met my eyes, her expression haunted. The wound on her arm was still bleeding, her previously white shirt smeared with crimson. And her golden brown skin had a sickly pallor, dark circles hollowing her eyes.

"Aveda," she whispered, "I don't feel so good."

"Don't worry, Pippa," I said, even as a sinking sensation took hold in my gut. "That is a nasty-looking wound, but I'm sure we can get it checked out and patched up, nothing to worry about—"

Before I could get any further, her face crumpled in agony and she fell to her knees screaming, clutching her arm even more tightly against her.

"Pippa!" I screamed, the most horrible feeling of helplessness overtaking my entire being.

And before I could do anything else, her body dissolved into a flock of bats, their beating wings creating the most awful cacophony of noise as they flew after Kat into the fiery golden sun.

Chapter twenty-four

THINGS GOT HAZY after that, as if time slowed way down—crushed beneath the merciless heat of late afternoon in LA. I tried with all my might to grab on to the bats with telekinesis. But it felt like I was haphazardly flinging my invisible feathers into the sky, and the mere act of doing so exhausted me every time—until I finally had to give up. I didn't understand. I'd moved the Auntie with no trouble at all; but trying to grab on to the bats felt like that day at the beach, when I'd struggled to tow Mercedes to safety.

What the fuck was going on with my telekinesis? Maybe Scott was right. No way I'd be able to handle a Zacasta-esque depowering mission.

I couldn't bring myself to simply give up, so I actually tried to chase the dual flock of bats through Little Tokyo, the beating of their wings roaring in my ears. But they eventually faded into the distance, and I'm not sure what my plan was going to be had I caught up to them, since my telekinesis was apparently on the fritz.

In that moment, I felt like I had to try *something*—running after the bats like a fool was the only action I could take, the only path I could follow. I couldn't just stand there, screaming and helpless, panic threatening to crush the air from my lungs.

Aveda Jupiter never gives up. But sometimes that means she doggedly pursues things that are actually impossible, refusing to admit defeat until she's run full throttle for miles and at last collapses into a sweaty pile of frustrated tears. Which was exactly what happened.

I managed to pick myself up post-collapse, but I had no idea where I was. The bustling warmth of Little Tokyo had given way to cold steel and dull gray buildings, and I had to do something I'd never actually done before: call an Uber. Well, to be more precise—I called Evie, and she told me *how* to call an Uber.

I was trundled back to the Beverly Hills Hotel in a sensible four-door Mazda sedan, shrinking into the back seat and trying not to think about how I'd managed to completely lose Pippa.

Evie pulled me into a tight hug as soon as I arrived back at our suite. Afternoon had given way to evening, that maze of taillights once again illuminating the hotel's huge windows. My heart sank even further when I realized Scott wasn't there. Maybe he'd gone home—or somewhere else entirely. Maybe he was never coming back.

"Tell me what happened from the beginning," Evie urged, leading me over to the banana-leaf couch. "You were all garbled on the phone."

I took a deep breath, tried to get my thoughts in order, and let them spill out in a halting mess.

"So I guess Kat is a vampire now," I said, wrapping up my tale. "And I guess she also bit Pippa and now Pippa's a vampire too and . . . and . . . *why* did she go after Pippa, though? I should have been there to protect her. I should have been faster about shoving that Auntie out of the way, or told Pippa not to go after Kat, or . . . or . . ."

"Annie." Evie patted my arm, her voice very gentle. "Please don't get trapped in the 'what ifs.' Pippa reacted on instinct, Kat may not be in control of herself, and as for the Auntie—*nothing* was gonna move her out of the way and you didn't want to fight an old lady. I'm not seeing anything in this situation that you could have actually done differently."

"My telekinesis could've worked," I mumbled, slumping

back against the couch. "And I'm sorry I didn't get you your mochi."

"That's . . . okay?" she said, sounding confused.

My eyes drifted closed and every spare bit of energy seemed to leach from my body in an instant. Why was I so tired? The exhaustion that kept overtaking me these past few days was overwhelming, a cloud descending over me at the most inopportune of moments. I needed to toughen up and be the formidable Aveda Jupiter I knew I could be.

And that started with finding Pippa.

"Let's FaceTime Bea," I said, squaring my shoulders and trying to recapture some of my mojo. "I'd like her insights on this."

"You sure?" Evie asked, pulling her phone out and tapping on the screen. "You don't want to rest before we break this down?"

"Pippa's *missing*, Evie," I spat out. "We don't have the luxury of rest."

She looked like she wanted to say something else, but just nodded and refocused on the phone screen as Bea's face appeared.

"Hey, olds!" she chirped. "Where's Pippa? Can y'all really not figure out the whole Batcave situation without her? 'Cause the view I'm currently getting is much more limited . . ." She leaned in, puzzling over the closely cropped screen we were presenting her with, just me and Evie instead of the whole suite.

"Actually, that's what we want to discuss with you, Bea— er, Pippa's absence. Not us being old."

"I can do both," Bea said. "Hit me."

I related the whole story again, my heart twisting when I reached the part about Pippa turning into bats and disappearing into the sky.

"All right, hold up," Bea said, raising her hands. "The theory we were batting around last time we talked involved the Otherworld demons using some kind of emotional energy to, like, activate vampirism in humans."

"And we speculated that said energy was feelings of failure, hopelessness," I said, nodding. "Which seems to line up with what Kat's been feeling—she's worked *so* hard for her dreams. But I remember her telling me her dreams don't feel good right now—she was saying that even before she was fired. The entertainment industry racism, Clint's shenanigans, and this feeling like she had to show up and be endlessly resilient and unbreakable no matter what—it was all getting her down."

"And now she feels like her career is over before it can even begin," Evie chimed in.

"Right, that all makes sense," Bea said. "But now Aveda has witnessed, with her own eyes, one of these Otherworld-created vamps making an all-new vamp through a more traditional method." She leaned into the camera until she was one big eyeball, ringed with heavy violet eyeliner. "Kat *bit* Pippa. She totally turned her!"

"We don't know that yet for certain," Evie said, holding up a hand. "We're still not sure what happened to Pippa."

"Except that she turned into bats," Bea retorted.

"Wait a second, we *have* witnessed that before!" I cried. "The turning-by-biting thing. Stan bit Kat in one of those first scenes we watched them shoot, remember? Maybe that's when Kat became, uh, infected with vampirism!"

"We're not one hundred percent certain on how Stan and Clint were actually turned," Bea mused, leaning back in her seat. "They could have been bitten as well. But say they weren't—say they got it the way we first theorized, via Otherworld demons manipulating emotional energy. But then Stan bites Kat and turns her, too, meaning Otherworld-created vampires can—"

"Make *new* vampires," I growled, closing my eyes. "This is all very, very bad."

"Possible vamp swarm on your hands," Bea said, nodding thoughtfully. "Wow. I wish I was there for this."

"Me too," I said, too tired to make my voice sound anything less than plaintive. "You know—"

THWACK!

I was interrupted by something heavy smacking against the window—it sounded like a bunch of wet towels flung at the glass with maximum force. The three of us all jumped.

"What the hell!" I growled, leaping to my feet.

"Ugh, looks like we gotta go, Bea!" Evie cried, tapping on the phone screen.

THWACK THWACK THWAAAAACK!!!

Adrenaline pumping, I zipped across the room to the window, just in time to see a massive black blur crash into the glass once more.

I leaped back instinctively, even though the blur didn't seem to be making the slightest dent or crack in the glass. Those fancy hotel windows were holding *tight*. Very tentatively, I moved just a little bit closer, narrowing my eyes as I tried to home in on what the thing was . . .

"Annie!" Evie hissed. "Don't get too close, it might—"

THWAAAAACK!

I jumped back again, but tried to keep my gaze locked on this thing. Slowly, my eyes started to make out shapes . . . a series of shapes . . . this blur was actually made out of a bunch of tinier blurs, all of them coming together to swing themselves at the window like a wrecking ball, the shadowy mass obscuring the glittering maze of taillights that was our usual nighttime view.

"Bats," I breathed out in wonder. "Of course. They're *bats*. We can't seem to get away from the fucking things."

The blur paused, hanging in mid-air—had it heard me?

"Hey!" I said, projecting my voice as loudly as I could. I felt ridiculous, trying to communicate with a flock of bats that was possibly a vampire through the glass of the window.

Then again, when was my job *not* ridiculous? Almost never.

"Hey," I called out again. "Hello. Are you trying to get in?"

The blur bobbed up and down frantically—almost like it was nodding?

"And is your purpose communication? Like, if I open this window you won't swarm in here and try to kill us?"

The blur bobbed up and down even more frantically. I tilted my head at it, trying to figure out what was going on. I swore I could recognize it's, um . . . body language? Was that even the right term?

"Pippa?" I said, voicing the hunch tickling the back of my mind. "Is that you?"

I was expecting another exuberant bat-nod, but this time, the tinier blurs broke apart and flew in an excited circle, as if trying to convey their "yes" as dramatically as possible.

"Okay," I said. "That's either Pippa or a bunch of bats who have figured out how to perfectly mimic her personality. I'm letting them in."

Evie nodded and crossed the room to stand behind me, getting into one of her firestarter formations—feet planted and hands raised, in case she needed to incinerate something.

I drew in a deep breath and reached for the window latch. Was I about to invite a murderous swarm of vampire bats directly into our current living space? Before I could think too hard on that, I released the latch and threw the window open. The over-eager bats wasted no time at all, swooping in with vigor, the beating of their wings sounding almost . . . joyful.

I stepped out of the way of the swarm, moving toward Evie. Her mouth was agape, her eyes following the bats' every move. They flew in a circle, drawing themselves closer and closer together until they were a single blur yet again—a storm cloud convening right over the banana-leaf couch.

The storm cloud of bats drew in on itself, constricting into a tight sphere . . . then exploded into what could perhaps be best described as bat confetti. Tiny black bits everywhere. Evie screamed.

And then Pippa was in front of us, landing on the couch with a decisive *WHOOM*, doubled over and coughing until she wheezed.

"Pippa!" I cried out, rushing over to her. I threw my arms

around her and pulled her against me, even though she was still hacking up a lung.

"Hey, AJ," she managed, her voice hoarse. "Remember last time when I fell from the sky? I'm really working the whole dramatic entrance thing."

I hugged her even tighter, tears springing to my eyes. She'd undoubtedly been through an incredibly weird supernatural ordeal, yet was still managing to crack jokes. And she'd figured out how to get herself to us, despite being in a totally not-human form. I had to admire her bravery, her bravado, her determination to never give up.

Dare I say, it reminded me very much of a young Aveda Jupiter.

"Pippa," Evie said, her voice soft as she moved to sit next to us. "What happened? How did you get to us?"

"Whoa, okay!" Pippa exclaimed, waving her hands around expansively. I smiled, still happy to see that her essential Pippa-ness seemed to be intact. "So I'm assuming AJ told y'all about our meeting with Kat, me getting bitten, and turning into a bunch of bats."

"Yes," Evie nodded. "It sounded terrifying."

"It was," Pippa said, her grin widening. "But also, like, the coolest thing that's ever happened to me?"

"How exactly did Kat bite you?" I asked, stroking her back. I couldn't seem to stop patting her, as if convincing myself she was actually here and this wasn't yet another hallucinatory moment. "Because I was busy mentally wrestling with a very stubborn Auntie at that time."

"Well, you saw Kat go after the mouse," Pippa said, her eyes going to the ceiling as she pulled up the memory. "I ran after her, and we got out to the parking lot. She kept trying to pounce on the mouse—like, I swear, she looked just like my mom's cat when he thinks he's got some kind of insect or rodent prey cornered—and I yelled her name, asked her what she was doing." She paused, pursing her lips. "I'm sorry, do you guys have any food?"

"I think I still have some crackers from when I was feeling

nauseous earlier," Evie said, rummaging around in her hoodie pocket.

"No, like . . . meat?" Pippa cocked a hopeful eyebrow.

"Let's order her an extra-rare room-service steak," I said, wondering if Pippa was sneaking longing looks at our tasty blood-filled necks. "With a side of steak."

"On it," Evie said, heading over to the rotary phone.

"Thanks, I'm *starving*," Pippa said. "So yeah, anyway, I yelled, and Kat turned around. Her eyes were all red and scary. And then she pounced on *me*. Started yelling all this stuff about how I was trying to take the mouse from her, how dare I! And then she sank her super sharp teeth into my forearm, and it turned into a blood spigot." Pippa rubbed her arm, wincing. I noticed it seemed to be mostly healed, just a faint pair of puncture marks marring the otherwise smooth skin.

"How did you get her off of you?" I prompted. "Because she seemed to have stopped with the biting thing once I got out there."

"I shoved her really hard," Pippa said. "It was weird, I had a sudden burst of, like, super strength? Maybe that's part of my new vampire powers." She grinned to herself. "But immediately after that, I felt like I was dying. My heart was literally on fire, about to consume the rest of my body. And the sun was like tiny knives, piercing my skin."

"Did you know you were about to turn into a swarm of bats?" I said.

"Not at all," Pippa said, her expression turning thoughtful. "It was more like . . . this sudden compulsion. Right after Kat turned into the bats, I felt like my body was drawing in on itself—constricting, getting smaller. I also felt this undeniable draw to all the bats in the sky. And then, just like that, I *was* in the sky." She shook her head in wonder.

"I tried to chase you," I said, struck once again by how useless I'd been. "Obviously it didn't work. But . . . I tried."

"I could sense you down there, AJ," Pippa said, giving me a warm smile. "But we flew for what felt like fucking forever.

I felt that compulsion again—that need to follow the other bats. Who I guess were Kat."

"And where did you end up?" Evie asked.

"The Pinnacle lot!" Pippa exclaimed. "The Kat bats flew over the lot—a very lovely aerial view, by the way—and then swooped low to the ground. I still felt compelled to follow, but little pieces of . . . I don't know what you'd call it? My actual consciousness? My own free will? Anyway, that started to pull me in the *opposite* direction. Even though I was absolutely starving and could pretty much only think of that and how much I wanted to follow Kat . . . another thought got in there. And it was telling me that I simply had to find Aveda Jupiter. I broke away, and I flew here."

Pippa's story was punctuated by a knock on the door.

"That must be the room service," Evie said, getting to her feet.

A few moments later, she returned with a room service cart topped by a whole mess of bloody meat.

"Oh my god, *thank you*!" Pippa gasped.

We were silent as she dove into her meal, her eyes rolling back in her head as she downed bite after bite of rare steak.

"Gaaaaaah," she moaned. "This *hunger* . . . I can't seem to get rid of it. This is really hitting the spot."

"Where was Kat going?" I asked, frustration clawing at my insides. "Why the Pinnacle lot? Was she trying to exact vengeance on the people who fired her?"

We sat there in silence as Pippa eagerly downed the rest of her steak.

"I say we all sleep on it," Evie finally said. "Pippa's back with us and safe. And the more we try to work this out, the more questions we seem to come up against. Looking at this with fresh brains might give us more insight."

"How can you even think of sleep at a time like this?" I grumbled, rubbing my eyes. White lights danced in front of my pupils, and I blinked to get rid of them. "There's plenty we can do. We can scour Pippa's vampire books for clues, or do more research on everyone involved with the show, or try to track down this elusive showrunner, or sneak onto the Pinnacle lot in the dead of night—"

"Annie." Evie gave me a look. "No. All of this stuff is just so you can feel like you're doing something. We'll be much more effective *with sleep*."

"Agree," Pippa said, leaping to her feet and going into a monster stretch. "I am *wiped*. Flying all over the city for hours on end really takes it out of you. I can re-read some of my vampire books before bed, Aveda, although I can't guarantee I won't just get swept up in the story. Or skip to the sex scenes." She skipped off to her bedroom, happy as a clam.

I studied Evie. Her eyes were blinking rapidly, her shoulders were slumped, and even her curls looked droopy. She clearly needed sleep too.

I could think of nothing I'd rather do less. Especially since my bedroom would be cold and empty, no Scott in sight. Just me and my tangle of thoughts and my need to *do* something.

"Good night, Annie," Evie murmured, hauling herself off the couch.

I gave her a slight nod, even as everything in me screamed to call after her, to tell her there was no way I could sleep right now, to convince her to join me in finding something—*anything*—to do.

My gaze skittered to my phone and I picked it up, desperately scrolling through my messages, my contacts. What action could I take at the moment? Maybe something *not* related to the investigation? I certainly still had plenty of spinning plates.

I finally landed on my mother's message thread, and a little spark of an idea pinged in my brain.

I tapped my mother's contact info on the screen before I had time to overthink it.

"Anne?" she said, her voice incredulous. "Why are you calling so late? Is there an emergency?"

"I'm sending you on a cruise!" I blurted out, forcing myself not to retort that it wasn't *that* late. "You and Dad. It's going to be so beautiful, so romantic—"

"Anne." I could practically hear my mother's disapproving headshake over the phone. "What nonsense are you talking? We cannot go on a cruise right now."

"Because you're getting a divorce?!" I exploded, unable to hold back. "Mom, I figured it out, you can—"

"Aiyah! My goodness." My mother let out a weary sigh that seemed to go on forever. "Where on earth did you get that idea?"

"You've been packing all your stuff in separate containers," I said insistently. "And you seem really mad at him all the time and—"

"We're not getting a divorce," my mother interrupted, her tone firm. "We're . . ." She hesitated, and I could practically hear everything contained in her silence. The calculations, the trying to figure out what my reaction would be. I waited, my heart thrumming loudly in my chest. I wondered if she could hear *that*.

"We are moving," my mother finally said. "This house, too big for us. I found a better place nearby, right next to the golf course. Your father loves it, too. And moving is very stressful, we have so many things to go through. Easier to categorize our separate things *separately*—I have a system, but it is a lot of work. If I seem irritable, that is why."

"Then . . ." My forehead crinkled as I tried to work it out. "Why didn't you just *tell* me that?"

"Because you do not like change," my mother said simply. "You have always been that way, going back to when you were a child and Evie accidentally ruined your favorite Barbie by trying to make it 'swim' in the toilet. We got you a new one, but you never liked it as much—you missed the first Barbie, and you swore you could tell the difference."

"Right," I murmured. I *had* been able to tell the difference. My original Barbie had a silky mane of raven hair, like mine. New Barbie had been blonde, because blonde Barbies were just way easier to find.

"And this is the house you grew up in, so us leaving it is a pretty big change," Mom continued. "I was trying to soften the news. First I sent you those pictures of oranges, because you like it so much when I send you fruit. I thought you would find the images comforting. When you protested that, I started sending you the photos of our things in the Container Store boxes. I thought maybe I could gradually break the news, and then it would hurt you less." She paused—and possibly for the first time ever in my life, I heard my mother's voice soften ever so slightly. "I see that I was wrong."

"N-no," I managed, trying to understand everything that had just come out of her mouth. "That's . . . that's very caring, Mom."

"You do not need to sound so surprised," she huffed. "I do care about you, Anne. Very much."

I didn't know what to say. I knew my mother loved me, even if she'd never been the best at showing it. Now she was really trying to show it—in her own way.

"Anne," my mother said slowly, "if your father and I were having a problem, I would not expect you to solve it. That is our job, mmm?"

"Sure," I said, still in a daze. "But . . . I guess I don't know how to look at a problem and *not* want to solve it? What else would I do? Just ignore you and not help at all?"

"No, no," my mother said, sounding impatient. "But you do not always 'help' by solving. Sometimes, it is enough to listen to the person. To be there for them. To let them know you are supportive. If you try to solve *everyone's* problems . . ." She clicked her tongue. "Well. You will run out of energy very quickly—turning exhausted, burned out, running on empty. And then you cannot even fix your own problems. You will be useless."

"This is such an Asian Mom pep talk," I muttered.

"You are always there for your friends, Anne," my mother continued. "This I know. I am sure they would like to be there for you now, when you are struggling."

"What? I'm not 'struggling,' I'm . . ."

"I know you," my mother insisted. "Whether you like it or not."

We fell into silence, neither of us willing to give an inch. Finally, my mother let out another long sigh. When she spoke again, her voice sounded more gentle than I'd ever heard it.

"When we are done with this move, Anne, maybe you and I should go on a cruise. A cruise sounds nice. But I *do* see your father every day. And I see you much less."

"O-oh!" I managed, surprised. "Well. Okay, Mom. Maybe we could do that, yeah."

"And if you have any problems you need someone to listen to . . . I know I am not Evie. I am not Scott. But I *can* listen, Anne."

"I . . ." I shook my head, unsure what to do with this version of my mother. She sounded so . . . open. Sincere. She really was trying to show me she cared, even if she didn't have the right words. She wanted me to know she was there for me, always.

That felt so *different* from the way our relationship had been for the majority of my life. Gratitude rushed through me, taking me away from all my worries for just a moment.

"Thank you, Mom," I finally said. "That means a lot to me. You . . . you've changed. These past few years."

"No need to get sentimental," she sniffed. "And you know, Anne, change is not always a bad thing."

And with that, she hung up. Before things could get too "sentimental."

I stared at the phone in my hand, my mind a whirl. There were still so many things I *did* have to solve, and I couldn't figure out where to start and I was still so *tired* . . .

I drew in a long, shuddering breath, letting that exhaustion sink into my bones. And finally acknowledging that no, it wasn't going away.

I couldn't just *will* myself to not be tired anymore. To not feel overwhelmed, helpless, trying so hard but accomplishing fucking nothing . . .

My mother was right. I *was* struggling. I'd just been too fucking stubborn to admit it.

Before I could think too hard about it, I tapped the phone screen to call the person I desperately needed to see.

"It's me," I babbled as soon as the voicemail picked up. "I . . . I'm sorry. I need you. Please come."

CHAPTER TWENTY-FIVE

AFTER I'D MADE my phone call, I collapsed on the couch. The exhaustion burrowed even deeper into my bones, making my entire body feel like it was suspended in molasses, heavy and slow and impossible to crawl through. Getting to the bedroom suddenly seemed like the most arduous task in the world, and before I knew it, my eyes were drifting closed.

Thankfully I didn't have any more dreams or visions or fantasies involving the images I couldn't seem to get out of my mind these days. Scott and Mercedes as the perfect California blonde couple. Sexy threesomes involving possible vampires. And of course, me all alone in my big, drafty Victorian. My body must have been too tired to dream.

When I stirred awake, the suite had fallen into darkness. It was late at night, most of the taillights had found their way home, and only a few cars still dotted the cityscape outside the window.

I also felt warm, cradled, surprisingly peaceful . . . and then I realized it was because a very familiar body was wrapped around mine.

"Scott," I murmured, blinking rapidly as my eyes adjusted to the darkness.

He'd pretzeled himself around me on the banana-leaf couch, one arm slung over my waist to pull me tightly against his hard wall of chest. My head was tucked into that perfect spot between his chin and shoulder, and he'd tangled his legs with mine so we'd both fit on the somewhat narrow surface area. I closed my eyes and breathed him in, his soothing summertime scent. And I let myself feel comforted.

No matter what happened with us, he would always be *home* to me.

"Hey," he whispered against my hair.

"Y-you came," I sighed. "I'm sorry, I know things are weird right now and we're technically fighting and you maybe don't want to see me at all, but . . ." My voice cracked and I tried to tamp down on the tears that were gathering in my eyes. "I really, really needed you. We've still got this weird vampire problem—which, by the way, has possibly just gotten even weirder. And Shasta is probably still after Evie's baby, the show about my life is going to be a whitewashed mess, I'm tired all the time for no reason, my telekinesis is on the fritz, Evie is about to go on a forever sabbatical, and I almost lost Pippa. And . . . and . . . *Lucy and Bea aren't moving back home*." The sobs rose up, and this time there was no stopping them. My words clogged in my throat, and I gasped for breath. I'd never felt so *useless*.

And before I knew what was happening, I was fully bawling. Heaving and gasping into his chest, soaking the soft cotton of his t-shirt. Every bit of helplessness and hopelessness, every worry of the last few days poured out of me in wild, uncontrollable tears.

He drew me closer, his hands stroking down my back, murmuring soothing nonsense words into my hair.

"Annie," he finally said, as my sobs quieted. "Of course I came. No matter what happens between us, I'll always be here when you need me—*always*. I promise."

"God, why are you so *good*?!" I snuffled. "And how did I get things so wrong? I love you more than anything in the world, you're my favorite person of all time—well, tied with—"

"Evie," he said, a hint of amusement threading through his voice. "I know."

"—but somehow I managed to convince you that you aren't enough for me?" I barreled on. "How did I even do that?

I apparently made you think the opposite of what I actually think—what I feel! I . . ." I took a deep breath, trying to get rid of the last of my tears. "I feel like *I'm* the one who's not enough, Scott. Or that I'm somehow both not enough *and* too much for you. I get so wrapped up in everything, all of these problems I think I have to solve, and then I forget things like our date. But then I'm also pushing you into things you maybe don't want, and I . . ." A sob rose in my throat again. I blinked back tears, determined to soldier on. "I just love you so much. And I *need* you so much. You're the only person who can calm me down, who can soothe me and make me feel like things are going to be okay—you did that on our wedding day, for god's sake, when I got scared and wanted to run away. You . . . you make the world make sense to me."

I broke off and set my sobs free again, burying my face in his shirt. He let me cry, stroking my back and smoothing my hair. Absorbing my messy stew of feelings into those gentle hands until my sobs devolved into sad little hiccups.

"Sweetheart," he finally murmured. "How do you not realize that you do the same thing for me?"

"What do you mean?"

"I mean my world doesn't make sense without you in it," he said. "And you keep talking about how I never put myself first, how my concern is always for others . . . but you do the same thing. That's what you've been doing this whole time, trying to make sure this whole job thing was what I needed it to be. And don't you remember the *other* drama from our wedding day? You stood up for me like no one ever has. You protected me, just like you did when the other kids tried to mess with me in middle school. And you made me realize I wasn't destined to become my father."

"You could never," I whispered into his soaked t-shirt.

"I love how *much* you are," he said. "You are so fucking fierce, you always show up for the people you love, and you throw yourself into protecting them with everything you have. But lately, I've been worried that you're giving so much, there's nothing left for you. I don't want you to feel like you have to be less. But I'm also terrified that if you keep going this hard . . . you won't be here anymore."

His voice wobbled, and his jaw clenched. My heart felt like it was simultaneously bursting and caving in on itself.

"I . . . I have been doing that," I said, my voice halting. Admitting it out loud made my chest feel like an overinflated balloon finally releasing all of its helium. "I started having panic attacks, and I didn't even realize what they were—Evie had to explain it to me. I have this burning need to fix everything. To save everyone. To complete all my missions before I run out of time on this planet. And I've always been that way, but lately it's been worse, I feel all of that *so much*. Ever since . . ." I trailed off, my eyes filling with tears again.

"Ever since Morgan," Scott said, his voice so tender that my tears spilled over. "You haven't really talked about it, but I know how you feel. You thought you were going to lose Evie. You thought she'd given up, that she'd lost all hope—"

"And I had to give it back to her," I finished. "I *had* to. She was so fucking defeated, so convinced she was *worthless*, she almost gave Shasta her baby. Her face . . ." I pressed my lips together, unable to go on. Evie's face in that moment had haunted me for months now.

"You've been extra protective of her since then," Scott said, brushing his lips against my hair. "You're always making sure food magically appears when she's hungry, or that she gets that nap when she needs it. And she's been squirrely lately, you know? She doesn't always make it easy for you. Some days it kinda seems like she wants to toss the superheroing to the side and escape to . . . well, anywhere else."

"Y-you've noticed that?" I asked, scraping a hand over my teary eyes.

"I notice a lot about other people," he said with a chuckle. "I have a harder time noticing things about myself." He paused, his hand rhythmically stroking down my shoulder. I closed my eyes, reveling in his soothing touch. "You were right about me, Annie. I do think about other people's needs before I think of my own. And sometimes that means I push my own dreams or things I want to the side. But . . ." He brushed a light kiss against my temple, and I felt his lips curve into a half-smile. "Remember when I decided to go back to school? When you helped me realize I didn't have to put myself in a box, I could make my future into whatever I wanted it to be?"

"Yes," I whispered.

"I never would have even asked myself those questions if it wasn't for you," he said. "That was the first time I *really* made myself think about what I wanted my future to look like. What my dreams could be. And I decided I wanted to feel like whatever I was doing, it was making people's lives better. Especially kids—kids like me, who maybe aren't growing up in the best of circumstances. I always want the kids in my classes to know at least one person cares about them."

An image of him talking to that shyest kid in class, the one too scared to go into the waves, popped into my head and my heart fluttered.

"Forging my own path in that, expanding the surf clinic— I do want to spend more time doing all that stuff," he said. "And when we fought last night, you reminded me of that."

"You light up when you work with those kids," I said. "I may not observe people as keenly as you do, but I see it every time."

"There's another thing I remembered," he said, his voice softening. "Something else I decided I wanted in my life all those years ago."

I lifted my head from his chest and turned my face up to look at him. I could not fathom why, but my heart was beating very fast. "Which was?"

"You." A shy sort of smile spread across his face. "You were my very first dream."

"Well, that came true, didn't it?" I said, a flush creeping up the back of my neck.

"It did," he agreed, chuckling. "But I thought a lot about

that after our fight last night. And I just think . . ." He pulled me even closer, our noses nearly touching. "Our dreams don't have to be so separate, you know? You and I have found so many dreams together."

"But you said our dreams weren't the same!" I protested, remembering his harsh words the night before. "That I didn't know how to . . . to comprehend any dreams that weren't exactly like my own."

"They might not be *exactly* the same," he said, laughing again. "I, for instance, like to work on any ambitions at a slower and more meandering pace than you do. But we are also very different people who just . . . go together. We fit." He gave me a squeeze to emphasize the point. "Why can't our dreams co-mingle in the same way?"

"Co-mingling . . . sounds a little sexy," I said, arching an eyebrow. "I like it. And I think it starts with us doing our best to be more open with each other." I bit my lip and buried my face in his chest again. "I'm sorry I didn't tell you about Mercedes. I should have. I just thought, you were having such an amazing experience and maybe she's changed—"

"I don't care if she's changed," he said, a rare bit of steel creeping into his voice. "She was racist, went out of her way to make you feel small, and she hurt you. And I know all of that must be hard for you to talk about. I'm sorry for failing to notice that she's *still* hurting you. I think . . ." He stroked my hair, that rhythmic motion soothing me once more. "Maybe I'm a little too open with complete strangers to begin with—"

"You always want to see the good in everyone," I murmured. "I love that about you."

"I think I confided in her because I felt like you were drifting away from me," he said. "And I did believe she was your old friend, so I thought she could help me . . ." He shook his head. "Anyway. I'm sorry, too. But Annie, please believe this: in my own meandering ambition kind of way, I do want to be part of Team Tanaka/Jupiter whenever I can. I'm going to try to focus on the other stuff I want to do more seriously, but I can't imagine the team not being part of my life. So please let me help. Let me be there for you. I *want* to be there for you—in every way I possibly can."

I turned my face up to his again, meeting his earnest gaze. Those brilliant blue eyes got me every time. We could be a thousand years old, having spent several lifetimes together, and I'd still get lost in them.

"Thank you," I whispered fervently. "Um. Well, maybe you can help me figure out what to do next, then? About this whole vampire . . . bats . . . Pippa situation?"

He brushed my hair off my forehead, his eyes studying me in that way where it just felt like he could see everything. All my messy thoughts and feelings and secret vulnerabilities. And I was happy to realize that I was back to loving it. I adored how well he knew me—even the parts I considered jagged and broken.

"How about a bath?" he finally said.

I pulled back from him, my face screwing into a look of total confusion. "Excuse me, what?"

"This is awkward," he said, pulling a look of faux concern. "You're this big, famous superheroine, this seems like something you should know. Okay, so you fill a tub with water, usually really hot water—"

"Oh my god, shut up!" I cried, thwacking him on the arm. Suddenly we were back at our favorite middle-school lunch table, him needling me until I relented and paid attention to him.

I opened my mouth to protest the bath—this was, after all, not exactly the guidance I'd been looking for—then closed it. My aching muscles perked up immediately at the idea of comforting heat sinking into my limbs and making me feel whole again. Physically, at least. And if I was going to face off against a bunch of actual vampires, I needed to be in the best possible shape.

"Okay," I whispered, curling against him again.

He gave me a last squeeze, then disentangled our limbs, eased himself off the couch, and extended a hand.

My instinct was, of course, to tell him I didn't need any help taking a freaking bath, but he was looking at me so earnestly and openly . . . and hadn't I just said our dreams could co-mingle? Maybe that meant admitting I was totally exhausted and accepting help regarding something as mundane as a bath once in a while.

So I took his hand and allowed him to lead me into our bedroom, and then the connecting bathroom. All of the bedrooms in this massive suite had their own palatial bathrooms—ours featured pink and black tile, delicate gold fixtures, and that ubiquitous banana-leaf wallpaper. And right in the middle of the room, a gigantic bathtub made for relaxing. My bones practically quivered with anticipation at the sight of it.

Scott dropped my hand and leaned over the bathtub fixtures, turning the knobs and then testing the water as it flowed from the faucet.

"Water's nice," he said. "Get undressed—I'll finish getting this ready."

He started adding various salts and other accoutrements from the countertop next to the tub, releasing soft floral scents into the air. I peeled my clothes off slowly, little shivers of pleasure coursing through me as the steamy air brushed my skin.

"There we go," Scott said, swishing the water around. He extended a hand. "Here, get in. It should feel *really* good."

I took his hand and climbed into the tub, sinking slowly into the water. The warmth enveloped me immediately, permeating my skin, my blood, my bones. And the soft scents of all the stuff he'd thrown in the water—lavender and gardenia, sharpened by clean notes of mint—floated through the air, wrapping me in a cocoon. I let out a long, pent-up sigh, my worries dissipating the tiniest bit.

"And the finishing touch . . ." Scott murmured. He closed his eyes, holding a loosely clenched fist in front of him. When he uncurled his fingers, a small assortment of brightly colored flowers sat in his palm. He scattered them in the water, then nodded slightly, looking satisfied. "New spell," he said. "Not really useful for anything but decoration, but now your bath is fit for a queen. As it should be."

He met my eyes and grinned. "I'll leave you to it. Do you have enough energy to yell if you need something, or should I find you a bell?"

I studied him, so many emotions sweeping through me. God, I loved this man. He'd come back when I needed him, he'd showed up, he'd done *actual magic* to create the perfect relaxing bath for me . . . and now he was just going to leave? I couldn't put any of what I was feeling into actual words—it was like gratitude and sudden calm and the biggest love all squished into one messy ball. But I could at least convey my most urgent thought.

"Don't go," I blurted out. He raised a quizzical eyebrow. "Stay here with me," I babbled. "Join me in, um . . . here." I gestured to the massive bathtub. "There's plenty of room."

His lips curved into a sly grin. "I thought you were tired . . . ?"

"I didn't say we were doing . . . that," I said, my face flushing. "I just think it would relax me even more if you got in, too."

His grin widened—he wasn't buying that for a second. I clamped my mouth shut so I wouldn't keep babbling and watched as he slid his shirt over his head and unzipped his pants.

I leaned back in the tub, letting the warmth sink into my bones even more. And not even trying to hide the fact that I was openly ogling all that lean, golden muscle.

"You feel relaxed yet?" he said, stretching and posing in an equally shameless way.

"Very," I managed. "Get in."

He eased himself into the tub and settled in behind me, pulling my back against his chest and nuzzling my neck. Now I felt even warmer, the pleasure of his arms around me and his skin against mine making my heart melt. I sighed again, and tears sprang to my eyes. I couldn't seem to stop crying—

but this time, there was no frustration, no helplessness. Just the sweet sensation of being cradled, held close, taken care of.

Letting people take care of me went against every instinct I had. But Scott always managed to do it anyway.

And that made me want to open myself fully to him. To say all the things I'd been thinking the last few days. To send all of that into those hands that always made me feel so soothed.

"Scott, there's something else—another reason I've been feeling so . . . like I have to go so hard and do everything. Fix everything."

"What's that?" he asked, dropping a kiss on my shoulder.

"I'm scared," I blurted out.

He stilled against me, then went back to nuzzling my neck. "Okay," he murmured. "Why?"

I closed my eyes, savoring this closeness with him. I felt so *safe*.

"I had this vision," I began, my voice soft and hesitant. "Something that pops into my head and won't go away, no matter how hard I try. It's . . . it's me. All alone in Tanaka/Jupiter HQ. That big, drafty Victorian. Wondering how my life that I thought was so perfect changed so fast, and how all the people I love are so far away."

"Where are they?" Scott asked. "Where am I? Where's Evie?"

"Evie has moved beyond the superheroing life, and she and Nate are off in some remote cabin with their baby—finally out of the way of danger and able to actually enjoy their lives and their hard-won family," I said. "And you're . . . ." My voice caught, but I made myself finish. "You've moved down here, to LA, where you're thriving as you've never thrived before, working at the Youth Center and married to Mercedes and you have two-point-five absolutely gorgeous, extremely 'All-American' blonde children."

"I'm sorry," Scott said. "But *what*—"

"Lucy and Bea have already moved out, so they're not

there either," I barreled on. "It's just me. Thinking about how I've failed at everything. I tried so hard to protect the world from evil. But the harder I fought, the bigger and more all-consuming that evil became, until it devoured everything in sight. And my dedication to this failed mission means I have completely alienated everyone around me and therefore have nothing except my own sad thoughts and a cold, empty home that's way too big for me."

Tears pricked my eyes and I blinked hard, trying to keep them at bay. Trust me to hurricane all over something as benign as a bath.

"Annie," Scott said softly—and the tenderness in his voice made those tears slip down my cheeks. "I know there have been so many changes lately: Bea leaving, Lucy moving out. Evie and Nate are about to become parents. And my job offer . . . well, we still need to talk about what might happen with that. But sweetheart . . ." He brushed his lips against my hair. "None of what you're seeing is real. Why do you think any of that would happen?"

"I . . ." I blew out a long breath, trying to get my thoughts in order. Then I reached down deep inside of myself, uncovering the truths I was always so afraid to admit. "I've always had this belief that if I mess up, even a little bit, if I am anything less than absolutely perfect . . . everything I have will go away."

I flashed back to Mercedes, enthusing about "affirmative action" and how I was so lucky to be the chosen one. Never mind all the *work* I'd put into it. All the training, all the "eating right," all the flawless hair, makeup, and costuming. All the fights against demons that left me bruised and bloody, my muscles screaming out in pain as I plastered on yet another dazzling smile and smoothed my hair into its pristine ponytail—not a single thing out of place. And yet I absolutely knew, without a shadow of a doubt, if I presented myself as anything less than perfect, it could all be over for me in an instant. Bye-bye to the "exotic choice," bring back the All-American.

"I . . . I guess I thought I'd finally gotten things right," I bulldozed on. "I worked so much on myself, I learned how to be a team, I repaired my friendship with Evie—and we made it better than ever. And I finally told you how I felt— how I *feel*—about you, even though it scared me to death. When you gave me that plastic ruby ring on my birthday, I don't think I've ever been happier." I felt him smile against my hair. "It felt like we all created this perfect family—Bea and Evie even stopped fighting. And then, just like that, it all changed."

"Life doesn't stand still," Scott said. "That's not necessarily a bad thing."

"And logically, I know that," I said. "But right now, it *feels* bad. It feels like everything is about to go away. And if I can't even protect Pippa—like, keep her from being kidnapped into the Otherworld or save her from being turned into a vampire—how can I expect to save the world? Especially when the demon threat just keeps getting worse and worse. I know everyone wants me to *relax*—Evie wants me to do vacation stuff and you want me to enjoy the beach and take time off, but . . . how can I do that? At the end of the day, I *do* have to save the world. I can't just not show up. The consequences for that could be . . . well, catastrophic. Everything *could* go away."

I leaned back against him again, exhausted once more.

Great, so now the mere act of *talking* was enough to wear me out. Scott was silent again, his fingertips tracing idle patterns on my bare shoulder.

"Annie," he finally said. "First of all, can you honestly imagine Evie 'roughing it' out in some remote cabin? She'd come screaming back as soon as she realized there's no Postmates."

I laughed a little. That was true.

"And she'd never be able to 'enjoy' her life if you weren't in it," he continued. "You said it yourself—this is a family. It's changing, it's growing—but it's not as easy to destroy as you seem to think. It's important to all of us. And we all want to work together to eradicate the demon threat. You don't have to carry that weight all by yourself—we're all right there beside you. We'll show up *with* you."

I hastily scraped my hand over my eyes. "I guess sometimes I worry that I need the family a little *more* than everyone else does."

He laughed softly. "I love you. I love that that even occurs to you—this idea that your heart is too big, and you'll end up needing people too much." He slid his palms up my arms, my shoulders, and started massaging a particularly stubborn knot on the side of my neck. "I know that's why it's hard for you to open yourself up to other people—you're afraid you'll have to rely on them. But needing each other isn't always a bad thing." He lowered his head, his mouth grazing my ear. "I need you," he murmured. "More importantly: I *want* you. I've always wanted you. And I'll always be with you in that big, drafty Victorian, even if everyone else goes away."

"B-but . . ." I could not seem to keep any coherent thoughts in my brain, especially when his mouth was that close to my ear.

"But nothing," he said. "And you know everyone loves you for more than just your superheroing prowess, right? We all love *all* of you. Well. Granted, I get to see parts of you that no one else does . . ." His lips brushed my earlobe and my breathing went uneven. "Now, let me ask one last burning question," he continued. "Why does your vision involve me being married to *Mercedes*? Your imagination couldn't find anyone better?"

"You know I can be jealous," I huffed out, even as his teeth nipped lightly at the delicate flesh of my ear. "And you kept telling her all these intimate things and talking about your dreams with her and the two of you look so perfect and blonde together. And . . . and she's really good at surfing!"

"You're right," he said, his teeth continuing to explore my earlobe. "These are all definitely good reasons to ditch the woman I've loved for a decade and a half. The one I pined for. The one I cast an anti-love spell over myself to forget—

and even then, I could *never* forget her, or the way she makes me feel."

I closed my eyes, tiny shivers coursing through me. "When you put it like that, it *does* sound a little ridiculous."

"More than a little." He pulled away from my ear and I could feel him looking at me with those blue eyes that always saw so much. "Maybe I haven't shown you just how much I want you lately."

He slid an arm around me and took my chin in his hand, turning my head slightly so he could kiss me.

Even after all these years, there was no sensation that swept me away quite so much as the simple feeling of his lips on mine. I sighed against his mouth and leaned into it, his thumb stroking my jawline. His tongue swept my lips open, and I sighed again, the steam from the bath whispering against my skin.

He pulled back and gently moved my head so I was facing away from him again, then nipped at my neck—the exact spot where I'd hallucinated the vampire version of Scott biting me. A ragged moan escaped my throat.

"Mmm." He chuckled, his voice deep and husky. "Are you thinking about sexy vampire threesomes again? Because imagining you in that scenario makes me think about . . . well, quite *a lot*."

"I'm thinking about *you*."

I felt his lips curve against my skin.

He reached over and grabbed a bottle on the counter—some kind of lathery-looking body wash. He poured some into his palms, the bottle releasing a tropical scent that made me think of beaches and coconuts and the gentle music of the waves lapping against the sand. He massaged it into my shoulders, his strong hands making me melt all over again. The feeling of the soap against my bare skin—deliciously slippery, cradled in his palms . . . I couldn't help but moan again.

"*Now* are you relaxed?" he asked, massaging the tight spot that connected my shoulder and neck.

I pressed back against his chest, that hard wall of muscle. I'd been worried about so many things only moments ago, but now I couldn't seem to remember a single one of them. The only things that mattered were his hands, doing such incredible things to my shoulders. His mouth, grazing my earlobe again.

"I'm not sure," I breathed. "I think you need to go lower."

He chuckled again—and now he sounded positively wicked. There was nothing quite so hot as sweet, earnest, *good* Scott Cameron when he wanted to be just a little bit bad.

His hands slid slowly to my collarbone, and I made a needy little sound in the back of my throat, urging him to move faster. To touch me where I wanted.

"Oh no," he murmured. "We're going *slow*. I really need to show you how much I want you."

"I believe you," I squeaked out. "Just . . . *please* . . ."

"God," he said. "I love making you come undone."

He traced his fingers over my collarbone, light as a feather. Then, *finally*, he allowed them to continue on their journey, skating over my skin, slipping underwater, and finally landing right above my aching nipples.

"Please," I whispered. "Please touch me."

He obliged, his hands moving lower to cup my breasts. Even then, he went maddeningly slow, thumbs lazily stroking the delicate skin—everywhere except my nipples. I let out a frustrated cry and tried to shift position so I could get his hands right where I wanted them.

"Stop that," he reprimanded me, a slight smile in his voice. "Let me take care of you—*trust* me to take care of you."

I stilled against him and turned to give him a pouty look, biting my lower lip.

"Oh, that is not fair," he said. "You *know* what that does to me."

He finally gave me what I wanted, his fingertips moving to my nipples. He caressed one, then the other, his hands still irresistibly slippery with soap. The sensation was almost too much for me to bear. My head fell back against his chest, a guttural cry rising from deep in my throat. He kissed me again, his fingers still working their magic. His mouth was hot and hungry, and I had that overwhelming feeling of being *devoured*.

"Convinced yet?" he asked, pulling back from the kiss. His breathing was ragged, his eyes dark with desire.

I could not, for the life of me, remember what I was supposed to be convinced of—but I was pretty sure the answer was yes.

"Keep going," I managed, my own breathing heavy and uneven. "I think I'm getting closer. To, ah, being convinced."

He kept one hand on my breast, his thumb lazily stroking my nipple, and slid the other one lower still, his fingertips landing on that most sensitive spot between my legs.

My head lolled back against him as he stroked—light at first, a ghost of a touch. Then, ever so slowly, he applied more pressure, building to that most delectable of rhythms. I closed my eyes and let myself fall into every sensation—his hands on me, his muscles hard against my back, his teeth grazing my earlobe, then my neck . . . the steam of the bath all around us, making things hotter, wetter. I could not remember anything outside of this bath. I felt too *good*.

"Wait," I gasped, my voice high and breathy. "I want more. I want to feel you inside of me. *Everywhere*."

I turned in his arms before he could protest, water splashing around us.

"Annie," he groaned, his hands going to my waist as I positioned myself, straddling him. *"Fuck."*

His eyes were wild with wanting as he searched my face, his hand reaching up to brush wet strands of hair off my face.

"I love seeing you like this," he said, his voice getting that ultra-serious tone that *did* things to me.

"Like what?" I said, biting my lip again. "About to come undone?"

"Vulnerable," he said, stroking my cheek. "Bare. Everything stripped away so it's just us. This part of you is just for me—only I get to see you this way."

"Only you," I agreed, my heart beating so fast I could feel it everywhere, thrumming through my bloodstream.

He pulled me close and kissed me, sweeping me away all over again. I sighed and just let myself *feel* it—that sense of unabashed joy coursing through me, that sensation that everything was perfect in this moment.

And if it wasn't perfect the next moment? Well, we'd deal with it. Together. That's what he was trying to tell me with this kiss, this baring of bodies and souls. It was okay to need each other—it was even beautiful.

I broke our kiss and gazed into his eyes, marveling at how much I treasured every one of his features—and how he looked back at me with so much love.

"I adore you," I whispered. "Thank you for making me relax."

I put my hands on his shoulders, raised myself up, and slowly lowered myself onto his cock. He growled low in his throat, his hands going to my back to urge me closer. And as we started to move together, he leaned forward and slipped my nipple into his mouth, sending a whole new wave of pleasure coursing through me.

I closed my eyes and gave myself over to sensation. All that mattered right now was *this*.

Everything else could wait until tomorrow.

CHAPTER TWENTY-SIX

NATURALLY, "TOMORROW" HAD a complete shit show waiting for me.

But at least the phenomenal sex I'd had the night before put a spring in my step the next morning, the blissful memory of Scott's skin against mine inspiring me to hum a little tune as I emerged from my bedroom.

Pippa was at the dining table, fussing over a breakfast spread with her phone jammed to her ear.

"Ohmygod, *yes*—the flying was so unreal?! We should see if you can do that too, Shel, can't ghosts fly? Or at least, like, float?"

She paused, a huge grin spreading over her face as she listened to the person on the other end of the line.

"Yeah, yeah, I'm super aware that you're way less of a daredevil than I am, but what am I always saying?" she squealed. "You gotta live a little! I know Kris will totally be up for some flying experiments—oh, Aveda's awake! Gotta go, Shel, love ya forever!"

She tapped the phone screen and beamed at me.

"Hey, boss! Feeling rested? You should be after last night—oh, so my new vampiness apparently means I have enhanced hearing as well. Sounded like you were having a *very* good time! You deserve it after all that hard superheroing work you've been doing." She paused to take a breath, her brow furrowing. "Where's Scott, though? I know he loves those little mini croissants, so I got extra!"

"He's taking a shower," I said, an amused smile pulling at

the corners of my mouth. I did *not* mention that I had also just been in the shower, which had proved to be as relaxing as the bathtub. And which I'd had to vacate so Scott could actually spend some time getting clean. "Pippa, was that Shelby on the phone?"

"Yeah!" she exclaimed, her face brightening even more. "I texted her last night and was just like, 'I'm feeling this distance between us and I know you're falling in love and I *love* that for you, but I also feel like we've gone from talking every second of every day to never at all and I hate that for both of us, and also you're my best friend of all time and this is the first time I've actually had a best friend of all time, so can we please reserve some *actual* best friend time, because I miss you and I really need that.'" She paused to sit down at the breakfast table and pop a mini croissant in her mouth. "She called me this morning and said she was sorry, she's still learning how to exist in the human world as a ghost girl and being with Kris has been so exciting, but of course she misses me too. So now we're reserving one afternoon a week as dedicated Shippa—Shelby and Pippa—time."

"That's wonderful, Pippa," I said, taking a seat next to her. "And it sounds like you told her about your new, ah, supernatural status?"

"I did indeed!" Pippa crowed, waving her mini croissant around. "I'm hoping there's some cool-ass vamp-ghost shit we can do. Of course Shel is a little nervous about that . . ." She popped the croissant into her mouth, her eyes getting a far-off gleam as she chewed.

Hmm. Shelby was probably right to be nervous.

"AJ!" Pippa polished off her croissant, and took a swig from her mini can of soda. "Thank you so much for helping me with this whole Shelby situation. You're a real ride-or-die!"

"Thank you, but I didn't actually do anything," I said, flashing her a slight smile. I'd spent so much time worrying about Pippa, furiously trying to figure out how to help her solve her friendship problems. And in the end, she'd done all of that herself.

"Not! *True!*" Pippa bellowed, slamming her tiny can down on the table. "Don't you remember our convo at Ms Chi Cafe? You listened to me spill my guts, reassured me I wasn't totally awful for feeling the way I feel. Just being able to talk about all that helped me see everything more clearly. And you mentioned how you and Evie put some effort into actually working it out. I realized that's what I had to do with Shel—I needed to tell her really honestly how I felt, open up the conversation instead of acting like everything was totally okay."

"I . . . oh," was all I could say. I watched as she hopped up from the table and scampered over to the minibar, liberating another soda.

"Now I can get to the main course," she breathed, returning to the table. *"Bacon."*

I pushed the heaping plate of breakfast meat toward her. My brain was still stuck on the idea that I'd helped her simply by sitting on my ass at Ms Chi Cafe and listening to her problems.

But then . . . hadn't that been what my mother was trying to tell me last night? That solving someone's problem in a big, dramatic fashion wasn't always the most helpful thing. That sometimes what a person needed most was for someone to simply *listen* to them.

"Pippa, I'm so glad you and Shelby worked things out," I said, smiling affectionately at her. "And I love the idea of a vampire–ghost girl team-up."

"Yeah, on that tip . . ." Pippa crammed three strips of bacon in her mouth and gave me a hopeful look. "I know I'm a super badass vamp now, AJ, but I'd still really love to keep working for you and Evie, like we talked about. This whole trip has been so fucking fun, even the part where I turned into bats! Actually, especially the part where I turned into bats."

"And we would still love that, Pippa," I said, reaching over to squeeze her arm. "You've been an absolute star."

"Awesome! We all love it, you know—me, Shel, Tess, Julie.

Being part of y'all's superteam is kind of the best thing ever," Pippa enthused. "I guess Shel has been talking a little to Shruti, something about how some of her ghost abilities might enhance Shruti's hair power? And Tess and Julie are going to start learning self-defense from Lucy—including *supernatural*-type self-defense." She grinned at me. "Imagine the next gigantic demon battle. You're gonna have a whole squad behind you, Aveda Jupiter!"

"I . . ." My voice had gotten thick, the beginnings of tears lurking around my eyeballs. I flashed back to what Scott had said to me the night before:

This is a family. You don't have to carry that weight all by yourself—we're all right there beside you. We'll show up with *you.*

Evie and I had built this, I realized. A sprawling found family of a superteam. Something that was bigger than us, something that would endure after we were gone. Yes, I hoped to eradicate the demon threat for good within my lifetime. But if I didn't? Well, there was a whole new generation of potential superheroines to pass the torch to. That was an important part of my mission now.

And that was a beautiful thing.

"With me," I murmured, almost to myself.

"What?" Pippa said around her mouthful of bacon.

"The whole squad will be *with* me, Pippa—not behind me," I said, warmth blooming in my chest.

"Sure, however you wanna say it," Pippa said, rolling her eyes at me.

"Morning, friends," Evie said, emerging from her bedroom with a massive yawn. "Ooh, croissants! And Pippa, you can still eat real food? You don't have major bloodlust?" She paused, her fingertips drifting to her neck. "Do I need a scarf?"

"Nah," Pippa said, waving a dismissive hand. "I still seem to be able to eat whatever I want—but I now want *meat* the most. Basically any formation of meat. I'm also sensitive to light, but it doesn't seem to, like, kill me." She gestured to the big windows, where she'd closed the curtains. "And I do sleep like normal. I wasn't sure how the whole sleeping thing would go as a vampire, like do I need an actual coffin? But nah, I slept like a log. And I had such cool dreams! So *vivid*. Way better than when I was a boring regular human."

"Like what?" I said. "Or is this going to end up being too spicy for the breakfast table?"

"You're one to talk after everything I heard you getting up to last night," Pippa sassed.

"Yeah, I'm kinda surprised at how not sound-proofed this fancy hotel is," Evie said, grinning at me. "But I'm very happy you and Scott made up."

"Your dreams, Pippa?" I said, my face red as a beet.

"I did have a pretty nice one involving several characters from the *Midnight Dreams* saga." Pippa smiled to herself, taking another swig of soda. "But then there was this other one where . . . well, I don't think it was just a dream. Certain vampires in the books I've read have the ability to enter your mind, or send you messages with *their brains*." She waggled her fingers around her head to really give us the full picture. "And they're especially able to do that during your dreams. I was actually gonna ask for y'all's take on this, because it's possible I received . . ." She paused for dramatic effect, her dark eyes widening. "A vampire dream vision. A *message*."

"And what form did this message take?" Evie asked, as we exchanged a look. We were going to have to parse which parts of Pippa's vampire experience were actually connected to our investigation and which parts were products of her overwhelming enthusiasm for all things paranormal.

"I *think* it was from Kat," Pippa said, her brow furrowing as she tried to remember. "She appeared—"

"Before or after the sexytimes?" I couldn't resist asking.

"After," Pippa said. "In general, vamps aren't gonna intrude on your dream orgies unless you ask them to. That would be *rude*."

"Of course," Evie said, sounding like she was trying to stifle a laugh.

"Anywaaaay," Pippa continued, "Kat popped up, and my surroundings dissolved, and I was in some kind of . . . it was like a really dark tunnel type of situation. Kat didn't say anything, she just beckoned me to follow. And being a natural adventurer, I did just that." She popped another piece of bacon in her mouth and chewed contemplatively, her head listing to the side.

"Did you recognize the tunnel?" I said. "Was there anything about it that was at all familiar to you?"

"No," Pippa said, shaking her head. "That's kinda why I thought maybe it was a vampire message. Sure, we can craft entire new worlds in our dreams, but this one was so . . ." She waved her hands around. "Like, *complete*? Fully realized, detailed. It wasn't like something my brain had imagined before, or something I'd cobbled together from places I know."

"So tell us about it," Evie prompted.

Pippa's gaze went to the ceiling as she tried to recall the details. "It was dark, damp. The walls were made of some kind of heavy-duty concrete—it was definitely a man-made tunnel, something constructed. And there were noises . . ." She frowned, gnawing on her lower lip. "But it was like they were coming from above."

"What kind of noises?" I pressed.

"Just, like, people going about their business," Pippa said. "Walking, chatting. Traffic sounds. Like we were under some regular city street."

"So a man-made underground tunnel," Evie said. "Are you sure you weren't in the sewer? The subway?"

"No," Pippa said. "It was more like, I don't know, the actual Batcave? All smooth surfaces, sealed off and secure. No grotty old sewer pipes, no trickling water sounds, no stench. It was like something that had been constructed for a very specific and secret purpose."

"And what happened when you followed Kat?" I asked. "Did she say anything?"

"I followed her for what felt like forever," Pippa said.

"Through so many twists and turns. I had this sense that she was leading me somewhere important. Like when we got to our destination, it would be the most momentous thing I'd ever experienced! But then . . ." She paused, chewing on her bacon.

"It wasn't momentous?" Evie asked.

"We reached a point where it was like we were near an entrance of some sort," Pippa said. "To another part of the Batcave. I could see light filtering in from around the corner, and I thought I could hear voices. Like, inside the cave, not just coming from above. And then, just as we were about to enter, Kat turned to me and gave me this deathly serious look. She put her hands on my shoulders, and she was looking at me so directly, like she really wanted me to get this . . ." Pippa paused and snagged another piece of bacon.

Evie and I were both leaning forward in our seats, practically holding our breaths with anticipation.

"And . . . ?!?" I prompted. "What did she say?"

Pippa closed her eyes, milking the drama of it all, and swallowed her bacon.

"She said . . . *CosmoBurger.*" She opened her eyes and looked at us expectantly.

"What?!" I exploded. "*That's it?* What does that mean?"

"Dunno," Pippa shrugged. "I thought you guys would understand, since you're the big superheroes and all."

"CosmoBurger." I shook my head. "Sounds like you were just hungry again. Craving all that meat."

"Hey, it's possible," Pippa said cheerfully. "But I gotta say, it seemed like a really cool vampire dream message. Kat wanted me to remember that, even after I woke up. Maybe I should try taking a post-breakfast nap—what do you think, will she send me another vision of some sort?"

"Maybe," Evie said faintly, but I could tell she was thinking the same thing I was—that this seemed very much like a dead end, Pippa's excitement over being a vampire amping up her desire for big, momentous things to happen to her.

"I'm gonna try it," Pippa said, polishing off the rest of the bacon and hopping to her feet. "One mid-morning nap, coming right—"

She cut off abruptly, her face going very pale.

And then her eyes flashed bright red.

"Pippa . . ." I jumped up from my seat. Evie did the same. "What's wrong?"

She opened her mouth as if to speak—but nothing came out. Then she crumpled to the floor, writhing in agony.

"AJ . . ." she gasped. "I can't . . . it's happening again . . ."

"What?" I fell to my knees next to her, scanning her body, my heart racing. "What's happening?" I demanded. "Pippa, please . . ."

"N-no," she growled. "No, this can't . . ." Her eyes rolled back into her head.

"Pippa!" Evie screamed. Her hands hovered over Pippa's form.

"Don't!" Pippa screamed. "Don't touch me, it will only . . ." She threw back her head and howled, her face screwed into a look of agony. Her body folded itself into a ball, tears streaming down her face.

I watched in disbelief as her body constricted in on itself, getting smaller and smaller . . .

Then she exploded into a flock of bats.

Evie and I screamed, pushing ourselves back from the creatures that were flapping their way around our hotel suite. They scattered, then got back into formation—that little storm cloud again. And they flew straight for the window.

"What . . ." I gasped.

The bat swarm smacked itself against the curtained window, a sound somehow even more awful than the ominous flapping of their wings.

"Evie!" I screamed. "We can't contain the bats here, and we don't know what will happen to Pippa if they keep smacking against the window like that! I mean, I guess the bats *are* her, but we don't know how it all works!"

Desperately, I reached out with my telekinesis and tried

to grab on to the bats. But something kept blocking me, sending my feathers reeling backward—it was like an invisible force field had erected itself around the swarm.

"I can't grab on to them," I growled, frustration coursing through me.

"Let me . . ." Evie called out.

She held out her hands and sent her fire careening toward the window, aiming at a spot just beneath the bats. The heat melted the curtain and the glass behind it in an instant, giving the bats a way out. And just before they flew into the city sky once more, one of them turned and . . . I'm not sure how I was able to tell this was happening, but it looked me straight in the eye.

I was overcome with a disorienting sensation, like someone had thrown a giant piece of gauze over my entire body and was trying to wrap me up like a mummy. I heard the faint sound of Evie screaming, but it was like she was a million miles away. I tried to look around, but my vision was narrowing, narrowing . . .

I stumbled to the side, trying to grab on to something, trying to keep myself upright as my vision narrowed to a single tiny pinhole of light. Was I having another panic attack?

"Annie!" I heard Evie shriek. She sounded *so* far away . . .

And then I was out cold.

When I opened my eyes, I was lying flat on my back in a place that was somehow familiar, even though I was sure I'd never been there before. It was dark, damp. Solid gray concrete all around me. Smooth surfaces, no pipes in sight. And up above, I heard the faint bustle of a city street.

I was in Pippa's tunnel.

And then Kat was peering down at me, her expression oddly blank. She looked as tired and lost as she had in the ramen shop the day before, the dark circles under her eyes highlighting just how pale the rest of her face was.

"CosmoBurger," she intoned. "You have to find Cos-moBurger."

"What the fuck is CosmoBurger?!" I spat out. "Help me out here, please."

Kat tilted her head at me, a slightly snarky expression crossing her face and making her look more like herself.

"Can you really not use Google, Aveda Jupiter?" she said, rolling her eyes. "Or Yelp? Anything?"

I just kept staring at her.

"Fiiiiiine," she said, getting to her feet. "Bitch, I'll *show* you."

The tunnel dissolved, and a new location came into focus around us. I blinked, trying to make sense of it all. I was still lying on my back, but now we seemed to be on a busy LA street, that relentless sun beating down on us yet again. And Kat was standing over me.

"Right *there*!" she cried, pointing emphatically.

I turned and there it was—the infamous CosmoBurger. It looked like an old-timey burger and shake joint, a squat, unassuming hut with a giant sign proclaiming its name in big neon letters.

"Awesome," I said. "So it exists. But where are we, ex-actly?"

Kat rolled her eyes at me again, and shifted her pointy finger to the other side of the street. I turned to look.

And realized CosmoBurger was right next door to Pinna-cle Pictures. Grouchy Stacey must have driven us past this joint multiple times, and I'd never noticed it before.

"Great," I said slowly. "So now we know where it is. But Kat, why is CosmoBurger so important? And if it turns out that this is all a ploy for me to buy you more carnivorous—or vampiric?—meals, then I am going to be so pissed. Of course I'll buy them for you, but still."

She shook her head, like she was ever so disappointed in me. Then she closed her eyes, took in a long inhale . . . and dissolved into a flock of bats.

"Wait, no!" I yelled, as the bats took off into the sky.

"Why does this keep happening! And am I just stuck in this vision now?! Because if so . . . well, I'm going to be *even more* pissed! Do you hear me, Kat?!"

But it was no use. The bats were already almost out of sight.

I realized I was still lying on the ground—very undignified, even for a mere vision—and tried to get to my feet. But I seemed to be stuck, trapped in molasses. That feeling of being wrapped in gauze surrounded me again, and I desperately tried to punch my way out . . . but I could barely lift my arm to get a good punch in.

I gave up on the punching and tried for a smaller motion, attempting to very slowly lift myself up again . . . and again . . . and then suddenly my vision was closing in on itself and everything went black.

My eyes snapped open a few seconds later and I was back in the hotel suite, still flat on my back. Evie and Scott stared down at me with twin expressions of worry.

"Annie!" Evie cried. "What happened?! You passed out and we couldn't do anything to wake you and you were just so . . . *still* . . ."

"I'm fine," I said, sitting up and squeezing her hand. "Really," I added, as Scott opened his mouth to protest. "I'm pretty sure I just received a vampire vision-slash-message of my very own."

I surveyed our suite—the empty bacon platter, the breakfast wreckage. The big, beautiful window that now sported a gaping hole, the curtain that had covered it flapping gently in the morning breeze.

"Get dressed," I said to Evie. "We're going to Cosmo-Burger."

CHAPTER TWENTY-SEVEN

COSMOBURGER LOOKED JUST as mundane and unas-suming as it had in my vision. I was hit by a weird sense of déjà vu as soon as Scott dropped us off, standing in front of that giant neon sign right across the street from the Pinnacle lot. The only thing missing was Kat being her unhelpful vampiric self.

"So no clues about what we're supposed to do now that we've found the place?" Evie asked, eyeing the nondescript hut. "Do we just stand here until a big swarm of bats descends on us yet again?"

"Let's not do that," I said, shuddering at the thought. "How about we go inside?"

The interior of CosmoBurger was also about as expected: cramped and greasy, a lone chef flipping burgers on a long metal grill behind the counter. The overwhelming scent of sizzling meat washed over us, and my stomach growled loudly. Evie gave me a curious look.

"You hungry?" she said. "'Cause this seems more like my kind of joint than yours."

"Mmm, true," I said, my mouth watering, my eyes locking on the burgers, their oily juices oozing onto the grill. "Perhaps Kat simply wanted us to sample the finest junk food in all of Los Angeles."

"Heya!" the chef called out. He surveyed the burgers and, apparently satisfied, took up a post behind the cash register, facing us. "What's up, people?" he said, his inflections full of the long vowels and surfer-esque nonchalance often associated with the part of LA known as the Valley. "Glad to see there are some other early birds who like to eat lunch at ten-thirty in the a.m."

"We're actually not here to eat," Evie said, sliding a side-long glance my way as I gazed at the delectable-smelling meat on the grill. "We, um . . ." She gave me a prompting look.

"Right," I said, tearing my eyes away from the grill. I assessed the guy in front of me. He seemed mellow, genial. Of course I knew that appearances could be deceiving, but perhaps a certain measure of friendly directness was the key here. He also didn't seem to recognize us—or maybe, like so many of his fellow Angelenos, he simply didn't care about our supposedly famous faces. My gaze wandered to his nametag, which read "Carl."

"Carl," I said, giving him my best Aveda Jupiter megawatt smile. "My friend and I are actually exploring some historical local landmarks today—we're from San Francisco—"

"Aw yeah, 'Frisco!" he exclaimed, giving a fist-pump.

"Uh, yes, quite," I said, widening my smile. "And we heard that we are very possibly in the vicinity of one of these landmarks, right here at CosmoBurger."

"CosmoBurger *is* a total historical landmark," Carl said, his chest puffing up with pride. "My granddad's granddad opened the place *way* back when, and we're definitely known as the spot where slacker kids and studio execs alike can pop in for a good old-fashioned burger and shake."

"Delightful!" I trilled. "Tell me more—I adore interesting trivia of all sorts."

"Aw, me too!" Carl grinned. "I knew you guys were kin-dred spirits. Well, our secret recipe has also been passed down through the generations—many have tried to replicate it, all have failed! And we've been used as a location in quite a few movies and TV shows. There's an extensive list on our website if you want to check that out."

"I most definitely will!" I said, my megawatt smile so big I felt like my face was about to split in two. "I imagine your close proximity to Pinnacle Pictures means you've been in some of their productions . . . ?"

"Tons!" Carl said, brightening even more. "For a while, our exterior was the go-to for any sitcom that wanted a good establishing shot for their neighborhood hangout of choice. We've been on TV as a coffee shop, a fast-food joint—one time we were even a record store! Nothing to do with food!"

"How cool!" Evie said, glancing at me out of the corner of her eye. I could see what she was thinking: this wasn't giving us anything that seemed to connect with vampires or the *Heroine* show or whatever Kat had been trying to tell us.

"And then of course, there's the other connection to Pinnacle," Carl said, leaning forward conspiratorially. "But if you guys are into weird historical trivia, I'm sure you already know all about that."

"Um, refresh our memories," I said, my ears perking.

"I'm talking about the Mistress Tunnel," Carl said, leaning in even more.

My heart started to beat a little bit faster. "Tunnel . . . ?"

"Yeah, the one that runs underground from here to Pinnacle," Carl said, jerking his thumb in the direction of the lot. "As urban legend goes, it's what execs back in the olden days used to sneak their mistresses on and off the lot."

"And is it an urban legend?" I said. "Or does it actually exist?"

"Oh, it exists," Carl said, flashing us an eager grin. "You can kinda see the old opening to it in our back storeroom—well, what *was* the opening. It's been patched up for decades."

"But there's still a tunnel behind it?" I pressed.

"Supposedly," Carl said with an elaborate shrug. "I've honestly never been adventurous enough to check. Hey, do you guys want to try a burger? On the house—special for fellow history buffs!"

"That sounds lovely," I said, my eyes going back to the sizzling meat. The scent invaded my nostrils again, and my mouth watered. "And would you mind if we took a little tourist photo of your back room? For all the history buffs back in, ah, 'Frisco."

"Totally cool," Carl said, turning back to the grill. "You want cheese on it?"

The back storage room of CosmoBurger was also exactly what one would expect: minuscule and crammed to the brim with various boxes of stuff. After I threw an unbelievably delicious cheeseburger down my gullet, we got to work inspecting every square inch of the space—which was extra hard to do, given the championship level of clutter. And Carl couldn't help us out since he was preparing for the lunch rush.

"Oof," Evie said, trying to move a gargantuan box of napkins away from the wall. "I don't suppose there's a map or something that details the exact location of this Mistress Tunnel? Also, are we sure Carl isn't spinning tales, trying to make CosmoBurger way more epic than it actually is?"

"The cheeseburger I just ate was definitely epic, I'll give him that," I said, hustling over to help her so she wouldn't try to lift the box herself. "Hey," I said, when she gave me a look. "I know your pregnant ass is perfectly capable of moving the napkin supply around, but Nate will murder me if anything happens to you or the baby, and I'm taking no chances. And anyway, I can just . . . well, at least I think I can . . ."

I tentatively reached out with my invisible feathers and shifted the box to the side—where it promptly rammed into yet another overflowing box of supplies.

Okay, so my telekinesis *did* still work. Perhaps my night of restorative relaxation had helped reset my system.

"Ugh," Evie said, leaning against the wall. "This is some extreme clutter. It would be super helpful if those bats . . . or Kat . . . or really anyone connected to this vampire business flew in here right freaking now to give us another clue."

"Indeed," I agreed, leaning next to her against the wall. I crossed my arms over my chest, feeling the cool slab of concrete against my back, and stared down at the dull, gray floor. Maybe if I stared hard enough, it would give me all the answers I was looking for. I stared at it for so long, my eyes started to cross, the floor blurring in and out of focus, its dull grayness shifting . . .

No. Wait.

I stared harder, then crouched down on the floor so I could study it up close.

"Annie . . . ?" Evie said tentatively, probably wondering if I was just a little bit delirious.

But I was pretty sure I was seeing things correctly—the gray hadn't *shifted*, there was actually a patch on the floor that was a slightly different color. Just a shade or two lighter, its edges blurry and indistinct. It looked like someone had tried to clumsily repair . . . what? I pressed on the patch with my fingertips.

And then I was falling.

It happened so fast, I didn't even have the chance to scream. Air rushed through my ears, and my hands grabbed fruitlessly at the emptiness all around me. I heard Evie shrieking my name, but I didn't know where she was, didn't know where I was, didn't . . .

I flung my invisible feathers out instinctively, trying to catch my body . . . and then I was suspended in midair, breathing hard, darkness everywhere . . .

Holy shit. I was really glad my telekinesis worked *that* time.

"Annie?" Evie called out, her voice sounding far away and echo-y. I twisted my neck this way and that, trying to follow the sound. "Up here!" she yelled.

I jerked my head upward and finally found a source of light—a small circle framing Evie's worried face, about fifteen feet above me.

"Did I just fall down an actual rabbit hole?" I blurted out.

"I don't know about the rabbit part," Evie chuckled. "But yes—the floor gave way under your hand and then you just fell into the ground. It would have looked incredibly cool if I hadn't been totally freaking out."

I tried to look around again, but everything was still so dark. "Am I in the Mistress Tunnel right now?! And if so . . . where's the bottom? All in all, this seems like a not very safe way of sneaking around."

"Wait . . ." Evie said—and her head disappeared from the circle of light. I heard the faint sounds of rummaging around, and then she returned, waving a small white object I couldn't quite make out.

"What is that?" I demanded.

"It's a plastic fork," she said, grinning at me. "I'm going to drop it down there to see where the bottom is. Can you move a little to the left?"

"Why do I feel like we should have a more technologically advanced and/or magical way of figuring this out?" I groaned, using my telekinesis to shift my position in the air. I wondered how long I could hold myself here. Maybe I could teach myself how to "fly" using my power. (Much better than a jet-pack, if you asked me.)

Evie held the fork aloft, then released it. It made a whistling sound as it soared down. For a second, I thought it might just keep soaring forever, that I'd plunged myself into an endless tunnel.

But then, a couple feet below me, I heard a telltale *clink*.

"Oh, I'm almost to the bottom!" I exclaimed. "Hold on, let me . . ." I very gently moved myself downward, reaching out with my toes like I was in a swimming pool, trying to find the deep end.

"Damn!" Evie exclaimed. "You found Kat's mystery tunnel! Can you use telekinesis to bring me down with you? And do not even try to convince me to sit my ass up here while you go off exploring."

"I wouldn't dream of it," I said, reaching my invisible feathers up toward the circle of light. "But let's go *very* slow. And let's maybe not tell Nate about this part."

Taking the utmost care, I painstakingly used my telekinesis to bring her through the hole in the floor and lower her to the ground. She pulled her phone out of her hoodie pocket and turned on the flashlight, sweeping it over our darkened space.

"What do you think?" she said. "Is this the same tunnel from your vision?"

I cocked my head and listened, my heart speeding up when I heard rumblings and chatter from the street above. "It does appear much like Pippa described—the Batcave atmosphere, all the smooth surfaces and such. And it looks like what Kat showed me."

Evie held the flashlight out, illuminating the path in front of us. "Should we walk until we find something?"

"That is probably what we have to do," I said, squaring my shoulders and trying to call up my usual determination. "Kat didn't say anything about how we were supposed to proceed once we made this amazing discovery."

We started shuffling forward, both of us on high alert, trying to keep track of our surroundings. The quiet hum of traffic from the street above wafted through, muffled car engines and honks sounding like they were being beamed in from another planet.

My eyes were at least starting to adjust to all the darkness—beyond the flashlight's glow, I could make out the concrete of the walls, the curved shape of the tunnel.

"I think we're crossing the street into Pinnacle territory," I murmured.

"I wonder if Carl misses us," Evie mused. "We've been exploring the back room like the dedicated history buffs we are for quite a while now."

I couldn't help but giggle, a welcome rush of release amidst the tension. I gave Evie a sidelong glance, now able to make out the vague shape of her in the shadowy dark. I could see that her brow was furrowed, her posture determined. And I felt an unexpected surge of warmth as we continued to shuffle our way through the tunnel. This was the kind of thing that would have terrified her just a few years ago: sneaking through a weird, creepy tunnel teeming with possible dangers. And with me, her headstrong daredevil of a best friend.

And now look at her—bravely striding forward, pregnant with her first child, badass superheroine written all over her.

Yes, she'd been, as Scott had put it, "squirrely" for a large part of our LA adventure. But she always showed up when it counted.

"Hey, Evie," I said impulsively. "Even if this ends up being our last mission—I'm glad we're doing it together."

She swiveled to look at me. "What do you mean 'last mission'?"

"You'll be heading into that last trimester soon," I said. "And then you'll be on maternity leave, and you keep talking about sabbaticals and the glories of vacations and time off and Little Tokyo walking tours. I understand that you want to make your life smaller, move beyond the superheroing of it all! And I want you to know . . ." I paused, swallowing the lump that had appeared in my throat. "I want you to know that I understand," I said, straightening my spine and willing myself not to cry. "I really do. And if I have to train some new superheroing partners, well! We have so many wonderful protégés to choose from. A veritable squad."

"Annie," she said softly, "I still don't . . ."

"I hope you have a beautiful forever sabbatical," I soldiered on. "With your beautiful family!"

Now she stopped dead in her tracks and turned the flashlight on me. I winced at the bright light shining directly into my eyes.

"*Annie.*" I could still make out some of her features—her face was deathly serious. "What are you talking about? You *are* my family."

"Oh, I know, I know," I said hastily. "But . . . you're creating a whole *new* family. And Aveda Jupiter *is* trying to better understand work/life balance!"

"The key word there is *balance*," Evie responded. "Not, like, all one thing or the other."

I squirmed uncomfortably as we both fell silent, her still shining that bright light in my face like I was being interrogated. She studied me for a long moment, cocking her head to the side. As if she was trying to peer into my brain.

Finally, she lowered the flashlight and let out a long exhale, leaning back against the tunnel wall.

"I'm sorry," she said. "I . . . I've been acting weird. And I don't think I realized just how weird until you said all that." She idly twirled the flashlight in her hand, the light playing across the dark surfaces of the tunnel. "I know I've been avoiding mission-related things. Superheroing-related things. That I've been speculating about sabbaticals and trying to escape into some kind of vacation-like bubble . . . and, yeah, we all *deserve* that kind of escape! But I don't think I realized just how alone I was making you feel." She pushed off from the wall and faced me again, regarding me thoughtfully. "The stuff that happened at Morgan affected me a lot more than I wanted to say. And I'm working on all the processing and stuff in therapy. But I've had to admit that it really did drain me, and my brain has had a hard time engaging with some of the tougher parts of our job—and the idea that yeah, Shasta might still be after my baby. I should have talked to you about that, probably. But like I said, I don't think I realized how bad it was."

"It affected me too," I said, my voice very small. "The stuff at Morgan. I thought I was going to lose you, Evie. And I couldn't bear to see you looking like you were about to lose hope, to give up—"

"*You* made sure I didn't give up," she said fiercely. "You always do."

She tilted the flashlight up again, so that both our faces were slightly illuminated.

"I know Bea's said I'm like the glue of Team Tanaka/Jupiter," she said.

"You are," I agreed. "You hold us all together, no matter what."

"But you're, like, the engine," she said. "You're the one

who lights a fire under our collective ass. The one who never gives up, backs down, or stops fighting. You make us *go*."

"What contraption has both glue and an engine?" I murmured.

"The best kind!" she retorted. "And I wouldn't have been able to deal with the ghosts of Morgan or Shasta's evil plan without you being that fucking powerful engine. You were being *tortured*, in indescribable pain, and you still kept yelling out encouragement, telling me to never give up. You fought back the whole time."

She gave me a slight smile. "I've noticed you being extra protective toward me since Morgan, making sure I eat and sleep and don't go flying off rickety golf carts to my death," she continued. "You push and protect all of us with everything you have, Annie—that's who you are, and I love you for it. But please know that we also want to protect *you*. And another reason I've been talking so much about sabbaticals and vacations is I think you could use one too!"

"I . . . probably could," I admitted. "I don't think I know *how* to take a vacation, though. I really am trying to learn. Or be open to learning. And I did realize last night that I *have* been going extra hard, depleting all my internal resources. I was thinking about things Kat has said to me, about how she's achieved her dreams, but they don't feel good. They *hurt*. I don't want that to be me. I still love superheroing with all my heart, and I never want that to change. And . . ."

I drew in a deep breath and tamped down on the beginnings of tears that had decided to make an appearance. Usually Evie was the sentimental one—the easy cry, the bringer of the feels, the one who showed all the emotions she'd spent years trying to suppress.

"There's been a lot of change in our lives lately, and I seem to be having some trouble coping," I continued. "Change just keeps happening, and I am powerless to control it, and that makes me feel . . ." I trailed off, overcome with emotion. "Sometimes I pause outside Bea's room because I'm hoping

I'll hear her tinkering with one of her projects or blasting loud music—that I will then yell at her to turn down—or goofing off with Sam and Leah. I don't know what I'm expecting, that she'll just magically appear?" I shook my head. "And yet, every time I *don't* hear her, my heart breaks a little bit."

My voice cracked on the last word and I was glad for the dark—so Evie couldn't see how embarrassingly red my face was.

"I do that, too."

"What?" I looked at her, confused.

"I stop outside Bea's door too," Evie said with a sheepish laugh. "And I always hope for the same thing, even though I know it's impossible."

"Oh." I wasn't sure what else to say.

"Don't you remember how completely fucking distraught I was when she told us she was moving?" Evie said. "The night after she left, I took a blanket she'd left behind on her bed and wrapped myself up in it. I told myself I was so scared for her, venturing out into the big, bad world for the first time in her life. We'd never been apart, not for the twenty-three years she's been alive. But really . . ." She shrugged and gave a rueful smile. "It was myself I was scared for. I didn't quite know how to exist without her."

"She said she'd come back," I said faintly.

"She did," Evie agreed. "But who knows if that will actually happen? She loves it out there—and she's thriving. She sounds so damn happy whenever she calls. So confident, like she's found her place in the world." She shrugged expansively. "Things change. Life changes. I'll miss Bea if she decides to stay there permanently, but how can I deny it's a good thing when it's so obviously amazing for her?"

"Well, yes," I said hastily. "And obviously, I am also happy for you and all the thrilling changes in your life—I know how excited you are for the baby—"

"Ah, but remember I *wasn't* excited at first," Evie said wryly. "I was scared shitless. I don't exactly love change either—but one thing that reminds me change is a good and necessary part of life is my friendship with you."

"With *me*?" I said, my voice twisting up on that last syllable.

"Yes," she said, laughing. "Imagine if you and I had stayed the same once we settled into our extremely unhealthy, codependent dynamic—we'd both be so much worse off. I'd still be a doormat, you'd still be a diva, and we'd spend most of our time resenting each other and never saying what we actually felt."

"Sounds miserable," I said.

"Yup." She nodded emphatically, her curls bobbing in the dark. "We *had* to change to get here. And look at us now."

"Right, but we *got* there," I blurted out, irrational panic rising in my chest again. "We were perfect. And now—"

"What, we're changing again?" She reached over and squeezed my hand. "Why do you automatically think that's bad?"

I thought back to the vision I'd shared with Scott the night before: me all alone in the drafty Victorian. And I thought of how he'd told me, with so much earnest feeling, that it would never happen.

So why did I keep thinking it was inevitable?

I swallowed the lump that had formed in my throat and squeezed her hand back. "I'm still figuring out how to deal with all this change," I said. "But please, Evie, no matter what happens, promise you'll come back to me. Even if it's different, even if you and Nate and little Galactus Tanaka-Jones decide to buy an isolated vacation home in the middle of the woods—"

"The *woods*?!" she said incredulously. "Why would I want to do that—"

"—don't leave forever," I pressed on. "I can't bear the thought of standing outside your door the way I stand outside of Bea's."

She swept me into a fierce hug. "Never," she whispered. "I couldn't bear that either."

One of the tears I'd been holding back slipped down my cheek, and I let out a long, shaky exhale I felt like I'd been shoving down forever.

"And just in case this wasn't clear," Evie said, pulling back from the hug, "I'm not planning on leaving the superheroing game behind. I love being your partner, Aveda Jupiter. This work, this life, is what I'm supposed to be doing. It's the thing that woke me up, that forced me to stop hiding. And I can't imagine *not* doing it. I just need a fucking break, and so do you. But even if one of us does decide to ditch superheroing? We'll still be best friends. That's forever."

"Thank god," I said. "I love all of our friends, but you're the only one I'd forgive for drowning my favorite Barbie in the toilet."

"Still hearing about that all these years later," Evie laughed, scrubbing a hand over her eyes.

"And you'll hear about it for many years to come—that's *also* forever," I shot back, returning her smile. "Now. Shall we keep exploring the Mistress Tunnel? At this rate, Carl will be sending a search party for us at any moment."

"Carl's gonna be super excited about our Mistress Tunnel adventures," Evie scoffed, training her flashlight on the path ahead. "It'll add even more mystique to the already mystique-filled CosmoBurger."

"I might need another cheeseburger when we return," I said, following the light forward. "All this lurching around in the dark is making me feel quite—"

I was cut off by a bone-shaking *ROAR*! Evie and I both jumped, and she swept the light around wildly, trying to find the source.

He came out of nowhere, a hurricane of snarls and teeth charging toward us. And when Evie's light finally found him, we saw that it was someone familiar: Stan the vampire, his fangs fully bared, his eyes flashing bright red.

CHAPTER TWENTY-EIGHT

"GET BACK, ASSHOLE!" I screamed, flinging my invisible feathers at Stan. But he slipped out of my telekinetic grip, moving lightning fast, and advanced on Evie and me. I ran toward him and landed a solid punch to his midsection, sending him doubling over.

He snarled and lunged, but I nimbly dodged out of the way.

"Annie!" Evie called out. "I don't want to start a fire down here, but—"

"No, you're right!" I called back, sweeping a roundhouse kick toward Stan's legs. He slid to the side, dodging me, and my kick landed against the concrete wall of the tunnel. I winced. "We're in an enclosed underground space, and fire is not going to play well with that," I continued. "Stay back for a minute and let me see if I can do this the old-fashioned way—oh, and give me some light!"

She obliged, sending her flashlight beam in my direction. Stan threw his hands up against the light, roaring.

"Keep doing that!" I yelled. "He's light-vulnerable!"

She turned the brightness up and Stan howled in pain, squeezing his eyes shut tight. Adrenaline pumped through my veins, and I homed in on the fight, landing well-positioned blows to his torso as he flailed his arms around, trying to make contact.

"What the fuck!" I bellowed. "Did Kat lead our asses directly into a trap, or—"

"*GRAAAAWRRRR!*"

I turned toward another roar, a *new* roar, which was not

coming from Stan . . . just in time to see Clint throwing himself at me with extreme force. He landed on top of me, but I managed to throw my arms around his waist and shift my weight, sending us rolling. I used the momentum to my advantage, pulling him along, and finally managed to heave myself on top of him, straddling him at the waist.

"Go down, you bloodsucking auteur *motherfucker*!" I screamed, punching him in the face.

"Annie!" Evie shrieked. "Behind you—"

"Oof!"

Now Stan was launching himself at me again, his hands clamping on my shoulders like vises. His fingers snaked up to grab my hair, yanking my head to the side so he could get at my neck—

"Stan, Clint—*stop*!"

The voice rang out through the tunnel, strong and clear. Evie moved her light and found the source—a shadowy figure emerging from the darkness and slowly cohering into a familiar shape.

It was Kat. And she looked different.

She wasn't quite her human self, and she wasn't quite the exhausted, defeated Kat I'd seen yesterday. He face was smudged with dirt, and her sloppy outfit was torn and grubby. I was somewhat amused to see that she still had her giant sunglasses perched on top of her head. Now she didn't seem defeated. She looked ready to *fight*.

Like she'd reclaimed that ever-important intensity. My heart swelled for her.

Kat stood tall and frowned sternly at Clint and Stan, projecting a sense of authority that seemed to take up the whole tunnel. They both stopped attacking and turned toward her, their expressions slightly fearful—like kids who'd gotten in trouble for eating too much ice cream.

"Wow, she's got some big vamp energy," Evie murmured.

"Remember your humanity—the things that ground you in this world!" Kat barked, putting a hand on her hip. "Stan, you love that connection you make with people when you're acting. You told me about all the joy you feel when you're doing theater, because that's where you can see their faces, all the joy you're giving *them*. And Clint, you still have so much more to create, so many stories to tell. We talked about that just last night."

Stan and Clint were still staring at her, as if hypnotized. I remained in position, straddling Stan while Clint's hand stayed clamped on my shoulder. They seemed to be listening to Kat, and I didn't want to do anything to disrupt that.

Her vampire self was so goddamn magnetic, I couldn't seem to stop staring at her either.

"You both have so many hopes and dreams for the future," Kat said, radiating empathy. "We can't forget that."

Clint released my shoulder, slowly getting to his feet. The red light in his eyes dimmed.

"You're . . . right," he replied, his voice hoarse. He shook his head, like he was trying to come back to himself. "Sorry, Kat. These weird vampire instincts we've been given are so fucking strong."

I did a double take. Clint sounded almost humble. Not like the big-headed auteur we'd become accustomed to. He'd apologized—to Kat. Had vampirism made him more self-aware?

"Sorry, Ms. Jupiter, may I stand up?" Stan asked, holding his hands up in surrender. "I did not intend to attack you, but as Ms. Kat mentioned, these vampire instincts are very strong. And your blood smells so *flavorful*."

"Uh, sure," I said, hastily scrambling to my feet.

Kat shifted her gaze to me, her face lighting up.

"Bitch, you found it!" she exclaimed, clapping her hands together. "I was hoping you understood the vision, but I'm so new to all of this, and I wasn't sure if I was clear. But Pippa reminded me that our girl Aveda Jupiter is so brilliant—"

"Hold up, Pippa?" I said. "Is she okay? Is she *here*?"

"Come with us," Kat said, beckoning me and Evie to follow her. "We have so much to talk about."

Kat led all of us further into the tunnel, until we reached a point where I could see the faintest light emanating from just around the corner. Once again, I was struck by that weird sense of déjà vu—this was something Pippa had described from her vision.

"Before we enter: I invite you both in," Kat said, beckoning for us to round the corner.

"I thought the vampires were the ones who had to be invited in," Evie said.

"We've discovered this weird thing with vamp 'force fields,'" Kat explained. "They only seem to pop up when a vampire wants to block people—or sometimes even their fellow vamps—from a location. It's not really a thing we're aware we're doing, it's like the subconscious asserting itself."

"That's why no one else could enter Edendale during our, er, discussion," Clint chimed in. "I am ever so sorry, Aveda, I was not in my right mind—"

"We'll get to all that in a sec, Clint," Kat said dryly. "Just let them come in first."

We rounded the corner and I was immediately smacked in the chest by a small bundle of energy launching herself at me with the force of the mightiest cannonball.

"AJ!" Pippa shrieked. "I knew you'd find us!" She pulled back and beamed at me. "This is so awesome!"

"Pippa!" I hugged her back fiercely. "I'm so happy you're okay! Again!"

I smiled at her, then scanned the section of tunnel we were in. The smooth surfaces and general state of dank darkness were the same, but we seemed to have entered a small pocket in the tunnel—like a hollowed-out room. The flickery bits of light dancing around the walls were coming from an eclectic collection of candles placed all around the space. They were different sizes, shapes, colors—I saw everything from tasteful Pottery Barn beige columns to a monstrous green novelty piece that was apparently supposed to stand in for Hulk's nether regions. Together, the flickering candles created a messy rainbow, a sliver of warmth cast over the meager furniture: a beat-up couch, a few old chairs, and an assortment of ratty blankets.

"Are you living here?" I said, trying to make sense of it all.

"Not by choice," Kat grimaced. "As far as we can tell, we were all compelled here by some greater force. That's the bit where we turn into those creepy bat swarms and fly off into the distance. We always end up *here*. Yesterday, when I flew away from you in the parking lot—that's the first time it happened for me. I've tried to escape the tunnel a few times, but I keep being drawn back."

"Just like I was compelled back this morning," Pippa said. "Ughhhh, that was so annoying. Thanks for burning a hole in the window, Evie, otherwise my batsona would've been toast."

"Of course," Evie murmured.

"I really need to know everything," I said. "Kat, were you aware of your vampirism before you turned into a bunch of bats?"

"No," she said, a contemplative frown crossing her face. "I just thought I wasn't sleeping enough or something. But since I've been able to talk things through with these guys . . ." She jerked her chin at Stan and Clint. ". . . I've realized I was totally experiencing the same symptoms they were. Exhaustion, light sensitivity, extreme mood swings. And *hunger*. My goodness. All I wanted was meat, all the time, the bloodier, the better. It was this all-consuming *need*, leading to me biting Pippa. But it was also hunger in, like, my emotions. I wanted to fix my shitty situation so badly. You saw how frustrated I was yesterday!"

"I did," I said, turning this over in my mind. I also remembered how tired she'd seemed back at Edendale, how she was distracted by the scent of cheeseburger potstickers when we'd been at the bookstore. And her ever-present giant sunglasses, always on hand to block out the light. "Do you think you were turned from Stan's bite?"

"Yes," Kat said, nodding emphatically. "We've been trying to piece everything together, figure out where this whole vampirism thing originated. But Stan and Clint don't remember being bitten at all."

"I am embarrassed to say that my recent, ah, *setbacks* as a thespian have driven me into the bottle, and I do not remember quite a bit," Stan said, grimacing. "I believe the day I bit Ms. Kat was the first time I've experienced vampiric traits, however. Hopefully I would remember *that*, at least."

"I told you, brother, I can't remember when I was bitten either," Clint said. He turned to Evie and me. "Stan and I remember a lot of the symptoms Kat's describing: the exhaustion, the hunger, the erratic emotions, all of that. I remember feeling so out of control at Edendale, like nothing made sense and everyone was out to get me, and then that turned into taunting you, Aveda . . ." He frowned. "I'm sorry about all that. After Stan and I both had our, ah, meltdowns . . . we turned into bat swarms and ended up *here*." He gestured to the tunnel walls.

"Do you recall when you started feeling these symptoms?" I asked, remembering what Naira and James had told me about Clint's change in demeanor at the first *Heroine* table read. "Was it after you'd been brought on to the show?"

"Yeah, I think so," he said. "It's weird, I remember having this really clear idea of how I wanted to do the show, how I wanted to make it so true to your actual lives. And then . . ." He trailed off. The flickering light from the candle rainbow danced over his face, making him look extra haunted. "It got away from me."

I exchanged a look with Evie. All of what we were hearing seemed to confirm what we'd discussed with Bea the day before: that vampires could be made from either Otherworld interference or a more traditional bite.

"We've been trying to figure out how the others became vamps as well," Kat said, as if reading my mind. "And if there is any purpose to it beyond locking us up in this weird tunnel."

"Wait a sec, 'others'?" Evie said. "There are more vampires than the four of you?"

"Yes, the others went on a tunnel exploration. Trying to find another escape route," Kat said. "They should be back—ah, well, here they are now!"

Evie and I turned to see several familiar figures rounding the corner. Naira and James. And . . . I blinked a few times, trying to make sure I was seeing things correctly. It was Dee and Carina—the two teenage girls who'd nearly gotten into a brawl the day I'd accompanied Scott to the beach. But before I could absorb their presence, Naira nearly pounced on me.

"Aveda Jupiter!" Naira crowed. "We were hoping you'd find us down here!"

"Ah, well, yes," I said, my face flushing. I flashed back to our last encounter, which had apparently been even more vampiric than I'd realized.

"Sorry we left so abruptly that day," James said, running a sheepish hand through his hair. "That was our first time turning into bats and shit. We had no idea what was happening!"

"Yes, we realized later that we'd both been feeling a bit strange for several days," Naira said, twisting her hands together. "We tried to put on our most professional actorly faces for you, but we know we were not at our best!"

"No, you guys were, um, great!" I said, my voice way too loud. Once again, I was glad for the tunnel's darkness, so no one could see my deepening blush. "Tell me something: were either of you feeling kind of drained before all this happened? Were you coming off a failure or really burned out or—"

"Goodness, Aveda, you certainly are *direct*," Naira said, releasing a tinkling laugh.

"She's intense," Kat said admiringly. "In all the best ways."

"We were both dealing with pretty bad breakups," James said. "So yeah, I guess we were kinda going through some stuff."

I nodded, my brain trying to put the pieces together. It seemed that no matter how you were turned, this particular type of underlying emotional energy made you a prime vessel for vampirism.

"So as vampires, you can all turn into bats and house a truly impressive amount of meat—but you're also trapped here and unsure why," I said, feeling it out. "Do you have any other new powers you've noticed? Kat, you mentioned something about visions—that you sent the one I experienced this morning, wherein you led me to CosmoBurger?"

"That's right!" she beamed. "We've all been experiencing various kinds of visions. Sometimes they're things that seem like gazing into a crystal ball—events that may happen in the future. Other times, they're fantasies or fears made real: vivid sequences that represent deep-seated desires or things we're especially stressed about. And there's also a version that seems to manifest as simple messages, images we can send back and forth to each other. That part is ridiculously cool!"

"Like vampire text messaging!" Naira enthused.

"Kat sent me that dream vision last night!" Pippa exclaimed. "Oh, just the tunnel part, to help us find it. Not the orgy, that was all me."

"I see," I murmured. "Ah, Naira, James: were you sending me any vision texts during our . . . rehearsal?"

"Oh goodness, no," Naira said, a distressed hand drifting to her chest. "We would never disrupt the work like that! Why?"

"No reason," I said hastily.

"Some of us have discovered that our vampiric energy can influence humans to produce visions of their own," Kat said. "But they are usually inspired by something that human's already feeling—so again, fears and desires dialed up to a zillion."

"Ah," I said, my blush intensifying once more. Perhaps my desire for Scott—and the undeniable sexiness of this duo— had harnessed that vampiric energy, producing my threesome fantasy.

"We don't know if we can do the vamp text messaging with humans, though—like, the sending of very specific images," Kat explained. "But I thought it was worth a shot to try to send you that CosmoBurger one. After all, you are a very exceptional human, Aveda Jupiter."

"So all of you are connected to the *Heroine* show," Evie said, gesturing to Kat, Clint, Stan, Naira, and James. "But you two . . ." She turned to Dee and Carina, tilting her head inquisitively. "Have we met? I feel like we have, but . . ."

"They're part of Scott's surf clinic," I said. "You may have seen them when you came to pick me up after I passed out at the beach. And . . ." I paused, another piece of the puzzle clicking into place. "I'm pretty sure they're the two kids that Scott mentioned the other day—the ones who went missing."

"Hey, Mr. Cam's girlfriend," Dee said.

"Wife," I corrected. "Are either of you connected to the *Heroine* show in any way?"

"Nah, we're not on the show," Carina said. "Except that we've had to hear about it freaking constantly because Mr. Cam won't shut up about it."

"Yeah, he's, like, bursting with pride," Dee said. "Kinda cute, I guess, that old people can still be so in love."

"Excuse me—" I bristled.

"Anyway," Evie intervened quickly. "Have you both been feeling lost lately? Out of sorts with the world—"

"We're teenagers, so yeah, that's kind of our daily existence," Carina said with an eye-roll.

"And when did you start experiencing vampiric traits?" I cut in. "Were you bitten?"

"We don't think so," Dee said. "But we do remember that on that day at the beach, we both started feeling weird. Like, craving insane amounts of meat, feeling kinda gross from all the sun . . ."

"And we were, like, super aggressive—our emotions were so outta control," Carina chimed in. "It's like Kat said, everything was hunger, and not just for food—any desire or want we had was dialed all the way up. Like, I *needed* Dee to understand why I hated her hair so much and then we got into that stupid-ass fight."

"You shoulda just admitted my hair was amazing," Dee grumbled.

"And when were you called to the tunnel?" I asked.

"It was later that night, after the whole beach incident," Dee said. "Carina and I both ended up here."

"The part where your body turns into bats is super gross," Carina said, shuddering. "It feels like you're being torn apart from the inside."

"Lovely," Evie murmured.

"So not everyone here is connected to the show," I said. "But they are all connected to *us*—to Team Tanaka/Jupiter."

I pressed my lips together, my mind twisting and turning. My brain felt like a hamster wheel revved up to an impossible speed, and if I kept trying to run, I'd inevitably fall off.

"What do you think this is ultimately about?" Kat asked. "We've been trying to figure that out amongst ourselves. Like, are evil forces trying to rattle Team Tanaka/Jupiter with a really bad TV show? But then, how do Dee and Carina fit in? And why did we need to become vampires for all of that to happen? Bad TV gets made every day with no supernatural intervention."

"It's my baby," Evie whispered.

I turned to her, trying to make out her face in the flickering dark. Her eyes were wide with worry, her mouth pinched. And her hands had gone to her belly, as if to ward off evil.

"The Otherworld wants my baby," she breathed, almost to herself. She met my gaze. "I'm sorry, Annie, I know you thought that all along, and I kept dismissing it. I just didn't want to believe it."

"Who would?" I said, reaching out to give her hand a reassuring squeeze. I turned back to the assembled vampires. "There are demonic forces that have been trying to get Evie's child-to-be. We foiled a plot a few months ago that utilized Otherworld-powered ghosts. And we've wondered if this is another version of that plan, using another kind of fictional creature. But I'm not sure *how* this is all working. Whoever's behind this has been keeping you all pretty locked up here, and given that you aren't attacking us right now, it doesn't seem as though being a vampire has automatically turned you against us or put you in some kind of baby-stealing mode."

"No," Kat said, a small crinkle appearing on her forehead. "We've also been talking about that, how a lot of our humanity still seems to be intact. We can still eat the regular food we usually enjoy, and while we don't love the sun, we're also not incinerated by it."

"But we do experience a certain kind of overwhelming bloodlust," Stan piped up. "It overtakes us without warning, and the hunger is unbearable—it's as if we can suddenly think of nothing else. That's why Clint and I attacked you in the tunnel just now—for which I am ever so sorry—"

"Yes, I get it," I said. "No need to keep apologizing. But Kat snapped you out of it by . . . what, reminding you of your dreams? Your humanity?"

"That does seem to work," Kat said, giving a helpless shrug. "We keep trying to remind ourselves that even as we're going through these downright bizarre changes, we are still our most essential selves at the core."

"But we're not sure what will happen when whoever's doing this to us brings us out of the tunnel," Clint lamented.

"Right, because we assume we're being created and assembled as some kind of vampire attack posse," Dee added. "That's logical, right?"

"Unless demons enjoy creating rando vampires for fun," Kat said.

"Demons almost never do anything just for fun," I confirmed.

"So whenever we're, like, weaponized, what if there's a point where we can't control the bloodlust no matter what?" Carina piped up. "What if we actually hurt people? Like this lady and her baby." She nodded at Evie, who was clutching her stomach even more protectively now. Even in the dim light of the tunnel, I could see her knuckles turning white.

I gnawed on my lower lip, still trying to work it out. I thought back to Morgan, Shasta's evil plan. How she'd come so close to succeeding . . .

"The demon trying to steal Evie's baby is still stuck in the Otherworld, as far as we know," I said slowly, trying to follow my train of thought to a logical conclusion. "She needed emissaries last time since she can't get to our world—so she had a human and a demon disguised as a human to do all her dirty work."

"Those two activated the Morgan ghosts," Evie murmured, still looking as if she was in her own world.

"Right," I said, pointing to her. "And since we've theorized that the vamps were activated in a similar way as the ghosts—using emotional energy from humans—it makes sense that she'd need an emissary this time, too."

"So who is that person?" Evie said, picking up the thread. I was pleased to see that she seemed to be coming out of her daze. "Someone else working on the show, maybe? Bertram?"

"I guess Shasta could have promised him some kind of ultimate Hollywood power—or whatever it is he wants in life," I mused. "That's how she got to Richard at Morgan." My mind boggled at the idea of an actual demon studio executive.

For some reason, that didn't seem that farfetched.

"Wait!" We all turned to see Pippa flailing around, waving her arms in the air as if to get our attention. "Remember how Bertram keeps saying he hired this amazing new female showrunner?"

"You think it's her?" Evie asked.

"Either that or there is no showrunner and Bertram's pulling the strings and told y'all an elaborate lie," Pippa said, her eyes narrowing. "No one here has actually met this mysterious showrunner yet. But listening to y'all talk . . . I think

I just realized where this climactic baby-stealing attempt is going to take place." She paused, looking at all of us in turn and lowering her voice conspiratorially for maximum drama. "There's a comic book convention tomorrow in downtown LA, and there's supposed to be a panel for *Heroine*. Rumor has it that they're going to reveal the *new* Aveda Jupiter—the person they cast to replace Kat—and the new showrunner."

"So the demon emissary could also be my replacement!" Kat growled. "This whole situation just keeps getting worse."

"But this is a prime opportunity for us to get some answers," I said, nodding approvingly at Pippa. "Excellent deductive work, Pippa."

"I don't know," Evie said. "That is some big, juicy bait they seem to be hanging out there. What if it's a trap, designed to lure us in . . ." She took a shuddering breath, her hand going instinctively to her belly again.

"Then we're going to run right into it," I said, drawing myself up tall and trying to beam out bravado. "That is the Aveda Jupiter Way."

"Does the Aveda Jupiter Way also involve having a plan?" Evie asked.

I smiled at her, bits and pieces of thoughts snapping together in my head as I envisioned our future battle. I just *knew* I had my Idea Face on.

"Oh, yes," I said. "And trust me: it's gonna be fucking brilliant."

CHAPTER TWENTY-NINE

EVIE AND I managed to leave the Mistress Tunnel by simply retracing our steps back to the hole in the floor of CosmoBurger. I tried to cover the hole with some artfully placed boxes, reasoning that the back room was so messy, it would take Carl a while to notice anything amiss.

When we returned to the suite, I assured a much-relieved Scott that his missing teens were safe for now, and that I'd even managed to get an explanation for their bizarre behavior at the beach. Then I called Bea and got her to walk me through the technical intricacies of setting up the mini HQ Batcave Pippa had developed. In short order, most of Team Tanaka/Jupiter was assembled—me, Evie, and Scott on the hotel couch; Nate and Bea in their FaceTime windows on the TV screen. I was just about to make with the master planning, when the communal iPad buzzed with another incoming call.

"Lucy!" I exclaimed, as Evie hit the answer button and Lucy popped up in her own little FaceTime window. "No cat grooming emergencies today?"

"I should think not," Lucy huffed, tossing her honey-colored hair over her shoulder. "I spent several days in a row helping Rose groom that infernal creature. I swear she is an actual demon in a feline body. Just look at this!" She brandished her wrist, which sported a pattern of rather impressive scratches. "Anyway, I know I've been a bit busy adjusting to my glorious domestic life with Rose, but I've been so envious of your LA jaunt, darlings. Wish I was there!"

"We wish you were too," I said, breaking into a very genuine version of my megawatt smile. "But I'm glad you're calling in now, because we have a lot to discuss."

In short order, Evie and I relayed everything we'd learned in the Mistress Tunnel, ending with Pippa's revelation about the comic book convention.

"Wow!" Bea exclaimed, her eyes widening as we wrapped up. "So Shasta—or at least we think it's Shasta—created a whole vampire squad to get Evie and Nate's baby? That is *bananas*. Then again, her plans are *always* bananas!"

"That's what we're thinking," I said, reaching over to give Evie's hand a comforting squeeze. "And we also think they're laying whatever this trap is at that convention panel. So I propose . . ." I threw my hands out in a *ta-da!* type gesture. ". . . a *counter* trap."

"Ooh!" Bea said. "I love counter *anything*."

"I was thinking back to our experience at Morgan," I said, homing in on the topic. "Evie defeated Shasta because she figured out how to give the last ghost we encountered closure. Shasta had managed to weaponize emotional energy from humans, true—but she never accounted for just how unpredictable that energy is. Even if it's being manipulated by the Otherworld, it's still a very human thing."

"And we, as a species, are very fucking messy," Bea said, twirling her purple hair around her finger.

I glanced over at Evie to make sure she was still with me. She nodded, absently rubbing her belly. I knew she was scared, but trying to prepare herself for whatever battle lay ahead. "And now, we think Shasta's doing something similar, yes?" I continued. "Only she's weaponized emotional energy that exists in living human bodies, rather than ghostly traces left behind at certain locations."

I hopped up from my seat and started to pace. I focused so much better when I was in motion.

"So let's say Shasta's plan tomorrow involves the vamp squad being called in to snatch and/or attack Evie at this convention panel. Or to take the baby from her, somehow.

Kat and Co. mentioned that overwhelming bloodlust, that *hunger* that overtakes the vamps. But when presented with a disruption—like Kat reminding Clint and Stan about all the stuff they still want to do with their lives—that hunger seems to dissipate."

"So you need to, what? Distract the vampire gang for a really long time?" Scott asked.

"Not exactly." I stopped in my tracks, my brain buzzing nonstop. "Evie gave her ghostly self what she needed to finally feel okay: words of reassurance, words of closure. Everything she needed to finally forgive herself. All of our vampires were experiencing some kind of failure, burnout, or sadness when they turned. Even Pippa was dealing with all of her friendship drama, convinced Shelby had left her behind. We think that's the kind of emotional energy Shasta preyed upon. And while there is no way to *fix* everything they are going through . . ." I shrugged and resumed my pacing. "Perhaps we can let them know that they are seen and heard. That we believe everything will be okay for them, and that most importantly: we are here and we are listening."

"This is a very . . . mmm, I'm not sure what the right term is, darling," Lucy mused. "Woo-woo? New age? A very interesting idea, to be sure. But not exactly what we expect from Aveda Jupiter." She gave me a teasing smile.

"That's only part *one*," I retorted. "After we hopefully soothe the vamp squad's bloodlust, we'll get into the next step—we'll take a page from our old pal Zacasta—"

"Who?" Nate asked, his brows drawing together.

"I'll explain later, Nate," Bea said.

"We're going to *pull* the Otherworld magic out of them—the element that's manipulated their energy and turned them all vampy," I continued. I stopped pacing again and put my hands on my hips, looking at everyone in turn. "Once we do *that* . . . well, if Shasta has an emissary this time, that person should be at least somewhat neutralized. Remember, Richard couldn't do anything without access to Shasta's good demon buddy, Leonora. And Leonora couldn't do much without her ghosts—except get pushed into an Otherworld portal by Shelby."

"So whoever the emissary is, you're setting them up for mondo defeat!" Bea crowed. "I love it."

"This is promising, but you've left out some important information," Nate said. "How are you going to soothe the vampires' bloodlust and pull Otherworld magic from their bodies? How did your, er, friend Zacasta do it?"

"Annie." Scott stood and crossed the room to stand in front of me, concern written all over his face. "Are you thinking of trying to pull magic from multiple people using your telekinesis? Like, all by yourself? Because . . ." He shook his head, trying to find the right words. "It's not that I don't think you can, it's just . . ."

"Oh no." A slow grin overtook my face. "Do you really think Aveda Jupiter would attempt something as foolhardy as that, Cameron? That she is at all like that self-centered fool Zacasta, who was so obsessed with being special, she didn't realize she was totally fucking herself over?"

"Still don't know who Zacasta is," Nate muttered.

"Darling, just go with it," Lucy said. "Have you learned nothing over the years?"

"Here's what I'm thinking," I proclaimed, tossing my ponytail over my shoulder. "We are finally going to try one of those *power combos* you and Bea keep talking about."

"Holy shit, yessss!" Bea gasped.

"Tell me how it works," I prompted.

"Scott does a spell," Bea began, "that gives us a temporary mental link with each other. Kinda like when I was having all my adventures on the brain plane, but we've worked on adding supernatural safeguards so it's not quite so dangerous."

"That's right," Scott said, picking up the thread. He was studying me, looking shocked and intrigued all at once. "Once our minds are linked, I can bring our powers together—they fuse into, as Bea has called it, a *mega-power*."

"That's . . ." I shook my head at him, in awe. "That's incredible. *You're* incredible. And you too, Bea," I added hastily when she loudly cleared her throat. "So then what happens, can both of you wield both powers at once?"

"Not exactly," Bea said. "It seems to work best if we designate one person as the traffic controller, the 'host,' if you will. That person's body is the conduit for both powers—but you're communicating on the brain plane, telling your power combo partner when to add a little of this, or pull back on that."

"So, for example—when Bea and I fuse our powers, she can use her emotional projection to aim my spells very precisely at their targets," Scott explained. "But *I* still have to cast the spell, while communicating with her through the mental link."

"Here's my idea," I said, pointing to Scott. "You're going to cast this spell. Only you're not going to fuse just two powers. You're going to fuse *three*. Mine, yours, and Bea's. Do you think you can do that?"

"Yes," he managed, meeting my gaze. "Yes, I can."

"Excellent. We will then proceed like this: I'll be the host. I'll send my invisible feathers into the vampires' bodies, as I did with Evie during her wedding. Only they will be bolstered by your magic and Bea's emotional projection powers. Bea will use her power to send those soothing 'we're listening' vibes to the vamps. You, Scott, will use your fabulous Otherworld magic-sensing abilities to find that magic within them. And then I'll use my telekinesis to pull it out."

"That sounds so exciting," Lucy exclaimed, pumping a fist in the air. "Goodness, I *really* wish I was there now!"

I held Scott's gaze. He was looking at me intently, his eyes unreadable.

"There's no way to practice this beforehand, is there?" he finally said.

"No," I said. I reached over and took both of his hands in mine, trying to show him how much I felt this, how I *knew* it would work. "But I believe in us."

He smiled then, that sweet, lopsided grin I was a sucker for.

"What will I be doing during all of this?" Evie piped up.

I turned to look at her. She appeared more energized now, some of the fight resurfacing in her determined hazel eyes.

"We may end up needing fire to contain Shasta's emissary, particularly if they are demonic," I said. "But also . . ." I dropped Scott's hands and crossed the room to her, resettling myself on the couch and meeting her eyes. "I think you and I should engage in a bit of trickery that's going to enhance our plan—and hopefully ensure that it succeeds."

She leaned in, intrigued, as I explained the rest of my plan to her. And was happy when she enthusiastically agreed.

"So, everyone's onboard?" I concluded.

"Of course we are, love," Lucy purred. "Though I suppose Nate and I do not have much to do as we are not there, nor are we capable of projecting our emotional states all the way from Maui the way Bea can."

"Your moral support means everything," I said, grinning at her. "And, you know, different missions always give different members of the team a chance to shine. Whatever demonic horrors we encounter next will surely be all yours."

"How absolutely thrilling," Lucy said, fluffing her hair. "In the meantime, why don't you and Evie come over for tea when you return home? I do adore my domestic bliss, but I miss seeing your faces every day. We can get petit fours and everything."

"I would love that," I said, my heart surging. "And, um. Maybe we could make that a weekly thing?"

"Smashing!" Lucy exclaimed, throwing me a wink. "I will purchase some extra lint rollers so you don't get Calliope's sheddings all over your beautiful clothes."

"Hey, I'm actually working on building an all new and improved lint roller!" Bea squealed. "I'll send it to you, Luce!"

As the room devolved into lively conversation about many disparate topics, I leaned back against the couch, purpose gathering in my chest. We were going to triumph, I just knew it. How could we not, with this amazing team?

"Hey," Evie whispered, reaching over to squeeze my hand. "That was awesome. See what I mean? You're the *engine*."

"My thanks to the glue," I said, squeezing back.

"And Luce misses you too," Evie said. "Even though she's not moving back in."

A slight smile played across my lips. "You told her, didn't you? About how I was feeling?"

"I told her," Evie confirmed. "But she was already planning on inviting you over for tea."

I laughed, my heart feeling light and free even though we were about to embark on one of our most dangerous missions to date. I reached over and snagged a pair of leftover mini croissants from the coffee table and handed her one.

"I love you, Evie," I said, holding up the croissant in a makeshift toast. "And I love our family. Here's to our *not* last mission."

She clinked carbs with me. "I can't wait."

CHAPTER THIRTY

"I'M NOT SURE about this." Evie cocked an eyebrow at me. Which was extra disconcerting, because it was *my* eyebrow. And my face, staring back at me.

"A little trust, please," I said, fluffing the tangle of dark brown curls that was now gracing my head. "When have any of my genius ideas ever turned out anything less than one hundred percent successful?"

"Well—"

"Never mind," I said hastily. "I should know better than to ask that."

We were standing outside the Los Angeles Convention Center, a cavernous, maze-like building done up in drab gray concrete. Today, the gargantuan bustling crowd piling inside gave it an endless parade of color: X-Men, Sailor Scouts, and Jedi jostled for space, all extra excited to celebrate their fandom of choice.

And Evie and I were settling into the first step of my brilliant plan, the one I'd explained to her in great detail the day before: we were disguised as each other.

I'd asked Scott to give us glamours, and the results were rather convincing. This wasn't the first time we'd posed as each other—but staring back at your own face is always quite bizarre.

My reasoning for the glamours had been simple: Shasta and this mysterious showrunner (and/or whoever else was behind this devilish vampire/Otherworld plot) would be going after Evie. So I'd suggested we switch places. I'd go to the convention as Evie, she'd go as Aveda, and we'd draw the vamps to me and take them down. We were hoping this clever bit of trickery would throw the demonic forces off— they'd be bracing for fire, not telekinesis. And definitely not a telekinesis/emotional projection/magic spell power combo.

"Got the passes!" Scott called out, jogging up to us and waving a trio of laminated convention badges in the air. "Somehow, Pippa reserved them for us."

I hopped from one foot to the other, anticipation humming through my veins. There is nothing Aveda Jupiter loves quite so much as the thrill of a big battle. Perhaps I would get to punch *many* things.

"This is weird," Scott said, gesturing between Evie and me. "You look like each other, but the body language is . . ." He shook his head, flashing a half-smile. "All you. Both of you. Wait, I think I just confused myself again."

"Just make sure you know who you're kissing," I said. "Hopefully that won't be confusing at all."

He grinned, reached over, and squeezed my hand. And as we walked into the convention center, on our way to what would hopefully be the climactic battle of our LA adventure, he didn't let go.

I leaned over and gave him an impulsive peck on the cheek. "I'm glad you're here with me," I whispered in his ear.

"Me too, Annie," he whispered back. "I mean . . . Evie? I mean . . ."

"Oh god, let's get a move on!" the real Evie groaned, giving him a little shove.

We fought our way onto the dealer's room floor and dove into a mass of people, Evie batting various cardboard swords out of her way. I took extra care with "my" pregnant stomach, dodging the wide array of bumps, elbows, and other bits of humanity intruding on my personal space. Yes, the belly was merely an affectation of the glamour, but I had to make it *look* real. If any of Shasta's minions were watching, they needed to be convinced that I was Evie.

"Hey, nice Aveda Jupiter costume!" someone dressed as

a giant Pikachu screamed at Evie as they zipped past us. "You really captured her diva aura!"

"At least we blend in," I said wryly, as Evie burst into giggles. "Well, for now. Once we get to the panel room, *not* blending in will be the order of the day."

"We're going to panel room A," Evie said, waving an arm at a distant point across the dealer's room floor. "Just over there and up the escalators."

We finally made it to the other side of the dealer's room and hopped on the escalator. As we ascended to the panel room, I gave myself a pep talk, drawing myself up tall and putting on my—or was that Evie's?—most ferocious game face.

This *had* to work.

We reached the top of the escalator and entered the room with the helpful "A" emblazoned on the door. It was a smaller panel room—not one of the big auditoriums reserved for the likes of *Star Wars*—but it was *packed*. Every seat was full, and all eyes were trained toward the front of the room, where a stage had been set up with a long table containing a line of microphones. A podium with its own mic was positioned at the end of the table.

But no one was onstage yet. Everyone in the audience was watching, waiting, the anticipation looming over the space like a cloud.

A skitter of nerves ran up my spine as I scanned the room, taking in the mix of colorful costumes, plastic swords and lightsabers, and overflowing merch bags. We weren't sure when the vamp crew was going to be summoned; I didn't see any sight of them yet. I was hoping maybe Kat or Pippa would be able to send me another vision text message, but my brain hadn't received anything. Maybe they were flying through the sky, an overwhelming storm of bats overtaking LA like an especially ominous rain cloud. Maybe their minds were not their own, compelled by a greater demonic force, bloodlust flowing through their veins—

I shook my head. This was not the kind of empowering thinking I liked to engage in right before battle.

"Well, well, well—what a crowd!"

I was jolted out of my thoughts by a booming voice, and my gaze went to the front, where an uncharacteristically jovial Bertram was striding onstage and taking up his post behind the podium.

"Good morning!" he said, flashing a too-big smile. "I'm Bertram Sturges, executive vice president of original series programming at Pinnacle Pictures, and I am oh-so-delighted to introduce our *Heroine* panel today! Folks, we are set to make some stunning revelations."

He did his weird holding for applause thing, only to be greeted with silence. Hmm. Wasn't this the type of forum where he *should* get applause? But the eclectic audience filling this packed room simply stared back at him, totally silent. Perhaps they weren't true Tanaka/Jupiter fans, and were, in fact, waiting for a future panel about *Star Wars*.

Don't get your feathers all ruffled over that, I thought sternly to myself. *Focus on the mission!*

"And at this moment, I am thrilled to tell you that this will be less of a panel and more of a *spotlight*." Bertram leaned into the mic, his eyes lit with glee. It looked odd on him—he was usually so bland, so completely nondescript. I supposed he felt he had to dial his stage presence all the way up for an event like this. "So without further ado, I am ever so pleased to introduce to you our brand-new showrunner—who also happens to be our *star*. That's right, she is your Aveda Jupiter! Let's bring her out: the beautiful, talented, absolutely iconic . . . Mercedes McClain!"

Luckily, the crowd chose that moment to come to life, screaming, clapping, and stomping their feet.

Because otherwise, they would have heard the *actual* Aveda Jupiter—currently disguised as her best friend Evie Tanaka—bellowing from the back: "Oh *hell* no!"

"Cannot agree with that sentiment more," Scott muttered, his eyes narrowing as he laid a soothing hand on my back.

As Mercedes swanned onstage, waving to the audience, I

felt Evie's hand clamp on my arm. Which was a good thing, since my first instinct was to storm the stage.

"Not yet," she cautioned, her eyes wide with surprise. "No sign of the vamps, and we have a whole plan, remember? But . . . wow. Okay. Was not expecting *that*."

I bit back my extremely uncharitable reply, and tried to tamp down on the rage currently burning through my bloodstream. What the actual fuck? Was *Mercedes* Shasta's emissary? A mere pawn for Bertram? What was she doing?!

Scott's hand stayed on my back, calming me a bit. I forced my shoulders to relax and trained my gaze on Mercedes. Evie was right, we couldn't outright attack her or try to capture her just because she was being her usual annoying self in a surprising new context. For one thing, this wasn't total confirmation that she was Shasta's emissary. And there was still no sign of the vamp squad.

So for now, we had to wait. And watch.

Mercedes settled herself at the center of the long table, smiling and tossing her shiny blonde hair over her shoulder. She was, I noticed, wearing an outfit that appeared to be a carbon copy of one of my signature superheroing costumes: a concoction of black spandex and shiny silver accents, topped with a pair of sleek over-the-knee boots.

"So, Ms. McClain," Bertram said, inclining his head deferentially. "How did this come to be? Because as I understand it, initially the show was going a different way with its portrayal of Aveda Jupiter?"

"I love how he's saying this as if he has no prior knowledge of anything—or any hand in the decisions," I muttered.

"That's right," Mercedes trilled, lowering her eyes modestly. Her eyelashes were encrusted in silver mascara—another key element I always included with this particular look. "They'd cast an entirely different actress, actually. Someone who was perhaps a bit more . . . hmm, what you'd think of when you think of Aveda Jupiter. You know: quirky, exotic, outside the box, perhaps a bit niche."

"Just say 'Asian,'" Evie hissed.

"I have never been called 'quirky' in *my entire life*," I seethed.

"I think it's safe to say she hasn't changed," Scott said, his hand tightening protectively against my back.

"But it was decided that a choice with more *broad* appeal was best for such a groundbreaking project," Mercedes continued, flashing a brilliant smile. "The studio wanted this to be a four-quadrant global smash rather than a cult classic. So they thought it best to cast someone who would be believable as an iconic superheroine!"

"B-believable?!" I sputtered. "I *am* an iconic superheroine!"

"I know there's a lot of talk right now about diversity," Mercedes said, narrowing her eyes in a way that she probably imagined looked thoughtful. "And as a woman, I certainly respect that trend. But when you're asking a worldwide mainstream audience to buy into the concept of a superheroine . . ." She flashed that brilliant smile again. "You have to have someone who really looks the part."

"I really, *really* want to use my fire power right now," Evie growled.

"And what of Aveda's superheroing partner, Evie Tanaka?" Bertram said, his expression twisting into a look of mock confusion. I had to commend him for his acting—perhaps he was angling for a part on the show as well. "She was a key part of the original concept."

"And she's still an important character in Aveda's story," Mercedes said, nodding emphatically and bringing a hand to her heart. "But we needed to focus our concept, and audiences seem to prefer solo superheroines more—lone wolves, you know. When we zoomed out and looked at the creative, we realized that she was more of a sidekick. And what superhero doesn't need a good sidekick?"

"And now I wish *I* had a fire power," I snarled, my hands clenching at my sides. "I don't think anything else is explosive enough to express what I'm feeling right now."

"Just wait," Scott murmured, glancing around the room. "Still no sign of the vamps."

"And we still don't know if Mercedes is the emissary," Evie whispered. "Is she demonically evil, or just, like . . . a total freaking jerk?"

"'Both' is also an option," Scott said.

"You're using a lot of 'we,' here," Bertram said, giving Mercedes a conspiratorial wink. "And that leads perfectly into my next announcement—you're also our new showrunner! How did that come about?"

"I'm so humbled and grateful," Mercedes said, smiling. "When I was cast, I just had so many ideas! As I understand it, they were already looking for a new showrunner after parting ways with the last one—creative differences, you know how it is! And since I came to the part with my own vision, it unfolded organically. Suddenly I was starring in *and* running my own show! How did that even happen?" She let out a tinkling laugh that set my teeth on edge.

"You must be phenomenally talented," Bertram gushed. "Because prior to this, you didn't have any acting or writing experience, is that correct?"

"Correct indeed!" Mercedes exclaimed, her eyes flashing with delight. "I was of course known as Magnificent Mercedes, LA's premier superheroine! So I had lots of real life experience to draw on." She and Bertram laughed together, and I resisted the ever-increasing urge to storm the stage and tackle her.

"Bringing this story to the screen is so important to me," Mercedes said, her expression morphing to gravely serious. "When I think of all the little girls who will see this and realize they too can be a superhero . . ." Her hand flitted to her eyes to brush away fake tears. "I feel so *moved*. The story we are telling is so *universal*—"

"Fuck you!"

I did a double take. Because while I'd certainly thought those words, I hadn't said them out loud.

Evie had.

Every head in the room swiveled to look at her—including mine.

Her face was red, her hands were balled at her sides, and she looked absolutely furious. Given that she was still glamoured as me, the effect was super weird. As if I was watching myself on TV.

"Excuse me?" Mercedes said, raising a hand to shield her eyes. "I can't quite see all of you, was that someone in the back?"

"You bet it was!" Evie barked. "And seriously, fuck you, Mercedes! Aveda Jupiter *means* something to women of color. Just because she's not 'universal' in your eyes—and let's be real, that's just code for 'white'—it doesn't mean she's not a hero to a lot of fucking people. Your thoughts on that say way more about you than they do about her."

"Um, Evie . . ." I whispered.

I was extremely touched by her impassioned defense of me. Especially since she was usually the quieter one, less likely to completely blow her top. But when she *did* . . . well, she always seemed to choose the most *interesting* moments.

But hey, maybe we *needed* to get Mercedes'—or Bertram's, or whoever was behind all this—attention. Maybe that would get her to finally call forth the vamps and we could set our plan in motion.

"You haven't changed at all!" Evie cried. "Everything that comes out of your mouth is a bunch of diminishing, undercutting, passive-aggressive—or sometimes *actually* aggressive—bullshit disguised as 'nice' white lady nonsense!"

I drew in a calming breath and surveyed the scene, once again scanning the room for signs of vamp life. The audience had turned to stare at us, their attention drawn by Evie's outburst. The weight of their collective gaze pressed down on us, and I shifted uncomfortably, trying to retain my battle-ready posture. Scott's hand was still on my back, that constant bit of warmth.

Evie finally finished yelling and silence descended over the room. I waited for the crowd to turn back to Mercedes.

But they remained fixated on us.

Sweat beaded the back of my neck and unease threaded through my gut. Something was . . . off about this audience. No, I probably wouldn't have been cheering for Bertram and Mercedes either, but they were totally silent. And they were all looking at us with the same disconcertingly blank stare.

"Well, hello to my old friend Aveda Jupiter," Mercedes said, her overly sweet voice finally breaking the silence. "Bertram said you might try to crash the panel. Oh, Evie, I almost didn't see you there. Always in Aveda's shadow, hmm?"

That's right, I was still glamoured as Evie. It was weird that Mercedes had said something so outright bitchy in front of her adoring public, but . . .

I frowned, scanning the crowd again. There was no scandalized murmuring, no phone cameras going off and trying to capture the moment.

No, now all of those Jedi, X-Men, and Sailor Scouts were staring at Evie and me with the exact same disconcertingly blank expressions. As if frozen in place.

I tamped down on the dread building in my chest.

This whole time, I'd been watching and waiting for the vampire army to show up.

What if they were already here?

"Scott," I hissed, "start the power combo spell *now*."

He pressed his hand against my back to show that he understood, and then I felt his posture stiffen next to me as he focused, preparing to access that Otherworld magic and connect his mind with Bea's.

"Mercedes!" I called out, trying to distract her further. "Just for the record, I am *nobody's* sidekick—"

"God, you're boring," she snarled, getting to her feet. Her gaze swept the crowd, and she gave them a queenly nod. "It's time, my glorious minions!" she barked. *"Get her."*

And the crowd's collective gaze flashed bright red.

In an instant, they were out of their seats, bearing down on us as a mob. I saw flashes of fangs, that *hunger* in their eyes as they swarmed toward us. I steeled myself, reminding my brain that *this was it*, this was why I was glamoured as Evie. It was time to be bait, to run directly into the trap—just as I'd planned. Out of the corner of my eye, I saw Evie-as-me dance out of the way, giving the vamps a clear path to their target.

"Scott," I hissed. "The spell . . . ?"

"Almost got it," he replied.

I stood my ground, planting my feet and trying to straighten my spine into a classic Aveda Jupiter power pose—even though I was glamoured as Evie. Every cell in my body was braced for impact, ready to fling those invisible feathers in the mob's direction.

And then I felt something brush up against my mind—a whisper that slowly shaped itself into a familiar voice.

Aveda! Bea shrieked in my head. *It worked! We're all power combo-ed up! Let 'em have it!*

The magic's holding, Scott's voice added. *Go for it, Annie.*

I closed my eyes even as the mob got closer still—I felt the heat from the crowd pressing in on me, heard the lustful panting as they scented my blood in the air . . .

And as I gathered my invisible feathers, preparing to fling them with all my might, I was surprised at how *strong* they felt. I could sense the magic thrumming through me, could practically picture my telekinesis as a column of glowing light.

That's right! Bea crowed. *It would look like some motherfrakkin' rainbows if you could see it IRL. So rad!*

I didn't realize this spell meant you could hear everything *happening in my head, Bea,* I thought back at her.

I won't nose around too *much,* she said, not sounding anywhere near convincing.

I refocused on my beautifully reinforced feathers, felt Scott's magic flowing through my brain, my bloodstream . . .

Then I heard Scott curse, and my eyes flew open . . . to see the vampire mob swarming right past me, eyes flashing and fangs bared. As if they hadn't seen me at all.

What the frak! Bea said in my head.

I swiveled around, desperately trying to figure out what was happening.

"Bring her to the lair!" Mercedes shrieked over the snarling din. "She's the key—*Aveda Jupiter is the key*!"

The vampire mob was converging on Evie. Who was glamoured as *me*.

"Wait . . . *no!*" I screamed.

I ran toward the mob, flinging my feathers out haphazardly. Maybe it was all that bright magic flowing through me, but I swore I could see them soaring through the air, as shiny and rainbow-hued as Bea had said. Determination gathered in my chest, powering me forward.

"Dammit!" Evie screamed in my voice. She was so mobbed at this point, I couldn't see her anymore.

My feathers flew toward the mob, and I prepared to send them into every vamp's body—true, this was way more people than we'd expected, but I could still do this. I could still—

THWACK!

I reeled back as my feathers slammed into some sort of invisible barrier, sending them flying back toward me.

"Fuck!" I growled.

What was that? Bea cried.

The vampire mob has some kind of magical force field, Scott said, his tone grim.

I ran toward the mob, but they were already sweeping their way to the exit. Evie was still in there somewhere but I couldn't see her between all the bodies. I knew she didn't want to hurt the humans spiriting her away—they were clearly under the influence of that supernatural bloodlust—but I desperately wished she'd make with the fire.

I flung myself at the exit . . . only to slam against the very same invisible barrier that had blocked my telekinesis. I tumbled back onto my ass, breathing hard. The vampire mob was already halfway down the hall and I couldn't even make it out of the fucking panel room.

"Whoa, awesome group cosplay!" I heard someone in the hall yell at the vampire mob.

"No!" I screamed, scrambling to my knees and watching helplessly as the mob—and Evie—disappeared down a nearby escalator. "Goddammit!" I pounded against the invisible barrier with my fists, angry tears gathering in my eyes.

"What is this?" Scott spat out, hustling up behind me. "Another force field?" I turned and saw that we were now the only people in the panel room; Mercedes and Bertram had exited the stage during all the chaos.

"Yes, I think it's one of the weird vampire force field things Kat told us about yesterday," I said, fruitlessly smacking the invisible barrier. "You can only get past it if a vamp invites you in."

I sat back on my heels, that sick sense of helplessness overwhelming my entire being as my fists clenched and unclenched at my sides.

Aveda! Bea exclaimed in my head. I nearly jumped out of my skin.

"We're still with you," Scott confirmed, meeting my gaze.

His face was grim, his mouth set in a thin line, his eyes darting to the exit. He was also trying to figure out what we could possibly do next. We had to do something, we had to save Evie . . .

Go over all your memories from the past few days! Bea yelled. *There must be a clue in there somewhere. I'll help— um, if that's okay with you.*

"Yes, fine, Bea, dig around in my brain," I said out loud. "Anything to figure this out."

Actually, I just saw some stuff I didn't want to, she said, sounding a little queasy. *Scott is like a brother to me, I do* not *need—*

"Gah!" I tried to tune her out, furiously going over everything Evie and I had done during our time in LA.

"Annie." Scott crouched down next to me, his hand squeezing my shoulder. "How can I help?"

"Just be here," I managed, grabbing his hand in a death grip. "Please. And help me remember . . ."

Images piled up in my brain in an incomprehensible mosaic, sights and sounds and smells jumbling together with no rhyme or reason.

I recalled how drained I'd felt for our entire trip—all my monster yawns, my sense of bone-deep exhaustion, my burnout that was never alleviated, despite all my protests to the contrary. My newly erratic telekinesis that seemed to drain me even more.

And . . .all that *hunger*. About everything. I felt it deep in my bones, that desperate need to solve every single problem I encountered, that inability to rest until I'd thoroughly conquered everything in my path.

That was a lot of emotional energy I was carrying around. Just waiting to be manipulated by demonic forces.

More images coalesced in my head.

I saw myself dragging Scott into the Edendale bathroom, overcome with sudden lust so overwhelming, it was almost painful—how I'd felt feverish and erratic in that moment, my moods swinging all over the place, my hunger insatiable.

I watched as I inhaled that delectable red meat marvel from CosmoBurger, its oily juices coating my tongue.

I remembered how the LA sun always seemed to beat down on me, making my skin feel like it was burning up.

And then, all the strange visions and dreams I'd been having recently converged in my brain, blocking out everything else.

Kat's voice from the tunnel echoed through my head.

We don't know if we can do the vamp text messaging with humans . . . But I thought it was worth a shot to try to send you that CosmoBurger one. After all, you are a very exceptional human, Aveda Jupiter.

Ohmygod, Aveda, Bea murmured reverently. *How did we not see it before?*

"See what?" Scott asked out loud.

"Scott . . ." I squeezed his hand, and got to my feet,

turning to face the force field. "Our whole combo power thing is still going, right? Can you maintain it even if I'm far away from you?"

"I think so," he said. "My link to Bea is holding strong, and she's many, many miles away. But where are you going, and why do you think I'm not coming with you?"

"Because," I said, studying the barrier, "where I'm about to go, I'm not sure if you *can* come with me."

I focused on the barrier, concentrating hard. Then I closed my eyes and envisioned the place I wanted to go.

"Come on," I hissed through gritted teeth. "I don't know exactly how this works, but I need someone to compel me . . ."

The invitation! Bea called out in my head. *Try the invitation!*

I took a deep breath and stared down the invisible force field, hoping our hunch was correct.

"I invite *myself* in," I intoned, projecting so loudly that my voice seemed to echo off the walls of the now abandoned panel room.

The pain was instant and sudden, a collection of metaphorical knives stabbing every conceivable place on my body. My chest felt like it was crumpling in on itself, all of my internal organs being crushed at once . . .

A scream tore itself from my throat, and I was vaguely aware of Scott yelling my name in the background, and the pain, *fuck*, the all-consuming *pain* . . .

And then everything went black and I was in the air. I was my own swarm of bats, flying triumphantly through the force field, down the escalator, and out the convention center doors.

CHAPTER THIRTY-ONE

BEING A BIG, ominous swarm of vampire bats was weird.

I floated in and out of consciousness, slivers of awareness flitting through my brain. I saw the vast floor of the convention center from my midair perch, the costumed spectators below goggling and yelling about the random bat circling above their heads. Patches of sunlight and clouds. A grid of jammed-up traffic, honking its way through the smoggy air. I kept trying to take in more, but every time I attempted to expend that bit of additional effort, my brain blacked out.

When my very human eyes popped open again, I was hit with a wave of pain so vicious, I had to curl myself into a ball.

"Not that super at the moment, are we, Aveda Jupiter?" a cloying voice cooed.

I forced myself to breathe through the pain, uncurling my body a little bit at a time.

I was in the tunnel again, darkness all around me—but as I kept blinking, various shapes started to come into focus. I saw some of the vampire mob from the panel standing off to the side, still silent and blank-faced and wearing their colorful cosplay. Somehow, that made things even creepier. I didn't see Kat or any of the original crew; hopefully they were okay.

And right in the center of things was, of course, Mercedes. Her eyes weren't flashing red, but that didn't make her appear any less malevolent.

"I guess you didn't hear me," she sneered. "I said—"

"I did hear you," I managed. "I just didn't want to dignify

the worst fucking joke I've ever heard with a response. It's also a nonsensical joke, because apparently I'm *extra* super at the moment—you know, being a motherfucking vampire and all!"

Mercedes chuckled. "So you finally figured some of it out. Oh, I can't wait until you hear what's in store for you."

I blinked my eyes furiously, trying to get the tunnel to come into focus. I could make out Bertram, standing right behind Mercedes. And curled into a ball on the floor in front of them was—

"Evie!" I screamed. Then slumped back over, the wind knocked out of me. "If you've done *anything* to her—"

"She's perfectly fine," Mercedes said, waving a careless hand. "Of course, we were extremely disappointed to learn that you two had engaged in some kind of *Parent Trap*–level scenario to switch identities. I wanted the real Aveda Jupiter, not some wannabe."

She sent Evie's limp body a disdainful look.

"I'm okay, Annie," Evie said, her voice very faint. My heart clenched; our glamours were no longer working, so she was herself once more, and hearing her voice like that brought tears to my eyes.

"Let me go to her," I managed through gritted teeth. "I just want to make sure she's okay—"

"I told you, she's *fine*," Mercedes snapped. "But then, of course you don't believe me—you never listen, do you?"

"What is that supposed to mean?" I growled, my gaze never leaving Evie. I still felt like I'd been run over by a bus, but I tried to rally. I felt around in my mind, frantically trying to locate Bea and Scott.

Are you still there? I thought plaintively.

No response. And I didn't feel the magic flowing through me like I had earlier.

"I tried to talk to you about all of this *years* ago," Mercedes said. "About how the people of San Francisco deserved a more *universal* heroine, someone *everyone* could look up to! I was dropping hints left and right, and still—you refused to get out of the way."

"What?!" I shook my head. "First of all, that is so fucking racist. Are you saying that so-called 'universal' heroines have to be white? That women of color are just expected to see themselves in white women, too? That me being Asian makes me . . ." Another massive wave of exhaustion hit me square in the chest. ". . . *niche*?!" I managed to finish.

Mercedes shrugged. "Sounds like *you're* the one making it about race."

"And you said nothing of the sort," I pressed on, gasping for breath. "You *congratulated* me—"

"I was trying to be *nice*!" Mercedes spat out. "I wanted to handle the situation with kindness, but I should have known you would be all aggressive about it—"

"I was *not* aggressive!" I interrupted. "I sat there and listened to your racist-ass 'kindness' because I couldn't believe the fucked-up words that were coming out of your mouth. I mean, 'affirmative action'? *Really*?!"

"That's exactly what it was," Mercedes said, her eyes sparking with malice. "I was right there, and I was *perfect*. The universal ideal of a superheroine. But because people wanted to show just how 'woke' they are, they fell all over themselves for the freaking diversity hire."

"That is rich," I choked out. "I seriously cannot believe the lengths you've gone to in order to twist that logic. The truth is, I was just better than you. And by the way, I had to be about a thousand fucking times better than you to get a fraction of the opportunities that were handed to you on a silver platter—"

"*Quiet!*" Mercedes bellowed. "You're as insufferably long-winded as ever. I can't believe Shasta thinks you're worth *anything*."

"Of course, Shasta," I muttered. "I knew this was her. But why *does* she want me? I thought this was all about Evie's baby."

"Ugh, looks like I'm going to have to explain this to you like you're a toddler," Mercedes glowered. "Very well."

She snapped her fingers at Bertram, who stepped forward eagerly. "Bertie, be a dear and take my minions to that darling section of the tunnel where I stashed Kat and company. It's time for *all* my beloved vamps to bond."

"Of course, Mistress," Bertram said, giving her a slight bow.

I watched in disbelief as he ushered the mob—which was still silent and blank-faced—away from us, leaving me with Mercedes and a barely conscious Evie. I called out in my brain again, and was answered by silence. Dammit. Where had Scott and Bea gone? Had my bats-plosion moment caused the spell to malfunction? Or severed our connection entirely?

All right. Fine. I didn't know what I was doing, but for now I had to keep Mercedes talking, at least until I could get a good plan going.

Luckily, she didn't need much encouragement.

"Hmm, where should I start?" Mercedes said, leaning back against the tunnel wall as she examined her nails. "I think we have to go way, way back for this one."

I smothered a groan. Even though I needed whatever information she was about to spew—and the time it would buy me—I still did not relish the thought of listening to her voice for another second. Why do supervillains always have the burning need to monologue?

"It was five years ago," Mercedes said. I sent out a silent thank you to the universe that she wasn't going all the way back to, say, her birth. "I was toiling away down here in the city of angels, assisting law enforcement with various traffic-related issues."

"Sounds thrilling," I muttered.

"It *was*," Mercedes said, her eyes flashing defiantly. "I know it may not seem that exciting to someone fighting all those fancy demons, Aveda Jupiter, but I was contributing to society in my own way. And the local public loved me." She said that last part as if she was trying to convince herself. "Then I heard tell of some things happening up north—how an earthquake near the original demon crash site had led to power level-ups for everyone in the vicinity."

"That's right," I said, flashing back to that moment in time. "And when we saw you up in Topanga Canyon, you said you didn't get one."

"No!" She glared at me. "And of all people, I certainly *deserved* one. Here I was, working my ass off, bettering myself and my community, and once again, Aveda Jupiter waltzes in and *takes* something that should have been mine."

"For the record, I didn't actually do anything to make those level-ups happen," I said dryly. "They just kind of . . . did."

"In any case," Mercedes continued, "being the proactive, empowered woman that I am, I decided to take a trip up to the Bay Area to check out the crash site. I thought maybe I could figure out how to get a level-up of my very own."

"And . . . that worked?" I guessed.

Her lips curved into a sly smile. "Oh, did it ever. I climbed down into the crater—the one that still exists to this day! I figured the closer I could get to the actual crash site, the better my chances. And . . ." She pushed off from the wall and threw her arms wide in a *ta-da!* sort of gesture. "I was right. A big bolt of supernatural energy *exploded* from the crater and hit me square in the chest." She tapped her breastbone to demonstrate. "And I passed out. When I woke up . . . well. I felt *different*."

"What was the level-up?" I asked, desperately wanting her to get to the point.

"It was a simply astonishing enhancement to my human GPS ability," she said. "Previously, I could really only track vehicles. But now . . ." She smiled to herself. "I can track *everything*. Humans, animals. If you asked me to locate literally any living creature, I could do it. Remember when I sought you out at Edendale? I tracked you in that way."

"I thought you tracked the rental car," I said, trying to follow the thread.

"I can do *both*," she beamed. "But it's generally more fun with living, breathing creatures. Anyway, more importantly: I discovered I could also track beings that were not in our world."

"Wait, what?" I frowned, trying to make sense of it all. "Like . . . you could track things in the Otherworld—*demons* in the Otherworld?"

"Exactly," she said, nodding in a self-satisfied manner. "I do love it when you surprise me, Aveda—you usually aren't this insightful."

"And did this lead you to make contact with the Otherworld?" I asked.

"They actually came to *me*," Mercedes trilled, preening. "It did take a few years, mind you. But eventually, Princess Shasta was able to connect with my mind one day when I was mentally poking around in the Otherworld. She recognized my greatness, of course—and she knew I was the one to help her achieve her ultimate goal!"

"Yeah, yeah, we already know about the ultimate goal," I groused, my gaze wandering around the tunnel. Evie had ceased moving at all and was lying very still—but I could see her breathing, ever so slightly. I was trying to find something, anything, I could use my telekinesis to bonk Mercedes on the head with. Then again, my telekinesis had been so spotty lately, I wasn't sure if that would even work.

"The ultimate goal," I continued, "is to steal Evie's baby. Which Shasta already tried to do once unsuccessfully, using another demon who's apparently her protégé or BFF or something." I cocked an eyebrow at Mercedes. "Sounds like you were the second choice. Again."

A faint hint of rage pierced Mercedes' sickly sweet smile. "That's a lie," she hissed. "That other plan was *practice*. I'm the real deal."

"If you say so," I said, injecting my voice with as much skepticism as possible.

"*Anyway*," Mercedes said, "as the first human who was able to access the Otherworld in this particular way, I am obviously very important to Princess Shasta. And she told me that if I helped her, she could help *me* get everything I've ever wanted."

"Which is what, my life?" I retorted. "My husband, my fame, my TV show—"

"Ha!" Mercedes scoffed. "You think you're hot shit with that show, don't you?" She crossed the space until she was standing over me. I was starting to feel my strength return, but for now I stayed on the ground. Still trying to buy time. "What if I told you that that entire thing was *fake*?" Mercedes said, her eyes gleaming. "That *I* made it all happen?"

"What are you saying?"

Mercedes knelt down next to me, her smile widening. "Shasta was able to give me access to my very own Otherworld magic. And I thought, what will get Aveda Jupiter down to LA? How about something that feeds her already ginormous ego—a television show based on her life."

"But the show . . . it's happening," I protested. "We got emails about it . . . we . . ."

"Didn't you wonder why you couldn't quite remember so many of the essential details of how *Heroine* came to be?" Mercedes said, her smile turning mean. "Why you knew virtually nothing that first day on set? Why it seemed like this TV show sprang from out of nowhere?" She leaned in closer, practically baring her teeth at me. "It was because it *did*."

"But there were real actors . . . real executives . . ." I trailed off again, my mind spinning.

"Executives compelled via Otherworld magic," Mercedes said. "Human minds are so susceptible. So *weak*. I did let our friend Bertram in on some of my plan since I needed one real executive who could help me manipulate people. Before this, he was a junior assistant at some podunk production company."

"So not actually a demonic exec—just regular old evil," I said dryly. "And how did this all lead to vampires?"

"Princess Shasta and I concocted that plan *together*," Mercedes gloated. "After the practice run at Morgan College, she realized that while that attempt failed, activating and manipulating humans' emotional energy was certainly worth trying again—because look how close she got to getting Evie to give her the baby."

I stole another glance at Evie. She'd managed to push herself up the teeniest bit. I tried to meet her eyes, but they were trained downward as she struggled to get her bearings. I kind of hoped she was focusing on this so hard, she wasn't hearing anything Mercedes was saying.

"When I use my power to locate people, I always key into their emotional states," Mercedes continued. "That's what I have to grab on to in order to track them. So *I* suggested that we try accessing emotional energy that already existed in people's bodies! Naturally Princess Shasta thought that was brilliant. And she wanted to know if we could perhaps tie this to another one of humanity's fictional fearsome creatures."

"So you suggested vampires?" I said. "Because that was probably the most interesting part of the whole scheme."

"Not exactly," Mercedes said, her eyes shifting to the side. "I actually voted for werewolves—"

Boring! I imagined both Pippa and Bea responding.

"—but Shasta was intrigued by vampires," Mercedes said. "Especially when we did some experiments and realized that when we gave my GPS power another little Otherworld-fueled boost . . . well, I could manipulate humans' emotional energy in such *interesting* ways."

"Like . . . making them act erratic, giving them mood swings and major meat cravings?" I said, remembering the symptoms Kat and the vamp squad had described. "Enhancing every type of *hunger* someone might feel, and maybe making them feel extra exhausted as well?"

"That's right!" shrieked Mercedes, clapping her hands together. "And Princess Shasta thought that was the perfect metaphor for vampirism—sucking someone dry."

"Yes, that is actually the most obvious fucking metaphor I've ever heard of," I said, rolling my eyes. "It's kind of weird you didn't think of that, Mercedes. Like, werewolves? That doesn't fit at all."

"Shut up," Mercedes hissed, that bit of rage passing over her face again. "The plan fell into place after that. I chose my potential vamps carefully—people who were already coming off some kind of failure, feeling hopeless and down-trodden. The pain was radiating off of them so powerfully—it was easy to find, to latch on to. And to manipulate. And whenever I felt they were ready, whenever they'd gotten *hungry* enough, Shasta and I used that Otherworld magic to fully turn them."

"And yet, not everything went according to plan," I said, my brain working furiously to figure it out. "Because then some of your Otherworld-created vamps found they could create new ones with the whole biting thing."

"Human emotional energy is quite unpredictable," Mercedes said, nodding sagely. "I did try to explain that to Princess Shasta—that's one of the reasons her Morgan plan failed, after all. When it came to Stan biting Kat, it seemed like a boon! We found we could access and manipulate her emotional energy as well—and she had that whole downtrodden, burnt out thing I was seeking in the first place. Pippa . . ." Mercedes' gaze turned dark. "Well, that was more unfortunate. Her emotional energy was much *too* unpredictable. So we scrapped our original vamp squad and created a new one."

"The comic-con crowd," I said. "Did you actually turn them *at* the convention?"

"Indeed," Mercedes gloated. "And I didn't dilly-dally this time—I turned them right away. So far, they've been easier to control."

"I doubt that will last," I muttered.

One might say that I was goading Mercedes simply because I enjoyed it. But the truth was, I could see how much it got under her skin. I was still killing time, trying to come up with a plan—and if I could unbalance her just enough, she'd make a mistake. (Okay, so I did enjoy it *a little*.)

"Back to me being a vampire," I said. "What's *that* all about?"

"You must see that you were a perfect candidate," Mercedes said. "You were draining yourself so well, you were completely burnt out and running yourself into the ground, and particularly after your adventures at Morgan . . .you were just so goddamn *hungry*. I barely had to do anything. Lightly enhance some of your existing emotions, mess with your telekinesis just a bit. Send you some lovely visions of your husband with the woman he's *supposed* to be with."

I flashed back to how I couldn't seem to stop envisioning Scott with Mercedes; I was extremely thankful that *that* wasn't part of my actual subconscious.

"And then some of your other visions . . . well, they were prompted by your own feelings, your fears and desires," Mercedes said. "That threesome . . ." She smirked and fanned herself. "I had no idea you had that level of *spicy* in you, Aveda. I mean, yes, your burgeoning vampirism put you in a heightened state—and being surrounded by James and Naira's vampiric energy probably helped things along. I arranged to have Scott sent to you—remember, the mysterious call he received from someone claiming to be Evie? I was hoping you'd go full vamp and I'd get to swoop in and stake you right in front of him."

"So much manipulation," I said. "That's a lot of fucking work to steal someone's husband. Especially when said husband has no interest in being stolen."

"Maybe not," Mercedes said, her eyes flashing. "But that didn't stop you from imagining him leaving you behind, did it? When it came to certain visions you were having . . .it didn't take much vampiric enhancement. You probably would have dreamed up that big, empty Victorian no matter what."

I took a deep inhale, trying to figure out what to do next, and snuck another glance at Evie. She was still on the ground, but she looked more alert now. And . . . I squinted, trying to see her more clearly. She was moving the tiniest bit at a time, trying to inch her way across the floor. She caught my eye and nodded in confirmation. A tiny spark of hope pinged through my heart.

"But . . ." I paused, trying to get it all to make sense. "I still don't understand why the vamp swarm wanted *me* and not Evie. What exactly is Shasta's plan, here?"

"That is a very interesting tale," Mercedes said, trying to give me an Aveda Jupiter–type imperious look. "As you noticed, we've had a few hiccups in our brilliant plan. But I was able to improvise along the way. Even when Shasta decided . . ." She cocked her head to the side, like she was listening to someone the rest of us couldn't hear.

"When she decided . . . what?" I pressed.

"Nothing." Mercedes got to her feet and stalked back across the room. "It doesn't matter. Because now that you're here, looking like the weak, pathetic failure that you are, Princess Shasta will realize—"

Suddenly, Mercedes froze mid-stride. Her arms shot out, as if she was trying to fend something off. Her movements turned awkward and jerky, and she very slowly turned around—but it looked like she was *resisting* that motion. Like she was a puppet trying to break loose from her strings.

"No!" she yelped. "No, I—"

"Shut up, Mercedes!"

I tried to push myself up again—but it was so hard, I did feel weak—and did a double take. Because *Mercedes* had said that. She'd just told *herself* to shut up.

"You're supposed to tell her!" Not Quite Mercedes continued. Mercedes' eyes looked furious, and she was still struggling in place, trying to break free of whatever force was controlling her. "Fine, then *I'll* tell her!"

The force propelled Mercedes' body forward, laboriously lifting one leg, then the other. Mercedes' body lurched toward me, even as her expression stayed resentful.

"Aveda Jupiter!" Not Quite Mercedes continued. "I know

we've met before and I did not exactly make the best impression, but I'm hoping that this time, we can have a meaningful relationship."

"Shasta?!" I gasped. "How are you speaking through Mercedes?"

"I am using her very special connection to me and the Otherworld, of course," Shasta-Mercedes said, flashing me a toothy smile. "Don't you love it? I couldn't do this with Leonora or Richard, and it's just so . . ." She gave a ghoulish stretch, extending her resistant arms over her head in jubilation. ". . . *freeing.* I've been able to watch you through Mercedes' eyes this whole week. And I had to make myself known when I heard her not executing my plan correctly."

"Excuse *you!*" Mercedes gasped, sounding like the real Mercedes again. "This is not *your* plan, it's a collaboration—"

"Not this part, my dear," Shasta said, retaking control. "Aveda, I realize we've had our differences, and that you had no interest in becoming one of my demon-human hybrids back in the day. But watching you this past week . . ." She awkwardly brought a hand to her heart. "I remembered how fabulous you are. There is no one quite like you—you're the only vamp who figured out how to turn *herself*! You realized what you needed to do to break through that force field and you made it *happen.* And that's the kind of energy I want in my inevitable empire."

"No!" Mercedes shrieked, wrenching back control of her body. She tried to pull herself toward the wall but remained frozen in place. "You weren't supposed to care about her, this was supposed to be about *me*! Finally, I was going to get everything I wanted, everything I always *deserved*!" She shot me a look of overwhelming hatred. "I'm the one who should have been the star. Who should have the gorgeous, attentive husband. The TV show—all of it!"

"You saying that does not make it true," Shasta said, reasserting her dominance. She even got Mercedes to roll her eyes. "I gave you the show, didn't I? Even agreed to you becoming the star *and* the showrunner, which seems excessive."

"So you're totally changing your original plan?" I interjected, trying to get us back on track. "I thought this was all about Evie's baby."

I snuck another glance at Evie and saw that she'd managed to drag herself closer to me.

"I want you *and* the baby," Shasta said. "The baby is going to help me establish that connection between my world and yours, so we can move back and forth freely, and I can finally rule humanity as I'm meant to. But I will need a liaison here on Earth, someone who gets it—"

"And that was supposed to be me!" Mercedes roared.

Mercedes' head shook back and forth a few times, as if wrestling for control. Then Shasta's smug smile appeared on her face yet again.

"It has to be you, Aveda Jupiter—that's what's always been meant to be. And now that you're starting to experience your very own vampire powers—"

"Wait a minute." I shook my head. "Why was I targeted for vampire powers, besides the fact that I was in the correct emotional state? It sounds like Mercedes wanted to get me out of the picture entirely."

"Oh, she did," Shasta said. "You weren't going to be part of the squad that was to attack Evie. Mercedes imagined a very elaborate scenario wherein you turned into a vampire and then she became Magnificent Mercedes, Vampire Slayer, and staked you in front of a cheering crowd, thereby cementing her place as a beloved heroine—"

"That's not exactly how I described it," Mercedes piped up, her tone peevish.

"It so is," Shasta insisted. "But as usual, I had a much grander vision in mind. Or at least I did once I witnessed you in action once more. Mercedes hadn't really thought about the long-term consequences of having all these Otherworld-created vampires roaming around on Earth. I supposed she imagined she'd stake them all too, to really drive home the whole Mercedes the Vampire Slayer thing. But I thought . . . well, why not keep them as a sort of demon enforcement unit? Something to keep all the humans in my newly acquired Earth dimension in line. And who better to lead them . . ." She flashed me her biggest, brightest smile yet. ". . . than *you*."

"What?!" I spat out. "So you did want me to become Aveda Jupiter, Vampire Queen? Just like in that scene I read with James and Naira . . ."

"*Now* you're getting it!" Shasta said, nodding Mercedes' head eagerly. "I wrote that scene myself to show Mercedes just how good it could be. She kept trying to add an ending wherein the *real* Aveda Jupiter—played by Mercedes, of course—bursts in at the last minute and stakes everyone."

"Shasta." I shook my head at her. "What in the world made you think any of this would be appealing to me? I'm not going to let you steal my best friend's baby, and I don't want to be your earthbound minion. That's all on the extreme side of ridiculous."

"I *know* you," Shasta insisted. "You're just like me— you've worked hard all your life, and now that you've achieved perfection, you want it to stay that way. I can *make* it stay that way! If you're a vampire, you'll be immortal. And you'll have all those lovely compulsion abilities—you can make Evie forget she was ever pregnant in the first place. You can banish all thoughts of Scott's new job offer from his mind. You can make your wayward teammates move back home. You can exist as you've been existing—surrounded by love and in control of your perfect life! Nothing will have to change ever again! Doesn't that sound incredible?"

I stared back at her, trying to parse each of her words, trying to understand—

And then I felt a hand grasp mine.

"Annie."

I turned to my left . . . and saw Evie, who had finally managed to drag herself over to me. Now she was clutching my hand tightly, her eyes meeting mine, her gaze so fierce and determined, tears sprang to my eyes all over again.

She believed in us—just like I had back at Morgan.

"Don't do it," she hissed. "Don't give in to her! I know it sounds tempting, but—"

"It doesn't."

She tilted her head at me, her grip loosening slightly. "What?"

"I said: it doesn't." I arched an eyebrow and gave her a small smile. "And . . .really, Evelyn? You think my dream is to mind control all my friends and loved ones into doing exactly what I want? Didn't we just go through this with Bea's Dark Side flirtation? And, by the way, our Bea also did *not* take that deal."

"N-no," Evie said. "I don't think you want *that*, I just . . .I know how it is when someone offers you something in the heat of battle, and it seems like the answer to everything you've been struggling with, and—"

"Evie." I squeezed her hand. "You were never going to give that monster your baby. And *I'm* not doing this." I turned back to the unholy Shasta-Mercedes mashup. "I don't want that," I said, putting as much steel into my voice as I could muster. "I don't want to fucking *control* people and I don't want my life to be frozen in some weird, static bubble. Change isn't always a bad thing. Sometimes it's necessary. Sometimes it's *growth*. And I have this life I love so much because I allowed that change to happen. Because *I* changed." I met Evie's eyes again and smiled. She squeezed my hand, her eyes full of tears. "In the end, I know the people I love will always be there for me—we'll change together, even as the most essential core of who we are holds strong."

I slumped a little, feeling drained again. I didn't know if it was Mercedes messing with me or if I was simply exhausted, but after all that speechifying, I could barely keep my head up. I couldn't fight, I couldn't push back, I couldn't do *anything*.

"See, she doesn't even want it!" Mercedes squawked, briefly regaining control of her body. "She—"

"Silence!" Shasta growled, jerking Mercedes' head to the side.

I flashed back to Pippa grinning at me across the breakfast table, talking about how I'd one day have a whole squad standing behind me. Standing *with* me.

I desperately wished they were here now.

I'm sorry, I thought, wildly trying to beam it out to Scott somehow. If this was it, if Evie and I were about to be defeated, then I desperately needed him to know—

You need me to know what?

I gasped, my head jerking up, my eyes going wide. Evie squeezed my hand again, her gaze full of questions. I glanced over at Mercedes-Shasta. They appeared to be fighting amongst themselves, grappling for control.

Scott? I thought, terrified to hope.

It's me, sweetheart, he said.

And me! Bea's voice piped up. *We lost you for a minute when you turned into the bat swarm thingy—which was majorly cool by the way, do you think you can teach me how to—*

Bea, Scott interrupted. I could practically hear his sweet, lopsided grin in my head, and the tears in my eyes spilled over. *Later. We've got stuff to do right now.*

"Annie . . . ?" Evie whispered, jiggling my hand.

"They're here," I muttered, tapping my head. "Scott and Bea. And I think I—*we*—know what to do."

I took a few deep breaths and felt Scott's magic flowing through me. I felt Bea's projection power fusing with that magic, and then they both seemed to surround my telekinesis. I imagined our three powers locking together inside of me, a bright thread of strength.

And suddenly I didn't feel so tired anymore.

"Hey, Mercedes? Shasta?"

The Mercedes-Shasta combo turned to me, looking confused. My voice sounded really fucking powerful, booming off the walls of the tunnel. I straightened my spine and got to my feet—still holding Evie's hand the whole time.

"Both of your plans fucking suck!" I hissed.

Then I gathered my invisible feathers and flung them at her body with as much force as I could muster, shooting straight for her heart. Her eyes widened and she stumbled backward as they plunged into her chest.

Scott? I called out in my mind.

No invisible force field around them, he said. *We're in.*

They must've been too busy fighting to even think of that, Bea said.

I see the Otherworld magic, Scott said, his voice lit with excitement. *I'm going to contain it for you, okay?*

Perfect, I said. *Bea . . . stoke her anger. Er, their anger. Play on the conflict between the two people currently trapped in this body!*

On it! Bea chirped.

"What are you doing?" Shasta hissed at me. She danced around, as if trying to break free from my mental grasp. "I've won, Aveda Jupiter. And now I'm going to take over this weak human body as my own."

"The hell you will!" Mercedes screeched, snatching back control. "I don't care if you're demon royalty, you evil bitch, *I'm* the one who's meant to be great—I've always been *special—*"

She sounds like Zacasta, Bea snarked.

"Shut up!" Shasta hissed. Her eyes sparked with rage. "Really, this is how you wanna play it? After I offered you everything?"

Her body jerked to the left, the rest of that sentence dying on her lips. Her eyes went wide with surprise, then switched to determination . . . then back again to surprise . . .

Satisfaction flowed through my veins—Bea's projection was getting them to really fight each other over who got to be the prettiest princess. Just as I'd hoped.

Annie, Scott said in my head. *It's right . . . here . . .*

And just like that, I felt bright energy brush against my feathers, weird and wild and definitely not of this realm.

The Otherworld energy, I said. *Is that all of it?*

I felt Scott and Bea surrounding my power again, a bright thrum of light that seemed to envelop my whole body. And I felt Evie, still clutching tightly to my hand.

Yes, he said. *Now's your moment. Do it, Annie.*

I closed my eyes, gathered all the strength they were surrounding me with, and yanked my invisible feathers with all my might.

"GAAAAAAAHHHHHH!"

Shasta-Mercedes fell to her knees and released a bone-shattering howl of rage, throwing her arms skyward. Gasping, she met my eyes and leveled me with a look of bitter hatred.

"This isn't over, Aveda Jupiter," Shasta hissed. "That baby *will* be mine. And when you're all screaming for mercy, I want you to remember that I gave you a chance to be on the winning side."

"Oh my god," I retorted. "Your dramatic villain speeches are almost as bad as your terrible fucking plans. Now get the hell out of here!"

I gave my feathers one more decisive yank, and felt that energy come with me.

Release it into the air! Scott cried. *If Bea and I have done everything correctly, she should be booted back to the Otherworld!*

Mercedes threw back her head and screamed, a horrible sound that seemed to reverberate through the deepest parts of the tunnel, bouncing off their hard surfaces and sending an endless echo into the very depths of LA.

I let go of the energy and slumped back to the floor, still clutching Evie's hand as tightly as I could.

There was a blinding flash of light. And then Mercedes—just Mercedes—collapsed to the ground, unconscious.

Scott, I thought. *Bea. Are you still there?*

We're here! Scott exclaimed, his jubilant voice ringing out through my head. *And we'll stay fused with you for extra strength—even though you probably don't need us anymore.*

I smiled, tears streaming down my cheeks. I felt Scott and Bea with me, giving my brain the equivalent of a group hug. I felt Evie's hand in mine, still unwilling to let go.

"No," I said out loud. "I do."

MAISY KANE PRESENTS: BUZZ BY THE BAY

By Maisy Kane, Half-Demon Princess Editrix

My dearest 'Friscans, I must say: there is an extra spring in my step and I am feeling quite delightful today! I can only guess it's because the city's most beloved daughters, Aveda Jupiter and Evie Tanaka, have at last returned to the Bay Area fold.

I know many of you rabidly followed their adventures down in the city of angels via social media, and our girls did end up getting into some major hijinks! But it appears they also found time to squeeze in a li'l ol' R&R—peep my exclusive gallery of snaps sent in by trusted sources, featuring the girls eating their way through the historic Little Tokyo district, exploring Griffith Park, and taking in a glorious-looking comedy show called Asian AF! Don't they look like they're having the best time?!

(Editrix's note: I will *not* be including the snaps someone sent me of Aveda indulging in some beach-set romantic moments with her hottie of a husband, Scott Cameron. Some things are meant to be private, people! All the best journalists—like yours truly—know that!)

I've also heard quite a few of you are disappointed that the TV show based on EVEDA's exploits, *Heroine*, was apparently some kind of supernatural scam that will not be moving forward. Cry it out, my sweet bbs—but I can tell you exclusively that you may soon be able to dry your tears, as rumor has it that the two actresses cast in the now-defunct show, Kat Morikawa and Michelle "Miki" Chong, have formed their own badass production company, and may have something *very special* in development!

Rumor also has it that Aveda Jupiter is headed down to LA yet again in just a few short weeks—is she consulting on a new show? Was her presence just so fabulous that she's now swimming in influencer-type partnership deals? Or is there more evil afoot down south—especially pressing as LA's former heroine-in-residence, Magnificent Mercedes, has been revealed to be an aspiring super-villain!

Time will tell! All your pal Maisy knows is something Aveda told me herself: 'Friscans shouldn't worry about her temporary absence—she and Evie have been training a li'l class of superheroing protégés, icons-in-the-making that you may have seen battling our garden-variety puppy demons all over town as of late!

Could it be that we are about to witness the birth of a whole new generation of heroines?

Stay tuned. This story's still developing . . .

Chapter Thirty-Two

"ARE YOU READY for this?" Scott flashed his lopsided grin at me as he dragged my overstuffed suitcase down the stairs of the Victorian. "Also, did you pack your *entire* closet, or . . .?"

"Of course I'm ready—and part of that readiness is having an outfit for every possible occasion," I said, flipping my power ponytail over my shoulder. "Aveda Jupiter has faced down demons of every stripe, a myriad of existential crises . . . and now ghosts and vampires. I'm fairly certain she can face *vacation*."

"I don't know," he said, reaching the bottom of the staircase. He looped an arm around my waist and pulled me in for a kiss. "It's going to be *a lot* of relaxation. You sure?"

"I'm actually *not* sure, but I'm assuming you will be able to guide me," I murmured against his mouth. "I'm guessing I might willingly sleep in at least one day. And whatever relaxing activities are planned, I'm hoping there will be a bathtub involved."

"I believe we're booked in the same suite," he responded. "Prepare for a future that very possibly involves nothing *but* baths."

I laughed and leaned into the kiss, marveling at how perfectly we still fit together. How we always did.

We were headed back down to LA for a whole week—but this time there was no TV show, no Mercedes, and hopefully no vampire attacks. And Scott had even talked me into making it a road trip—Lucy had loaned us her car, and it was waiting for us outside.

The *Heroine* show had been shuttered once Shasta had been banished back to the Otherworld—on account of it being completely made up in the first place. And Mercedes had been taken into police custody, but not before she'd snarled at me for "ruining everything" and stealing what was hers. So much for superheroine sisterhood.

Scott and I were going to relax, go to the beach, and explore the various options that might be available as far as him accepting the job at the Youth Center. He hadn't officially said yes, but I knew he wanted to—and I knew we could figure out a way to make it work. Perhaps we would become a glamorous dual-city couple. Perhaps I would try my hand at LA living for a bit since they were now down a superheroine. Perhaps we would be fabulously long distance and become experts at astoundingly creative phone sex.

There were just *so many* possibilities.

"Let me go say good-bye to Evie," I said, patting him on the chest. "I'll meet you at the car."

I marched into the kitchen and found Evie at the table, in the midst of chowing down on some very delicious-looking tacos with Pippa.

"And as it turns out, I do have some kind of super speed power now," Pippa was saying. "So I zipped myself down to LA and back—isn't that the best? We can have these tacos *every day*!"

"I love that that's what you want to use said power for," Evie said, giggling. "Bravo, excellent work."

I leaned in the doorframe, affection rising in my chest as I studied them. Once Shasta had been banished back to the Otherworld, the vamps created exclusively by Mercedes had simply reverted back to their human selves—good news for Clint and Stan, who were back to pursuing auteur-level greatness in Hollywood. I'd been hoping their brush with the Otherworld would result in some much-needed humility, but Kat told me their personalities were back to being mostly insufferable. As for the vamps created via bites from other vamps . . . well, they seemed to have retained some of their powers. Kat could still turn into a flock of bats on cue—but now she was able to control it, and she never found herself compelled back to the Mistress Tunnel. And Pippa was, of course, overjoyed that all of her paranormal dreams were finally coming true. As for me . . . I'd noticed a few changes. Like that I now had a *much* greater fondness for bacon.

We weren't sure how long-lasting these effects would be, if the extra powers would fade with time. But I was open to whatever was next, and I hoped Pippa was, too.

I was thrilled that Kat was also flourishing. She and Miki had teamed up to start their own production company, and were already hard at work developing some exciting projects featuring women of color—including a potential TV show starring the two of them and Naira, who was now officially dating James. I understood they had also employed Grouchy Stacey as one of their assistants—as it turned out, when she didn't have to work for guys like Clint, Grouchy Stacey was actually quite pleasant.

Kat and I had made plans to meet up again during my vacation and go shopping in Highland Park, and I couldn't wait. We'd been talking constantly, trying to work our way toward fully loving our respective dreams again. I was starting to rediscover that sense of purpose and giddy delight I'd felt when I'd decided to become a superheroine—that feeling I'd had watching *The Heroic Trio* for the first time, reaching over the battered old movie theater seats to grasp Evie's hand. And Kat was reconnecting with her deep passion for acting. It felt good to be able to hash all of this out so thoroughly with someone who understood—our shared goal was to be disgustingly happy pursuing our callings, doing the things we felt we were meant to. And I had complete faith that we'd both get there.

"Yeah, bitch!" Kat had crowed during one of our most recent hours-long phone sessions. "We're gonna own that intensity all day long!"

"Oh hey, AJ!" Pippa exclaimed, spotting me in the doorframe. "You wanna say a sappy, tearful goodbye to Evie? 'Cause I can skedaddle. Shelby and I have plans to see if we can get our ghost and vamp powers to interact! Bea's going to call in and help, since she and Scott were so successful with their power combo spell."

"Sounds fun and not at all dangerous!" I said cheerfully. "I'll see you when I get back?"

"Eh, I might pop down and visit you during your trip," Pippa said with a wink. "I do love this whole super speed thing."

And with that, she was gone—moving so quickly, I could barely see her.

"That should be an interesting afternoon," I said, laughing a little.

I crossed the room and sat down next to Evie, snagging a taco for myself.

"So you'll have everything under control here?" I said. "You're sure you and our protégés can survive for a week without me? You can call any time if there's an emergency. Even if it's really early or super late—"

"Annie." She laughed. "Everything will be fine. I've got Shruti on call, I've got Pippa and Shelby and Lucy and everyone else—we're ready. Please, just enjoy yourself."

"Mmm," I murmured. "Pippa and Shelby are pretty cute, no? They kind of remind me of . . . well, us." I nodded at her belly. "I know you haven't given birth yet, but don't you feel like we kind of have our own kids now? The next generation of superheroines."

"I'm hoping they'll have way less to fight than we do," Evie said with a laugh. "But damn, Shasta sure is persistent. And she just keeps finding new minions. Speaking of, any idea how Mercedes is doing?"

"I can honestly say that I don't care," I said, finishing my taco. "Even after I saved her ass from permanent Shasta possession, she still acted like she was entitled to my entire life. Like I'd stolen it from her, even though she has nothing to do with any of it. I can't believe she wasted so much brain power obsessing over me instead of, I don't know, focusing on herself."

"That's some extreme white lady entitlement in action," Evie said. "But do we think there's any way she's still in touch with Shasta?"

"Multiple tests were done on her—there's no supernatural energy present in her body," I said. "We're theorizing that once her connection to the Otherworld was severed, it took everything. Even her original superpower."

"So Mercedes is just Mercedes now," Evie said. "No more human GPS, no more 'Magnificent.'"

"Nope," I said with a shrug. "I guess that's a big shift for her, but you were right about her personality, Evie: she hasn't changed."

"But you have!" Evie beamed at me. "And now look at you: going on vacation, taking time off to relax with your husband, and you're even starting therapy and shit. And did I hear that you're going on a cruise with *your mom*?! I do believe you've actually grown up, Aveda Jupiter."

"And it only took me thirtysomething years to do so," I said, grinning at her and getting to my feet. "Don't burn anything down while I'm gone, okay? And do *not* have that baby."

"Wouldn't dream of it," she said. And then she gave me one of those best friend telepathy looks that said *everything*—more than words could ever convey.

I bounded out of the kitchen, down the hall, and out the front door. When I finally got to the car, Scott was waiting for me, patient as ever.

"There you are," he said, pulling me in for another kiss. "I should have known you and Evie would need an epic good-bye. I probably could've driven to LA and back again by now."

"Hilarious," I said, arching an eyebrow. "Let's get this show on the road—you ready?"

"Always," he said, those brilliant blue eyes sparkling with

humor and mischief—and something so tender, it made my heart swell. I realized that he had that look I kept wanting for him, that expression of being all lit up.

He always looked that way . . . when he was looking at me.

And I knew I was looking at him the exact same way.

"What about you?" he asked.

"I'm ready for whatever comes next," I said, settling myself into my seat and facing forward. And I realized that what we were doing didn't feel like the end of something— inevitable change that would destroy everything.

It felt like the *beginning*. And the possibilities were endless.

I smiled at him. "In fact, I can't wait."

ACKNOWLEDGMENTS

Thank you to my readers—I appreciate your love for Evie, Aveda, Bea, and their ever-growing found family more than I can say.

Thank you to all my superteams, who always make me feel like I can take over the world (and that we will be doing so as a squad): The Girl Gang(s), the Shamers, Heroine Club, the incredible Asian American arts community of LA, Asian American Girl Club, Team Batgirl, the Millsies, the Kuhn-Chen-Coffey-Yoneyamas, and all the writing sprint support threads and convention crews.

Thank you to my awesome agent, Taylor Haggerty, and everyone at Root Literary—you have made me feel so at home already, and I could not ask for a more supportive group. Here's to all the vision boards!

Thank you to my editors, Katie Hoffman and Betsy Wollheim, for caring about Aveda's journey as much as I do. And thank you to Alexis Nixon, Josh Starr, Jessica Plummer, Sheila Gilbert, Leah Spann, Lindsay Ribar, and everyone at DAW Books and Penguin Random House for continuing to support all the *Heroine*-ing.

Thank you to Jason Chan, who always brings my girls to life beautifully, and who did extra fabulous work on their outfits this time—Evie and Aveda look just as heroic and stylish in Hollywood as they do in San Francisco!

Thank you to everyone who fed this book in some way—Jenn Fujikawa, Rebekah Weatherspoon, Tom Wong, Amber Benson, Javier Grillo-Marxuach, Sarah Baker, Christine Dinh, Mel Caylo, Andrea Letamendi, Amy Ratcliffe, Christy Black, Liza Palmer, Janet Eckford, Maurene Goo, Diya Mishra, David Perkiss, Jenny Yang, Erik Patterson,

Phil Yu, Jenny Bak, Michelle Chong, Keiko Agena, and Will Choi. I am gazing at all of you with major heart-eyes.

This book was obviously heavily influenced by some of my own favorite LA haunts and events, and you may spot fictionalized versions of them throughout. Thank you to Big Bud Press, Asian AF, Edendale, Porto's, Shootz, Guisados, Kogi BBQ, Astroburger, Fugetsu-Do, and basically all of Little Tokyo for the inspiration. And extra special thanks to The Ripped Bodice, Ms Chi Cafe, and their respective proprietors—Bea and Leah Koch and Chef Shirley Chung— for always being there for me and my books.

And thank you to Jeff Chen for everything—you make the world make sense to me.